Also by Ryan Van Loan

The
MEMORY
in the
BLOOD

Ryan Van Loan

TOR

Tor Publishing Group

New York

THE MEMORY IN THE BLOOD

Maps by Tim Paul

A Tor Book
Published by Tom Doherty Associates / Tor Publishing Group
120 Broadway
New York, NY 10271

www.tor-forge.com

Tor® is a registered trademark of Macmillan Publishing Group, LLC.

The Library of Congress has cataloged the hardcover edition as follows:

Names: Van Loan, Ryan, author.
Title: The memory in the blood / Ryan Van Loan.
Description: First Edition. | New York : Tor, a Tom Doherty Associates
    Book, 2022. | Series: The fall of the gods; 3
Identifiers: LCCN 2022008307 (print) | LCCN 2022008308 (ebook) |
    ISBN 9781250222640 (hardcover) | ISBN 9781250222633 (ebook)
Classification: LCC PS3622.A5854945 M46 2022 (print) |
    LCC PS3622.A5854945 (ebook) | DDC 813/.6—dc23
LC record available at https://lccn.loc.gov/2022008307
LC ebook record available at https://lccn.loc.gov/2022008308

ISBN 978-1-250-22265-7 (trade paperback)

Our books may be purchased in bulk for promotional, educational, or business use.
Please contact your local bookseller or the Macmillan Corporate and Premium Sales
Department at 1-800-221-7945, extension 5442, or by email at
MacmillanSpecialMarkets@macmillan.com.

First Tor Paperback Edition: 2023

For you, Dear Reader, who stayed with Buc until the end

Kanados

Port au' Sheen

The Southern Expanse

The Ring of Fire

N
W E
S

THE
SHATTERED
COAST

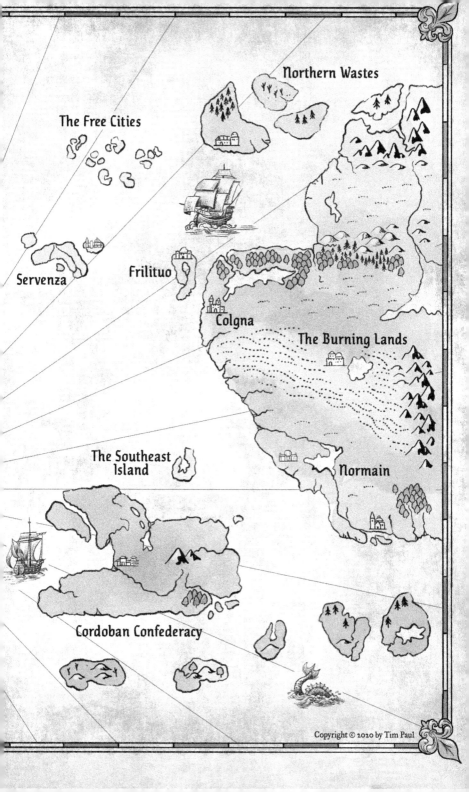

Northern Wastes

The Free Cities

Servenza

Frilituo

Colgna

The Burning Lands

The Southeast Island

Normain

Cordoban Confederacy

Copyright © 2020 by Tim Paul

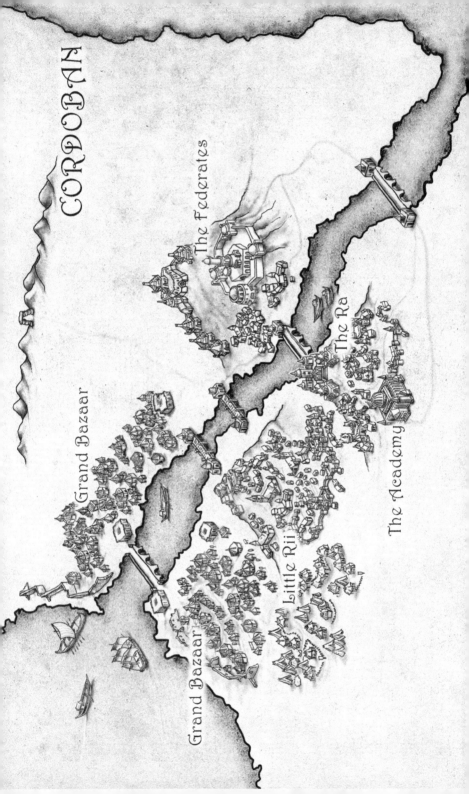

CORDOBAN

The Federates

The Ra

Grand Bazaar

The Academy

Little Rii

Grand Bazaar

NORMAIN

The Old City

The Dead Gods' Citadel

Mercantile Row

The Fingers

1

Rage is a winter's gale so cold it burns, filling your veins with a liquid hotter than the sun. Not living fire, but something far deeper. Harder. Brighter. I discovered that when I lost Eld and everything within me burned away in the frost that froze my chest and lungs. Now it burns within me so brightly that I wonder any can look upon me and not be struck blind. Once, I was Sambuciña "Buc" Alhurra, now I am become Incandescence, Goddess of Rage.

Eight months ago, I left Servenza, bent on revenge and convinced I knew what rage was. Then I lost Chan Sha, nearly lost my mind, and discovered what rage truly was, a freezing fire that seared away the fog and let me see clearly for perhaps the first time since I'd taken Sin into my mind in a ritual on a deserted island to defeat a horde of Shambles and the Ghost Captain who commanded them. Only, that wasn't the truth. Leastwise, not all of it. The full measure was I'd done it to save Eld and in so doing brought an enemy between us. An enemy buried deep within my once-brilliant mind. Sin hadn't meant to betray me. It was in his nature to want to reunite with his Goddess. To convince me to complete the Rite of Possession. A rite that would have turned me from demi-Goddess in my own right to little more than one of the slaves the Burnt were said to keep in their sandblasted lands. I'd thought I was winning when in truth I was being played, and it took falling out with Eld, defeating Sicarii who was but Chan Sha in disguise, and finally, fatally, losing Eld to realize how badly I'd been beaten.

Chan Sha giving me the slip had been the final olive pit cracked in the press that truly broke me, but with that breaking came insight. When I was ten and six, I sought the power to challenge the Gods and their hidden forever war, to break the chains they wrapped around the throats of the world and give people a chance to breathe on our own. When I was ten and seven, having found that power, I discovered what so many did before me: power is a conniving bitch.

Now I'm ten and eight and wiser for all my failures.

Alone, as I was at the start, after Sister passed and before Eld found me. Everything burned away save the knowledge that Gods can be bested. If they can be bested, they can be killed.

Aye, but it will take a special flame to consume both the Dead Gods and Ciris. I used to fear fire, but now I'm frozen and can't be fucked to care. Incandescent. Rage. Me.

"You upset with me, amirah?"

I glanced down at the little girl, who was barely more than eight. A faded, pink rag was tied through her hair, which had been blond once and was now brown from dirt. I felt the heat of the sun's harsh rays, though Sin's magic kept me from sweating. It wasn't the heat that made me move deeper into the alcove provided by the door, shifting my weight away from the child.

"No, little one," I answered in Cordoban, shaking my head and setting the bangles threaded through my loose braid into motion. The words were strange on my tongue—another of Sin's gifts. "You pulled me out of my thoughts, is all. They like to wander, same as you," I added. *You could have stopped me.*

"I'd like nothing less," Sin whispered in response to my thought, his voice echoing in my mind. "You muse on little else but anger and machinations these days, and the last time I tried to intervene, you locked me in a dark corner of your mind for a month."

"It was a week," I replied mentally.

"We were on Southeast Island one moment and when I came back, we were in Colgna!"

"Maybe it was a fortnight," I admitted.

"So, little one," I said out loud, forcing myself back to the moment. Sin wasn't wrong; given half a chance my mind focused on either the rage fueling me or all the delicious paths I aimed to trod while spelling the ruin of the Gods. "You've word for me, Denga?"

"Aye," Denga said, picking at a thread that had pulled loose of her brown dress. If she pulled many more, there wouldn't be enough fabric left to earn the name, but she'd refused my offer of better clothes. After seeing a lad wearing silks above his station get jumped by half a dozen others and left with little more than his torn undergarments, I thought I understood. "I spotted another limper this morn."

"Oh?" I started to lean forward, but my right arm—stretched behind me—protested. I held myself still. "Was it like the man with the sleeveless vest you saw last week, Denga?"

"I'm not dumb," Denga said, pouting in a way that displayed her cracked lip.

My eyes burned with Sin's magic, zooming in on her skin, but there was no bruise there. *From the sun, then.* Denga had decent parents whose only crime was being too poor to have a child. I guess that meant the father's crime was being too slow to pull out, but isn't that every man's sin?

"And how would you know?" Sin asked with a grin I could feel in my mind.

"Why did I let you out again?" I felt his amusement turn to a sulk and I chuckled soundlessly.

"You said the stranger you wanted was a woman and this limper is a woman," the girl continued.

"An old woman?"

"Older than you, amirah Buc," she agreed.

"Aye, but as old as your ma's ma or your ma?"

"Ma."

"Cordoban's lousy with strangers, little fish," I reminded her. "And the sun's baked the bricks so badly they've cracked . . . limpers aplenty with streets like that."

"You said this one would have her hair in braids down to her arse?"

"I did that."

"And she'd probably hide her face beneath a hat?"

"Aye."

"To hide her missing eye," Denga said, this time not making her sentence a question.

"Now that . . . ," I said, straightening up so quickly that I felt something twist in the wrist I still held behind. It began to burn as Sin's magic fixed the sprain I'd just given myself. ". . . is interesting. Very interesti—wait!" When Sin's magic kicked in, my hearing went, and I'd missed a few of Denga's words. "What'd you say?"

"You didn't say that she'd speak Cordoban," Denga repeated. Her sunburnt cheeks dimpled when she saw my expression. "Did I do good, amirah?"

"You did." The cold maelstrom inside me was rising to tempest levels but I held the breakers at bay. *The second sighting? In as many days?* I couldn't allow for hope, but this was worth further investigation. I tossed a coin to the girl; she whooped when she saw silver flash in the sun instead of copper. "Where did you sight said stranger?"

"Watching the harbor," Denga said. "Lots of ships come in—Ma says on account of fighting twixt Servenza and some other place? Whatsoever ship she wanted, she didn't find it because her face was . . ."

"Long?" I suggested.

"Scary."

"You've nothing to fear from that one," I told Denga. "What'd she look like?" The child's description matched the one I'd gotten yesterday—a divided riding dress in a shade of brown that nearly matched the woman's skin and hid her limp from all but the most studious types: children. "You did good," I repeated. "How're you coming along in your studies?"

"The m'utadi says if I can find a word that I don't mangle I will be able to read before next season's rains."

"And arithmetic?

"She just sighs and says a word Ma said would earn me a lashing."

I laughed. "But she does teach you."

"Every other day," Denga confirmed. "Ma doesn't understand why one of the apprentices to the"—she said a word that even Sin couldn't fully translate, rendering it as "Most Esteemed Knowledge Bearers"—"would bother teaching one such as me."

"But she does teach," I repeated. If Denga's ma knew what leverage I had over said apprentice, she'd understand just fine— the Cordoban Confederacy understood blackmail even if they didn't have a word for it. "And if you pay attention, you'll be able to sit for the exams come summer's end.

"Then I'll be a m'utadi?"

"You will," I promised her. "I'm going to stop by tomorrow, Denga, and you can read to me. Then I'll tell you if your apprentice is right or not, aye?"

"As you say, amirah," the girl said, her cheeks showing the first color other than dirt. Denga was impossibly proud of being able to read, however poorly, but embarrassed as well. Her parents were still trying to decipher my angle, but could see no harm in learning to read—which showed their ignorance. If Eld hadn't taught me to read, I'd have never realized how fucked we were by the Gods and never set out to balance the scales. There were dozens who'd let slip their mortal coil who could tell Denga's parents the dangers of my reading, but the dead can't talk. Not without a Dead Walker, anyway.

"Call me Buc," I told Denga. "Now, run off before you melt into the bricks. Oh"—my voice stopped her midturn—"if you ever want to skip out on your m'utadi, or wonder why you chose such a path when the maestros are beating the soles of your feet for mistranscribing a tome, just remember, Denga . . . that coin I gave you? Anyone with quick fingers or a blade can steal that." I tapped my head. "But knowledge? That's a wealth that can never be stolen, only squandered. Savvy?"

"I don't ken that word?" Denga said, her accent suddenly heavy to my ears. "But I won't let you down. I promise."

"Don't," I told her. She bowed slightly and turned to leave. "And while you're at it," I shouted at her back, "don't let yourself down either, girl!"

I waited until I saw her pink scarf, waving like a banner, disappear around the alley corner, then pivoted and caught the body I'd been using one arm to hold up out of her sight. The Sin Eater's head lolled against my shoulder. A trickle of dried blood ran from her lips down to her chin like a faint scar against her mahogany skin, but elsewise she could have been sleeping. I eased her down in the alcove, setting her back against the brick with her feet blocking the door, her azure robes unwrinkled despite the abuse. Over the last six months, I'd learned, with Sin playing my own reluctant m'utadi, that one has to be careful when murdering Sin Eaters—take too long in the murdering and they'll call others of their kind to them or, Gods forbid, Ciris herself.

"Ciris wouldn't come in physical form," Sin said. "For you, though, she might possess the Sin Eater."

"Wouldn't that be the same thing?"

"It would be semantical," he confirmed.

"Uh-huh."

I leaned the woman forward and her black, shoulder-length hair shifted, exposing the hilt of the short blade I'd driven through the back of her neck. It's hard to call anyone, let alone a Goddess, when your brain stem's been severed. The blade caught on a vertebra, and I had to twist it a bit to get it out, the woman's head jerking back and forth and the sound of steel on bone loud in the silence cast over the alley by the oppressive heat. *Give it up, woman.* The blade pulled free and the Sin Eater fell back against the door with a dull thud, her sightless eyes slipping closed as I wiped the blade clean on her robes.

Ciris would realize one of her own was missing eventually, if the other Sin Eaters in Cordoba didn't first, and one way or the other they'd trace her to this stoop. I was counting on it. After slipping the blade into its sheath beneath the thin jacket I wore, I tucked a scrap of paper into the fold of the dead woman's collar, arranging it so the edge of a blade drawn in red ink that could have been blood was just visible. *Sicarii's calling card.* Servenza thought Sicarii dead, but the Gods—both sides—knew she was still out there. For the past six months, Sicarii had been murdering their mages and . . . most deliciously of all, each side thought Sicarii was working for the other.

I straightened and inspected my green sleeves, bright as spring, but I'd put the blade where I wanted and there was no blood to give me the lie.

I couldn't keep the grin from my lips as I stepped away. It'd taken me murdering my way through two enclaves of Sin Eaters and burning the Cathedral of Colgna down around a dozen mages of the Dead Gods—destroying some of the Dead Gods' bones worked into their altar in the process—for actual war to break out between the Gods. Once it had, the clergy on both sides had set to with a motherfucking will, taking the world as their battleground.

As for Sicarii? She had been Chan Sha. Now she was a hollowed-out husk, on the run from me.

I'd lost her in that blur of the first month after Eld died, but at last I had her. She'd finally returned to the place I'd least expected, her old stomping grounds: the Cordoban Confederacy. Oh, I'd moved on, redoubling my efforts to destroy the Gods.

I owed that to Eld, who'd died so that I might live. I owed it to Sister, who'd done the same many years before. And I owed it to the little street rat I'd once been, a girl who read a few books and dared to dream. But that didn't mean I couldn't spare a moment for Chan Sha if she'd gone to all this trouble to pay me a visit.

I rounded the same corner Denga had a few moments before and felt the sun pale before my black skin, bursting with rage. I was incandescent.

2

I stepped out of the alley, and the port of Cordoban spread out before me like a giant's beating heart, pumping its lifeblood from the great, yawning bay into the wide river that ran through the city and then down south and east for hundreds of leagues, across the entire breadth of the country. The city was built upon three hills that shadowed the port, which was usually packed with ships of every size and description; the confluence of port, hills, and river created a seemingly never-ending bazaar that bustled both night and day with trade, food, drink, and entertainment of every kind, plus a few expected and unexpected pleasures. Al-kasrs, with their resplendent gilded domes, rose from sunburnt brick buildings, adding pops of color to the landscape of vermillion and terra-cotta.

Even here, on the smallest of the rii—what the locals called the hills and a bastardization of the Cordoban word for "blade"—the wind carried the sound and scent of the bazaar. The thrilling blend of spice was somewhat tempered by the pungent, sweetly sick smell of refuse baking in the gutters running down either side of the winding cobblestoned streets. I breathed deeply, feeling a pang of homesickness. I never thought I'd miss Servenza—and this wasn't Servenza; the spices and language were wrong and the air was too dry. But I guess even a street rat misses their hole every now and again. Not that my palazzo was a hole—it was as nice as many of the al-kasrs here in Cordoba—but the principle stood.

I eschewed the bazaar's center, which was reserved for Cordoban's banks, or qarsi, and their money exchangers. All around were stands of every size and shape, offering a dazzling array of goods for any with coin. Here and there the rainbow sea of cloth that enclosed most stands was parted by crumbling walls that offered a view of the port. Likely Chan Sha was lurking around one of these, trying to see the ships below. If she'd gone down to the hodgepodge of brick, mud, and wood that formed the docks, she wouldn't have been able to see a damned thing.

I stepped up onto one of these minor promontories. The sea wind kissed me, its salty licks once again reminding me of Servenza. Two nearby stall owners were complaining about the confederation— why were the princes and princesses who oversaw the city-states that made up the Confederacy allowing unrest in the streets and murders at night?—but neither trader seemed to realize these were skirmishes in a larger war being fought by the Gods and their followers, bleeding their lives out in the name of a holy war we'd no part in. I scanned the water and a thousand scraps of sail. Some ships were anchored between immensely tall, brightly colored staves driven into the seafloor, while others were hauled into—or out of—place by teams of rowers. The pilots' guild over-saw all ingress and egress of the bay.

I shifted my boots on the wall, sending bits of ancient mortar tumbling. Two centuries ago this wall had stood twenty spans high and encircled the capital. Servenza, then a budding empire, and Normain had briefly allied in a bid to bring the Confederacy to heel after Cordoban's privateers took too much wool from the other nations' merchant flocks.

One night, Servenza and Normain's combined forces had come over the walls and poured into the city like rats in a grain shed, not realizing the entire civilian population had disappeared into the rocky dunes that led to the interior of the country. With their enemies inside the city, the Confederacy sprung their trap, flooding the street with whale oil that was then set alight. Both Servenzan and Normain had burned like human torches.

A fraction of the great host survived to limp back to their

countries, their alliance shattered irrevocably, and Cordoban never bothered with walls again. The bay soon gained a massive set of chains that could be drawn across its mouth to prevent fleets from entering, but otherwise, the Confederacy trusted in that for which the hills that ringed their capital were named: the blade.

"Sin," I said under my breath, trying and failing to keep the need from my voice, "let's see if she's still here." I swept my gaze back from the port and over the bazaar sprawling before me. "Start with limpers and we'll narrow it down from there."

"Limpers, aye," Sin said, and my vision burned, the stall-holders' grousing suddenly fading as my hearing went, but with its loss, I gained an eagle-eyed view of a hundred paces around me. I stopped turning at Sin's nudge and focused on an uneven movement within the crowd. A scrap of cloth resolved into a bent old man with a shambling gait; he bumped into one of the tents and got cuffed by a broad-chested woman twice his height. I saw her lips forming a variety of insults . . . and the gilded cup he'd slipped into his other hand. I shook my head and my vision leapt back, wider, Sin resuming his search.

We went like that for a good half bell and I was beginning to believe Chan Sha'd called it a day, if she'd even been the limper Denga had seen, when Sin focused on a shadow that turned into a woman. She was striding down the narrow divide between the backs of the rows of stalls, her brown skirts swishing back and forth. She hitched one leg, catching her weight with a cane of plain brown wood. On another step, her braids fell away from her cheeks, and I saw the one-eyed face that I'd been dreaming of for more than half a year. *Chan Sha.*

I was moving before I knew it, peripherally aware of one of the stand owners finally realizing I was there and cursing me out as only a fishmonger could for darkening her bench without the decency to haggle over her catch, whether I wanted fish or no. Another time I might have paused to listen, profanity being a poetry all of its own, but I could *just* make out the back of Chan

Sha's brown dress as she slipped through the ranks of stalls farther down the hill. *You gave me the slip before. Not again.* I took a right and paralleled her, dodging a towheaded teenage boy shouting about the cockles he was selling and feeling too clever with himself by half for the dick jokes he slipped in amongst his cries. A flurry of movement farther uphill drew my eye—and half my blade from beneath my thin coat—before I realized it was just a dagger fight over rights to beg on that particular corner. I shifted direction, cutting the distance between us. *Never again.*

"The amirah is wise!" the reedy-thin man practically shouted at me. I was too dark to be from Cordoba, which apparently meant I was deaf. He gestured at the lamp in my hands. "It contains the soul of a Dejen, amirah."

"A magical construct that takes the form of whatever I desire?" I asked him in my flawless, properly accented, Sin-assisted Cordoban.

"It's a Dejen," he said by way of agreeing. "Look. There! The script says . . ."

I held the lamp up as if studying the swirling bullshit the man had likely carved himself, but my eyes were on the woman, who'd pulled her wide-brimmed, floppy hat down low—protection from the sun that also served to hide her features. Everything in me froze solid, setting my insides aflame. It'd taken me another half bell, and drawing a blade on a would-be pickpocket, to cut the distance between us to a mere slingshot's reach. My fingers itched to pull my slingshot from the slim, leather pouch that hung crosswise acrost my body and let fly. Or else to call Sin's magics to me and put a blade between her shoulder blades. The Buc of eight months ago would have done just that, but then I hadn't appreciated the frost that rage required, the utterly cool delivery it entailed. I did now.

So I didn't out steel and draw a bloody smile across Chan Sha's throat. *Yet.* Instead I tossed the lamp back to the thin man, who caught it and switched instantly from selling me on the brilliance of the Dejen within the lamp to telling me where I could stuff it. In some ways, the cursing, more than anything else, made me miss Servenza. With me not far behind her, Chan Sha made for the edge of the bazaar that led toward the inns and houses of the tallest hill, or rii, that was filled with outlanders. It was right about here that one of my other little fishes had caught sight of her yesterday. He'd trailed her into the city, where she'd hung around the section that played host to the Sin Eaters' conclave— the official one, at any rate—then followed her back to a small alley in the poorest hovel of this rii.

Drive low into her back when she passes an alleyway. Kick out her bad leg. Pin her left shoulder to the ground with a blade when she tries to rise. Mind the punch she'll throw, likely with a fistful of blade. Break the bad leg and then . . . tear her apart. I could see it all in my mind's eye, variation upon variation, all ending with her torn and bloody as my frozen rage consumed her. My breath was ragged in my ears and my expression must have been more than a little unsettling because as two women passed me, one recoiled so hard she knocked her companion into a table full of tin cups of all shapes and varieties. The resulting cacophony drew Chan Sha's attention and forced me to turn into a doorway to avoid her gaze.

Patience.

There were only two inns on the corner the little fish had followed her to, but not even a mouse trusts itself to one hole, and for all her faults, Chan Sha was no mouse.

"Sin Eaters never are," Sin said. "Not even former ones."

The woman was barely two score paces in front of me. It could be that Chan Sha'd laid me a trap to find and step into—it'd be like the wench to do so and have me thinking it all my own idea. I didn't believe that was probable, but possible? Sure. More than that, I hesitated because killing her now wouldn't get me what I needed: answers. First, to what the fuck Chan Sha's endgame had been with her Sicarii front, but secondly and far more importantly: was anything still lingering in her mind from her days as a Sin Eater that might help me kill the Gods? A former Sin Eater was dangerous, aye, but also capable of giving me what Eld and I had been working so hard for.

Eld.

His name stole my breath away like a blade between my ribs.

"Let her go," Sin suggested. "She seems to be following the same route today she did yesterday, and we know she can't have been here many days before our little fish found her. You've a meeting with the Artificer you're overdue for. Chan Sha will keep."

"Aye," I said, letting go of the hilt I'd been gripping along with the breath I'd been holding. I watched the tall woman, bent slightly over her cane, hobble around the corner. I felt like someone had picked a scab off my heart, but as sharp as the pain was, I couldn't let it consume me as it'd done before.

"She will. And the Artificer may have word. Finally."

3

I found the Artificer on the second-floor balcony of A Sharp Word, one of the taverns perched midway up the middle rii, known as the Ra as it was where the nobility lived and did their business. The hills were blades, and the name of every tavern, bar, and drinking hole seemed to contain some corresponding pun. As taverns went, the Sharp Word was fairly tame, perhaps owing to its proximity to the Royal Academy. Gearwork ceiling fans provided some semblance of a breeze to cool the patrons, many of whom eschewed alcohol for stimulants. In Cordoban they liked to drink their kan mixed with cocoa, piping hot despite the blazing summer heat. Half the population drank watered wine chilled in cellars deep in the rii, but the scholars wouldn't dare muddle their wits, not when words so easily led to actual steel and certainly not when many of them had access to both words and blades aplenty.

I wove my way around tables that were packed with wealthier m'utadi—third or fourth children of the nobility—in brown and cream robes with their cowls thrown back. Farther back, away from the sun's searching rays and closer to the largest of the fans were the futuwwa—maestros of the Academy—resplendent in their bloodred robes sewn with thread o' gold. They argued just as fervently as the m'utadi about matters of history, law, trade, politics, and a dozen other disciplines. Strangely, it was the astronomers who were the loudest, one woman standing up to spit obscenities: a disconcerting metaphor about a comet and another's arsehole. Ignoring them, I made for where the Artificer sat, beneath an awning on the cream-marbled balcony. He lifted a hand when he saw me coming.

"Cocoa?" the man asked, indicating the steaming mug in front of the empty seat. His own drink was half-gone, despite the sweat pouring down his pallid features. He adjusted his thick wired spectacles—only three rows of lenses lined up in front of his eyes today—and smiled.

"No kan, aye?"

"Of course not," he said, sweat dripping from the tip of his long nose. "I only made that mistake once and that was in Colgna, Buc. You're not very trusting, and so forth," he added, taking a careful sip of his kan-laced cocoa and smacking his red lips together despite the obvious distaste he had for the brew.

"You can't trust him," Sin whispered. "He's weak, willing to turn that straitjacket of a coat to whoever's twisting his arm. He worked for Sicarii!"

"Trust is the sound of death," I told both of them. *He's strong enough, in his own way. And he turned on Sicarii before I was in a position to twist anything of his. Not even his nose.* Sin was quiet in my mind, as close as he ever came to owning that I was right.

"You play your part well," I admitted, dropping into the seat opposite the Artificer. "Even if you hate kan and the heat. You know, if you ever get the futuwwa to grant you scholar access to the Academy, they'll let you wear robes instead of that ridiculous jacket."

"My jacket's not ridiculous," the man said, running his hands along the plum-colored, tight-fitting jacket he wore buttoned to his neck. "It's their tawdry dress that's ridiculous," he added half under his breath, glancing at me and then away as his cheeks blushed to match his red lips.

"You Normain," I said, kicking my feet up on the edge of the balcony and letting the darker-green, close-fit, divided skirts I wore fall back, exposing the barest edge of my calves where my tanned leather boots ended, "are the world's most fucking prudes, I swear. It's hot enough to boil water, man!"

"That would require a temperature precisely double the current air temperature," the Artificer said, looking away. "Ah—you jest," he added after a moment. His spectacles clacked together as the lenses shifted, putting a different pair in front of his eyes. "I've news, Buc. Things you may be interested in hearing and so forth."

"I've news of my own," I told him, reaching for the red lacquered mug. "Go on, you first. Brains before beauty and brains."

"You laugh at my appearance," the Artificer said, "but I may be wearing a robe soon enough."

"They let you in?" I hissed, pausing with the mug halfway to my lips. "Finally?"

"Into the Halqove," he said with a nod, unable to hide his grin as he ran a hand through his close-cropped, corn-silk hair. "I know it's but the first step, Buc. Give me a few more months and so forth and they'll let me past the outer ring and into the Marlqive proper."

"You did well," I said, following his gaze past our balcony and to the resplendent al-kasr that rose up like a flower across the street from us. A white plaster wall ten spans high ran in a graceful, curving perimeter around open courtyards that were dotted between the three large towers that rose up into gilded balls, like glasswork half-blown on the tube. They were connected by massive, white corridors covered in indigo-and-gilt scrollwork with arrow slits designed to admit light. The Academy was huge, dwarfing even the Confederacy's al-kasr, but we both knew looks were deceiving. While its library was famed throughout the world, the Halqove was mostly filled with tables of m'utadi who were transcribing older works and attending lectures.

There were library stacks, aye, but not many. The true trove lay within the Marlqive and within something known only to the futuwwa—and to the Artificer and myself—the Mamnuan Xuna. The Forbidden Library. It was practically impossible for outsiders to be granted admission to the Marlqive; the Artificer's vigorous efforts had only gotten him into the Halqove—the Academy—and that had taken more than a fortnight.

"I'd given them up ever letting you pass—comes of Normain keeping too tight a lid on your genius."

"Comes of scholars not appreciating engineering," the Artificer said with a shake of his head, his voice as close as it came to anything resembling anger. "You're . . . not impressed?"

"It's not that," I told him. "It's just I can't afford to give you a few more months to maybe cajole these old arseholes into letting you have a red robe." I tapped the mug against my lip. "I can feel time slipping through my fingers like sand, Arti."

The war, and you could pick whichever you wanted: the mortal one between the Servenzan Empire—still Doga-less and, according to Salina's last letter, the nobility increasingly unhappy at the Empress's delay in appointing a new leader—and Normain. Or the deific one between Ciris and the Dead Gods. Regardless, the war was the best opportunity I was likely to get to take them all down, but until I knew exactly how to kill them I was struck blind. Which had led me to the Forbidden Library.

I said as much and added one of my new favorite lines. "'When the time for action arrives, the blade that strikes first, strikes deepest.'" *451.* Amirzchu had been one of Cordoban's most famous princesses, fighting three feuds at the same time and melding the city-states into a single bloc over the span of five years. She'd also somehow found the time to write a memoir, a fascinating blend of philosophy and military stratagem, that, being Cordoban, prized speed, surprise, and aggression above all else. It'd worked for her and, two generations on, her family was still a powerful force in the Confederacy.

"Didn't she die of poisoning?" Sin asked.

"Aye, her eldest daughter didn't want to wait for the Confederate Seat," I admitted. "But I don't have any daughters to watch out for."

"No, just every deity and their followers in the world," he murmured dryly.

"You mean to trust this—" The Artificer leaned forward, dropping his voice. "—this dog you've brought to heel?"

"You know," I said after a moment, "I always thought it a mark against them that they give their apprentices the same name as a mutt, but in hindsight they do train them well and quickly."

"You're dodging the question," the Artificer said. He gestured with one of his ink-stained hands. "And so forth."

"I entrusted her with something small," I reminded him. "And Denga says she's still doing her job."

"How well is the question."

"Something I'll find out tomorrow," I said. I took a sip of the cocoa, the bitterness twisting my tongue, and suppressed a sigh. *I'll add sugar to the order next time.* "Or you will. I promised Denga I'd listen to her read, but that may not be practicable any longer."

The Artificer frowned. "Why's that?"

"Because on my way to see you, I ran into an old friend . . . Chan Sha."

"Chan *Sha!*" he hissed, fumbling his mug and nearly dumping it in his lap. "Here?"

"What I said." I nodded toward his shaking hands. "Might want to set that mug down before you ruin that jacket." My needling him worked; I saw his hands steady even as he followed my advice. "So you see, events race on whether we will it or no and I *need* the information in that secret library."

"That we don't know for sure exists."

"The whole reason this m'utadi is staying blackmailed is because she let slip in her cups that it does exist," I reminded him. *After I noticed her smuggling a book out to study.* That offense alone was enough for her to lose a hand or an eye depending on her sponsor's mood, but then I'd gotten our frightened m'utadi drunk and she'd spilled all the cocoa beans she had in her.

"The child truly has no luck at all," Sin muttered.

"Child? She's barely a year younger than me," I whispered mentally.

"Look, Arti, the proof is right there before you," I continued. "Would she have offered to tutor a street rat for free? To give me the exact dyes used in the futuwwa's robes?" I snorted. "She's so scared we'll let it slip that she's been teaching Denga mathematics as well, to keep me happy."

"Even if this library is real," the man hurried on, speaking in clipped tones before I could interrupt him, "we've no way of knowing if said library holds the information you seek."

"Ergo, our need to do some hands-on research," I said. "The only reason our poor m'utadi knows it exists at all is because the Dead Gods' priests came here two years ago, a whole coterie of scholars seeking knowledge that their ancient archives don't have."

I left unsaid that the timing suggested they'd left with an idea on how to destroy Ciris, setting the Ghost Captain and Chan Sha on paths that eventually intersected with my own. Everything was coming full circle, but then I'd read that the stars above ran in infinite loops, and Jerden—a northern mystic writing two centuries before who also apparently had a fondness for a hallucinogenic found in a particular mollusk—claimed that time ran in a loop as well and everything had, or would eventually, repeat itself. I wasn't sure about any of that; the man's prose was beautiful but he seemed to be living in a fantasy contained within his mind.

Either way, it was clear the library contained something important. The Royal Academy didn't collect only dissidents—like the Artificer—but also dissident books and forbidden knowledge. Knowledge dangerous enough that my m'utadi's sponsor had nearly cut his own throat when he realized what she'd witnessed.

"You can't trust a Cordoban," the Artificer said, cutting through my thoughts as he dropped his voice to a bare whisper. "Gods, Buc, they don't even trust themselves! Entering the outer ring without the proper pass is enough to earn a laming. Entering the

Marlqive without a robe or pass will see you blinded and run out of port on a plank and so forth. Can you imagine what they'd do if you found this Forbidden Library?"

"Only too well," I admitted. "That's why you're going to hear Denga read tomorrow. If the girl does credibly, we'll have the measure of the m'utadi."

"And if she doesn't?"

"Then our apprentice won't have to imagine what will happen to her if she's found out," I said grimly.

"I don't like it," he said, dry-washing his hands.

"Clearly."

"Where will you be?"

"Cutting through Chan Sha," I said, unable to keep the growl buried in my throat.

"We must be careful, Buc," he said, hesitantly reaching out a hand and then, when I didn't move away, putting it atop my own. "She was a Sin Eater once, a pirate queen, Sicarii . . . we don't know what she is now."

"A dead woman walking."

"Buc!" He squeezed my hand. "She nearly overthrew the most powerful city-state in the world and came within a hair of besting the most powerful woman I know." I smiled, despite myself, at that and he grinned, too. "She didn't come here by accident," he added, his smile fading. "Not when she could have lost herself in the Shattered Coast if she'd given up whatever demented dreams she sees behind her eyelids."

"Lid." I tapped my eye with my free hand.

He snorted, his lips turned down. "We've got to assume she has a plan and that plan may include you."

"Or you," I reminded him.

"Fine, us, then."

"What are you so afraid of?" I asked him. I leaned forward and let the winter-deep rage within me trickle out. "I as good as took her eye and her magic from her. I destroyed her plans and sent her fleeing like a rat before a dog. She's a bare husk of what she was before. When I take her—and Arti, I am going to lay hold of her with both hands and give her a steely kiss—she'll be naught but a memory!" I didn't realize I was nearly shouting until one of the nearby apprentices raised their mug and yelled approval while the rest of her compatriots asked her to translate what I'd said.

"That," the Artificer said, watching the other table in disapproval, "is precisely what I am afraid of. You were calmer than this when we faced her on Southeast Island, and when she slipped your grasp it was . . . unpleasant. Face her like this, Buc, and she may slip away again, and I worry what would come of that." He cleared his throat. "I—I just—worry."

"Worry." I sat back in my seat, blinking back scalding tears as my chest ached as if I'd run the length of Servenza. "Eld used to worry," I said after a moment. I glanced at the Artificer's hand, pale atop my own, which was the color of the ebony table, and smiled. "I'd forgotten what that was like, I think."

"I've been . . . concerned," Sin chimed in. "It's not in my nature to worry."

"Save about what a failure you are at convincing me to pledge my heart and soul to Ciris?"

"Save that," he admitted.

"What do you do, Arti, when you're unsure of an outcome? When you're running experiments?" I asked the man.

"Ah, well, experiments are by their nature the first of their kind, so I'm never exactly sure what will come of them. I have theories, of course, supporting documentation, research—" he began.

"Sure," I said, cutting him off before he really got going. It was always a risk asking the man about his methods; he could talk for hours. Days, even. "But in the moment, when you were making Serpent's Flame, what'd you do?"

"I used a control," he said, unfazed at my interruption. "Several, actually. The first was simply gunpowder, which I knew to be explosive. I measured its effects in order to set a baseline against which I could compare the explosions from that which would eventually become Serpent's Flame. I started with one ingredient and as I added more, I kept each previous concoction so I could compare them across a range of ingredients. It gave me, well, control over how I proceeded."

"Control," I mused. Right now I was in control, but a moment before, I'd lost all semblance of it. That's what I needed, some mechanism to control my reaction such that no matter what Chan Sha stirred within me, I'd be able to hold my rage steady.

"I am your control," Sin whispered.

"You were, once," I admitted.

"I could be again. If you—"

"If that happens it will mean I've decided we're both done for," I told him.

Once, I thought I'd had control of Sin, but it'd been the other way around. I hadn't known that not only could he respond to my commands, he could direct the feelings and sensations running beneath my consciousness. Similar to the way the body remembers to breathe without being told. Sin had made me forget my love of food because enjoyment beyond nourishment wasn't necessary. He'd made me forget how I'd fucked up and let power blind me, how I'd destroyed some of the very ones I'd set out to protect: children and the poor and downtrodden.

When Eld and I had torn apart, I'd realized the extent of Sin's control. Pain had given me the ability to wall Sin away from me. I still did that from time to time, when he was truly aggravating, but mostly I kept him so close within my consciousness that he could do nothing I didn't allow. Letting him influence my emotions would give him a gap in my armor that I knew he would plunge through. I needed to find another way.

Time is a circle that spins out before us so quickly we imagine it to be a line, or at the end, a wall. I snorted mentally. Jerden had been off his rocker—apparently, smearing mollusk toxins over your body will do that. *Jerden. Hmm.* I stood up suddenly and the Artificer, who'd been silently waiting, stood up with me.

"Returning to the al-kasr with me?"

"No, you go ahead," I told him. "I know you want to get that automated piston running more than one in a dozen throws."

"I had thrice in a dozen yesterday, then it stripped a gear," he said with a smile. He reached up and twisted his spectacles, putting yet another set of lenses before his eyes. "And where will you be, Buc?"

"Finding control, Arti." I squeezed his shoulder as I passed him. "Finding control."

4

"Blood from the liver of a sand hind combined with this one, dearie," the apothecary said, touching a tin whose label bore a word even Sin couldn't translate, written in a spidery hand, "heals all sorts of maladies of the blood.

"If it's an issue of the mind," she continued, pushing her broad body upright and moving slowly back behind the polished hardwood countertop, "it's desiccated magefish brain, ground into a paste and mixed in with . . ."

I let the older woman natter on as she pulled various jars and tins from the built-in shelves along the back wall. Her clothing was plain, a large grey dress that looked dark against her faded tan, cinched tight below the fold of her stomach, the skirts cinched tighter still so that they almost looked like trousers. *I miss trousers.* Her hair, gathered over one shoulder and threaded through with bangles and silks that could be drawn across the face like a veil to provide shade if she ever left her shop, was of a color with her dress. I'd tried three other shops, but I'd known as soon as I stepped across the threshold of this one that I'd come to the right place. There was a feel about it, the organized clutter and the rotating gearwork chandelier that cast faint light across the entire floor, but it was her eyes, angled and black and piercing, that convinced me.

"Pardon, saydechu," I said, letting Sin give the words to my tongue. "My dear da has a toothache that wine nor sahju won't touch. He's tried. More than usual."

"How much sahju?" the woman asked, bending to look at the drawers beneath the counter.

"Two."

"Two drams?"

"No. Bottles," I said. Sahju was a Cordoban alcohol made from some heinous combination of fermented rice and seaweed. Two drams would have you feeling on top of the world. Two bottles should put you out for life.

"*Bottles?*" The woman stood up so fast her arthritic knees cracked. She leaned against the counter, her brow furrowing to add more wrinkles to the ones already there. "And he is still in pain?"

"He is. We can't afford a physiker, saydechu," I added. "I hoped you had something that could lessen his pain. And his anger."

She nodded thoughtfully. "I've a tincture put by that comes from the splintered rainbow mollusk," she said as she sifted through a drawer. "Gets its name from the beautiful colored pattern on its shell. Beautiful to us, a warning to any would-be predators." The woman pulled out a small bottle and set it on the counter. Reaching for a pair of thick gloves, she added, "The slug inside exudes a deadly toxin that seeps into its shell, giving it the pattern. The older ones have half a dozen rainbows in their shells and are so deadly that picking up even an abandoned one that washes ashore can still put you to sleep for a brace of days or more."

She carefully used a dropper to transfer half a dozen drops of the liquid in the vial to a small brown glass, speaking as she did so. "You'll want to mix a drop of this into a full mug of water or wine—not sahju. That'll put him to sleep for half the day or better and there's enough here to last a week or so. Perhaps the tooth may mend on its own."

"Are you sure, saydechu? My dear da *really* needs sleep."

The older woman snorted. "Any more than that, child, and your da may never wake up."

"That would be a shame," I said, touching the faint bruise on my face, made with brushes and powders. "But he really does need his sleep. The deepest sleep." I met her eyes, Sin making them tear up. "I was told you helped women in need, saydechu. I've not much, but . . ." I dug into the ragged pouch I'd purchased from a begging woman and pulled out two silver coins. "Can you help me?"

"Oh, my dear child." The older woman sighed. She rested her thick forearms on the counter and took one coin, pressing the other back into my hand. "I'll help. The Gods send I shouldn't have to, but then the Gods all seem to have lost their minds these past few months." She slipped the thick leather gloves back on and tripled the amount of drops in the small brown bottle. "Put the lot in his next dram of sahju and your da *will* sleep well."

"Thank you, thank you," I whispered, faking a tremble as I took the bottle from her.

"Just mind you don't let any touch your skin when you pour it," she said, her thick lips twisting in a humorless smile. "A drop absorbed through the skin will make you see all manner of things that aren't really there. If you've a cut and it gets into your blood it'll put you down for a bell or two, if it doesn't stop your heart.

"And see that you throw that bottle in the gutter when you're done, in case there's someone that does actually find your da dear," she called as I left the shop.

I slipped out of the rough overcoat I'd worn to the apothecary's, tossing it to a different beggar on the corner before taking the nearby alleyway that led through a warren of shops and stalls. Sure, I could have gotten what I'd needed for less coin in the Grand Bazaar, but I'd no need for anyone to remember a short woman a shade darker than most Cordobans frequenting apothecary stalls . . . and even less to risk another run-in with Chan Sha. The next I saw her, it would be on my terms, dancing to a tune of my choosing.

The alleys darkened as the sun sank below the horizon; lamps strung across the thoroughfares gave light where needed. With

Sin, I didn't need much light at all, which was just as well, as the path I took back toward the small al-kasr the Company had purchased a few years ago as a safe house avoided all of the larger streets. The Company's actual place of business was a magnificent al-kasr that lay a stone's throw from the Confederacy's, and I didn't want to attract their attention. *Not when the Company still has me on the books as missing, presumed dead after the clock tower in Servenza blew up.* Salina, who knew otherwise, had made sure the house was at my disposal before I'd even arrived. Palaces, small with but one gilded dome or none at all, replaced the bricked buildings on either side of me as I moved farther up the rii.

"Show me it again, Sin."

"Buc—is it wise to torture yourself like this?"

"Show me."

Sin sighed and shifted in my mind and suddenly, I was in two places at once. I still walked along the chipped and broken cobble of the increasingly narrow alleyway, sidestepping dross that had been tossed over a wall here and there, but I also stood in a blackened room with no walls, floor, or ceiling. I wasn't alone.

Eld was there.

"Buc . . . if you're seeing this or hearing this?" Eld shook his head, his blond hair drawn back in a loose ponytail, both hair and skin bright in the darkness, his blue jacket immaculate, brass buttons shining with a light of their own. He ran a hand back along the side of his hair and shrugged. *"I don't know what this Sin can do, but if you received this message, it means something happened to me. Yesterday a pickpocket tried to knife me when I caught her reaching for my coin and another joined in. It happened again today and a rusted blade can kill just as easily as a polished one, so I don't want to take any chances. Not with you . . . asleep."*

Eld looked directly at me for a long moment and sighed. "Two days ago I pulled you out of a warehouse as it burned around you, Buc. You were bleeding from your head and half a dozen other places and when you woke yesterday you were half-crazed. Your Sin calmed you down and revealed himself to me." He swallowed, his sapphire eyes bright with tears. "I don't know what's going to happen, Buc, and I'm torn up inside that I haven't spoken to you sooner. Told you the truth."

He took a deep breath, his broad chest straining the vest beneath his jacket. "The truth is that I realized a while ago that I feel something stronger than friendship for you. I—I held back because I didn't want to betray your trust in that friendship and I'm terrified it will ruin what we have. I can't let that happen. You're my best friend, Buc."

"You're mine, too, Eld," I whispered, seeing both the wall a few score paces ahead where I'd need to angle up the hill to the al-kasr and Eld before me.

"I know things have been . . . awkward since the Shattered Coast. I've been a fool, Buc. I hate magic and you know that and I know you only did what you did to save me and . . . Gods," he said in one long breath. He shook his head and looked away. "I should have told you all of this and let you decide what you wanted. I've kept that from you, but I promise if you wake up from—when," he amended, "when you wake up from this and your mind heals, I'll tell you everything and you can decide where we go from here. But, Buc?" He smiled. "No matter what you decide, friends or something more, or nothing at all. I'll always be there.

"I'm not going anywhere."

"Oh, Eld." I bit back a cry. Half of me hated listening to this, knowing that soon after, Sin had convinced Eld that telling me the truth of what happened at the warehouse would drive me insane, forcing a wedge of lies between us. The other half? The other half couldn't stop listening to his voice. It'd been so lonely and strange the last eight months with only the Artificer and Sin for company.

"You're bloody fucking welcome," Sin hissed, and I felt his pain at my remark.

"Eld taught me to read; you just taught me you're only loyal to your Goddess," I snapped.

"I helped you defeat the Ghost Captain and save Eld's life," he rejoined. "You always judge me over the one thing I have no control over! I can't help my nature."

"Let it go," I told him. "All of it."

Eld disappeared, fading into inky darkness, transforming from bright and alive before me to dead and pale in my memory. *I'm not going anywhere.* I blinked back tears, looked up toward the dim stars popping into the night sky overhead, and bit my lip. *Godsdamned emotions.*

I turned the corner toward the al-kasr that passed for home these days, trying to swallow my thoughts with a deep breath that physically hurt. My head full of Eld and past mistakes, I didn't see the ambush coming until I was in the center of it.

Emotions: they'll get you every time.

5

I realized something was wrong as soon as my boots scraped on the gritty cobbled alley that ran, crooked, up the hill before me. I drew a stiletto from the sheath that hung beneath my armpit, inside my jacket.

"Easy, Sambuciña," the woman said, pushing herself upright from the crouch she'd landed in when she'd dropped from above. Two other hooded figures landed behind her, making the ten-span jump from the top of a darkened al-kasr look like a leap from a few stairs. She brushed a few errant strands of red hair back from her pale cheeks and smiled. "Wouldn't want us to think you had reason to fear us."

"Save," a man's deep voice said from behind me, back in the alley I'd just turned off from, "you lied to us and then tried to disappear. Not the actions of an innocent."

"Did Ciris go and create some legal system while I wasn't paying attention?" I asked, sliding to the right so that the al-kasr's wall would offer me some protection. *Unless the bastards are going to jump from there, too.* My ears burned with Sin's magic for a fraction of a heartbeat, but I didn't hear any noise above. So: at least one opponent behind me and three in front. Not great odds when we were all playing with the same magic. "I've nothing to fear," I continued, "and nothing to be guilty of and, last I checked, no reason to lie to you."

"Keep Her name from your tongue," the woman snapped. One of the black-hooded figures stepped up beside her with a growl. "You've lied to us for the last time, girl."

"Can you at least tell me which lie it is I told you?" I asked, showing my teeth. "There's been so many, you know."

"Bitch," the man beside her snarled.

"Efram," she said, and he visibly reined himself in. "You told Katal and Jesmin about Chan Sha's final showdown with the Ghost Captain in Servenza this winter. Recall?"

"Eh, that tea was pretty weak," I said. "Stronger now, though, aye?"

"What?" Efram asked.

"Ignore her," the woman said, "she's obfuscating. We've been to the Shattered Coast, girl."

"You, personally?" I knew that was unlikely; she was right, I *was* stalling.

"Sin Eaters," she said, her eyes locked on mine. "We're all one. With Her. In the Shattered Coast we found the Arawaíno and the island. We know the truth. Chan Sha never made it off those shores and neither did the Ghost Captain, but whatever it was that was buried on that island isn't there any longer."

"You have it," Efram growled. So much for his patience.

"And you've come to Cordoban to confirm its authenticity before selling it to the Dead Gods."

"Seems you've got everything all figured out," I said slowly.

"Don't try anything stupid," the Sin Eater said. She smiled, baring white teeth behind her red lips. "You've another blade or two on you, I wager, but you're no match for me, let alone the rest of us. Ever see a Sin Eater in action, girl?"

"A time or two," I muttered dryly.

"Careful, Buc," Sin whispered.

"If they wanted me dead," I whispered back, "they'd have rushed me straight off, but they think I have something hidden away, which means they need me alive." *Ciris didn't tell them what was on that island . . . interesting.* "'Sides, Sin, we've an advantage they don't."

"What's that? You?" he snorted.

"Me . . . *and* you." I felt him freeze within my mind before he grudgingly nodded. I felt the blade in the palm of my hand. Not balanced for a long throw, but within a dozen paces? It'd do. *Stiletto overhand, edgeless blade up left sleeve, crossbow, or slingshot?* Decisions, decisions.

"As I said, you've got all the sums totaled," I told the Sin Eater in front of me. "But I am curious. After all these months, why here? Why now?"

"You hid yourself well," the woman admitted. She shrugged. "But you should know better than to trust a Cordoban, especially a scholar."

"Oh, M'utadi," I muttered. "You double-crossing bastard."

"You fucked up, Buc," the Sin Eater said.

"Maybe," I admitted. *Sin? Now.* "But so did you."

I whipped my hand forward at an impossible speed, eyes and arm burning with Sin's magic as my hearing and other senses shrank to make room for what I was about to do. The stiletto I'd drawn scythed through the air so fast none but a Sin Eater could see it. Unfortunately, everyone in the alley, present company included, was a Sin Eater. The woman snapped her head to the right and the blade passed her by. Fortunately, I'd accounted for that— and as fast as Sin Eaters are, they can't stop what they don't see coming.

The hooded figure who hadn't stepped up with Efram collapsed in a heap, my blade jutting from where their forehead likely would be. Efram shouted and the woman cursed, both drawing short swords and pistoles.

"Forget about me?" a deep voice behind me rasped.

"Not—" I twisted my wrist, pirouetted, and drove my edgeless blade through the bottom of a large man's chin, driving it up and back, where throat met chin. His momentum slammed us both into the wall, but I didn't stop. Sin's magic made my hand burn like it was on fire as I rammed my fingers up through the bloody hole created by the steel. I thrust the cord-wrapped hilt of the short blade through blood and tissue and fat until my fist drove the blade home.

Into his brain.

"—even for a moment," I gasped, spinning to put the large corpse between me and the two remaining Sin Eaters.

His body jerked and the boom of pistoles eviscerated the night, reverberating down the length of the narrow alley. Shoving the dead man toward the Sin Eaters in front of me, I assessed the shorter, thinner figure who stood half a dozen paces behind the man I'd just killed. They'd thought to take me alive, but they'd been planning on a human, not a fellow Sin Eater. *Slingshot? Too fast.* I drew my jacket back, exposing the narrow crossbow that hung from a string beneath my arm, and flipped it up, catching it in my hands and firing from the waist.

Bolts zipped through the air and the figure jerked—a woman, by her scream—as I rocked my index and middle fingers against the trigger, sending half a dozen bolts into her. I let the momentum of the gearworked crossbow—the Artificer's invention— carry them up the length of her body. An alley piece like this one didn't have much range, but up close it was as deadly as any gun. The cylinder clicked empty as she fell in a heap. I released the crossbow and threw myself into a roll just as another cacophony of gunfire riddled the alleyway, blazes of light erupting from where the two Sin Eaters fired rotating pistoles.

"Sin!" Time slowed as we spoke literally at the speed of thought. "Grenado?"

"Left inner pouch. You're going to come up against the wall of the other al-kasr in two more rolls."

"Rebound and toss?" I asked.

"Rebound and roll."

"Aye," I agreed.

The world came back in a blur as I somersaulted toward the wall. One hand supported my body weight as I vaulted back across the alley; the other found the smooth sphere in my jacket. Thankfully, it hadn't broken. The Sin Eaters had unloaded a dozen rounds between them in the blink of an eye, but I knew, none better, that they had used their magic to do so, and that meant they had to pay a price. To move that fast, they had to sacrifice either their vision or their hearing. Being deaf in a fight is one thing, but being blind was a death sentence.

Which is why they might have seen me roll the grenado across the cobble toward them but wouldn't have heard the glass break when it hit the hilt of the sword belonging to the large, dead Sin Eater lying in the alley. For a blink of an eye nothing happened. Then the powder inside the sphere came into contact with the still-wet blood the man had coughed up while dying, and the entire alleyway was illuminated by a sheet of flame that drowned out the shrieks of the Sin Eaters.

I took my time coming to my feet and drew my slingshot from the satchel slung crosswise around my shoulder. I wasn't quite deaf, but I'd chosen to keep my night vision in the dark, and as the flames coalesced around two figures dancing in writhing pain, it was but the work of a moment to put a lead ball through each head. They dropped to the ground, still burning.

For a moment all I heard was the rasping breath in my ears, muted against the buzzing from all the gunfire, and then my limbs began to tremble. I let go of the slingshot, which clunked to the ground, and dropped my arms to my sides.

"D-damn," I wheezed. "Serpent's Flame certainly lives up to its moniker."

"You could say that again," Sin muttered. "I—I can't believe we just killed five Sin Eaters."

"They were overconfident . . . didn't expect an ordinary-looking woman to be able to do what I just did. What we just did," I amended.

A scuffling sound made my head whip back around just in time to see a flash of skirt disappear around the corner. I leapt after her and rounded the corner in time to see the Sin Eater I'd shot up with the crossbow sprinting away supernaturally fast with skirts gathered high in one hand. *Damn it.* There was an awkward lurch to her gait—she was badly injured and running on pure magic—but there was no way I could catch her. I whipped my jacket back and drew up the crossbow again, holding my aim well over her head to account for the distance.

"Sin!"

"Buc—"

Cursing, I squeezed the trigger without his magic. Click. The cylinder gave a faint puff as it tried to cycle, and I realized I hadn't reloaded. I glanced back at my slingshot, lying on the cobblestones a dozen paces away, and cursed again. The Sin Eater cut into an alleyway and disappeared from view. Shaking my head, I moved to collect my slingshot. *Looks like the m'utadi showed me her worth tonight. Nearly pulled off her betrayal, too.* It was the work of a moment to retrieve my blades, and then I trotted off toward my own al-kasr. It was past time to be gone. Once the local militias realized mages were involved, they'd take an interest in what had happened here. *With luck, they'll think the Sin Eaters were killed by the Dead Gods' priests and dismiss it as just another skirmish of the war.*

"Fuck me." I stopped so fast I nearly fell over. I'd still been half in shock from the sudden violence of it all that I didn't realize what I'd done. I'd killed five Sin Eaters in as many breaths, and the one who had gotten away had seen it all. Seen that I hadn't turned into a Veneficus to do it, either. Which meant she knew I wasn't human, and I didn't belong to the Dead Gods. And if she knew it, soon Ciris would as well. *Only Ciris knows what was on that island.*

"Me," Sin whispered.

"You." I cursed again. "Fuck me."

"Fuck both of us," he said.

6

―――――――――――――◦◦◦◦◦――――――――――――――

"W-who's there?"

"An old friend," I whispered, striking a sulfur match, putting it to the end of the wick, and swinging the small window closed. Light flooded from the gear-wrought globe I held, revealing a young woman with large, owlish eyes that were still full of sleep, a nose that dominated her face, and full lips that might distract the right lover from that nose. "Good morning, M'utadi."

The m'utadi's eyes grew even larger and she opened her mouth to scream, but I'd been anticipating that. I leapt across the bed, dropping the globe onto the sheets and clamping her mouth shut with my hand. She fought me, ramming her body into mine and slapping at me with the arm I hadn't pinned down. I dodged her hand and palmed a blade, halting it a fraction from her left eye.

"Eh-uh, woman," I whispered. "I lied just a moment ago. It's not morning, nor is this likely to end well. You see, I didn't come here to have a toss in your sheets. I came here to have a little chat, just you and I. You scream and you'll never scream again because I'll cut you from ear to ear and it's damned near impossible to scream when choking on your own blood and it *is* impossible when your vocal cords have been cut in twain like a piece of string. So you're not going to scream. Savvy?"

She made a throaty sob beneath the palm of my hand, tears pouring down her cheeks, then nodded slowly.

"All right then." I rolled off of her and stood up, then picked up the lighted globe—one of the Artificer's inventions kept the outer glass from growing more than warm—and pointed to the small table in the center of the room. "Let's have a palaver, just the pair of us."

The woman sat up slowly, trembling, her tanned skin dark beneath the thin, sky-blue nightgown. She ran a hand across her nose and took a ragged breath. "I—I pissed myself," she whispered.

"Terror will do that," I told her. "Say, what's the Cordoban word for 'friend'?" I asked, switching to Imperial.

"There isn't one," the m'utadi said after a moment, answering me in the same tongue.

"That's right," I said, gesturing toward the table. "So I don't give a fuck that your undergarments are soaked through. Move. Now."

She flinched, shrinking back against the headboard, then stood up slowly, walking with her head down, black shoulder-length hair covering her face like a veil. I followed, giving the m'utadi a push in the direction of the chair in the corner so she wouldn't get any ideas about trying to bolt out the door. She was a full head taller than me and there's plenty that think height equates to strength.

The corner was close to the window I'd used to climb in, but she'd have to be a Sin Eater or a Veneficus who could grow wings to make use of it, so I wasn't worried. I slid into the other chair, setting the lantern down on the table, and plucked a handful of dates from the plain ceramic bowl that lay beside a pitcher and a cup. I'd eaten enough for two back at the al-kasr, but I had a long night ahead of me and I was going to need all the magic Sin could conjure up, which meant he needed all the food I could stuff down my gullet. *A long night, thanks to this one.* I slammed the slightly curved blade into the table, my hand tingling from the power Sin gave me to put it a full finger through the wood, making the m'utadi jump, and popped a date into my mouth.

"You betrayed me, M'utadi, sold me out to the Sin Eaters in hopes I'd take your secrets with me to the grave." I spat out the pit, hitting her on the nose, and she flinched. "That doesn't bother me, not really," I lied. "What bothers me is: does this betrayal mean all you told me was but half truth and half fabrication, meant to trip me up if I went through with my plans?"

"I—I didn't lie," she pleaded, her low voice thick in her throat. "I swear upon the Gods, old and new, I didn't!"

"What's your name, M'utadi?"

"Kanina," she muttered, her voice hoarse. "Kanina Kyomi."

"How's that translate?" I asked her. "'Possibilities,' 'Opportunities'?"

"Close enough," she answered in Imperial, clearing her throat.

"Take a drink, Kanina," I told her, nodding toward the pitcher and cup and popping another date into my mouth. "You've got a lot of talking to do."

"I was being punished for mistranscribing one of the works of Fu- tuwwa Senxrit, made to put away the entire day's returns of books in addition to my usual chores, and it was well past midmoon be- fore I finished," Kanina said. "I had two tomes left and I was the only soul in the library. Or so I thought," she said, pausing for a gulp of water, and muttering something about the Gods and their humor beneath her breath. "I was returning a volume to its shelf and when I turned the corner of the stacks, I saw a futuwwa and two of the Dead Gods' priestesses in their bone-white robes dis- appearing into the floor."

"Disappearing? How?"

Kanina's lips curved in a grin, which, taken with her tousled hair, made her look almost a child. "I was young and foolish. I thought I was seeing magic, but when they'd sunk beneath the floor and I worked up the nerve to move forward I saw that it wasn't magic, but a set of stairs carved beneath the walkway be- tween the stacks. The wood slid back to reveal a hidden passage." She swallowed hard. "I wish I'd never taken that step."

"Why?"

"B-because," she said, wrapping her arms around herself, "when I looked down, I saw the three of them walking with a pair of the Almaush—the Death Dealers."

"Death Dealers?" I bit back a curse. The Almaush were a secretive warrior sect that supposedly had sworn a blood oath to the great winged dragon that had united Cordoban into a confederation centuries earlier. Pledged to train from birth to defend their chosen Federate, they were said to be the greatest hand-to-hand warriors in the world. Cordobans being Cordobans, who believed the best defense was an attack, they were famed to be the deadliest assassins as well.

"It gets better," Sin said. "They mix kan with other stimulants and build up their tolerance until they can take megadoses that allow them to move faster than any but a Sin Eater. It makes them stronger than normal, too."

"Wouldn't that kill them?" I asked in my mind.

"Eventually, sure, but only if they take too large a dose. There's a saying about a grey-haired Almaush having a small mouth," he said. "Because it's the only reason they haven't swallowed enough to die by that point," he added, answering my unasked question.

"That's . . . a saying," I muttered after a moment. I pulled myself out of my head and glanced at Kanina. "I thought they only served the princes or princesses of the Confederacy?"

"What they guard is far more valuable than a single Federate." Kanina snorted. "When the Dead Gods' priestesses moved past the Almaush I saw what they were guarding . . . the Mamnuan Xuna."

"The Forbidden Library," I repeated. "If it's forbidden and hidden and secret . . . how does everyone know its name?"

"They don't," she said. "You know it because I told you."

"And because I read the right books," I reminded her.

"And that," she admitted. "Although the heretical texts are not allowed outside the Forbidden Library . . . were you caught with them in your possession they'd execute you on the spot," she said slowly, as if just realizing what she'd said.

"Beginning to regret going to the Sin Eaters when you could have just gone to the futuwwa?" I asked her. "Don't get any ideas in your head." I touched the hilt of the blade I'd stuck through the table and added, "I've taken steps to ensure you don't betray me again."

"B-but I told you the truth! All of it," she said, beginning to tear up.

"You told the same story as the first time," I agreed. "Save you didn't mention the Almaush then."

"You don't understand," she pleaded. "It takes a decade to be allowed into the futuwwa and who knows how long after to be told of the Mamnuan Xuna's existence and allowed entry. My sponsor's been a futuwwa for a dozen years and even he didn't know of its location until I told him what I'd seen."

"And then he tried to kill himself?" I asked.

"He only considered it," she said. "After he saw his own blood he dropped the knife from his wrist."

"Probably fainted," I muttered.

"Learning of the Forbidden Library isn't punishable by merely death." Kanina yawned, despite her angled eyes being wide with fright. "My sponsor said that we would long for death for seasons before they granted it to us."

"Don't get caught," I said. "Good to know."

"You're actually going to try to sneak in?"

"No, you are," I told her. She sat back hard against her chair, mouth working soundlessly, and I let her hang on that hook for a few moments before releasing her. "Gods, no." I laughed. "You'd never make it past the Almaush. But, Kanina?" I asked, leaning forward. "Cut the shit and tell me all. Now."

"I did!"

"You did not," I growled. "You're terrified. I get that. But if I don't believe you, you're not going to have to worry about the futuwwa torturing you, because I will. And if I don't make it out of that secret library alive, you won't survive the night. Savvy?"

"That's not an actual word, you know," she whispered after a moment.

"You've sand, woman," I said, "I'll grant you that. And it is a word, just not in your spiny-arsed tongue. Now," I snapped, "what haven't you told me? I already have to figure out how to slip into the inner passage with just a pass to the outer ring. I don't need any other surprises."

"It's not in the Marlqive," Kanina said.

"What?"

"I was too young to be allowed past the Marlqive unsupervised, even to return books," she said slowly, her tongue fumbling at some of the words. "The Forbidden Library is in the outer ring, just past the first set of stacks. Take a left and . . ."

"Genius," I whispered when she finished. "No one would think to look in a place so many can access."

Kanina fought back another yawn. "They've been right so far," she said slowly.

"Hmm, there's still a lot to steer by feel on this one," I mused. "I'd have liked another few days, but thanks to you forcing my hand, I need that information now, before—" I cut off. *Before Ciris finds out everything and puts a watch on the Royal Academy and comes hunting for me personally.* I'd realized, once I got back to the al-kasr and had a moment to catch my breath, that I had to take Ciris out first. The Dead Gods had shown little interest in the machinations of nations before Ciris awoke. All the histories I'd read about the time before that sounded as if the Dead Gods had been content to be the only soul merchants in town. So if I eliminated Ciris, that should calm them down, let them feel they'd won, and buy me enough time to slit their undead throats when they weren't looking.

"You really think this library has that kind of knowledge and Ciris didn't know about it?" Sin asked.

"I think the Dead Gods and the Ghost Captain thought so. 'Sides, the Cordoban Confederacy has been welcoming dissidents and heretics for centuries . . . if any place would have that knowledge, it'd be here. Mayhap there's a reason why they've never invited any Sin Eaters, eh?"

"Maybe," Sin said after a moment, discomforted at the thought of a blind spot in his deified vision.

"I—I d-don't feel well—right," Kanina said, slurring her words. Her eyes weren't wide any longer, mere slits as she fought to speak.

"Ah, well, you wouldn't," I told her. I flashed her the brown bottle the apothecary had given me and grinned. "Turn and turnabout, woman."

"Wh-what you do?"

"Are you familiar with the splintered rainbow mollusk?" Kanina tried to say something, but all that came out was a moan. "Me either," I admitted. "I'm told it's incredibly deadly, but I wasn't sure how fast it would hit you. I poisoned your cup," I said. The woman's eyes flickered and she collapsed, smacking her cheek on the table before rolling onto the floor. "Pretty fast for the dose," I added.

"You could have caught her," Sin said.

"Let her feel it," I told him. "She nearly got us both killed a couple of hours ago and you're feeling chivalrous?"

"Not really," he said. "I've just been trying to fill that void, lately."

That void. *Eld.*

"C'mon," I said, standing up and ripping the blade out of Kanina's table so hard that I tore a fist-sized hole out of the wood. I threw open the window and whistled like one of the thrushes that flocked about the rooftops of the city. A moment later a figure crossed the street and leveled something large at me. With a dull crack, a projectile flew toward me. Sin's magic let me snatch the grappling hook out of the air with ease. I quickly hauled up the rest of the rope and tied it into a makeshift sling. With Sin burning in me it was but the work of a few moments to slip the sling around Kanina's still form before hauling her over to the window ledge.

Bracing myself, I rolled her out the window and, hand over hand, lowered her down to the street. When the rope went slack, I glanced around the room, but—hole in the table aside—there was no sign anyone other than m'utadi had been here. I caught up the globe the Artificer had loaned me and stowed it beneath my coat before levering myself out, hanging on by the fingertips of one hand and pulling the window closed with the other, then climbed down along the drainpipe that ran down the side of the brick building.

"Whew," I muttered, landing beside the Artificer, who was still untying Kanina. "That was more work than I'd have liked, given what's left for me to do."

"And what's that?" the man asked, glancing up through his spectacles.

"Oh, you know," I said lightly. "Same old, same old. Find a hidden library, face deadly assassins, discover the secret to killing the Gods, and escape with life and limb still intact."

"Ah, that old fig," he said lightly.

"Exactly." I frowned. "Say, did you just make a joke?"

"I'm learning," the Artificer said with a grin, his eyes magnified behind his spectacles. "So now what?"

"You got the robes?" I asked.

"And the pass," he said, pointing toward the handcart hidden in the shadows of the alley across the street.

"Then we make a trade. I get the robes and the pass and a chance to die horribly for the second time tonight and you get the woman who is responsible in no small part for both of those." I helped him lift Kanina, picking her up beneath the arms, and we walked her limp body to the cart, the Artificer huffing and puffing from the effort.

"If I'm not back by first light," I said, pulling the blanket over Kanina's face and tucking it in around her so that the cart looked like any other, "go straight to the Company's headquarters with that letter I left on my nightstand and they'll smuggle you back to Salina. She'll know what to do." *I hope.*

"What about the girl?" the Artificer asked, taking a moment to buff his spectacles. He blinked at me. "What do I do with her?"

"I haven't decided," I lied. I'd already let one loose end dangle: the escaped Sin Eater. I couldn't leave the m'utadi to pull another thread loose. "Let's see if she's still breathing, come morn. Then we'll figure that bit out." I shrugged out of my jacket, tucked two stilettos into my belt, and pulled the crimson robes on over my head. Once my arms were through I wiggled around to get a feel for the fit. "How do I look?"

"Like one of the futuwwa," he said, handing me the pass he'd been given earlier that day. "Should I bow to you?"

"Only if you want to be a m'utadi," I told him.

"We're all m'utadi, if we're doing it right," the Artificer said.

I snorted. "That's something the futuwwa seem to have forgotten," I said, shaking his extended hand, "but maybe I'll have time for a lesson or two."

7

The guard returned my pass with a slight nod of his head, no full bow for a visiting scholar who required a pass because they didn't have proper scholar's robes—I'd removed the robes as I wouldn't need them until after I was inside—and was back to jacket and dress. I thanked him in broken Cordoban—sans Sin—to keep up the false persona I'd created, then marched into the outer courtyard. It was dimly lit by globes suspended from wires above; gearwork plates set within the cobblestone triggered their movement so that faint light followed me as I walked past fountains that were still in the humid, midnight air. Topiaries made for hulking shapes in the shadows, the mournful cooing of a nightwing and the faint buzzing of insects the only sounds at this hour. I reached the edge of the courtyard and, rather than following the wall around, kept walking straight through the corridor that led into the library proper.

The corridor before me looked tattooed by the indigo lines that traced intricate shapes across its white walls. The wide archway, which disappeared into darkness above me, held massive doors in its maw. The doors were resplendent with images of books and gilt lettering proclaiming this place the "House of the Most Esteemed Knowledge Bearers" or perhaps the "Citadel of the Highest Learned," or two or three other translations. The Cordoban were a complex people and their language equally so.

I realized I was stalling and forced myself to stride forward as if I expected the doors—slightly ajar—to open fully before me. As I neared and realized just how massive they were, I saw that there was just enough of a gap between them to walk through. There was no one else in sight. According to Kanina, the Halqove was usually empty at this hour, save for an unfortunate m'utadi who was performing some form of manual labor as punishment. There were guards at the entrance to the inner Marlqive, but thankfully I'd no need to go there. I stepped through the doorway and felt my breath leave me.

The stacks were few, lining the walls on either side for the first dozen paces and filled with ragged covers that had seen much use. Kanina had told me the Hall of Learning—or as she'd put it, "the Hall of Discovery, Thought, and Intent"—held only primers and introductory text for the lecture halls. Most of the space beyond the wide hall I now found myself in was closed off at the opposite end by another archway and doors that lead into the inner library reserved for futuwwa. I glanced into several open rooms—empty at this hour save for a woman scrubbing at what looked like a bloodstain on the floor by one of the lecterns—as I walked past. Many were filled with rows of seats arrayed around lecterns; at least one was clearly a waiting area—perhaps its far door led to audience chambers.

The smell of parchment and ink hung thick in the air, filling me with longing. I'd been a voracious reader since Eld taught me my letters, but here was a place where that love was formalized. Where I wouldn't be a freak because I looked as if I belonged in the gutter but always had a book to hand. Here I'd be amongst compatriots thirsting for knowledge, debating what scholars long dead had meant their writings to convey, defending theorems and theories, reciting histories. Servenza had her own academies and Colgna her university, but I'd never had the occasion to go to either. I thought books themselves were all I needed, but setting foot in this place, I knew I'd been wrong. Books were blades for the mind, and here was the whetstone.

"You could wait until morning and sit in on a class," Sin whispered in my mind. "I'm sure you'll get a lot out of it . . . right up until two score Sin Eaters show up with Ciris possessing one, if not all of them."

"She can do that?" I hissed.

"She's a Goddess. The only living deity in this world, Buc. When will you grasp the import of that?"

"Likely not until long after I've slit her throat and seen her tossed in the waves," I muttered.

"If you understood what I've been trying to tell you, you'd understand how ridiculous a thought that is," Sin said.

"Hey, take it easy. I've never been to school, remember?"

Before he could frame a rejoinder, I moved away from the classrooms and turned to the right at the intersection before the closed archway of the futuwwas' hallowed library. Immediately the hall opened into a labyrinth of bookshelves that rose from floor to halfway to the ceiling, laid out before me in even rows that ended—sometimes abruptly—only by other shelves that ran perpendicular to the rest. Here and there, flickering lantern light indicated where a visiting scholar—such as I claimed to be—or a m'utadi or servant was moving about. A wealth of knowledge lay in front of me, even in these "lesser" stacks, but I had no idea how they were organized . . . and tonight, no time to figure that out.

It was but the work of a moment to find the stack Kanina had described, built into the outer wall of the inner sanctum, and then the book with red binding that was thrice the width of its companions. I slid it out. Kanina claimed she'd nearly died of fright, but the woman had had the presence of mind to look around, trying to understand what had caused the floor to open up . . . and had noticed a book out of place. Such a thing was impossible in the stacks, because the m'utadi were in charge of returns and the futuwwa expected each copy to be flush with the next. The mistake had jumped out to her, leading her to the next secret. *Lucky me.* I held the cover up, but it was scrawled in a language I'd never seen before—Kanina thought it made-up gibberish, although looking at it, I wasn't so sure.

"It's definitely a language," Sin said. "One I've not seen either, though, and it would take a fair bit to translate it."

"That's fine. We're not here for that." I glanced around, but there was no one in this particular stack, which was only dimly lit by the chandeliers overhead. Reaching beneath my jacket, I undid the string that kept the robe tied around my waist. I'd tried the fit earlier because if it didn't look custom-made then there was no hope of fooling the Almaush. I shrugged into the bloodred robe, pulling it over my clothes. Then I felt along the smooth wooden shelf where the book had been, my fingernails catching the edge of the hidden compartment and prying it up. Within was the lever that would reveal the hidden staircase.

I couldn't afford to let any get close enough to see my face . . . I was about two decades too young to be granted access to the Mamnuan Xuna. So I pulled the cowl up over my head, tucking my loose locks back and letting the fabric throw a shadow over my features. Weapons inventory: a stiletto on either hip, a blade on each wrist, and another strung around a cord and hanging down the middle of my back. I'd killed half a dozen Sin Eaters with little more than this, but the Almaush were nearly as capable and just as deadly. If I had to fight, that would mean I'd lost any hope of discovering the means by which I could end the Gods and their chokehold upon the world. *No pressure.* I snorted and pulled the lever up. For a moment it held, then it shifted, sliding smoothly up into place with a click that echoed behind me as the floor trembled with a steady vibration that hinted at more gear-work beneath my feet.

A section of the wooden floor sank down a bare finger's breadth, then slid aside, beneath the rest of the floor. Stairs cut into polished grey stone led down to where two figures stood just outside a pool of red lamplight. Both swiveled to stare up at me as I nonchalantly slid the thick red book back into place, knocking the lever down, and stepped onto the first stone, a ticking sound just barely audible as I entered the passageway. Putting my hands together so that they disappeared into the wide-sleeved robe, I descended the stairs processionally, as if I were a queen deigning to give her due to the commoners.

Up close, the Almaush were as intimidating as the rumors said they were. A woman who would have rivaled Eld for wide shoulders stood tall in a thin, mail tunic that covered her tightly from neck to knees. Leaving little to the imagination, it showed her heavily muscled torso off to great effect; the red lantern light cast bloody shadows over her shaved head and thick, gold earrings. She shifted her weight but didn't reach behind her for a pair of axes, nearly as tall as me, resting in brackets mounted on the wall. Her compatriot was a short man with flowing dark locks and enough muscle to put the woman to shame, his neck as thick as my leg. He didn't wear armor, just a sleeveless vest over a pair of trousers that ended at calves the size of tree trunks. His hand strayed toward the hilt of the short sword that looked more like a cleaver in his belt, then stopped. His gaze told me he'd weighed me to the barest coin and assessed me no threat. Yet.

Though I'd seen plenty of fighters in my time, these two in particular reminded me of Eld: not fighters but warriors. *Sin?* He shifted in my mind. *If either moves for a weapon, give me everything you've got. I want them dead before they realize what we are, aye?* I felt him nod assent, but a layer deeper, I felt his hesitancy, and that, more than anything else, sent a chill through me. Sin considered himself next to a God, and if he was nervous, I should be petrified. *No one ever won by holding on to the cup. Toss the dice and play your roll.* Old Buc made me smile. One lesson she'd taught me is that if you've enough nerve, you can accomplish wondrous things.

I didn't bother to glance at either Almaush until I reached the door, then I gave the slightest fraction of a nod. After an endless pause, the man moved—perhaps at some hidden signal from the woman—sending Sin's magic coursing through my body in a tingling, burning flame before I realized he was just opening the door. I was being admitted to the most secret library in the world.

I strode boldly through the stone archway and down a row of marble statues that led to a dais in the center of an open circle ringed with tables. A man and woman moved slowly but purposefully between a handful of waiting scholars, all in robes that matched my own, and the dais, where a single figure stood before a long table. Slips of paper were passed, the figure bent, and I realized the table wasn't a table, but a massive cataloguing system.

Unlike the Kanados Trading Company's library, the Mamnuan Xuna was reserved for works by dissidents, heretics, and all manner of shadowy figures. There might be untold wonders on its shelves, but I needed to find a specific thing—if it existed—and quickly. I ducked into the outermost aisle before any glanced my way, and began walking quickly down the row. Shelves hewn into sandstone and lined with thin fur were on my right, while proper shelves of dark wood polished with scented oil curved sinuously away on my left. The row wasn't straight because the rock wasn't straight: the shelves conformed to the space, not the other way around. In a dozen steps I was out of sight and I paused to pluck a book at random.

"What am I looking at, Sin?" I asked, flipping through the pages slowly enough that I could scan each page, but too quickly for me to take in more than a word or three, even if it had been in a language I recognized.

"It looks like a book of songs on sexual conquests and insults," Sin said after a moment. "At least three centuries old, by the archaic Cordoban it's written in, and not fond of the Prince Federate of Umant, considering the three verses dedicated to the diminutive nature of his, um—"

"Block and tackle?"

"Aye."

"Sometimes making it into the history books isn't everything it's cracked up to be," I muttered. Slipping the book back onto the shelf, I moved farther down the row and paused when a gentle current of air tickled my ear. Two stories above, a gap in the ceiling allowed for some sort of ventilation; while the air wasn't bone-dry, my tongue was beginning to cleave to the roof of my mouth. *You're not here for the architecture.* I glanced back at the shelf and plucked out a thinner volume, flipping it open. "This one?"

"Songs on the nature of the Gods," Sin said. He made a noise. "They seem to be suggesting that the Dead Gods are the Father, Ciris the Mother, and we all her children."

"Definitely heretical."

"And stupid," he muttered.

"Uh-huh. I won't argue that one with you."

I kept moving from stack to stack, periodically removing books from the shelves to see if they were useful, trying to determine where the information I needed might be located. By the time we'd walked down a good two-thirds of four stacks, I was growing wary. I couldn't walk up and declare myself to the master librarian—that had to have been the figure taking book requests from their assistants who spoke to the other futuwwa—because they would instantly recognize I was too young to be there . . . or would realize I shouldn't be there at all. While the Royal Academy had several hundred scholars in residence, those granted access to the Mamnuan Xuna were far fewer and would know one another intimately. I had to rely on Sin deciphering the cataloguing system. Books were numbered, but with single digits, and were shelved by no discernible method save that some appeared to be in alphabetical order by title.

"The longer we're here, the more the odds increase that we'll get caught," I reminded him as we entered another row.

"I'm working as quickly as I can," Sin said. "There's only so much I can do with such limited information to work with. The rows seem to be arranged by subject, then further divided into additional subjects within the row, but the numbers don't make sense and I'm not entirely sure I trust the numbering system."

"Clearly the futuwwa don't trust themselves either," I muttered. "That's why the need for the master librarian—to control access to the shelves."

"It's very Cordoban of them," he agreed. "Wait . . . flip back a page?" I flipped back to the title page and Sin chuckled. "Fucking clever arseholes."

I glanced at the title page, which looked brighter than the rest of the text, flipped to the next page, and cursed. "The title pages are fakes, added in after the fact."

"To sow further confusion," he said with a mental nod. "All right . . . I think I understand now. Take a step back."

I walked to the beginning of the row and followed where Sin indicated. "The numbers on the ends of the rows are a repeating sequence that equates to the Cordoban alphabet and that allows one, if calculated correctly, to grasp the subject by the numbers carved along each shelf. . . ." I could see numbers carved into each shelf a dozen paces into the row. "Then," Sin continued, "the title page has a few numbers that indicate the sub-subject and the actual title page the title. Perhaps the title is the actual book title?"

"You're losing me," I told him.

"Your brain losing out to your beauty, Buc?"

"Fuck you."

"Nothing beautiful about your mouth," he muttered.

"Oh, I don't know, there's a certain poetry to cursing," I said. "Walk the docks of Servenza when sailors are loading or unloading and you'll hear it. Probably learn a new word or two in the bargain . . . so do you know which row we need to be in?"

"Two down," Sin said, pointing mentally toward the back of the library, farther from the entrance. "We'll—"

A gong sounded, growing in strength until it reverberated loud enough to shake the shelves for a moment before disappearing.

"What was that?" we asked at the same time.

"I thought you knew," we both repeated.

"Damn," I said, and Sin held up before we repeated each other for a third time. The sound of boots scuffling on the floor drew away from us, and I risked a peek around the corner of the next row in time to see a red-hooded figure disappear from view around the final curve before the central opening. A few more steps forward granted me a glimpse of another walking past one of the marble statues, throwing their hands up in the air as they moved toward the dais.

"Some sort of roll call?"

"Looks like," Sin agreed.

"This is the most secret library in the world . . . there can't be that many of us down here," I muttered. "What are the odds they send one of those assistants out to walk the rows after everyone's shown up?" I asked. "To make sure there isn't some demi-Goddess infiltrating their bloody secrets."

"I wouldn't take that bet," he said. "Look!"

A woman in a purple cloak walked past the row we were in, marching toward the stacks nearest the door, followed by a similarly garbed man who likely would take the other half of that outer aisle. Several moments later they both called back, "Clear." With Sin's magic burning in my ears, I heard them walk to the end of the first row and start down the second. *I've no time.* There were half a dozen rows between me and them, eight now as I moved to the row Sin indicated. *Almost no time.* For a moment I hesitated, doing the sums, but this wasn't a time for thought. This required action. Fast action or violent action in seven rows and counting. Biting back a curse, I sprinted toward the far wall, catching myself there for an instant and nearly upending a shelf full of books before running the last two rows to where Sin had indicated. I began pulling books at random.

"I hope you've got your motherfucking reading specs on, Sin," I growled as I began flipping pages. "We don't have—"

"Next one," he interrupted. "The time," he finished for me. "I know. That book," he added as I plucked and opened another, "was just on powers of the Gods. Next," he said after I flipped two pages. "Move a quarter of the way down and switch to the other side."

"Sin," I muttered as I plucked books without looking at them, "if you're playing me, I'll make that time back at Colgna look a single night's sleep compared to how long I'll lock you away."

"If you're not going to trust me, Buc, you picked a poor fucking time to do it," he snarled. "I'm not going to help you actually murder Ciris—I'll choose Ascension first—but there's still time for me to change your mind."

"What's Ascension?" I asked, aware that he'd capitalized it in the same way he did Possession."

Silence.

"You're lying."

"I'm not," he whispered.

"To yourself if no other," I told him, picking up another book. "Nothing's going to change my mind about ending Ciris."

"You've a mind like few I've encountered," he said after a moment. "You can't not respond to new stimuli, incorporate them into your decision-making process."

"Aye?" I flicked through the pages. "What of it?"

"When you learn the true nature of Ciris," he said, "you'll change your mind."

The certainty in his voice made me pause, but I shrugged it off. Sin had been trying to get me to agree to complete the Rite of Possession I'd accidentally began a year ago, and so far he'd not just been wrong, he'd been badly mistaken about his ability to succeed. This was just more of the same. *I hope.* I turned the page and made to turn to the next.

"Stop!" Sin hissed.

"What?"

"This is it. Quick—flip through this one and the ones on either side of it."

I did as he suggested, nearly dropping the second book when

Sin fed the details of the first into my mind. I winced, the sudden shock of knowledge like a pickax to my brain, and I felt my skull begin to tingle with his magic. "S-Sin." I tried to speak, but couldn't find a scrap of wind to breathe, let alone talk. Spots flecked my vision and my stomach somersaulted, and for a moment it was all I could do to remain standing, keep turning the pages. I wanted to melt into the floor. The pressure grew, focal points of pain dancing through my skull. "S-Sin."

"Next book," he said. "I know it hurts, but we've got no time, Buc. Next book."

Sweat blurred my vision, or maybe it was tears, but somehow I managed to put the book back on the shelf and grab the final volume. It shook in my hands and my sight narrowed to a fleck of light that let me see barely more than one sentence at a time. Knowledge, three books' worth, catapulted into my mind like iceberg juggernauts smashing into one another. No, that wasn't quite right—it was more like mountains collapsing into one another, crashing into a hundred thousand pieces, and immediately reforming. *Can't do this.* I'd always known the truth: knowledge hurts. It'd just never been physical like this. *Much longer.* My mind was going to break apart and there'd be no picking up the pieces.

Suddenly the pressure disappeared and the space it left behind was so vast I nearly fainted. A heartbeat later, I became aware that I was leaning against the shelf, panting as if I'd run a marathon, with a dull headache pounding behind my eyes. I began to ask Sin what the actual fuck he'd just done to me, then realized: it was all there, within my mind. All of it. *The weaknesses of the Gods.* The Ghost Captain had the right idea—I needed to introduce a virus into Ciris and it needed to be delivered by someone who could interface with the Goddess . . . but that didn't require the altar, though the Dead Gods thought it would. To kill Ciris required a willing host and a willing Sin. It required the unthinkable: a traitorous Sin Eater. *The Ghost Captain was right. He needed me all along, but not the Buc of a year ago.*

"He needed the Buc of today," I whispered.

"Scholar?" a voice asked from the end of the stack.

Shit. Between the pain of absorbing all that knowledge and the breakthrough of understanding, I'd completely forgotten why Sin had force-fed me in the first place.

"What are you doing?" the purple-robed woman asked, walking slowly toward me. "Did you not hear the sound of the gong?"

I'd discovered exactly what I needed, aye, but it was useless if I didn't make it out of the Forbidden Library alive.

"Scholar?"

8

Thirteen paces. Knife. Throat. Underhand, release at the midriff and follow-through will carry it higher. Silence. Sin moved with me and I twisted my wrist, the blade sliding into the palm of my hand at the same moment I heard another set of boots behind the woman, about to round the corner. *Fuck.* I could kill her silently, but I couldn't kill her companion when I couldn't see him and if he sounded the alarm . . . *Double fuck.* Even if I killed them both, the guards weren't going to allow me to leave in the midst of their roll call. *All the fucks.*

"I was lost in thought," I called back to her, dropping the pitch of my voice slightly. I shrugged and crossed my arms, using the motion to slide the knife back up into the sheath on my wrist. "I'm sure you've experienced the same."

"Of course, Scholar." The woman inclined her head. "Would you allow me to escort you to the Master Librarian? The Elmakti is adamant about the laws."

"As befits their station," I agreed. I motioned for her to lead on and kept my face as much within my hood as possible. The man, heavy brow furrowed, waited for me to move before slipping in behind me.

"Now what?" Sin asked.

"I think of a plan."

"You've got about forty-five more steps. Forty-four. Forty-three."

"You want to help?" I asked him. "Take care of this fucking headache you gave me."

"You wanted the knowledge to destroy the Gods," Sin growled. "You got what you wanted."

"I can't help but think there's some element of punishment in the method," I said dryly. "For gaining the knowledge to kill your Goddess along with the Dead Gods."

"I—am on it," he said after a moment, his hesitation giving him the lie.

"Good." I kept walking past the rows of books, head straight, eyes taking in the rapidly approaching main passageway before us and the statutes that led toward the dais where half a dozen futuwwa were gathered around the man standing behind the large desk dominating the platform. "Think they know I'm an impostor?"

"Tough to say if they're just being Cordoban," Sin said, "or if they have actual cause to not trust you. This Elmakti isn't going to be satisfied with a distracted-scholar excuse, though."

"I know."

"You're going to have to come up with something more than 'I snuck into your Forbidden Library to learn how to kill the Gods.'"

"I know."

"Then—"

"Sin," I snapped. "I fucking know, aye?" I just didn't know what story was going to satisfy this Master Librarian if he demanded that I lower my hood.

"Ah!" The Master Librarian greeted the woman in front of me as she stepped into the central area. "All accounted for, then, Niall. We can—" He cut off at the sight of me, his tanned features darkening beneath the spotty, black-and-grey beard that clung to his cheeks like bits of grit. "Who is this?"

"A scholar who lost themselves in the stacks," Niall said, bowing at the waist. The depth of the bow told me where this Elmakti ranked amongst the futuwwa.

"Scholar?" He made a sweeping gesture over the table that filled the dais. "Where is your name amongst my roll? You know the penalty for failing to sign your name? Well, what say you, Futuwwa?"

I reached up and slowly pulled my hood away from my face, letting it fall down my back. Sin hissed. Let a man sense weakness and he'll grab hold with both hands, but shove that weakness down his throat until he chokes, and he'll swallow it whole. "I am not one of your futuwwa, Elmakti. You stand in the presence of an Eldest of Baol, of the Dead Gods."

"Look at the pair on you," Sin muttered.

"Balls were made for kicking," I told him mentally. "That's why women run the world."

"I thought you looked familiar," the man who'd followed me after Niall gasped. "You're one of them from before."

"Aye." I nodded fractionally, turning farther away from him so he couldn't see my features and realize his mistake. "I apologize for the secrecy, Elmakti—but your Academy is being watched and I could not risk being as open as we were two years ago."

"You've violated our trust," the Elmakti snapped, his thick lips pulled back to reveal yellowed teeth from years of drinking cocoa. "This cannot stand, we—" He paused, tilting his balding head. "Being watched? By whom?"

"By what," I corrected him. "Ciris's mind fuckers have been stalking every institution of learning since they learned of our Ghost Captain's attempt on her life."

"An attempt you assured us would succeed," he said as if reminding me. "I do recall a younger one amongst your party, but you look very young indeed to be an Eldest."

"We're at war," I said. "I've come up in the last two years."

"Others of your kind have come down, you mean."

"We're at war," I repeated.

"Baol . . . you are Servenzan?"

"Of late," I agreed.

"You speak Cordoban like a native."

"The Gods work in mysterious ways."

"So what is it, then," the Elmakti asked, folding his arms in his robes, "that brings you here, a literal thief in the night? Even if we are watched as you say, surely you could have declared yourself once within these walls."

"I could have, save you don't trust your own scholars enough to let them enter and leave as they please," I said, giving him a smile. "I couldn't risk you not giving me leave to read the works we read last time."

"Why revisit what you already know?"

"'Because wisdom is a beach to be trod carefully, each grain of sand simultaneously unique and uniform,'" I quoted.

"Your knowledge of Cordoban scholars is impressive," the man said after a moment. "Lauxnu Lamin?"

"*An Education of a Wandering Mind*," I agreed. *461.* I'd only just read it a few weeks ago and was still mulling over some of Lamin's beliefs on framing an education. "We misinterpreted some of the texts," I said after a moment. "That is why the Ghost Captain failed. That is why Ciris is hunting for knowledge to hoard and destroy," I added, playing a hunch as to why the futuwwa would take a side amongst the Gods. "That is why I'm here tonight."

"Find the answers you sought?"

"I did, Elmakti," I said, inclining my head slightly. "With an apology again, for intruding upon your sanctum, and your permission, I will now depart as I came."

"I understand your motives," Elmakti said after a moment. By the way the rest deferred to him, it was within his power to let me go . . . or not. "I will leave you to return to your kind, Eldest," he said, fixing me with a hard stare, "but know this. If you return again, without permission, you will never leave these halls again. Do you ken?"

"Savvy," I said, touching my nose and pointing at him. "Never again," I added, turning around. I pulled up short when I saw the Almaush a dozen paces away, blocking the exit. The broad woman, leaning against the long battle-ax at her side, ran a hand over her shaved head while the short barrel of a man simply stood with his arms crossed, war hammer jutting from the sling on his back.

"Before you leave, Eldest?" the Elmakti asked from behind me. "You've blood coming from your nose. Do you require a physiker?"

"Just another vial of blood," I said, running a hand over my nose and feeling it come away wet. I could feel something leaking down the lobe of my ear, too. That knowledge really had come with a price. "Surely you've seen our relationship to blood," I added.

"Indeed I have. You remember your Ghost Captain?" I turned half back around at that. "We dined together that final night before your leave-taking and while he was too sure of himself, he had a quick mind. He told me of many things, including"—he flashed me a yellow-toothed grin—"some of the way your magic works.

"It pains me to have forgotten a fellow scholar," he said with a sigh. "Will you tell me his name, that I might add him to the lists?" He pointed at a tapestry that hung behind him and was covered in writing.

"You honor him, Elmakti," I said slowly. *Shit.* "He would appreciate that," I added. *Name. Sin, did he ever give his name?* I felt Sin's headshake and bit back a curse. *Name.* "His name was Eldritch," I said, speaking before I could think, "Nelson Rawlings."

"I wondered what you would say to that," he muttered. "You lie well, Servenzan," he added in a louder tone, stroking his patchy beard with ink-stained fingers. "Quickly, too. But I stopped believing the words that come from others' lips long ago. No, I only trust the words we leave to parchment, and them only some of the time." He spread his arms wide. "I've read of your magics, but only one kind of magic have I ever read of that would cause bleeding from the brain. Mind magic.

"Sin Eater."

"Well," I said, showing every tooth in my mouth as I smiled, "aren't you the clever fucker."

Sin? Give me everything.

9

I spun away from the Elmakti, grabbing the short man who thought he'd recognized me, and driving him forward in front of me like a plow. He tripped over his purple robes, tried to catch himself, then windmilled, boots slipping and sliding as I pushed him hard before me. Sometimes, you make a mistake and no one's the wiser; sometimes you're made to pay. He caught the female Almaush's war ax in the shoulder; the fearsome weapon slammed him to the ground, smashing through his torso and into his sternum, where it caught against his rib cage, making the same sound a chopping block made. The man screamed, a wild, inhuman cry, jerking like a bug on a pin. *Fuck me.* Warm blood splashed my face, but I was already sprinting. Away from the woman and toward the shorter Almaush, who was broad enough to almost make the woman look thin.

The man was all muscle, but as with the war hammer he had half-unlimbered, it takes energy to get that much mass moving. I, on the other hand, was shorter, smaller, and tossing loaded dice thanks to Sin's magic. My legs burned, moving faster than the Almaush could have thought possible, and I reached him before he'd done more than half draw the war hammer. Remembering what I'd told Sin about men and their balls, I used my momentum and the magic-enhanced strength of my legs and kicked the man as hard as I could.

Right in the danglies.

I expected him to scream, choke, go purple in the face, and fall to the ground from me putting his bits through one of the marble statues behind him. I didn't expect him to grunt in obvious pain as my boot connected not with his balls, but with his pelvic bone. I certainly didn't expect him to stiff-arm me in the chest with his fingers straightened so that it felt like I'd been stabbed more than hit. My breath left in a single whoosh of air that got lost in the searing pain that radiated from my core as I suddenly reversed direction. I was dimly aware of traveling through the air at speeds not recommended for prolonged life. Something approaching soft broke my flight and I tumbled to the floor, rolling over until I came up hard against one of the marble statues and saw black.

I came to after what can't have been more than an eyeblink, my ears ringing and my heart in my throat. Niall lay crumpled before me, her head twisted at an impossible angle. *How?* A roar drew my attention—my vision flecked with spots when I moved—and I saw the woman Almaush rip her ax free of the man she'd just killed, practically tearing him in two. *Oh, that's right.* She turned toward me, her bald head covered in bloody splashes like birthmarks, and showed her teeth. The man beside her had drawn his war hammer, which he now swung once or twice, as if to get the feel for it. *Godsdamn.* I'd thought myself unstoppable, but I'd just met something that was unmovable. I'd been expecting to put him down with that kick, but he didn't have balls or the rest, damn it.

"He does have a bloody fuck of a right hand, though," Sin growled. "Now what?"

"N-never let them see you down," I told him, pushing myself to my feet, using the statue behind me to catch my weight as I wobbled my way back to standing. With Sin, I was nearly indestructible, but Sin had one major weakness: hit me on the head and you knocked him, too. Knock hard enough and he'd be out completely, and until he came back, I was just a short woman carrying a lot of blades. Not that they were likely to help me now. I reached into my pocket, blindly feeling for what I was looking for. Weaving on my feet, the thought of Sin's magic made me nauseous, and it was looking like the only way out was if I burned this place down around us.

"You'll want," I said, speaking slowly as the pair moved toward me, "to let me leave here before things get too damned hot."

"They're only going to get hotter from here," the Elmakti cried out.

I breathed in deep, blinked twice, and shrugged. "Don't say I didn't warn you!" I said, tossing the grenado I'd managed to pull from beneath my robes. The orb wobbled, hurtling through the air, but Sin wasn't going to be back to normal for another few minutes at least, if not a full bell, so it would have to do. The female Almaush swung her ax like a stickle-bat player aiming at one of those bouncing balls, trying to knock it back to me. The ax-head connected, smashing the grenado into a thousand pieces, spilling out over the blood-soaked metal, and a sheet of fire erupted in every direction, catching the woman's head with shards of flame that leapt in gouts as they caught on the wet blood across her features. She opened her mouth to scream and took the flame in with her breath, the Artificer's powders feeding almost gleefully on their new source of moisture.

The Almaush made it another half step toward me, then danced away in flames and made awful choking sounds as she tried to scream through a blistered throat with desiccated lungs. Stumbling, she fell toward the books. The Elmakti shouted something and the other Almaush took three strides; hesitated for a second, his features hidden by his long dark hair; and then swung the war hammer up and around and brought it down on her flame-wreathed head. Her skull split like a scorched melon and she crumpled, most of her falling one way and bits of her head going the other, and the short man stomped on the flames as if kicking out a campfire and not his partner's corpse. The fire licking its way along her ax went out with a hiss that sounded like a dying woman's last breath.

"I did warn you," I said in the sudden silence. "Now, you know the truth, Elmakti," I added, tapping the shaved side of my head with a finger. "That means Ciris knows, too. She may want me to begin the cleansing here, tonight."

"You wouldn't dare," he began.

"To burn this heretical pit of vile lies to the ground?" I hissed. *Sin, where's the other grenado?* "Watch me."

"You used it, Buc," Sin said.

"No, I didn't. I used one just now and I always carry two."

"You used the other on those Sin Eaters earlier in the night."

"That's a problem," I muttered.

"A predicament."

"Aye, exactly."

"So?" he asked.

"Improvise?"

"I'm—" He hesitated. "I'm still knitting all of our connections back together, Buc."

"Kill her!" the Elmakti howled, pointing at me. "Kill the Sin Eater!"

The Almaush growled and took a step toward me at the same moment I thrust my hand in my robe and pulled out a small, brown bottle that barely filled the palm of my hand.

"Stop!" I held the bottle over my head. "Do it and I won't kill him," I told the Elmakti, turning so I was facing the stacks. "I'll do what I threatened . . . burn this motherfucker down to the stones it was built upon." I shifted my arm and one of the scholars screamed while the others made sounds as if sicking up. "All your carefully hoarded knowledge . . . lost."

"You've a mind witch's cunning," the Elmakti said after a long moment. "And their arrogance in believing only Ciris holds the answers we seek."

"I don't know what answers She holds, but I know one of Her Sin Eaters holds your library in the palm of her hand. Funny, how something so small is so destructive." I shifted my arm again. "And so heavy," I added. "What's it going to be, Elmakti? Death by fire along with all you hold dear or are you going to tell your Almaush to stand away and let me leave?"

For a moment, I thought he was going to risk it, which would have been a shame. The mollusk poison the apothecary gave me would likely kill the Almaush, but not before he did serious damage to me. 'Sides, I'd have to go back to the apothecary with a Godsdamned mummer's farce of a story to get her to give me more poison. Finally, mouth twisting, the Elmakti jabbed a finger at me. "Go," he snarled. "Out! Let the Sin Eater leave," he spat.

"Buc!" Sin growled, cutting off my retort. "For once in your life, just leave it go."

I went, sliding past the Almaush and pulling a growl from him when I trod on his partner's corpse. *Oops.* I felt Sin roll his eyes in my mind and fought to keep the smile from my lips—no doubt that would push the Almaush over the edge. What can I say? Pissing people off to the point of madness is a gift.

10

"What? W-where am I?" Kanina sat up from the coach bench slowly. Her eyes went from angled slits to their usual wide-eyed fluster when she saw me sitting opposite her. "You?"

"Me," I told her, flashing my teeth. "You're in a coach, heading down the rii as we speak."

"But—but I'm not dead?" The m'utadi clasped her chest as if feeling for her heartbeat. "You poisoned me!"

"Sickened, let's say," I suggested. "And you're altogether in one piece, so no complaints, aye?"

Kanina frowned, then sat up slowly. "I—" She glanced around the interior of the coach, the mustard-colored silks and pillows warm in the sunlight that filtered through the cracks of the closed windows. "I don't understand?"

"Clearly," I said, unable to keep from smiling. "We're heading for the docks, where I've booked you passage on a brig that sails for Servenza within the hour. There's a letter of introduction to the Chair of the Kanados Trading Company in your handbag," I added, nodding at the small clutch on the seat beside her. "And a comb as well—turns out being drugged and hidden in a cart all night tends to put knots in your hair. It also keeps you from being murdered, so there's that."

"Murdered?" Kanina squeaked, then made a louder sound when her nails caught on one of the knots in her black, usually straight hair.

"I don't think the futuwwa have caught on yet," I said, waving her question away. "Perhaps they never will, but they're going to be looking hard after someone infiltrated their Forbidden Library, murdered an Almaush, and faced down their Elmakti. That's the head of your order, I'm pretty sure," I added. Kanina's lips moved soundlessly.

"Look, you're a bit reckless for Cordoban, Kanina. Luckily, the Chair knows how to deal with reckless young women." Kanina cringed and I snorted. *Honestly, Cordobans believe everything is a knife.* "She'll also be able to get you seated at one of the universities," I added.

"I can complete my studies?" she asked, sitting up.

"Aye, that's the idea."

"But . . ."

"Why?" I suggested. She nodded. "Why didn't I kill you? Why am I helping you now?" She nodded again. "Because I admire a woman whose back is to the wall but still has the will to try to turn the tables on the one who put her there." *And nearly succeeded.* "You helped Denga with her studies, so you've got skill," I added. Another girl's face flashed before my eyes: Marin, whom I'd let down in Servenza, and let die as well. I knew Denga and Kanina weren't going to fix that—death can't be fixed. This was . . . reparations, in a way. The coach shook itself to a halt and I heard the short, clipped tones of a sailor's voice.

"We're here," I told Kanina. "You've got a chance at a fresh start, girl. You've got the brains, now you just need to learn to use them, savvy?"

"That's not a word," she protested as the door swung open.

"It is where you're going," I told her, motioning for her to step out. A porter and a sailor in sea-warped trousers and a sleeveless vest stood waiting. "Luck, girl!" I called after her, pulling the door shut and sinking back against the cushions. I was bone-tired and hadn't slept more than an hour, but now that things were heating up I couldn't afford to wait.

The old Buc of even eight months ago would have killed Kanina last night, framed her as the one behind my infiltration of the

Forbidden Library. The old Buc might have fit in better in the Confederacy than I did . . . she'd always believed in reaching for the blade first. Now? I wasn't so sure. Sometimes there's another play, another toss that can win more than steel alone. I slid the blade I'd hidden from Kanina in the fold of my vermillion skirts back into the sheath in my jacket and sat up. I hit the side of the coach and we began moving again. Where I was going next, I had only one toss to throw and it was going to be a sharp one. After all, when in Cordoba . . .

I practically guzzled down the wide-rimmed cup of cocoa the lad placed before me on the ebony table, barely waiting for him to slip back behind the sheer curtain that afforded patrons of means the privacy from the rest of the kan house. *Mmm.* I'd asked for sugar and they'd given me just the right amount, sweet enough that it would have complemented the shortbread cookies that came with it, save I'd not been able to keep from cramming them down before he'd brought the cocoa. Sin's magic gave me endurance seemingly beyond measure, but even he wasn't as good as a night of sleep, and I was going on close to two full days with barely a wink. The energy spike from the cocoa and sugar was deceptive, but it kept me from yawning as I swiped crumbs off my lap and pulled the thin, gear-wrought telescope from beneath my jacket.

I'd chosen the kan house not for its brew but for its location overlooking the bazaar. One of my little fish had followed Chan Sha past the Sin Eater's al-kasr before tailing her through the bazaar to the docks. I didn't think Chan Sha had noticed . . . for one thing, the little boy I gave the fistful of copper to was still alive, and for another, she hadn't changed her routine. I shifted the high-backed chair so that it faced out, and kicked my legs up on the edge of the white-bricked balcony before settling the telescope against my eye.

The bazaar leapt into view as if I were standing amidst the

multicolored stalls, shops, and street hawkers. I picked out the landmarks the boy had given me, and it only took a few more moments and some adjustment of the gears that whizzed within the telescope to locate my quarry.

"She likes the look of that sloop," Sin said. "I recall it lay in port yesterday as well."

"She likes the cheapness of it," I said, shifting my gaze past Chan Sha to the sloop, a weather-beaten wreck of a ship with tattered sails and a hull that hadn't been scraped in years. "Her dress is the same as yesterday and I suspect she chose brown fabric because it hides stains and will wear better than most colors."

Swiveling back to her, I felt the rage within my chest spike. Her braids, thicker than I remembered them, hid her face, but her throat and hands were darker from the sun, her once-olive skin now something within a shade or two of mine. "There's a bulge where that cloth belt goes over her hip and another just between her breasts."

"She probably has another blade in her boots," Sin commented.

"Maybe tied around her ankle—she's wearing sandals," I said.

"So . . . two or three blades."

"And something else we won't be expecting," I reminded him. "That's always been her way."

"Unpredictable," Sin agreed. "We could let her keep," he suggested, "return to our al-kasr and leaf through all those pages from last night."

I winced at the thought. The knowledge needed to settle; right now it was still like a living thing trying to force its way out of the prison of my mind. "Chan Sha's obviously contemplating something, but undecided." I squinted through the lens. "I don't want to wake tomorrow and found out she's made up her mind."

"Fair point," Sin said. "I wonder what she hopes to do? Staring at ships."

"And Sin Eaters," I said, putting away the telescope. I stood up and tossed a few coins on the table, shrugging my shoulders to feel my own blades. "Let's go ask, shall we?"

The sun was just beginning its descent and its heat tore through the few paltry clouds the sky tossed at it, radiating back off the cobblestone so that everyone around me was soaked through whether wearing wool or silk or—a few martyrs—leather. I strode through the edge of the bazaar, blissfully cool, a pit of jagged ice in my stomach, waiting to explode. Chan Sha hobbled on her cane, the back of her brown skirt looking black from sweat as she tried to navigate the midday crowd.

A woman shrieked about her flowerpots full in my face and I told her where to shove them. Her wrinkled creases disappeared in her angry expression, but whatever she'd been about to say died on her sunburnt lips when she took me in, pale-red jacket thrown wide open to show a sheer vermillion top that grew thicker where it ran into my skirts. It wasn't the fine cut of my clothing but my expression, darker than my skin, that set her teeth together. I tossed her a coin without looking, more for the confidence she gave me than anything else, and cut down the nearest row that led out from the bazaar.

I followed Chan Sha as I had yesterday. Sin gave me the image of a detailed map of Cordoban and I recognized two potential points to take her where none would be the wiser. The first was at the approaching corner, where a break between houses dead-ended, and the other was just before the alley that she'd want if she intended to spy upon the al-kasr that was the Sin Eaters' headquarters. *Which hole to trap her in?* Decisions, decisions. I felt a smile slip across my mouth.

"Signorina!"

I turned at the cry and saw a woman of my age but a head taller beckoning toward me. I stepped around the old man trundling along with a pack on his bent back and into the shade of the tailor's shop awning. The woman's light dress was obscured by a thick auburn dust cloak despite the heat, hanging on her thin frame. She had the strange look of northerners, amber hair pulled back in a strict knot so severe it made her cheeks look pinched.

"Aye?"

"Are you Buc Alhurra?"

"Say I am," I said, glancing down the street, but despite the few passersby, there was no way Chan Sha had heard her. *Guess I'm going with alleyway number two.* "Who the bloody fuck are you?"

"He said you had a tongue like a flint," the woman said with a sniff.

"There's something off about her," Sin whispered.

"Here," she added, thrusting a cream-colored envelope at me.

"What is it?" I asked, struggling with the feeling that I should have a blade in my hand. Sin was right, something *was* off about the woman. . . .

"Take it or toss it, I care not," she said.

I took the letter after a moment and she sniffed again and turned away, everything in her step making the space between my shoulder blades itch.

"Who are you?" I called after her.

"You ask such obvious questions," she said, pausing, her yellow eyes burning like orbs in the sun. "I do not know what it is about you." She shook her head. "Truly, I don't." And then she was gone, marching down the street, cloak whipping back behind her.

I stared after her a moment longer. *What was that about?* Shaking myself, I turned around and cursed when I didn't see Chan Sha. *Eyes on the prize, Buc.* I tucked the letter into my jacket pocket and broke into a trot, dodging around the others in the street and quickly passing the bent old man who'd walked by a few moments before.

"Say, I know what was off about the woman," Sin said as I neared the end of the street.

"Aye? What's that?"

"She smelled."

"Smelled?"

"Like metal. No . . . metallic. Like blood."

11

I dodged the blade in Chan Sha's fist, slapping her past me with my right hand and slashing her arm with the stiletto in my left. *Shove. Lower back. Watch hidden swing. Disarm. Headbutt.* My blade nicked her, catching the sleeve of her brown dress and tearing it instead of her flesh. When I shoved her, the woman cried out as her weight fell fully onto her bad leg; she lost her cane and pitched headlong into the alley's rough wall. She caught herself before her head connected with the plaster even as I rushed in to finish her off.

Mind the trap. She whipped around, blade in her left hand now, driving up low for my guts, and I stepped inside, trapping her arm between my own arm and my body, and dropped my weight. I felt her wrist crack and she grunted, her dropped blade clanging off the cobblestone. Chan Sha swung around, braids windmilling as she rolled with the lock I'd caught her in, and I released her arm and slammed my head into her chest. Hard. She grunted again, breath whistling between her teeth, and I caught the thrust of her hidden blade against the hilt of my stiletto.

"Nice try," I told her, shoving her back against the wall.

"You?" Chan Sha hissed, her taut features frozen.

"Me," I growled, icy rage breaking within me as I launched myself at her.

We went at it hammer and tongs. My blade drew blood twice. Thrice. Chan Sha managed to nick my shoulder, the material of the Artificer's design sewn into the interior of my jacket keeping her from ramming her weapon into the artery that ran along and up into my neck. She lost that blade, produced another, lost that one, too, and made me drop mine from nerveless fingers. It landed beside her cane. She stumbled, dropping to a knee beside her cane, and I drew another blade with my left hand, my right still tingling from the blow she'd given me and Sin's healing magic, and moved to finish her off.

Clang!

"There's the surprise," I muttered, straining to keep the sword cane she'd unsheathed from sliding up the length of the palm's breadth of steel I held in my own hand. Her dress had torn further, hanging completely off one shoulder. The sweat coursing down her tanned face and the look of murder in her angled, green, almost black eyes were the only signs she was straining with every fiber to run me through.

"I thought," I said louder, "you'd have gone for a pistole."

"Tied to my ankle and damned inconvenient," she said, speaking through clenched teeth. "I knew it was you. After Servenza. I felt you within a prick's hair of me on Southeast Island and then I gave you the slip." She bared her teeth in a grin. "Must have drove you mad, knowing Eld's murderer walked free. Had bested the great Sambuciña Alhurra."

"And yet, here we are," I snarled.

"And yet."

My left arm coursed with ice so hot it burned, and I flung her blade away with a shove of my own, the force spinning her onto her back on the ground. I brought my right arm up, flicking my wrist. The little contraption the Artificer had made especially for me hissed as the cylinder within it fired. Chan Sha jerked as she was hit, hands clutching at her chest, then a look of confusion filled her eyes as she stared from the small, feathered dart in her bosom back to me.

"A pin won't kill me, girl." She laughed.

"Aye, the dart won't, but the splintered rainbow mollusk poison what's coating its tip will." Chan Sha's eyes went wide with terror at the same time her hands fell to her sides and she slumped slowly back against the stone. "You see," I said, crouching down beside her. "It will kill . . . if I want it to." I plucked the dart out of her chest and held it up where she could see it between eyeblinks as the poison robbed her of consciousness. Rage suffused me, pushing so hard against my chest that I felt it was on the verge of exploding out and taking Chan Sha's head with me.

"I've had a few months to think of all the things I want to do to you, and this"—I shook the dart—"would be too quick. I'll see you soon, Chan Sha." I stood up, forcing a laugh.

"In your nightmares."

12

Clink. Clank-clank. Clink.
   Clink. Clank-clank. Clink.

I stood silently across the stone-cut basement from where Chan Sha hung, strung up between two pillars, manacles overhead stretching her arms taut, the ones at her feet pulling her slightly back so she hung forward, slumping in defeat. She shook her head, possibly fighting to control the panic that I hoped was stealing her breath. She looked up, though with her Sin's magic stripped away from her back on that beach in the Shattered Coast, all she'd see was pitch-blackness, devoid of any lights save the white sparks and stars her eyes would show her. No magic there, just tricks of the body. She drew in a ragged breath and straightened as much as she could with her weakened leg pulling her slightly off-center.

Clink. Clank-clank. Clink.
   Clink. Clank-clank. Clink.

I waited for her to look up again—thanks to the stress position I had her in, that was the best way for her to try to draw a deep breath—then yanked the release cord. The triple-thick canvas fell to the floor, revealing the signal lamp pointed at her face. Chan Sha screamed in pain as the light flooded her night-blind pupils. I'd closed my eyes, which were tingling with Sin's magic, but even so I felt a slight stab from the sudden onslaught of brilliant white fire. I walked over and twisted the aperture so that a few glass walls swiveled into place between the flame and the hole, reducing the light to merely bright instead of a good approximation of the sun.

Chan Sha's screams quieted as I walked forward. She squinted at me, blinking through tears. She opened her mouth as if to speak, but only a racking, wheezing cough came out. Licking the spittle on her lips, she tried again.

"W-who—?"

I kept walking, picking up the short length of rope that hung half-out of a bucket on the stone floor, and swung it hard. Chan Sha's question turned into a startled yelp of pain, and I spun in a circle, the water sluicing off the knotted rope as I caught her on the other side of her ribs, the sound of rope and flesh connecting cracking like a wave off the side of a dock. This time she screamed, and it took everything in me not to loose my rage through my limbs and beat her bloody and blind.

Instead . . . I waited. After a few moments she drew in a frothy breath, shaking her thick braids out of her eyes. She could see me clearly now; I could tell because she shuddered when our eyes met. She opened her mouth; I drew the rope back and she swallowed her words so hard she choked, coughing and hacking and crying out in pain. This time when she stopped, she simply stared. Waiting.

"Remember what you did to Eld and me when you thought us a threat to you?" I asked. "Back when you were the Widowmaker and I was just a slip of a girl." She opened her mouth and I raised my eyebrows. Her teeth snapped shut and she nodded grudgingly. I swung the rope, and it touched her side, gently this time, but she flinched anyway. I didn't try to keep the laughter from my lips, and she stiffened before my mockery. "And back then, Chan Sha," I whispered, "I was without my Sin."

She looked up at me, a bruise darkening one cheek, another just above her right breast from where I'd headbutted her, and red welts rising on both sides of her rib cage. One of the cuts from our earlier fight had opened, and blood ran down her arm. For all that, for the fear that clearly coursed through her veins . . . the woman wasn't broken. *Yet.* I hid the feelings that roiled within me, churning the icy rage to a froth.

This isn't what I want.

I'd been building this moment up in my mind for eight months. This was where I was supposed to loose my rage, let Sin turn me into the Goddess he thought Ciris was, and rip Chan Sha limb from literal limb. I still wanted that . . . but somehow, torture no longer appealed. Dead was dead. There was no way for me to inflict on her the level of hurt and suffering that she'd visited on me. Looking at her now, naked and on the verge of starving, judging by how her bones jutted out, I had no stomach to do more than open her throat. *And then what?*

I didn't have an answer and I felt Sin holding himself back. He didn't care for Chan Sha either—not after what she'd done in Servenza to undermine her former Goddess—but he didn't want to see me hurt more than I already was.

"It's a Godsdamned thing to have her where I want her and not give a damn anymore," I whispered in my mind.

"She's already lost everything that ever mattered to her," Sin said after a moment. "Mostly through her doing, yet also through some of yours. It didn't feel like it before, but I see it now. You've already had your revenge on her."

"Aye, you're right," I agreed. "But she doesn't know that."

I turned my back on Chan Sha, dropping the rope back into the bucket as I crossed to the light. I picked up the canvas and tossed it back over the signal lantern, restoring the inky blackness of before.

"W-where are you going?" Chan Sha whispered. "Buc? W-what do y-you want?"

As I circled the room to the door behind her, Chan Sha's question reverberated in my mind. It was a good one. If it had been asked about the Gods, I had an answer. It was strange to not have one for the woman I'd spent so much time chasing. It'd felt good in the moment and if the dart hadn't worked and I'd ice-picked her to death I think that would have felt good, too. This? I didn't know what this was, but it wasn't good. Chan Sha shouted behind me. *If it doesn't feel good for me*—I pulled open the door and stepped out, letting it swing shut, cutting off her shouted protestations—*at least it doesn't feel good for her either.*

I walked through the wine cellar that contained the hidden door to Chan Sha's prison and up the flight of stairs to one of the smaller rooms of the al-kasr. It'd been intended as a servant's room, no doubt a former vintner's apprentice who would choose the amirah's wine. I'd taken it over as my study. One wall was a built-in bookcase that went from floor to ceiling—I used a rolling ladder to get to the upper shelves—with a cushioned couch and a writing desk set before it. Long tables sat along the other three walls, until recently piled with papers and maps and drawings of plans and half plans and notions that might be plans some- day. Now those papers were strewn about the thick, Cordoban carpets, hiding the triangles and other geometric patterns sewn into the rugs. After returning with Chan Sha, I'd realized I was half-mad with all the knowledge I'd taken in from Sin's reading of those three books. It had to come out of me, so I'd alternated between quaffing down all the cold chicken curry and soggy rice the Artificer could get me whilst scrawling down new plans and diagrams and notions.

"We may have gotten a little carried away," I murmured.

"You don't say," Sin drawled. "We can sleep on this, you know that, right?"

"We could," I agreed, fighting back a yawn as I slipped into the wood-backed chair behind the writing desk.

"But we're not going to, are we?"

"Soon," I lied. "Let's put these notes into some semblance of an order and that might calm my brain down enough to let us sleep."

"I've magic," he reminded me.

"That I don't allow to touch my mind in that way," I reminded him, shrugging out of my jacket. My toss missed the table and I grumbled to myself as I moved to pick the garment up. The corner of a cream-colored envelope jutted out from the paper-strewn floor beneath it, and suddenly I remembered the strange woman who had distracted me while I was tailing Chan Sha. I remembered pulling the envelope out of my jacket and tossing it on top of some papers after locking Chan Sha up, but by then my skull was pounding and the madness had driven the missive completely from my mind. *Sin?* His magic made my nose tingle as I sniffed the thick paper, made my eyes burn as I looked for any discoloration, and finally made my tongue tingle when I touched it to the fold. Satisfied that there was no poison waiting to kill me by degrees—no simple matter when it comes to a Sin Eater, but not out of the realm of possibility—I broke the plain seal and opened the envelope. Several pages were folded within.

"What's this?" I asked as I unfolded the sheets to reveal lines of indecipherable doggerel. I squinted. There was something vaguely familiar about them. The way some of the letters were formed tickled the back of my mind, but— My breath left my lungs in one swift gasp that whistled between my teeth.

"What is it, Buc?" Sin asked. "Do you need me to decipher it?"

"No," I whispered. "This cipher is of my own making."

Five years previous, when Eld had taught me to read and to write, I wanted to make my own language . . . more to see how it was done than for any real need. The attempt had eventually turned into a cipher. I'd shared it with just one other person in the world.

Eld.

Impossible. My eyes burned with tears, not magic, as I forced myself to read the first line.

If you're reading this, you probably wonder how it is that I'm still alive. And if I am still alive, why haven't I found you sooner. I've become one of them, Buc. One of the Dead Gods' mages. I've become a Veneficus. . . .

13

"To serve the dead, you must be from the dead, but not of the dead." The Eldest standing at the front of the classroom pointed at the diagram she'd drawn in chalk on the board. The chalk dust blended seamlessly into her pale robes, which made her skin—the color of wizened bone—look almost tan. "You, every one of you, came to us in the midst of your passing, but the sanctity of blood spared you. There is a transformative property found in—"

"Who am I?" The words, in a woman's voice, sounded more like a song than a question.

He sat up in his seat, squinting to try to clear his vision. Somehow he knew it shouldn't be blurry, full of haze and halos around the lights from the chandeliers, but he didn't know why that was wrong any more than he knew the answer to his question. *Who am I?*

A girl with red locks that were shorn on one side where half her skull was crisscrossed with stitches and scars pushed herself half out of the desk. "Who am I?" she repeated, giving the words a gentle lilt. "Who am I?"—singing an octave higher. "Who am I?"—back in her normal register.

"That's quite enough, child," the Eldest said, her voice shifting from grandmotherly to the sound of bone scraping bone. "When was the last time you communed with our Gods' blood?"

A man beside him piped up in a deep bass that was rough and gritty, as if his throat had been cut—and it might have been, given the thick bandages wrapped around his neck. "Who am I?"

"Remember your prayers. From darkness you were rescued by the truth of blood. The Gods guide us with their life force and with them all manner of things are possible. Through the purity of blood, the sanctity of blood. Say it with me."

The Eldest's words swept past, meaningless. He opened his mouth, intending to voice the same question as the others, but found the words caught against his teeth. "Whhh. Whhh."

"Oh, damn," the Eldest growled. "I've got a circle forming," she shouted. "I need vials—now!"

"Whhgggg," he said, the word stuck in the back of his throat, his mouth a rictus of pain. "Wgghhh," he snarled, his arm fighting to free itself of the sling that bound it. He began choking. Suddenly the Eldest was there.

"Easy! Easy, man," she whispered. He looked up into her dark eyes and she smiled, the vaguest hint of wrinkles and the grey braid that hung from her shoulder giving the lie to her apparent youth. "I've a need of your blood."

"Whhggg!"

"Shh," she said, pricking his hand where it flopped uselessly on the table, then pinching the flesh until blood trickled into a little vial she held, mixing with some dark and viscous substance. Shaking the vial, she offered it to him. "Here, a drop of Gramorr added to your own will unlock your tongue. Aye, and keep you mending."

"Hhh?"

"Open your mouth," she said. He whimpered helplessly and saw disgust flash across her features. Someone grabbed him from behind and he tried to fight—knew he could fight, was good at it, but his body betrayed him, one leg uselessly pushing against the other so that all he managed was to twist in the hardwood chair. Claws pried his jaws apart and something warm and biting filled his mouth and it was all he could do not to drown.

"Sleep," someone whispered, and he felt thought fleeing, leaving behind but a single bread crumb to clutch in the darkness.

Who am I?

"You're getting stronger by the day!" a passing priest said, showing his teeth. His companion, a shorter woman muttered something as well.

He ducked his head and nearly fell over when the broom supporting his weight slipped on the slick, marble floor. His feet shot one way, then caught against a marble pew. When his body caught up, his feet shot back out and he almost fell. He caught himself with his good arm around the back of the pew and slid, by degrees, to the floor. By the time he recovered, the pair were at the end of the pews, heading into the foyer, the woman hooting with laughter. He wondered at what, then realized it was because he'd nearly slipped and fallen. His right arm was in a sling, his left weak, and he couldn't walk without a terrific and terrible hitch to his step. Still, sweeping with one arm was preferable to trying to carry water. They'd given up on that after he kept returning to the kitchens with more on his black tunic than in the bucket.

"T-the truth of blood. The p-p-power of blood," he said, his voice a halting, grating whisper. The rites helped calm his mind and after a moment he pushed himself carefully to his feet and took hold of the broom, which had fallen against the pew. "Blood c-c-calls to blood," he said, and began slowly sweeping the floor that had been swept by another like him the hour previously and would be again when he finished.

Who am I?

He felt more than heard the question in his mind. It'd become his personal catechism, not one taught by the Elders and not one he ever expected to solve, and so paid it no more mind than he did the way that woman's cheeks had shook when she laughed.

The hour was nearly up before he realized why that image had stuck with him.

He could see clearly again.

"That work in the yards put the muscle back on you, lad," the Eldest said, trying to squeeze his arm through his tunic and laughing when she could barely fit her hand a quarter way around his bicep. "Now," she continued, reaching up and tapping his temple, "we need to work on building up your mind. Make it strong, but not so bulky as your arms. Lithe . . . sharp. Savvy?"

"Savvy," he heard himself say, but something in his expression must have given him away because her lips pursed.

"What is it? Something came back to you?"

"M-my name," he whispered. "I think . . . no, I know. I know my name," he said, grinning.

"That's wonderful," she said, leaning against him. "What is it?"

"Eld," he said slowly, savoring the word on his tongue. *That's who I am.*

"Eld." *Me.*

His memories returned along with his health. Painfully and by degrees at first, in bits and flashes that were hard to grasp between the lectures that filled his days and the studying and chores that filled his evenings. He remembered a man's face, pale and bloody and full of fear, and he remembered the shiver the sword made through his arm when he passed it through that man's chest and saw the life leave his eyes. It was a fortnight later, in the middle of a lecture on the thaumaturgical processes required to create a Handbook of Glory—the tomes used by Dead Walkers—that the name of the man he'd killed came to him. *Seetel.* With the name came an outpouring of memories.

His parents sending him to the Academy. News of war; fear

and excitement and graduating a full two years early to join the army in the Burning Lands. Pride at the shiny rank pinned to his collar. Seetel giving orders. Sin Eaters. His men and women torn apart because of his failure. Gnawing guilt and searing pain, rage, and grief, all finally expunged with Seetel's last breath, leaving behind only an emptiness. Something, Eld sensed, had filled that emptiness, but though he prayed to Baol, Gramorr, Mmemnon, Talshur, and the rest of the divine, nothing more came to him.

He spiked a fever and lived in delirium for three days after that, but when he woke up, Eld remembered being a soldier. He was reasonably sure he could put the swordswoman the Eldest had begun introducing to their fighting lessons on her arse if he wanted to. But that wouldn't be polite. *Who am I?* Eld, yes, but there were so many layers to those three letters, and with every memory that returned, he realized how many more remained to be discovered.

The days became rote. Morning drills with staff, blade, and fist. A hurried breakfast on the way to lectures in the morning followed by practical classes later in the day. After, chores and hard labor until dinner, with studies consuming his evenings before he drifted off to bed.

There were a score of acolytes like himself, freshly returned to their bodies and still going through Reawakening, which was the name the Eldest gave to the process of those who were still discovering their memories. Reawakening could take weeks or months or even, in the case of one acolyte who giggled to herself when she thought none were watching, the better part of two years. It was both aided and hampered by the daily doses of the divine they were given. A tiny pinprick of Gods' blood combined with a thimbleful of their own aided healing and drew them farther away from the corpses they'd nearly become, closer to the people they'd once been.

The blood did things that made the memories hard to square up between past and present. Eld knew he'd been quick before, but he was faster now, stronger, and his thoughts were quicker, too—moving so fast at times that he felt nauseous. That, along with some of the darker aspects of the divine—a taste for raw meat, feeling others' emotions and knowing how to bend them if he desired—didn't square with the life or values he found in his past.

There were two score acolytes who were on the verge of Transcendence—when they would say the litany and complete the ritual that would transform them forever more into Dead Walkers or Veneficus. The council, which only appeared on feast days to lead everyone in prayer, seemed to have accelerated the training of Eld and his peers, intent on graduating his lot with the more seasoned acolytes. The war with the Sin Eaters demanded direct action and that meant there was a need for more Veneficus. Sword and stave practice vanished, replaced by lessons on animal husbandry, the properties of different beasts and predators, and how best to use their natural gifts for both spying and violence. Eld had also seen the storerooms in the labyrinths below the Divine Cathedral, packed with Shambles who stood motionless . . . waiting. Until more Dead Walkers were created to control them.

Perhaps because of the increased workload, Eld did not recover any more memories. He could feel an almost solid barrier between his days in the army and what followed after . . . a period of several years, if he had the scope right. What led to his death was a complete blank. He hadn't died, of course, but it'd been near enough that the Dead Gods had accepted him into their fold. Other acolytes seemed to recover themselves more and more, but none seemed to have the block he had. *If I had a moment's peace, perhaps I'd remember more.* That was the real issue: he had no time or space to think. They lived communally, sharing everything from toiletries to sleeping arrangements, and whenever he found a crack in that wall between him and his past, he never really had a chance to pry it open before someone was pulling him back to the here and now. He almost believed that was the intent of the Eldest: to keep him from fully reconciling his past, but that went against their teachings. They'd already saved his life . . . there was no reason for them to lie.

"Rumor is we're all to be brought before the council within the next fortnight to be tested," Sheira whispered breathlessly as they bent over their tasks in the scriptorium. Eld noticed that her red hair had finally grown long enough to hide the damage done to her skull. She was the youngest of them and did everything breathlessly.

"Aye, there's been assassinations and outright raids by the Sin Eaters," Petre said, lowering his voice as the Eldest marched past their desks and entered the stacks beyond them. He kept his quill moving, but Eld could see it wasn't touching the parchment, which was just as well. Miscopying one of the ancient works was punishable by three days' hard labor with no food and only a mouthful of water each morn. "Someone called Sic-something has been leading the teams."

"Sicarii," Xulet said, her voice harsh. She was a curvy woman who had been approaching middle age when a cutpurse decided to cut her throat for good measure. She'd been brought back from Cordoban and was the fastest of the lot at reclaiming her memories. She shrugged in her robes and raised a dark eyebrow. "It's a word of my homeland," she said. "'Sicarii' means 'blade.' Or 'blades.'"

Sicarii.

Eld paused in his own copying, the dusty tome of theories on how to be both Dead Walker and Veneficus forgotten as the word caught at Eld's mind like silk on a nail. The others' voices rose and he felt the meaning behind the name slipping away. *Godsdamn it.* If only there were a way for him to think, speak, or write without the others intruding. A way to find a moment's privacy. Lightning flashed through his mind, searing and bright, and when he realized what he was doing he'd pulled a fresh sheet of parchment out and filled half a page with . . . gibberish?

Only . . . as he leaned closer, the letters rearranged themselves in his mind. Not gibberish. *A cipher.* It was . . . a memory?

I felt a hand on my purse, slapped it away, and nearly took a palm's length of steel in the ribs. A short, dark-skinned girl in a ragged, midnight-blue dress was trying to stab me! I caught her wrist in one hand and she drove the heel of her other hand into my ribs, yelping when she connected with hard muscle. I caught that hand, too, and for a moment we were face-to-face, her bright-green eyes glaring into mine.

"Usually I like to catch the name of a lass before she tries to slide a blade between my ribs," I told her, forcing a smile.

"Usually I like to whisper it to men while they're bleeding out, fuck face," she snapped.

"Sorry to disappoint," I said, noticing the way the dress hung on her, the pinched look to her cheeks. "Since it doesn't look like you're going to succeed, how about a truce?"

"Truce?" the girl asked. "What's your terms, soldier boy?"

"Why do you think me a soldier?" I asked.

"Your head's on a swivel, your shoulders are too damned straight, and you walk like you've a stick up your arse. Either a soldier or a noble and your coat's not fine enough for nobility."

"Perceptive," I muttered. "I'm afraid I'll disappoint you on both counts," I lied. "My family did give me an education, and a fine one at that . . . until the book trade went out last summer."

"I'm fairly certain you're a terrible liar," she retorted. Then her lips parted and she made a noise in her throat. "Books? I've always wondered about them."

"Can't you read?"

"You ever met a cutpurse that could?" she asked.

"You're the first I've had the pleasure of," I admitted. "If you're not

going to kill me and I'm not going to let you steal my purse, how about we move along before the Constabulary takes note?"

She glanced around and saw what I'd seen, that more than a few passersby were giving us increasingly long looks as we stood locked with each other. "Your lucky day, soldier boy."

"I told you, I'm not a soldier." I sighed. "You wanted terms, aye? There's a meat-pie stand, just around the corner. I pay, you eat, and we see if we can settle our differences without a blade?"

"Deal," she said, twisting her hand free from my grip. She spat on it and held it out and I laughed and did the same, feeling her calloused palm against my own. "You say," she leaned in, "that you're not a soldier, but those calluses aren't from carrying boxes nor are they from knives . . . those come from holding the hilt of something a bit more substantial."

"Say you're right, what then?"

"We renegotiate terms," she said. "After you feed me my meal."

"What's in it for me?" I asked.

"My company?"

I snorted, but motioned for her to lead on. "You drive a hard price. What's your name?"

"Sambuciña . . .

". . . but you can call me Buc."

"Buc," Eld whispered, the name tearing from his lips and ripping down the wall within his mind. Memories fell on him like an avalanche and suddenly he was atop an impossibly tall building, laughing as explosions rent the air around him, the floor buckling and coming apart. He tumbled through the air, one chunk amidst thousands as debris rained down below him and he knew he was about to die, but it was okay. He'd done his part. He'd saved Buc. Years of memories slammed down upon him with the weight of an entire city and darkness consumed him. Dimly, distantly he heard shouts, pinpricks in the black pitch, and then nothing.

Buc.

14

Blood, thick and cool and pure, filled his mouth. Eld choked and tried to sit up, and the spike that had penetrated his brain exploded in pain and he fell back against his pillow, unable to stop the bloodcurdling scream that tore from his throat. Hands pressed him down, fingers pried his mouth open, and he felt more blood flow into him as words, bereft of meaning, rang out around him. The cool, metallic tang turned warm, then warmer still, and that warmth flooded through him, banishing the pain, ordering his thoughts, putting the memories away into drawers that he could pull open as he wished, and his mind cleared. After a moment that lasted an eternity, Eld opened his eyes.

"Easy, man," the Eldest said. She smiled, her white teeth bright against her dark skin and looking darker still by the white locks she wore in braids that reached to his sheets. "You've Reawakened and that is ever a painful thing. Like being born again."

"Is he ready for this, Ismiralda?"

The Eldest's face flashed with annoyance that she kept from her voice when she answered the man behind her. "If we had the time, I'd give him another week."

"You know we don't have that. As the council's sole Veneficus, I bear the burden of defending our brothers and sisters in blood from the mind witches. I need him."

"I know," she admitted. "I'll see Eldritch bathed and dressed and oiled, if you will send for the others?"

"I'll attend them myself and see the rites are prepared. The Archnemesis asked to attend this one personally."

"I'm not surprised," Ismiralda said, "given what we learned from his blood." She leaned forward and whispered in Eld's ear. "I wanted you for one of mine, boy, but maybe you'll be the rare Veneficus that thinks with its brain and not its muscle."

"I don't understand," Eld said slowly. Only, he was afraid he did. *I need to escape.* Eld saw the crimson vial hanging around her throat, bright against the bone-white gown she wore. *One of the council. A Dead Walker.* Her words reverberated through him and everything clicked into place. They'd studied the memories in his blood; they knew who he was, who Buc was, what they'd intended. *I need to find Buc, to warn her.*

"I summon thee, Eldritch Nelson Rawlings," she intoned, "this very hour, to be tested through the ritual and rite of Transcendence and join our ranks as one of our brothers, by blood, through blood, and in blood."

It was too late.

"Eld!"

"Petre!" Eld clasped hands with the portly man, although the term applied to him less and less as the harsh drills ate away at the flesh he'd gained in his former life as a coin counter in Port au' Sheen. "I heard you were raised," Eld said, studying the man's dark eyes for any hint of which branch of the family Petre had been chosen for. There was something *off* about Dead Walkers, something that came from communing with the dead that kept them apart from the living.

"Last week." Petre laughed and pulled up his sleeve, exposing the brand there, twin to Eld's own. Eld's itched when he saw it. "Veneficus, same as you. Although, I'd hoped—" He glanced past Eld, motioned for Eld to follow him into the shaded end of the cloister, and spoke more softly. "You've been away what, a fortnight?"

"It feels like thrice that," Eld admitted. "The Sin Eaters tried to follow up on Sicarii's murder spree in Colgna and we've been fighting them in the canals and across the rooftops, trying to hold them off long enough to rebuild the cathedral."

He'd Transfigured twice. The first as a trial against Ciris worshippers—not Sin Eaters, just folk seeking the Goddess's aid—and again when actual Sin Eaters attacked the small chapel the Dead Gods had been using as a temporary shelter. Both times he'd transformed into a bull with steel horns, very much like the one that had attacked him and Buc when they first went to work for Kanados. Both times he'd felt a passenger in his new body, half-blind with pain from the physical transformation and half-mad with the bull's rage at the mind witches who were anathema to his very blood. Afterward, coming down from the Transfiguration felt almost as good as sex. It almost but not quite made him forget about the way his body was ripped apart during the change, each limb breaking like a gunshot and then being reknit. The catechisms they were taught helped him recenter himself, but with his memories returned, he knew the litany to be dross. The Gods were dead and had been dead for untold millennia before the first priests figured out how to tap into their Wellspring and unlock their gifts. Bereft of belief, it felt less like holy transmutation and more like a twisted cult.

"Why, what have I missed?" Eld asked quickly when he realized he hadn't been able to keep the shadow of his thoughts from showing on his face. "Besides your own Transcendence? Did the rest rise, too?"

"Sheira did," Petre said after a moment. "And a few others." He scratched at his beard. "They were chosen for the newest form."

"Newest form?" Eld asked. "What do you mean?"

"The council, well, I guess the Archnemesis, really, created a new ritual and we were all tested for it. I thought for sure I'd be chosen, but I guess they figured with my size I'd make a better Veneficus." Petre's shoulders slumped. "It would have been an honor to be named Plague Walker."

"Plague Walker?" Eld felt his hackles rise. "What is a Plague Walker? What do they do?"

"Eldritch!" a woman's voice rang out.

They both turned and Petre grunted. "You want to know, ask her."

"Ismiralda?"

"Just the man I've been looking for," Ismiralda called out from the archway. The woman marched toward them, robes billowing out behind her, caught up in the trade winds that were being used by Normain to position their ships for war.

"She's the Eldest who's in charge of them," Petre said. "Given a new title, too. Plague Mistress."

"We thought we'd found a scalpel in the Forbidden Library of Cordoban two years ago," Ismiralda said. "How to wield it was the question." She tapped her lip with a long nail. "I gave the answer to one of my brightest students that he might draw that scalpel across Ciris's throat. A man you knew as the Ghost Captain."

"The Ghost Captain," Eld hissed.

"You know how well that fared."

"E-Eldest, I apologize for the role—"

"Not your concern," she said, waving his objections away. "That was a different man, a different time." She leaned back from her desk, studying him with black eyes that shone in the candlelight. "I saw what was coming then. That Ciris would begin spreading past her initial interests in coin and influence amongst the rich. When she first awoke, she was weak and we thought she'd be easily crushed. Then she found friends in high places and we recognized the task before us, but we thought we had time. Centuries more, surely. Time." She spat the word like a curse. "After that summer, I knew it was only a matter of time before she began gathering the masses to her. I underestimated how quickly she'd pivot. We all did."

"You mean, with her offering free healing by Sin Eaters?"

"Usurping *our* traditional role within society," Ismiralda growled. "She's done that and more, and with war about to erupt with Normain, she's begun wrapping the Empress around her finger. Once she's confident that she has the Imperial armies at her command, armies she's trained to rely on her mages in order to operate in the field effectively, she'll attack openly, overwhelming us with the numbers she's been courting these past few years."

"Why now?"

"She's insane, Eldritch," Ismiralda said. "Motive cannot be ascribed to madness. She isn't content with proxies anymore—she made that clear when she attacked our brethren the same night you came to us in the streets of Servenza. She's been using this Sicarii ever since, to whittle away at our numbers." She stood up and moved to the shelves behind her desk, framed by massive sconces with flickering candles, and plucked a freshly bleached skull from beside a book. "There can be only one end in this for her: destroy what remains of our Gods, their bones and their blood, silencing them . . . and us . . . forever."

"W-what would you have me do?" Eld asked, his throat dry.

"We tried using a scalpel with the Ghost Captain," Ismiralda said, studying the skull. "We can't just kill Ciris, not with her power spreading through the world by the passing of the sun. We need to remind the world of *our* power."

"Is this tied to the new ritual?" Eld asked. He almost asked her if the skull she held was the Ghost Captain's—Buc had decapitated him, after all—but wasn't sure he wanted to know. Everything was coming full circle and he felt like he was swimming in a pool of blood, watching sharks knife toward him, jaws spread wide.

"We've deciphered some of our oldest texts," she said after a moment. "Amongst their pages is a contagion and its cure. The plague, we believe, will prove deadly, certainly in the long run, but perhaps the short as well, to Ciris and her ilk. Creating the contagion is straightforward enough, but the cure will take some time."

"Ingenious," Eld lied. "How will we introduce it to the Sin Eaters? They aren't likely to take a peace offering from us. Not after the Ghost Captain."

"Hardly," she agreed. "So we don't even try. Instead, we introduce it to the world, let her sundry connections all become tendrils of disease that lead back to her."

Eld frowned, felt his sunburnt lips crack. "It's tailored to mind witches?"

"A plague is not a scalpel," Ismiralda said as if speaking to a child. "You know how painful it was, undergoing Reawakening." She turned away to set the skull on the hardwood shelf and when she turned back, the look in her eyes sent a chill through Eld. "The world requires the same, to be brought to the brink of death, Ciris expunged, in order to have that chance at rebirth."

"You're going to unleash a plague on everyone and wait for the Sin Eaters and Ciris to die off," Eld whispered.

"Aye. The cure is a year or more in the making, but we need not wait to begin. That's why I sought you out," Ismiralda said. "You drew the council's attention in Colgna. The Veneficus are puffed up about your fighting prowess, but I was more intrigued by how you reestablished our lines of supply after the attack, using Colgna's smaller port. The truth is, Eldritch, this war won't be won by fang and claw or by Shambles. It will be won by the mundane calculations required to spread this plague as quickly and effectively as possible. It will require the logistics of an army. Who better to design them than one who witnessed such efficiencies firsthand?"

"You want me to help you unleash this upon the world?" Eld asked, surprising himself by not choking on the words. *I've got to warn Buc.* Only, he had no idea where she was. While he was certain the latest assassinations by Sicarii were her work, it'd been more than a month since the last. *She doesn't know I'm alive, let alone what's coming.* If he couldn't warn her, he had to do something to give her the time to work her own magic. Surely she was still plotting the downfall of the Gods?

"I do," Ismiralda said, baring her teeth in a smile. "What say you, Eldritch? Will you be the Quartermaestro of Death to my Plague Mistress?"

"I would be honored," he said after a moment, willing his face to maintain the lie by focusing on the real question at hand. *Where are you, Buc?*

15

That's why I haven't come to you, Buc; I've been trying to prevent this plague from being created, from being sent out into the world. I've been trying to buy you time . . . but I fear I've failed. There's something else you need to know—

The words disappeared as my vision became a blurry haze of tears. *He's alive. Eld's alive.* Emotions swirled within me like a dust storm as I tried to take it all in. *A Dead God's mage. A Veneficus, but—* Alive. I drew in a ragged breath and read the last few lines.

They sifted through my memories when they pulled me half-dead from the rubble of the Lighthouse and again after I Reawakened. They know everything I know, Buc. That you killed the Ghost Captain. That you're as good as a Sin Eater. That you're looking to kill them. I found you, finally, because they did. The council dispatched a team on the same ship that bore this letter so if you're reading this, Buc . . . they're already where you are. You must be careful! You must—

The sound of the al-kasr's double front doors being torn off their hinges ripped me out of the letter. Sliding across the marble floor, the wood and metal shrieked like a haunted woman from a Cordoban tale, one who screamed men into insanity. A servant's startled shout ended abruptly as she slammed the door to the living areas shut. The heavy locking bar thudded into place moments before a roar filled the air as whatever demonic thing was attacking us thudded into those doors.

"What the actual fuck, Sin?"

"I'd say Eld was right and we've been discovered."

"I know that," I told him, pushing myself up from the desk and marching across the room.

"That door's not going to last more than two blows and then they'll be in amongst the servants like a fox in a henhouse."

"I know that, too," I growled. "Flip it and reverse it . . . what don't they know?"

"That you've a hidden door that opens to the side?"

"Aye, that," I said, catching up one of the Artificer's repeating crossbows from where it lay on the table. I plucked the cylinder out of it and slapped in a fresh one, then grabbed a second crossbow with my free hand. Moving into the gap between tables, I kicked open the door that was cunningly carved seamlessly into the wall. "And they don't know who they're fucking with, either," I added, stepping into the broad foyer.

A goat the size of a small horse with steel horns that curled in spirals around either side of its head stood facing the main door. Its head swung around, red eyes blazing at me, and it snorted as a growl built in its throat. Behind the goat, a woman fell to the floor on cats' paws, her skin shimmering as she took on the form of a lioness, her screams of pain turning to the howls of a predator. A third Veneficus flanked the pair, already transformed into a dog the size of a wolf. Its snarl revealed steel canines thrice the size of those of any wolf I'd ever seen before.

"I think they might, actually," Sin muttered.

"You sure know how to make a woman feel loved," I told them. The were-goat made an inquisitive snorting sound. "How about you let me return the favor?" I asked, leveling the crossbow in my right arm. I didn't give them a chance to answer, feathering both my index and middle fingers against the trigger. The weapon lurched slightly with each shot, puffs of air from the cylinder and the whine of the bolt the only sounds for a split second. Then the dog howled and leapt back into the doorway, its jowls pincushioned with steel.

The goat roared and charged across the foyer. *Roll. Go for the stick sticklies.* It lowered its horns as it reached me and I threw myself into a roll, managing to kick its front hoof as I did so, and the creature's hooves slipped on the marble, sending it crashing into the wall with a scream of fury and the wet thud of meat on wood. The lioness landed atop me, her claws sending pain flaring through my shoulders, but momentum turned us until we were face-to-face with my back against the floor. Then I put the crossbow against her soft underbelly and pulled the trigger. Once. Twice. Thrice. Her feral scream flecked my face with spittle and she tore new rents in my flesh as she leapt away.

I came to my feet, breathing raggedly, arms screaming with Sin's magic and pain from the Veneficus. Through the hole where the doors had stood, the night was broken by the soft glow from the magical book in the hand of a Dead Walker, who was flanked by a dozen Shambles bearing swords and axes. The dog and lioness retreated, disappearing as the Shambles surged forward. All I had were two crossbows—one of those empty—and a few blades hidden in my jacket. Too few for what confronted me. *Fuck.*

"A reputation is a motherfucker," Sin said.

"Seems like," I said, dropping into a crouch. I hurled the empty crossbow at the lead pair just as they crossed the threshold, hissing. Before I could follow it, the road transformed from night to day with a cacophony of gunfire. Shambles fell as their limbs were cut from beneath them. Something lanced through air and pierced the book *and* the Dead Walker, pinning them both to the wall behind them. *What the—?*

The demonic goat screamed in rage as it charged me from the side. . . . I'd completely forgotten about it in the few heartbeats since I put it down and it was upon me before I could do more than jump. Luckily, with Sin's magic infusing my bones, I didn't need more warning than its cry had given me and I surprised the beast by landing on its back. Twisting around, I pointed the crossbow at the back of its head, at the space where the horns met, forming a small circle of flesh unprotected by steel, and held the triggers down. The crossbow leapt in my arms, sending half a dozen bolts into the back of the Veneficus's head. That alone might have been enough to kill it, but the cylinders I'd loaded weren't filled with steel bolts. They were silver—poison to a Veneficus.

The goat's throaty rage turned to a high-pitched scream that cut off abruptly as it collapsed, throwing me backward over its head. I slammed into the wall so hard the al-kasr shook and the breath was knocked from my lungs. I landed beside the beast, gasping. The goat's body began to twist and writhe, bones breaking like gunshots, and an instant later the face of a bearded man was staring sightlessly at me. The corpse was naked, with saggy folds of skin around thickly muscled arms. I stared back for a moment, until I remembered I wasn't alone, and scrambled to my feet.

The lioness leapt at me; gunfire blasted from behind it, sending sparks off the marble floor. The big cat fell, its feet shot out from beneath it, revealing a woman holding smoking pistoles. She stepped aside and the Artificer, of all people, moved forward, leveling a crossbow like my own—save his was a full-sized version, not the alley pieces I'd been using. The weapon thrummed like a muted mill saw, turning the lioness into a veritable pincushion. It tried to rise, slipped, and fell heavily onto its side, tail lashing. The woman raised her pistole: flame leapt from the barrel, and when my vision cleared, I saw the cat turning back to a woman, half her head shot away.

The final Veneficus was snarling and leaping at a dark-skinned man in a short, white jacket. The man blocked the massive dog's snapping teeth with a large club that he then swung around to slap its head to the side. The dog lurched, tripping over the Shambles crumpled in the road. In a flash, the man was upon the dog, lifting the mace high overhead. Moonlight reflected off shards of stone or metal embedded in the weapon's head. He brought the club down with a cry. A meaty thunk cut off the Veneficus's growling like a string being snipped. The dog's head rolled one way, the body the other, both twisting and writhing as they returned to human form.

"W-what the fuck," I wheezed, "are you doing here?"

The woman blew smoke away from the ends of her pistoles and smiled. "It's nice to see you too, Buc," Salina said.

16

Anytime you wage a small war in an affluent neighborhood in the middle of the bloody night, questions will be asked. A lot of questions. Even in Cordoban. I had been ordering the servants to pack our things and wondering what I was going to do with Chan Sha, who was still chained up in the cellar, when Salina stepped in and smoothed everything over in a matter of moments. She sent a servant running to the Company's al-kasr to get the local representatives to apply pressure to the militia and the city's council—with luck that would keep word from reaching the Federates.

Another servant went off to the Sin Eaters' enclave so word could be spread, warning of possible attacks against Company holdings by the Dead Gods. A third returned from an errand I hadn't caught just as the militia arrived—a full complement in bronzed helms and ringmail, sporting pikes and muskets. The tall man, who walked half-bent, was soaked with sweat as he produced bags of coin from under his jacket. His had been the most dangerous task, I realized. Sprinting through the streets at night with that much gold wasn't just tiring, it was practically begging to be robbed or worse.

It was a breathtaking performance—Salina orchestrated everything like a captain general, including bribing the local police to look the other way despite the half a dozen dead bodies, one of which was clearly wearing the robes of the Dead Gods. Still, she was, after all, the Chair of the mighty Kanados Trading Company. What Kanados wanted, it usually got.

"Doubloons," she told the commander as the panting servant

handed over the money pouches. "For you and your troop. Some-one once told me," she added, glancing at me, "that they were easier to spend than lire."

"A thousand blessings be upon you, amirah," the woman said. The man beside her was twisting his mustaches so vigorously, his eyes bulging in shock at the bags of coin, that if he wasn't careful, he'd tear them off. The commander nudged him; he barked an order to the rest of the militia and they cleared out, taking the bodies with them.

"You're a fast learner," I told her.

"I had some good teachers," Salina said. "And some pains in the arse."

The woman before me had changed a lot in the past eight months. The ease with which she gave orders spoke to that. The alacrity with which she was obeyed was new, but then again she looked the part in her royal purple dress, cut in the latest Cordoban fashion. The skirts were so tight around her legs so that they almost could have been trousers and the fabric cut through with thread o' gold in wavy patterns that matched the silks tied throughout the thick braid in her blond hair.

"What the fuck is the Chair doing here?"

"Beyond saving your arse?"

I laughed in spite of myself. "Beyond that, aye."

Salina laughed, too, and touched my hand. "It's good to see you, Buc. Truly." I squeezed her hand gently. "Bar'ren, who claims he knows you, and a strange letter brought me here."

"Bar'ren?"

"I told you once, that we'd meet again." The man who'd decapitated the were-dog stepped forward into the light of the foyer's chandelier and at last I recognized him. *The old man from the island. Who gave me the canoe.* His braided hair was white as the animal skin he wore around his shoulders, but his tanned skin was smooth and muscled and he held the mace in his hand lightly despite its size and the razor-sharp rock shards embedded along in its head. His face broke into a sardonic grin. "As I recall," he added in a gravelly voice, "you thought it unlikely."

"As I recall," I said slowly, matching his grin, "I said that something would have to have gone seriously fucking wrong for it to happen."

"Something has," Bar'ren said, his grin fading. "Sin Eaters came to our shores, like the Dead One before them."

"The Ghost Captain, you mean?"

"Him," he agreed. "They were looking for him and wouldn't listen to me or our elders. They seemed to think we knew stories other than the ones we told and when we couldn't say what they wanted to hear—"

"They moved on to torture," I muttered.

"Didn't you mention Bar'ren by name when the Sin Eaters were questioning you back in Servenza?" Sin asked in my mind.

"Might have done," I whispered. "But I'm not telling *him* that. He just cut that Veneficus's head off like it was an olive branch. And my head is one branch not in need of trimming."

"In a manner of speaking," Bar'ren said. "They slew a few of us, it is true, but we are not weak. We fought them off, only they had knowledge of the Arawaíno that they should not have. Hidden knowledge, secret knowledge."

"What knowledge?" Salina asked, finally unable to stay out of the conversation. I'd watched her lips twitching before she spoke. "The same knowledge that told you where to find me? To find Buc?"

The man's mouth clamped shut, his expression warring with itself. He turned his stony, grey-eyed stare from me to Salina and back again before he exhaled, shoulders sagging, and let the club in his hand slip to the marbled floor with a clatter. "The Mother warned me I would have to do that which no Sha'amen has ever done before."

"Mother?" Salina asked.

"What taboo are you to break?" I asked over her.

"You're both overeager, but the Mother is not to be gainsaid."

He nodded slowly, his braids swaying. "You know of the Gods of the Dead and of the mind Goddess, but there is a third divinity, the only one truly of our home," he said, gesturing to indicate he meant all of us and not just his people and their island. "Mother Waska."

"A third God?" I asked, my chest tightening. *How many of these motherfuckers must I kill to free us?*

"She told me to tell you, child"—he winced at my expression—"her word, not mine—that she poses no threat to your aspirations. In neither the short nor the long term. Her intent was never to dominate like these false Gods, but to provide insight to those who would have it."

"Insights like where we were at in the world," Salina murmured.

"And what my name was without me telling you," I said, suddenly remembering our conversation out in the middle of the Shattered Coast. "Proof enough of her magic, but how do I know she speaks true?"

"She's found within a certain type of plant that grows on a rocky outcrop just within eyesight of our island."

"You eat the plant and she speaks to you?" Salina interrupted. "That makes no sense."

"That's a child's answer," he said simply, and I laughed. Salina opened her mouth, but I lifted a hand to forestall her. It sounded awfully similar to the out-of-body experiences Jerden hallucinated on mollusk poison—save that in this case, it appeared the hallucinations were real.

"There is preparation required, of both the mind and the body," Bar'ren continued. "The Mother is also prepared. Once she is ingested . . . over time she speaks to you. It is not," he added, "a pleasant experience. Knowledge hurts, and the Mother provides much knowledge."

"She warned you the Sin Eaters would come," I guessed.

"She did. When we wouldn't tell the Sin Eaters what they

wished to be true, they burned the sacred grove on the island. They"—his voice sounded like sharp rocks smashing together—"thought they destroyed the Mother, destroyed our power."

"They didn't?" Salina asked.

"They burned the groves, but there would have been seedlings left behind," I said. *At least Ciris took that Goddess off the table for the time being.* There was no need for me to turn full-on serial killer to the Gods. *Yet.*

Bar'ren nodded and I continued, "They didn't destroy the Mother, they simply locked her away for a time."

"You see far," he whispered. "She told me you did. The Mother told me much. That I had to leave my people, and what to take with me when I left my home. How to find this one"—he nodded at Salina—"and that she would know where you would be, Sambuciña."

"Buc," I told him.

"Buc," he said, rolling the word over his tongue. "Sharp. Like yourself. The Mother told me to remind you that you recognized the debt owed to us by our help with the Dead One. That we now call that favor due."

"Aye?" I said, unable to keep the incredulity from my tone. "And what favor would you have of me, Bar'ren, Sha'amen of the Arawaíno?"

"My people are peaceful, with no intention of forming an empire. We intentionally sought a place within the Shattered Coast to remain apart from the troubles of this world and yet—"

"And yet its troubles have found you. Because, Bar'ren, the Gods don't care about what you want, only what they want. And what they want is to rule the whole world, to see us all bend the knee and bow the head."

"The Mother agrees with you," he said, his lined face tightening. "She saw a future of fire, like the one that touched her groves, but spread across the world, consuming us all. Unless you stopped it."

"Me?" I whispered.

"You, Buc, are to be her instrument of revenge. I ask that you let me aid you in your war." He tapped his chest. "'Sha'amen' means 'speaker' in my tongue. Let me speak for my people. Let me speak for the Arawaíno."

"Here I thought you were going to ask me to go find your Mother for you," I said. "If that"—I pointed at his bloodied club—"is your language, then you can speak for me any day of the year, Bar'ren. And you name the day."

"I—" He paused, scrunching his nose up.

"She means you're part of the crew," Salina said, clapping him on the shoulder.

"You're all still standing out here?" the Artificer asked, appearing in the doorway that led into the al-kasr's living space. He adjusted his spectacles several times until the yellow-tinted pair that helped him see at night settled in front of his eyes. "When I saw you, Salina, I said we'd have much to discuss. Admittedly, I didn't know our arrival here would be so . . . fortuitous and so forth." He dry-washed his hands. "I believe a council is in order?"

"A council?" Salina asked.

"Aye," I muttered, remembering the letter I'd been reading right before a Veneficus tore the doors off the al-kasr. "A council of war."

My words hung in the air until Bar'ren grunted agreement. "Over food, one hopes," he said, picking up his mace and sauntering past me.

"I'd like to clean up first," Salina said, brushing at her cheeks, which were tattooed with powder burns and blood. She went to move past me and I stopped her.

"Salina, you said Bar'ren brought you here, but also a strange letter?"

"Buc," she said slowly, her amber eyes meeting mine, "I don't know quite how to tell you this, but there were two letters. One addressed to you, which I opened, because," she added hastily, "I doubted the first . . . but it was in gibberish."

"You doubted the first because you knew Eld died that night the Lighthouse of Servenza came down," I whispered.

"I—how did you know?" Her eyes widened and she gasped. "Is it true?"

"Possibly," I said, hearing myself speak the words as if they were from another person. "I, too, received a strange letter, moments before the Veneficus attacked. I've reason," I added, "to think those two events are not unrelated."

"I don't know what to say," Salina said after several moments. "I brought the letter." She reached into her jacket and pulled out a cream-colored envelope with a dark wax sigil embossed across it. "How is he alive? Where has he been? What's this all mean?"

"That's the ten-thousand-lire question," I told her, taking the letter slowly. "I've another ten thousand thoughts to go with them if the letter I read is true." My mind raced ahead as I spoke, Sin powerless to stop them if he'd wanted to. *Eld. Alive.* I'd planned to use the information I learned in the Forbidden Library just a day before to introduce a number of . . . mind viruses, for lack of a better term, to take out Ciris. Most of the ways to achieve that could severely injure me, would likely kill Sin, leaving me a mortal woman when I faced the Dead Gods. I'd a plan there, too, a suicidal one, but if Eld was alive that tempered my willingness to die. It'd be good to see his face again, even if just to make it blush. *Either way, the sums have changed.* This plague meant I needed to go after the Dead Gods first. And fast. *For that, I'll need even more information. All of it.* I knew a lot already and the Forbidden Library had given me more, but there was someone else who had a couple of decades more knowledge with Sin than I did. And the only ones who hated the Dead Gods more than me were Ciris's lot.

"You've a plan?" Salina asked. *Knowledge.* I touched the key in my pocket and smiled. I'd an idea I had just the right type of coin to exchange for that knowledge, too. "Don't you?"

"Always."

17

By the time I'd finished my bath and taken care of a few things—including getting a barrier erected until the broken outer doors could be replaced—everyone else had settled along either side of the long dining table. The servants had laid out bowls of bright, fish-curry stew, spiced lamb over yellow rice, and half a dozen shellfish dishes ranging from steamed to raw, along with pitchers of chilled wine and cocoa, as was their wont. My allies had tucked in with a will and made significant dents in the mounds of food.

I studied them from the doorway: The Artificer in his yellow tunic buttoned up to his throat—the color and pattern almost matched the wallpaper behind him. Bar'ren, still in his blood-spattered animal skin with multiple empty bowls before him, rapidly emptying yet another serving of the fish stew. Salina, picking at her lamb while using the small sips she stole from her wineglass to spy upon her companions.

An unlikely lot to take down the Gods, but there was power here, from the Artificer's inventions to Bar'ren's hidden knowledge and more obvious physical strength to Salina's command of the most powerful trading company in the world. An army couldn't defeat the Gods, not when thousands of their followers would rise to protect them, but a small team of specialists? That was something I could get behind.

"C'mon," I grunted over my shoulder, then sauntered in on the Artificer's side of the table, making it half a dozen paces before the clanking behind me drew everyone's eye. The Artificer's face turned purple behind his spectacles, Bar'ren paused with a full spoon half raised to his lips, and Salina muttered an oath, drawing the pistole at her side.

"You!" she growled. Bar'ren reached out with his free hand, pushing the pistole lower, and she turned her murderous gaze on him. "You don't know what this *creature* has done," she spat.

"You're right," he agreed. "But Buc's just learned something and we'd do well to hear her out before killing yon cripple."

"I have learned something," I said, pulling hard on the chains to move my prisoner along. Chan Sha stumbled, unable to keep up with me thanks to her injured leg. I met Bar'ren's grey eyes and wondered what else his green goddess had told him, but that was a question for another time. Instead, I wrapped the chain in my hands around one of the candle sconces in the wall so that Chan Sha had just enough slack to sit on the bench that ran along the table. "Sit and keep your fucking mouth shut," I told her, before moving to sit beside the Artificer.

"Uh, Buc?" He leaned forward, dropping his voice. "If you aren't going to kill her, perhaps it would be polite to offer her some food?"

"She tried to murder Buc," Salina said, murder bright in her own voice. "She did murder Eld and the Doga and set in motion what looks to be a world war. And you're worried about her nutrition?"

"Arti likes to stay on everyone's good side," I told Salina, straddling the bench. "And he's polite. Like Eld was." Salina's eyes flashed at the name, but she didn't say anything. "Dump out some of the lamb and rice on the table, then," I told the Artificer.

"What?" Chan Sha's voice sounded like a rusted, busted-up hinge. "Don't trust me with a plate and fork?"

"Consider it a compliment," I suggested. "Now," I continued as the Artificer stood up, "I'd like three or four bowls of that stew since I'm running on no sleep, piss, and vinegar, and I topped off the chamber pot afore I came in." Bar'ren laughed and Salina rolled her eyes, muttering about some things never changing. "In between bowls," I added, taking the steaming bowl of bright-yellow curry that undulated with fish and peppers and greens, "I'm going to tell you all a little story about a—" I bit back the tears that suddenly stung my eyes and took a deep breath. "—about a friend of mine I thought long dead."

"So the Dead Gods apparently decided that if they couldn't knife Ciris they would just poison her—and all of us along in the bargain—instead . . . even if it means they'll end up ruling a world of the dead." Silence reigned after I finished telling them everything; well, almost everything. I hadn't held back on the important bits, about the plague and no sure cure and the rest.

"The Dead Ones embrace death as a lover," Bar'ren growled.

"And Eld's become one of them?" Salina asked. "Does that mean they can control him the way Ciris controls her mages? Not that I don't trust him, Buc," she added quickly when she saw my expression. "But we have to be careful. After all, they sent a trio of Veneficus and a fucking Dead Walker after you, and knew exactly where to find you."

"Eld didn't know this place existed," I reminded her. "I may have . . . made a few enemies recently who would have reason to want me dead."

"Surprising," Salina drawled.

"Right?" I shook my loose braid, still wet from my bath, and drew my auburn robe tighter around me. "I don't think"—I shot a look over my shoulder at Chan Sha, who'd cleaned the table before her of food and was trying to watch all four of us simultaneously—"they have the same level of control?"

"They wish they did," Sin grunted.

"They don't," Chan Sha agreed. "Though if they could, they would," she added, matching Sin's tone.

You two are a fucking pair.

"She took Possession," Sin whispered. "She became what you

will not and once twinned with your Sin, the two are nigh indistinguishable."

"Tell me that's not creepy as fuck," I muttered back.

"So for now we assume a few things," I said out loud, and raised a finger. "First, that Eld is alive. Second"—another finger— "that he's a Veneficus, but hasn't bought into their bullshit. And third"—I held up a third finger—"that given the Dead Gods' plans, we have to put them in our sights and pull the trigger."

"A big fucking trigger," Salina said.

"Why is that when things look darkest, you all turn to profanity for comfort?" the Artificer asked. "'Fucking' and so forth?"

Salina exchanged looks with me and guffawed. Even Bar'ren's mouth moved in the semblance of a smile. "There's something comforting in the obscene," I said after a moment. "To return to the subject at hand. We know the Dead Gods have a plague, but we don't know where they plan to strike or when."

I ignored Salina's unspoken question, bright in her eyes. I hadn't been able to bring myself to open Eld's second letter. I still couldn't believe the first, despite having reread it when I was in the bathtub. I'd thought him dead, along with most of my reason for enjoying the breath in my lungs. Once, I'd said that need was a noose we tied 'round our own throats, waiting for the world to draw it tight, and I'd believed that.

I needed Eld. Then I lost him. Forever. I wasn't dead and didn't intend to die until I saw the Gods repaid in full for the bondage they'd put the world in. But I hadn't been alive either, not really. Losing Eld had been like losing colors, and in the greywash of this existence, I found little to satisfy me. His letter had changed everything, but it also reminded me that I'd abandoned him when he needed me most. *I'm so sorry.* It hadn't even been a full day before I was aboard a ship, chasing my revenge against Chan Sha across the ocean's waves. Eld wouldn't have abandoned me so easily. He would have searched the rubble for my body, if only to see me have a proper burial. In the hours after his death, I'd killed two women and framed the lot, setting up the world war that Salina laid at Chan Sha's feet. Because a world at war made enemies of us all, and that meant the Gods wouldn't know which of us was the true enemy until they felt my blade at their throat. All it had taken, in the end, was me sacrificing the only thing beyond revenge that I cared about in this world. The only person that had cared about me.

Eld.

"As to that," the Artificer said, breaking the silence, "I may have found something that could be of use." He dug into his tunic and pulled out a roll of treated parchment. "I found this in the pocket of the Dead Walker," he said, rolling it out onto the table. "It's in a cipher text that I thought I could break with some of the machines I've created . . . but it's untranslatable. Machines are not so bright as the mind, it turns out. Even ones created by me and so forth."

"And so forth," Bar'ren said, clearly not understanding the other man's verbal tic. "May I see?"

"Ah, it could be an islander tongue," Arti said, his expression brightening behind his spectacles. "I hadn't considered that," he added, passing the parchment over.

"We do not have a written language," Bar'ren said. "But I was taught to read Imperial and I've read the tracks of animals and humans that others have failed to discern."

"I suppose," Salina said slowly, "that it's possible to convert a verbal language into a written one using another language's letters?"

"A phonetic language," I mused. "That's—that's brilliant, Salina."

"I didn't get the Chair just on your vote alone, you know," she said, her cheeks turning a shade of pink.

"Noted," I told her.

"It's not that," Bar'ren said, cursing in his own tongue, and passed the parchment to Salina after a few moments. She studied it for a while, letting me finish my third bowl of stew before giving up with a sigh and offering the bit of parchment to Chan Sha.

"If you lot can't discern it, doubt I can either," she said, her voice lubricated from the wine the Artificer had given her. She now only sounded like a broken hinge instead of a rusted one, which likely matched her twisted mind. "Why don't we quit with the farce and just have Buc read it out for us?"

"I'm sure she'll try," Salina said, "but even a genius can't know everything."

"There's genius, and then there's preternatural genius," Chan Sha said, a smile growing on her thin, pink lips.

"No," the Artificer groaned beside me.

"Why don't you share your true nature, Buc?" the former pirate asked.

"What's she talking about?" Salina asked.

Chan Sha's remaining eye glinted in the candlelight, the other dark, hidden behind one of her braids. "C'mon now," she said, her voice hot, "you can't expect me to play nice every step of the way, surely?"

"You don't have to do this," Sin whispered. "Run her back down into the cellar. Chain her up. I know everything she does, Buc, I assure you."

"Save you were trapped in that altar for a century or better and haven't communed with Ciris since. She has," I reminded him.

"I don't think this is a good idea."

"Me either," I said. "It's a question of allies or cannon fodder. Friends or acquaintances."

"I—I—" I took a deep breath. "A little over a year ago Chan Sha tried to take back something her Goddess, Ciris, had lost."

"She's a Sin Eater?" Bar'ren growled, reaching for the long knife that hung at his side.

"Was," I corrected. "The Ghost Captain cajoled her into touching an altar of Ciris . . . but it was a trap, and in the process of defusing it, her Sin was torn from her body."

"Torn. Ripped. Mutilated," Chan Sha said, her voice sounding as if from another person. "I was left a husk."

"Hence her hatred of Eld and me," I explained to Salina. "She blamed me for what happened."

"You. Are. Godsdamned. Right." Chan Sha bit off every word, spittle flecking her lips. "Seeing as your hand was on the tiller the whole time!"

"Sounds as if she blames you still," Bar'ren muttered.

"Ergo the chains." I bit my tongue until I felt blood fill my mouth. I'd spent the past eight months alone save for Sin and the Artificer. One I couldn't trust and the other was more interested in what uses I could put his machines to than anything else. I wasn't sure I could trust any of them, not with this. "Trust" wasn't a word in my vocabulary save when it came to Sister and Eld and it hadn't served either of them very well. *You've come this far.* "After Chan Sha lost her shit, the Ghost Captain tried to turn Eld into a Shambles. There was only one way to save him," I continued. "I had to touch the altar."

I told them, haltingly at first, then faster, what had happened. Not nearly everything . . . but enough. "So I have Sin within me, but unlike Chan Sha and all of Ciris's other puppets, I'm not a Sin Eater. I haven't allowed Sin to Possess me, so Ciris is unaware that I'm alive. Unaware of what's missing from her altar."

"You?" Salina asked, her voice catching in her throat. "This whole time and you never told me? Buc! We tell each other . . . *everything.* I've been doing your work for the past eight months, unable to explain half the reasons for the orders I give to anyone, fighting with the Board and with the council stuck running Servenza until the Empress chooses a new Doga. Gods' breath, Buc, I had to attend the Empress *thrice* because of your orders!" Her voice broke. "Do you know what that woman is like?" She closed her eyes and tears traced down her cheeks. "I can't believe you didn't tell me. Didn't trust me."

"I wonder," Bar'ren said slowly, "if perhaps I didn't misinterpret the Mother's words . . . if perhaps you weren't to be the instrument of her revenge, but the instrument upon which she *should be revenged*," he growled.

"Is that a big knife you're holding below the table or are you just happy to see me?" I asked. Sin groaned. Bar'ren shifted slightly, evidently surprised that I'd caught the motion he'd sought to hide. "You think I'm one of those that killed some of your friends and burned your Goddess to the ground?" I snorted. "I killed nearly half a dozen Sin Eaters just the other day. I've been killing them, aye, and your Dead Ones, too, for months now."

"She's telling the truth," Chan Sha said, and the man's gaze snapped to her, but he kept his body and blade facing me. The woman held up her hands, chains clanking together, to show the manacles she wore. "The girl's never brought me anything but pain and misery—which, if you hate Sin Eaters, is something you should find comforting. I don't know how she found a way to keep Ciris from her, but she's done so for better than a year and I've no reason to doubt she'll do it for another. You want to kill a Sin Eater, try that pigsticker on me. I'm not one anymore, but I was for decades."

"I . . . know what the Mother told me," Bar'ren said finally, not bothering to hide the blade as he slid it back into the scabbard. He rested his forearms on the table, his hand twitching as if missing the feel of the hilt. "She said the waters of your shores would be murky."

"As for you, girl"—Chan Sha pointed at Salina—"you're upset your friend here didn't tell you what, exactly? That she had a shard of a Goddess stuck in her mind? That it was urging her to betray everything and everyone she believed in?" She snorted. "That's not something you tell a partner, let alone someone you're just coming to terms with." The woman shook her braids. "You forget I was once Sicarii, and I watched you all more closely than you realized. I—"

"Was told to sit there and shut the fuck up," I said, cutting her off. "I know, I know, you were building up to your big crescendo about how mighty you were. *Were.* Past tense. At the moment you could be eating your last meal, if you don't convince me you're worth more than the effort it would take for me to open your throat."

Chan Sha's taut cheeks blushed. "I was the one," she said in a low voice, "who suggested you could break the cipher," she reminded me. "I just kept everyone from losing their shit at finding out your true nature."

"Which they wouldn't have in the first place if you'd kept your mouth shut," I pointed out.

"Aye, another secret you'd have to keep from them. You want to kill Gods and Goddesses, Buc?" She smiled humorlessly. "You're going to have to decide to trust someone at some point. There's just too many ways this can go wrong and send us all down to the bottom. You've a need for friends."

"I said that once," Salina said quietly.

"Almost the first thing you said to me," I muttered. "I didn't believe you then."

"And now?"

"I'm sorry I didn't tell you, 'Lina," I said after a moment. She looked closely at me at that. "I might have done after the night Eld died . . . or almost died. Only, I left the next morning and this"—I tapped the side of my head—"isn't something you just mention in correspondence, casual or otherwise."

"No," she said, her mouth twisting in a faint grin, "I suppose it's not. So, do you really? Have Ciris's voice in your head?"

"Gods, no," I said quickly. "It's not Ciris, it's just a portion of her power. That's what Sin is, a shard of her within me. He's able to share that power with me and that's what fuels most of the magical things that Sin Eaters do."

"What's he saying right now?" she asked.

"That I'm just as pleased as a drunk pirate that you all know I'm alive," Sin muttered.

I repeated what Sin said and Salina laughed and slid the parchment across the table to me. I picked it up, aware of everyone's gaze, and glanced down at a page filled with letters crammed beside one another.

"Well, Sin? Can you break the code? Because I think everyone's going to be really disappointed to discover you're not omnipotent."

"Even Ciris isn't omnipotent," he said. "As good as, sometimes, but not always and in some areas she's as blind as the rest of us. Where you and I are concerned, for example."

"Perhaps not anymore," I said, remembering the Sin Eater who'd gotten away from that failed ambush.

"Aye," he whispered. "Hmm, so there is a code here that relies on a mathematical repetition, which should mean that the first letter, then the next first letter, then the second after that, the third after that, the fifth, the eighth, the . . ."

"Nature's Equation," I whispered in my mind. *Of course. Number sixty-seven.* I'd read Fivvonasi's work, *The Cornerstone of Nature: Chemical, Engineerical, and Physical Maths,* in order to understand some of the more complex books I tackled on astronomy, biology, and chemistry. The woman had been a fine teacher, beginning with the most elementary addition and subtraction before working up to advanced proofs and theorems. Nature's Equation was named such because its sequence was found throughout the world in everything from plant life to chemistry to architecture. "That means—"

"We just need to figure out the demarcation between words," Sin finished. Between the pair of us working in concert the letters began to pop out on the page, then form words, sentences.

"It's a letter of introduction," I said, looking up. "From the Plague Mistress to the Dead Walker Bar'ren killed."

"He had some help," Salina put in. "Just noting it for the record," she added, taking a sip from her glass, and Bar'ren chuckled.

"The Dead Walker everyone killed," I amended dryly. "Apparently they were to escort one of these Plague Walkers to the cathedral here, the one dedicated to Talshur." I glanced down at the parchment, the letters and words that Sin deciphered popping out to me so that I almost couldn't see the rest between them. "This Plague Walker has a final ritual to complete within the inner sanctum that will activate the plague within them, making the very air they exhale contagious."

"Why here?" Salina asked.

"How do we know it's not everywhere?" Chan Sha asked. Everyone looked at her, and the former pirate smiled. "I was plotting something similar myself, after all. Empire domination, not world domination, and though I decided to use the existing power structures to accomplish my ends, that doesn't mean I didn't consider plagues. At length. Tell them, Artificer," she added.

The Artificer flinched at her naming him. The man had turned against her before it made sense to do so, but I knew he prized learning and his own skin above all else. He knew it, too, which is why he kept close to me. Tugging at his collar, he shrugged. "If they are confident of the efficacy of the disease, then the best way to ensure they take down Ciris before she has a chance of creating an antidote would be to do so in one, world-consuming swoop." He spread his arms. "And so forth."

"And so forth," Bar'ren whispered, his skin ashen.

"Luckily for us," I murmured, "they aren't confident. That's why they've come here to test it. If it works as intended, then Cordoban, being the neutral party between the Empire and Normain, serves as a wonderful melting pot of merchants from across the world. An easy place from which to spread the infection. If it doesn't work, it'll be written off as some fever that a merchant brought in from the Shattered Coast."

"Gods," Salina said. "That would do it."

"Aye." I tapped the parchment. "Their plan is to set the Plague Walker free here and then rendezvous with a ship at this longitudinal bearing," I said, digging out a crumpled scrap of paper and a quill of the Artificer's invention that held an internal well of ink. I scrawled the numbers and put the scrap in the center of the table.

"That's less than useful," Salina said.

"Why?" Bar'ren asked. "What is this number?"

"It's a means by which one can navigate the world," the Artificer said, slipping into his lecturer's voice. "Imagine there are lines of direction running north to south along the world such that . . ."

"What it means," Chan Sha said after the Artificer made his point and slipped into relating the discovery of nautical direction, "is that without the latitude we'll only know how many degrees west of the principal line this ship will be. We need the second part—where it will be north or south of the equator—to discern its true position."

"You'd be right," I agreed, unable to keep the excitement from my voice, "save there's some contextual clues within the document and a queer bit of fungus growing along this tear in the upper corner," I indicated. "Which suggests the location to be Southeast Island, and the longitude is at such a point that it can only be one of two potential ports. One is a small landing on the western coast and the other is a natural islet that is sometimes used by smugglers." I sat back smugly, looking up to see a sea of confused faces. "What?"

"You figured out where the ship is going to be off a pinprick of fungus?" Salina asked.

"Well . . . more than a pinprick," I said. "If you scrape your finger across the edge you can feel it raised off the surface where the tear exposed the nonoiled parchment to it. The jungles of that island hold a particular genus that—"

"Do you believe her?" Chan Sha cut me off. "Artificer?"

"I'll have to test it with some of my chemicals to be sure," the man said, "but she has Ciris's knowledge in addition to her own not inconsiderable intellect, so I expect I'll but confirm her hypothesis. What were the contextual clues, Buc?"

"Their plan requires them to wait at a port of call within a few days' sail of Cordoban," I said, holding up a finger. "There the letter indicates they'll meet up with another ship carrying more Plague Walkers. If it goes as their Mistress believes it will, they'll use their planned anchorage as a jumping-off point to disperse themselves amongst a hundred ports of call."

"Southeast Island is the only place along that longitude that makes sense," Salina agreed.

"This changes everything," Chan Sha said. "You know that, right? We can't play fucking games, not when they've put all their coin on this toss."

"What are you saying?" Salina asked.

"The pirate's right," I said, surprising myself at how quickly I agreed with my former, perhaps still current, nemesis. *She didn't kill Eld.* That was a large part of it, but not the full measure. I'd bested Chan Sha, the Sin Eater, but as Sicarii, she'd nearly bested me. In many ways she was the proof to my hypothesis: people were better without the Gods than with. Also, her mind trod similar paths to my own and I could use that. "I told you," I continued, my eyes refocusing on the present, "this was a council of war, Salina."

"We're going to war?"

"We're at war," I said, nodding at the parchment on the table. "This is a declaration, or good as. We've got to find this Plague Walker here. Now."

"Before it completes the ritual," the Artificer said quietly. "Before it leaves the cathedral and begins to spread death throughout the city and so forth."

"And so fucking forth," I agreed.

18

After that, everyone began talking at once, offering a score of suggestions that ranged from the implausible to the outright impossible. The Artificer suggested warning the Federate, but Salina pointed out that by the time he finished bribing his way into an audience, it'd be days too late. As Chair of the Trading Company, she could arrange a meeting with the princes and princesses in a few hours, but she'd have to divulge enough information that when said information was eventually sold to the Dead Gods—and in Cordoban, that was simply a matter of price, not time—they would know the Kanados Trading Company was aiming for their throat. Salina suggested bribing some of the local toughs and guilds—gangs were outlawed here—to attack the cathedral, but the cost was prohibitive and the odds of success, terrible. Bar'ren mostly listened and Chan Sha kept opening her mouth to speak, then looking at me, then pressing her lips together in a way that suggested she was constipated.

"We need to know the lay of the land before we do anything," I said finally. "Aye," I cut Chan Sha off, "I know you wanted to say that half a bell ago, but it's good to let everyone work out their batshit-crazy ideas before we get down to the practical ones."

"I'll go," Bar'ren said.

"Go where?"

"To scout this land." He leaned forward. "Before I was speaker, I was both hunter and scout for my people. And even after, it was useful for a Sha'amen to appear unseen in unexpected places."

"Half of religion is performance," I agreed. His lips twisted but he didn't say anything. "When I say land, though, I mean city. Brick buildings and open streets and tall al-kasrs. You don't exactly blend in, you know."

"A man can change clothes," he said dryly.

"He did find his way to me on his own," Salina pointed out. "Even made it past half the guard before someone thought to question what he was doing roaming the halls of the Company's headquarters."

"The rooftops and alleyways of this place are strange to me, true," he said. "But they aren't so dissimilar from the palm trees and open sand dunes of my island. I'm used to climbing with few handholds and stalking pigs and monkeys that are constantly on the alert for the hunter. Compared to them, even these Dead Ones are not so wary."

"That's all well and good," Chan Sha said. "I saw your people fight the Ghost Captain, so I know what you're capable of . . . but you won't know what to look for. It's not just a different environment, it's different architecture, different lines of sight. Every danger will be a stranger to you. You need someone who kens not only a city, but the Dead Gods themselves. Someone who has plotted such assaults before. You need me."

"The fuck you're going anywhere," I told the woman.

"As if," Salina sniffed.

"But I—"

"Will only slow Bar'ren down with your bad leg and even if you didn't, there's not a Godsdamned chance I'd let you out of my sight."

"She's not wrong," the Artificer said after a moment. We all turned on him and he sank back on the bench. "I just mean that Bar'ren may be able to get close, but he's less versed in everything she mentioned. If he overlooks something of import, that could be as dangerous for our plans as if we were to go in blind."

"You volunteering, Arti?" I asked.

"The man's afraid of heights," Chan Sha said. "He can't go scampering across rooftops."

"He's not," I objected.

"I—uh—am paralyzingly afraid, actually."

"Arti!" I turned back to him. "You flew hundreds of paces above the ground in that crazy orin-contraption-thingie in Servenza. In the middle of a fucking storm, no less."

"That was different," he protested, pushing his spectacles up on his nose. "The ornithopter was of my design, a machine without fault. My balance, on the other hand, I am less sanguine about."

"Let me go with Bar'ren," Chan Sha pleaded. She leaned forward, her braids shifting to reveal the patch she wore over the eye she'd lost on the sands of that Godsforsaken island the Ghost Captain had brought us to, what felt like centuries before. "Remember what you told me? About it not being found? About having to earn it? Buc, give me that chance. To earn it. Please?"

It was the word and the emotion behind it that gave me pause. And the conversation we'd had before I brought her up out of the cellar. At the start I'd not been sure I shouldn't just kill her then and there, but then we'd talked and . . .

"Come to kill me then?" Chan Sha's voice smoldered like coals burned down to their last. She blinked in the lantern light. "Or do you want to carve on me some more first?"

"I haven't put blade to flesh yet," I reminded her, forcing my hands to remain by my sides and not run her through and be done with it.

"Sometimes—" She tried to straighten in her chains, then sagged, grunting when the metal bit into her flesh. "—the mental cuts are the deepest. I'm not sure how much more damage you can do that hasn't already been done, but you've always been an inventive one, eh, Buc?"

"That almost sounded a compliment," I told her, moving forward so she could see me more clearly.

"I never did like the cut of your jib," she admitted. "We're too much alike, you and I, in mind and temperament, and most days I'm too much for myself, let alone a double portion."

"You're cunning, in your way," I said.

"A compliment?" Her laughter disintegrated into a cough that racked her naked body, showing the lines of her ribs with every gasp. "It doesn't matter how cunning you are, Buc—Ciris can't be killed. Surely your Sin told you that?"

"First thing he said," I admitted. "Whenever everyone is quick to dismiss something as impossible," I said, speaking slowly, "I hear another word: opportunity."

"Your funeral," she growled. "Ciris is quite literally beyond your ken. Or mine. Or any of ours. You can't defeat that which you can't understand."

"You do sound like him," I said, tapping my head. "Almost a faint echo of the voice in my mind. I can't tell if it's because She inspires such devotion or if it's the magic She uses in your mind."

"Ciris welcomes two types at the start," Chan Sha said. "Those who are true believers and those who have vast potential. Brilliance is a prerequisite, of course, but the Goddess knows that over time those with potential will come to believe and those who believe will unlock their full potential."

"You actually love her, don't you?" I asked.

"I did . . . once." Chan Sha drew in a ragged breath and shook her braids out of her face. "She was my first family, really."

"It's a twisted sort of love that demands unquestioning obedience," I said.

"You ever been in love with any but yourself?" Chan Sha snorted.

"I've loved a couple of times," I said. Sister. Eld. "I'm no expert, it just seems to me that you didn't have much agency in the matter."

"The damnable thing about you," Chan Sha said, "is that you're always smart, but seldom wise, and then you come off with some shit like that and I wonder if your lack of wisdom is really all an act. You're too young for it not to be real and yet . . ."

I'd come down to see what Chan Sha had to say that might convince me not to slit her throat. If I hadn't just learned Eld was still alive, I wouldn't have hesitated: she'd be a corpse. Now, though, I was beginning to wonder what uses she could be put to.

"You said you loved Ciris once . . . but I saw you hanging around the Sin Eaters' al-kasr," I said. "You were figuring out how to return without them killing you on the spot or, worse, invading your mind, destroying it, and leaving you to wander the streets mumbling to yourself until someone took pity—or your threadbare purse—and put a blade through you."

"I was weak," she said slowly. "It's my biggest flaw. When the Goddess sent me off to become a pirate, to become the Widowmaker, I never expected it to be anything more than a role, but turns out it's nigh impossible not to come to care for your crew at sea.

"Weak," she added. "They keep you alive in countless ways and you return the favor. Storms, leaky boards, kraken, the Imperial navy, other pirates, there's just a thousand ways to die at sea and the only reason you don't is because of your crew. I never thought to find my family in the pinprick islands and endless waters of the Shattered Coast, but I did.

"In the end"— she inhaled shakily—"I betrayed them for Ciris. We didn't have to keep after the Ghost Captain and it became harder and harder to spin tales as to why we did." She snorted. "They weren't stupid, they should have seen through the obfuscations and half-truths I fed them."

"Love blinds us all."

"Just so. I felt a debt to Ciris and I'd been her creature for years before I turned pirate, so when she commanded, I went. I could feel her urgency, her need for what I was tasked to do. It made me feel . . . special." The woman made a sound in her throat. "I betrayed my family for my Goddess, and then on that rotted-out deck that hid that fucking altar, my Goddess betrayed me." Her voice hardened like a flint that's hot from striking against the starter. "Her betrayal took everything from me. My crew, my sight, my leg, my magic, and with it, my Sin, who was the only family I had left."

"Why didn't you go kill Ciris then?" I didn't think she was lying, but I didn't believe she was giving me the full truth, either. I wouldn't. It was the truth I needed, though, if I was going to use her for anything more than a sheathe for my blades. "Why come to Servenza and start your Sicarii bullshit?"

"I was feverish with loss, with anger that seethed in me like a living thing," she said after a moment. "Losing Sin broke my mind and what reformed just wanted to spread the pain." She looked up. "I hated you, Buc. You and Eld, the pair of you. You led me down the plank and fed me to the sharks. I hated Ciris, too, aye, but she was an afterthought and all I could see clearly through the haze of my hatred was you two. That fever broke when you tore my dreams apart at the Lighthouse."

"You and I share something else," I said when she finished speaking. "We don't do anything by half measures."

"No," she chuckled grimly, "we don't. Now, as much as I enjoy not being tortured or murdered . . . why don't you tell me why we're having this chat, Buc? What do you want?"

"I want all the things," I told her. "A few hours ago, I would have killed you and been done with it. I still might. But as you once told me, a change of breeze is but a wave away. And some things have changed. Important things. Here's where I stand. . . ."

When I finished telling Chan Sha what I'd learned of Eld and the Dead Gods, she simply nodded. She hadn't interrupted me once and for a moment I thought she'd fallen asleep, but then the light caught her good eye and I saw that she was listening with every fiber of her being. "The question that remains is: are you worth sparing?"

"You know why I hated you specifically?" she asked, answering my question with a question. "Back in Servenza?"

"Say I don't."

"Because when I realized you had magic, but weren't one of Ciris's . . . I realized the difference between us was one of strength. You had the strength to say no to your Sin, to choose your found family over magic. I . . . couldn't," she whispered. "When I was faced with it, I turned tail and let them all sink to the depths below.

"If you're looking for a reason to kill me, I've got a thousand." She lifted herself in her chains and tried to smile. *"If you're looking for a reason to let me live, I'm not sure I'm my own best advocate at the moment."*

"I could give you terms, a parley," I suggested. *"You liked that before."*

"Aye, and we both know how that turned out," she muttered. *"No terms. Terms are what Ciris offered and you saw where that leads."*

"Obligation."

"Requirements," she hissed. *"I'll help you, Buc, give you what I know, but for me"*—she raised her head—*"all I want is what you had. Have. I want that family and that's what I've been searching for."*

"The funny thing about family," I said slowly, *"is that it isn't just found . . . it's earned."*

"I might be willing to suspend my disbelief long enough to give you a kernel of trust," I told Chan Sha, then jabbed a finger at Bar'ren. "But he won't and he's the one who's going, so I think you'll be sitting this one out." I sighed. All I wanted was a few hours' sleep, a small repayment of the debt I'd collected over the past few days of running purely on adrenaline and magic. "I guess that leaves—"

"She can come with me," Bar'ren said, interrupting me.

"What?"

"You spoke of trust, and it is true that I don't trust this, this Chan Sha," he said, fumbling her name. "But it's equally true that trust must begin with an act of faith."

"You have faith in her, old man?" I asked.

"I have faith in the Mother. She told me that the sin of Ciris would betray her, and Chan Sha is a former Sin Eater."

"That's one way of looking at it," I admitted. I left unsaid that another would be that I was using her Sin against her by never becoming one of her own. "She won't have any weapons, but she's dangerous in her own right. Cunning beyond measure." Chan Sha sat up straighter. "She's also half-blind and crippled," I added, watching her redden, "so I don't know how much help she'll be in a fight."

"We'll cross that island when we come to it," he said, standing up. "If it is to be done, let us do it. You," he said, speaking to Chan Sha, "will slow me down."

"Maybe I'll surprise."

"Maybe," he agreed. "Take care how you do so." He tapped the knife at his side—it was really more of a small, broad-bladed cutlass. "In my eyes, you're still a Sin Eater, and I swore an oath to the Mother to kill every Sin Eater."

The two locked eyes across the table, staring each other down, until finally Chan Sha broke the tension with a grin. "I may join you in that oath."

"You're going to allow this?" Salina whispered.

"Bar'ren's right. I have to start trusting her sometime or I might as well have left her in the cellar to rot. Arti, get them whatever gear they need," I said, pushing myself up from the table. "I'm taking a nap."

I left unsaid that as bets went this was a pretty safe one. It's not like Chan Sha could betray me to the Dead Gods—as a former Sin Eater, she'd be on their hit list—and she had had plenty of time before I captured her to have gone to the Sin Eaters if she wanted to return there. Besides, some of my little fish, who were on their way to becoming window thieves, were waiting to follow any who left the al-kasr. If Chan Sha had more betrayal on her mind, she wouldn't get very far with it. There's trust and then there's trust, savvy?

19

"Buc?"

I sat up at Salina's voice in the doorway. I'd woken up when she loudly shut the outer hallway door, which told me the Artificer had warned her about startling me. Close to a year ago I'd been nearly killed by falling masonry when I went into a burning warehouse to save a child. It'd been my warehouse, my fault the child was there in the first place, and while Chan Sha—Sicarii, then—had started the fire, that didn't absolve me of my own sins. Eld had pulled me out of the burning hulk after I'd been struck. After that, we had changed, Sin and I. There was an edge to me now that hadn't been there before—and before, I'd still been plenty sharp enough to cut. Now, startle me and you'd be lucky to find yourself against a wall, my blade to your throat. The unlucky ones choked to death on their own blood.

"Is it morning?" I asked, letting the covers fall to my waist.

"Mid," Salina said, entering with one of the Artificer's gear-wrought lanterns, which shone more light than should have been possible. A servant followed in after her with a slow match and began lighting the candles around the periphery of the room. I'd mostly gotten over my fear of fire, but Sister had also died in flames. *Also my fault.* I tapped my leg with the fingers of my left hand, trying to concentrate on the beat rather than the fear. I didn't believe in the luck of three, but I didn't aim to tempt fate either, so there were no candles in the chandelier over the bed nor by my bedside, but between the candles lining the walls and Salina's lantern, there was plenty of light.

"Bar'ren and Chan Sha just made it back. I'll let them tell you what they learned, but I think we have time enough until tonight."

"The Dead Gods canceled services for the day?" I stopped tapping.

"How'd you know?" Salina asked, moving into the room, skirts swishing softly as she walked around the bed. She'd reverted back to Servenzan fashions, her blond locks falling over her left shoulder in a series of interlocking braids; lace spilled out of the left sleeve of her amber dress, hiding her left hand, concealing her marital status. Not that the woman was married. Her first love had died in a storm at sea, as did many Servenzans, and now she was wedded to her work.

"It was the only answer that would have kept me from setting out within the hour to burn the motherfucking crypt to the ground," I said. I hid a yawn behind my fist and gestured at the dark, mahogany table that matched the color of my hand. "Also, Eld's letter suggested the ritual would take a full day and night, perhaps longer." I smiled wanly. "I should feel like an olive put through the press, but I don't."

"Sin?" Salina asked.

"Him and learning Eld's alive," I agreed, nodding. "And seeing you. I've missed our talks, 'Lina."

"Me too," she said, sitting on the end of the bed. "Early on, I didn't have time to think, and neither did anyone else in the wake of the murders of three of the leaders of Servenzan society."

"Especially with some turned traitor to Normain," I added dryly.

"Especially that."

Before I left Servenza to chase my revenge, I'd led everyone to believe that the Chair—the head of the Kanados Trading Company—and her number two, the Company's Parliamentarian, were the ones behind the unrest that Chan Sha, as Sicarii, had fomented. I'd also convinced everyone that they were Normain traitors who'd murdered the Doga, ruler of Servenza and the Empress's cousin. Salina knew that Chan Sha had been Sicarii, but she didn't realize that neither the Chair nor the Parliamentarian were actually traitors. I'd needed them all removed—including the Doga, who *had* been working with Sicarii—in order to create the power vacuum necessary to get Salina named Chair. That it had also led to a shadow war between the Empire and Normain at the same time as a real war erupted between Ciris and the Dead Gods was merely a bonus. I'd left that mess for Salina to clean up, and the woman looked sharper than I remembered, but fresh as well, so she must not have been doing too badly for herself.

I said as much and she laughed. "It only took a month for the rest of the Board to rouse themselves from their stupor and begin trying to pull the boat in a dozen different directions," she admitted. "Unfortunately for them, by that time I'd gotten the Empress on my side, and since she hasn't replaced the Doga, the Empress's word is both Imperial and Servenzan law at the moment. That, of course, lends itself its own set of problems. . . ."

I listened to Salina talk, but more than that I watched how animated she grew as she told me of some of the trades they'd begun undertaking, preparing to capitalize on the ensuing war. She listed a dozen initiatives the Company didn't realize it was supporting with its new profits, like the clothing manufactory dedicated to simple, well-made garments that were distributed to children who showed up at Kanados's factories. To work, true, but thanks to some of the Artificer's schematics, Salina was automating some of the most dangerous jobs.

"You'll love this," she added. "I've ensured that some of the redesigned timing belts and turning keys are still in smaller areas— which means we continue to employ children. But now there's no danger of them being caught in grinding gears or turning belts. The best part"—Salina smiled—"is that the work now requires some reading and simple arithmetic."

"Street rats can't do that," I protested.

"No, so I had to bring in one of the retired governesses from the guild—at a pretty coin to satisfy the guild that we weren't encroaching on their domain—to teach them."

"You started a school," I whispered.

"A very base one," Salina said. She reached out and touched my hand. "But it's a start. Children are no longer dirty and naked in the streets, some are learning, and I've begun stockpiling food-stuffs for when the war inevitably kicks off."

"Godsdamn it, woman," I said softly, sitting up all the way and wriggling in excitement. "I've been planning universities and ways to build wealth from the streets up with pathways to educa-tion for all, but this . . . this is the mortar between the cracks that I'd never concerned myself with. No, it's bigger than that. This is the bedrock of my vision."

"I do read your letters, you know," Salina said, feigning a sniff. "Speaking of . . ." She pointed at the opened letter on the night-stand. "What did Eld say?"

"Most of it"—I shifted the sheaf of papers—"is repetitive of the letter I received. A fail-safe if I didn't get it, but he must have sent it after the first one, because this has an added page."

"I doubt they traveled by Cannon Ship as we did," Salina said.

"Quite." I felt my stomach flip at the mention of the ship. I was born on an island crisscrossed with canals, but my stomach didn't have a liking for the famed Cannon Ships—they shot water through complex gear-wrought tubes, propelling the ships across the water at speeds that shouldn't have been possible. Physics agreed with my stomach, but Sin Eaters' magic made all manner of impossibilities possible. *Like Eld's letter.* "He said that we need to come to Normain," I said after a moment. "I know," I added when Salina made a noise in her throat. "We'll have to disguise ourselves and the ship to get anywhere near their coastal towns, let alone the capital."

"Why there?"

"It's the heart of their power," I said.

"The Dead Gods." She shuddered. "I've always heard the city is made from the bones of the Gods."

"The Old City," I said, tapping my head. "From what I have seen in drawings, some of the Dead Gods were used in the architecture—some form entire cathedrals—and their cathedral cum citadel is carved whole cloth from three of the hoary old bastards."

"Drawings, or Sin showed you?"

"Both," I said, smiling. "I know you're pissed I didn't tell you, Salina, but it feels good not to have to hide it now."

"So," she said, her eyes flashing while avoiding the subject, "we don't have to worry about Eld being in the Cordoban cathedral when we blow it up? That's good."

"He's become the Plague Quartermaestro, which, if I'm reading between the lines"—I scanned the page—"hasn't endeared him to some of the other priests and priestesses. He's tried to slow their machinations down as much as possible while making it seem the opposite, but they aren't fools and with their Shambles they are legion." I looked up. "We need to go to him fast, Salina. Not only to rescue him, but to save the world before they create enough Plague Walkers that they doom us all."

"I'll help you," Sin said, breaking his silence. He'd been quiet after I told everyone our secret. "I can't help you defeat Ciris. Every good thing in your world, Buc, has come from her. Every scrap of gearwork, every lesson. She's the only way we'll save this world, whether we stop the plague or no. Certainly if we fail, we'll need her wisdom to devise an antidote, but set that aside," he added quickly, sensing my anger. "Set aside the evilness of the Dead Gods . . . I'll help you find Eld and I'll help you rescue him."

"Noble of you," I murmured. "To agree to what I've already decided."

"It's not that," he said slowly. "It's about . . . atonement? I fucked up back in Servenza. Aye, it was ultimately to force you to take Ciris fully within you, but I was wrong in how I tried it. Wrong to meddle with your memories and worse to try to turn you and Eld against each other. I fucked up and you'll never forget that, but if we save Eld together and defeat the Dead Gods?" He paused, his voice quiet. "Maybe then you'll grant me another chance. Like you did with Chan Sha. Family is earned, you're right about that."

"Thanks, Sin," I said, surprised. I didn't trust him, and he knew that, but I was touched.

"I'll go rouse the others," Salina said, rising. "Bar'ren and Chan Sha are sleeping, but I think the Artificer's locked away in his laboratory."

"He's playing around with some explosives," I said, waving a hand. "And those two can catch a few more winks yet."

"Explosives?" she choked. "Should I be worried?"

"No, but the Dead Gods should be," I said, smiling. "How about we catch up over breakfast?" I yawned. "Or lunch? Then we'll wake the others, hear what they saw, and decide how, exactly, we're going to blow these undead motherfuckers away."

Salina laughed, but her skin paled. "We're really going to do this, aren't we? Destroy the Gods."

"Aye," I said. "It starts tonight."

"You've found more cannon fodder," Sin said when Salina had left. "First the Artificer, then Bar'ren and Salina, and now Chan Sha."

Cannon fodder. I swept the covers aside; put my bare feet on the cool, marble floor; and paused. "Aye, but what if this time . . . what if they aren't?" I asked myself and him.

Being alone these past months had taught me that I couldn't treat everything like the streets or I'd never be able to create something better than what I'd experienced. I meant what I'd told Salina. I was going to blow these motherfucks sky-high and watch their corpses dance in the flames. I would bury a mind spike so deeply in Ciris's skull that she'd bleed Sin for days when she died. Before, I thought the world nothing more than fodder for my cannons, but that attitude wouldn't take me where I needed to go. No, what I needed, what I now had, was something more.

Allies.

20

"Go on, Denga," I told the girl. With Sin's magic burning in my ears I could hear Chan Sha limping closer down the hallway. "You did good."

"Promise?" she asked, her button nose wrinkling.

"Promise," I said, squeezing her shoulder. I swung my legs around the bench and so did she, the skirts of her new, peach dress swishing loudly. The garment had more thread than any three dresses she'd had before put together. "Now run along. And tell your ma I want to hear she's hired that new tutor, next I stop by."

"S-she already did," Denga said, smiling as she pulled at the scrap of yellow cloth tied into and around her blond hair—clean for once. "Starts after the feast day."

"Then you'd better get to studying, eh?" I asked, giving her a smile. The girl winked at me and disappeared through the door, yelling at the servant to open the door as if she'd been born to coin and not the street.

"You really do care for them, don't you?" Chan Sha asked. She stepped into the room, wearing a white shirt and black, leather trousers that were tight at her thighs but loose enough below her knees that they almost looked like the dresses most wore in Cordoban. Leaning on a blackthorn cane, she walked over to the table and rested against it, catching a breath before slipping onto the bench opposite me. She studied me for a moment, swiping her braids out of her eyes. "I didn't think you cared about anything."

"You don't think much at all," I said, switching from Cordoban to Imperial, "is the problem. Aye," I added when she opened her mouth, "I care for her. I care for them all, which is why you and I met in the first place."

"I curse the day," she growled.

"I bet."

"I do," she said. "Before you, every toss came up higher than the last, and ever since, it's been pips in every cup."

"Cheers," I told her, raising my glass of white wine that was mostly water. "Bar'ren coming?"

"In a moment," she said, plucking up a pomegranate from the table. "I don't think the man's ever had hot water doused over him before."

"Likely not," I agreed.

We descended into silence then, until one by one, the Artificer, Salina, and Bar'ren made their way into the room. The glasswork in the ceiling showed the sun had just fallen below the horizon and full dark wasn't that far in the offing. I waited for them to get settled on either side of the table, Bar'ren surprising me by choosing to sit next to Chan Sha, Salina and Arti flanking me.

"All right," I said, picking at the hem of my dark-grey dress. It was of Cordoban cut, so it might as well have been trousers and a tight blouse, but it didn't fit the same as pants and a blouse did, nor like a true Servenzan dress. "What'd you learn yesterday?" I asked, trying to set the annoyance of the dress aside. "Is the Plague Walker in the cathedral?"

"Likely," Chan Sha said.

"Definitely," Bar'ren said at the same time. They exchanged looks and he shrugged. "We could hear chanting." He glanced at me and smiled. "I could smell the incense on the air and Chan Sha says they only use that for rituals."

"That's true," we both said at the same moment. She smiled wryly and inclined her head. "The Dead Gods' priests believe that incense imbues them with certain powers or aspects of power."

"And it doesn't?" Salina asked.

"It does," Chan Sha said when I gave her a nod. "Save it's not the incense, but the scrapings of bone and other detritus left by the Dead Gods that are mixed within the incense. It's less like imbuing, to be honest. More like . . ." She tapped her finger against her chin.

"Creating an opening within them that can be filled," I finished.

"Aye," she agreed. "Something like that. There'll be blood involved, too. Always is, with that lot."

"So, whatever this ritual is," Salina said, speaking slowly, "it's utilizing bits of the Dead Gods, which we know are magic, to activate the plague within these new priests."

"Plague Walkers," Bar'ren growled.

"Plague Walkers," Salina said. She half pulled the cowl of her cloak up, stopped herself, and shuddered. "They'll be finished shortly, if they aren't already. What do we do?"

"Fire kills every instance of plague known to us," the Artificer said. He pushed his spectacles up on his nose. "Extreme cold, too, but sometimes that keeps it suspended rather than outright destroys."

"And we're in the deep south," I reminded him. "Cold isn't really an option."

"So, we waltz in there and light the place up," Chan Sha said with a grin.

"We'll need to ensure none can escape," Bar'ren said in his stony voice.

"Thank the Gods they suspended services," Salina muttered.

I left unsaid it was a strange thing to thank the Gods one was about to kill, but I couldn't help but point out the obvious. "If we bring the cathedral down around their ears, they would have nowhere to escape to."

"I don't think you understand the scale of the cathedral," Chan Sha said.

"It's nearly the size of the one in Servenza," Salina said by way of agreement. "You'd have to be in a dozen places at once to light enough fires."

"Two dozen," Chan Sha said.

"You're forgetting that you've got a genius and an artificer in your presence," I reminded them.

"The Artificer is a two-for-one," Chan Sha agreed.

"I meant the pair of us," I growled. I'd speed-read, with Sin's help, *Gunpyders and Their Arts,* by a madwoman who tested all manner of powders and bombs in the countryside on the Confederacy's eastern coast. Chinshu Feng had written a good two-thirds of what she intended, but the rest would have to wait until they found all the pieces her final experiment had left her in. Apparently the crater her workshop left behind was a bit of a local attraction. *Number 471.* "Arti, tell them."

"Well, uh," the man said, dry-washing his pale hands, "as to that, it's straightforward enough. Buc calculated the explosive load required to bring down the cathedral. There are, uh, one moment," he said, unbuttoning his coat halfway down before pulling out a thinly rolled piece of parchment. Unveiled on the table, it turned out to be a schematic of the cathedral. "There are," he said, pointing his thick finger at one of the arched ceiling intersections, "several points where key beams connect and so forth. Buc noted that a dozen well-placed charges, timed to go off in concert, should produce enough of a shock wave to shake the mortar loose here, here, and here. That, along with the explosions themselves and aided by falling debris, would do the trick."

"There are only five of us," Bar'ren said. He frowned, adding a dozen wrinkles to his suntanned face. "How can we be in two places at once?"

"You won't need to be," I assured him. "We'll have timers."

"You can't trust match cord for that," Chan Sha said. "You'll remember I used to string them through my hair when I was a pirate?"

"I recollect."

"Aye, well, they burn at different rates according to half a dozen factors. I once had a long cord burn all the way through during battle. By the time I realized it was my hair that was burning, I lost the whole braid." Chan Sha made a noise in her throat. "Nearly lost a full head of hair."

"As to that," the Artificer said, unable to keep the smile from his face, "I devised a gearwork timer like that of a clock."

"Gearwork?" Salina asked. "Did Buc help you?"

"Not magic, signora," the Artificer said. "Uh, that is, Chair." He blushed, brushing at his receding hairline. "I am capable, quite really, of creating my own gears. They are different, but—"

"And if Ciris or her Sin Eaters find that out, they'll kill him," I said, showing my teeth. "Unless we kill them first, right, Arti?"

"Your companionship appeals to me on several levels."

"See? Several levels," I said.

"That's the plan, then?" Salina asked, her brow furrowed. "All of us climb atop the cathedral and set these timers off together."

"Not quite," I admitted.

"I'm afraid of heights," the Artificer reminded her.

"And Chan Sha has a broken flipper," I added. "If we have to depend on her scaling a cathedral's tower . . . we're fucked."

"So kind," the woman muttered.

"Seems plain enough," Bar'ren said.

"Aye and it would be," I agreed, "save that my little fish tell me the Sin Eaters got wind of the ritual."

"They know the Dead Gods' plan?" Salina hissed.

"No," I said, as Chan Sha shook her braids in dissent. "They don't know what the ritual intends, just that it's going on and has been for a long enough time that they'd rather not see it succeed."

"That seems fortunate," Salina said.

"It would prove a distraction," the Artificer added.

"From what Denga told me, it's devolved into a running street battle that's enveloped half the rii," I said. "Worse, it's also drawn in the militia." Everyone save Bar'ren groaned at that. The Cordoban militia really was more akin to an army than a police force, with each prince or princess donating companies to patrol the city. With three sides fighting one another the city would be trapped in pure chaos.

"We observed from here and here," Bar'ren said, indicating one position southwest of the cathedral schematic and one to the northeast. "To reach the points of the cathedral, we'll have to fight our way through here," he said, making a motion on the table to indicate a street. "It shouldn't be more than two of your blocks."

"They could fit threescore in that space," Chan Sha growled. "With pike and shot and more besides."

"We're not fighting," I said. Despite the past few days, I hadn't been relying on Sin as much as I had before leaving Servenza. He was like kan, a drug that I liked, but liked too much. With him in me we could have fought through that threescore provided they were mortal and not mages, but we'd have drawn every eye to us. The Buc of old, before Sin, never would have considered that, and while the past eight months hadn't seen me slip fully back to my old ways, some of that sense of discretion and waiting for the moment to stab from the dark had returned. At everyone's questioning looks, I explained. "We fight and we'll have them all on us. Where two could slip through last night, perhaps five can as well?"

"Likely there'd only be token forces on the rooftops," Salina mused.

"It's a good plan," Chan Sha said.

"Will your leg be up to it?" Bar'ren asked. She nodded. "Even after last night? It must be knotted and stiff—"

"It'll be fine," she said, cutting him off.

"I've a coconut oil with me that when heated and applied—"

"I said," Chan Sha growled, "fuck off."

Bar'ren rolled his eyes, but nodded.

"And I've a fear of heights," the Artificer said. "Falling and so forth."

"Then don't look down." I stood up and clapped him on the back. "All right, here's the plan. We retrace Bar'ren and Chan Sha's footsteps from last night across the rooftops. When we get there, Bar'ren and I sneak over to the cathedral and plant the bombs while you three provide overwatch. Salina and I will gather up what we need while Arti rounds up his bombs and makes sure they don't blow our arses off while we're jumping from rooftop to rooftop."

"And what about me?" Chan Sha asked.

"You?" I smiled. "You're going to let Bar'ren rub that oil into your busted leg so you don't slow us down." The color drained from Chan Sha's face and she opened her mouth to argue. "Or you can stay here," I cut her off. "I won't have you slowing us down, savvy? We don't know when that ritual's going to kick off nor what we'll run into along the way. We've got to take down that whole damned cathedral in one go. Burn the rubble to glass to prevent the plague from spreading. You want a front-row seat to that? Take your fucking medicine."

Chan Sha crossed her arms, lips pouting, but didn't say anything. Bar'ren simply nodded while Salina fought to keep from laughing and the Artificer looked bemused at all of our expressions.

"All right." I slapped the table. "Let's burn this motherfucker down."

21

"All right," Buc said, tossing aside the wooden beam she'd been carrying to help them traverse some of the gaps between rooftops. It landed with a clatter. "That wasn't so bad, aye?"

Chan Sha fought to not roll her eyes at the girl's bravado. It'd been worse than the night before. Aye, the beam had helped, as had Bar'ren's oils; she could walk without the cane, but after moving at a breakneck pace across half the city her leg burned with a fire that twinned the one in her missing eye. A year ago that pain had driven her half-mad, uniting with her anger to create the persona known as Sicarii. Now, she was able to control it. *Just.* They'd had to run at a half crouch to avoid detection; they'd frequently slammed into the edges of rooftops, then leapt onto the wooden board and run to the next. She reached down absently, fingers kneading the twisted muscles around her knee, trying to work some of the tension out.

Twice they'd run into others: first, a Dead Walker who'd used a rooftop vantage point while controlling a score of Shambles on the ground. She'd thought to summon her undead to her, but Bar'ren had distracted her with that half knife, half sword of his long enough for Buc to put a pair of silver balls through the woman's eyes with that slingshot. The Dead Walker's glowing book dropped from her dead hands to smash into pieces on the cobblestone below. *I wonder why the Sin Eaters didn't try something similar?* Chan Sha snorted to herself. She knew why. Sin Eaters weren't stupid, but they were arrogant in the same manner as Veneficus, both styles of mages believing their magic made them invincible. Dead Walkers seemed to have more sense, although it was a sense that bordered on the lunatic if the Ghost Captain was anything to go by. *I hope that hoary bastard's rotting in the sands of that Godsforsaken island.*

Two rooftops before they reached the overlook she and Bar'ren had used the night before, they ran into a trio of militia with long-barreled muskets who had been sniping at any who tried to cross the intersection below. The crossing of these four streets seemed to separate several small battles going on between Sin Eaters and Veneficus or Dead Walkers and their Shambles. Salina had surprised them all by immediately cutting loose with a rotating blunderbuss that she held at waist level, the five barrels spinning in their gearwork settings and tearing the militia to lifeless rags on the graveled rooftop.

Glancing down, Buc added, "No need for quiet, not with those idiots down below."

The "idiots" were a squad of militia that had somehow gotten separated from their company and barreled into the ring of Shambles deployed in the streets surrounding the cathedral. A score of these Shambles, who clearly had been locked in the catacombs below for years, if not decades, judging by their level of decay, were mindlessly throwing themselves at the half-dozen Cordobans who had erected a hasty barricade from a cart and several abandoned merchants' stalls. The cacophony of gunfire, the groaning of the undead, and the faint sounds of more distant battles provided some measure of concealment.

Salina collapsed beside Chan Sha, letting the pair of muskets she'd taken off the men she'd killed fall against the crenellated edge of the roof. Sweat poured down her face and her cloak was sodden through from both their footrace and the humidity that had rolled in along with the coming storm. Salina drew a rasping breath, reaching for the water bag at her side. The Artificer crouched beside her, his pale features a queer shade of green that looked as if he were about to sick up, as he'd done on the rooftop with the dead militia. *From the corpses or from the heights?* He glanced past Chan Sha at the cathedral rising above them and swallowed hard, suppressing a shudder. *Heights, then.*

"Show me where you think footholds can be found, Bar'ren," Buc said. The girl—woman—moved about as easily as if she'd just finished a midnight stroll. She opened the sacks most of them had carried, sorting the bombs—each was made of several grenadoes tied together by match cord, with a smaller grenado on top, all secured within an intricate gearwork frame—into the two larger packs. "Sooner in, sooner out."

"There, you see the northern corner where the spout runs out of that flying dragon's mouth?" the older man said in his graveled voice. He crouched beside Buc, draped in a large, thin piece of fur that had a hole for his head; the rest just hung off his shoulders. Whatever animal it'd been—it seemed larger than any creature Chan Sha had seen on the man's island—its mottled pattern in black, grey, and brown offered excellent camouflage. "The . . . what do you call it?"

"Gargoyle," Buc muttered, her black dust cloak fluttering in the breeze as she worked a gear-wrought telescope. "I see it."

"The span below that, there's a broad gutter that runs the perimeter, and below that—"

"There's a drainpipe that runs down almost to the ground," Buc said. "Aye, that'll do. There's another series of pipes and gutters the next span up that seems to run almost to the spire." She handed the telescope to Bar'ren and grinned, her teeth bright in the dark. "Bloody perfect. Arti, you're up." The pale man stood up slowly, one hand on his stomach, the other clenching the rooftop's edge. "Go over how these things work, one last time. I'd hate to blow my own arse off trying to do the same to theirs."

"Embarrassing," Salina agreed in a light tone, and both women shared a look that twisted Chan Sha's mouth.

Why? The question caught her off guard. A little over a year since she'd lost her Sin, and she still wasn't used to the gaping space within her mind. The loneliness of her thoughts. Worse, she knew the answer. *Jealousy.* The Chair of the most powerful trading company in the world, born with a gilded spoon stuck in her mouth, friends with an orphaned street rat who sought to destroy the world's corrupt societies. It didn't make a spit of sense and yet . . . *Did Gem and I make sense?* Her first mate had been as close a friend as she had, a rough-and-tumble pirate of even meaner birth than Chan Sha herself, with a strong sense of honor that she'd found endearing, if inconvenient at times.

There'd been others, of course, but it'd been a long time since she'd seen women as close as Buc and Salina were. *I'm tired of being alone.* Her Sin's suicide meant she was more than alone. She was empty.

"Right." Buc's voice snapped her back to the present. "You three keep a sharp eye, and Bar'ren and I will skip over and present these gifts to those undead bastards. I hope they enjoy the unwrapping," she added.

"What will we be doing if said sharp eyes show trouble?" Salina asked.

"Put that musketry to use," Buc suggested.

"My people use hand signals when hunting to remain silent," Bar'ren said. "We could do the same? Use these scopes"—he hefted the one in his hand—"to see one another."

"We'd have to keep looking back," Buc said with a shake of her long braid, then ran a hand along the shaved part of her head. "No, speed is our friend here. We go in, do what we need to do, and get out. If we hear you three shooting, which we should given it will be in our direction, we'll know something's up and have a look." She hefted the pack over her shoulders, adjusting the straps. "Give us half a bell."

"You've only a tenth of a bell once you start the first timer," the Artificer reminded her, his spectacles shifting lenses from an amber one to a verdant lens that caught the sliver of moonlight poking out from the clouds above. "Make sure your sequence is timed right."

"If it's not, I'm not sure we'll be the ones who know," Buc said dryly.

"We plant them front to back," Bar'ren recited. "Setting them as we go so we can haul arse on the return."

"That's the plan."

"Be careful," Salina muttered. "The pair of you," she added, but her eyes were on Buc.

"Best be about it," Buc said lightly. She nodded at Salina, her gesture taking in Chan Sha as well, and clapped the Artificer on the back. Bar'ren tossed a rope over the side, tugging it hard to ensure it was secured to the crenellations. He went over and Buc followed, shooting the other three a final grin as she did so. Then they were gone, the inky blackness of night swallowing them up.

"When Buc told me you were Sicarii, I wasn't surprised," Salina said.

Chan Sha arched an eyebrow from behind the lens she held to her good eye, following the pair of shadows that were halfway up the piping of the cathedral's side. *So far, so good.* "Oh?" Her damaged vocal cords made the question sound harder than she intended. "Why's that?"

"The Chair—the one before me—said you were a venomous chameleon. You changed your colors as it suited you. I saw you once," the woman added, tapping the stock of the long-barreled musket she held. "You wouldn't remember, there were a dozen of us in the boardroom when the Company sent you off to become pirate queen of the Shattered Coast—not knowing your Goddess had other plans. Then you returned as Sicarii and Buc had you in her sights. . . ."

"Well." She hefted the gun. "I never thought to find you alive after that. You've lived a dozen lives."

"Aye," Chan Sha said, blinking tears away as she stowed the telescope. Her eye always watered when she strained her vision and there was no sense looking any longer now that the pair had spread out, running along either side of the gutter. *It's up to you now, girl. Buc.* "I lived a lot of lives," she agreed, "and they all ended the same: in blood and flame."

"Mayhap this time will be different," Salina said.

Chan Sha snorted. Experience suggested otherwise. *Ma and Da failed me. I failed Gem and my crew, every last one. Failed my Goddess. Failed myself.* She ran through the list, but couldn't deny that a portion of her—small and stupid, to be sure—wondered if perhaps Salina wasn't right. *If we can kill the Dead Gods together . . .* Buc had used her before, but Chan Sha had used Buc, too. This time, though, if they could be true allies, if there was a chance at earning some measure of trust, then maybe it would be different.

Failing that . . . there was always Ciris. Chan Sha clenched her teeth at the wave of nausea that rose within her. The Goddess had forced her to betray everything and everyone, and yet she still hadn't been able to dislodge the deity's tentacles from within her mind. Not fully. Worse, she knew returning to the Goddess was a possibility, thanks to Buc. *Her truth, the woman doesn't realize what she has with that Sin.* It shouldn't have been possible for Buc to have access to Sin's magic without accepting Possession, and yet . . . It had something to do with that altar on that Gods-fucked island, Chan Sha was certain. A faint memory rose within her mind, but wouldn't coalesce. *Maybe Sin doesn't fully appreciate the uniqueness of their situation either.* That meant there was still a chance for her there, an opportunity. A—

The sound of the pistole's hammer being drawn back snapped her out of her reverie, and she turned only a fraction before she felt the cool metal against her cheek.

"Your face is a study, Chan Sha," Salina whispered. The woman

had been hiding a pistole in the folds of her dress the entire time!
"I grew up in rooms where entire sagas were told in the shifting
of a glance, the raising of a brow. You even *begin* to think about
playing us false and this will be the last life you live." The barrel
shifted away from her cheek and Chan Sha turned her glare on
the other woman. "Best make sure you don't turn this life into
that self-fulfilling prophecy of blood and flame," she added.

"You—"

"Ahem." The Artificer cleared his throat, pulling both wom-
en's glares onto himself. "There's something happening. D-down
there." He pointed, looking past them and then away, swallowing
hard. "The cathedral doors have opened."

Chan Sha glanced down and cursed. Light flooded out of the
arched opening, bathing the steps in brilliance that framed a tall,
hooded figure—more shadow, really—and then other figures
without hoods began filling the doorway, flanking the first. There
was something in the way they held themselves that told Chan
Sha exactly who they were.

"Is that—" Salina asked.

"Plague Walkers," Chan Sha confirmed.

"Gods," the Artificer choked, dry-washing his hands. "They're
starting the plague now."

"We've got to stop them," Salina said, holstering her pistole
and reaching for the rope Bar'ren had left hanging over the side.
"What are you doing?" she growled when Chan Sha grabbed her
arm.

"Shooting a bunch of Shambles from behind when they are
crowded together in an alley or cutting down some surprised militia with a Godsdamned scattergun is a world away from facing
Veneficus or Dead Walkers on their home turf." Chan Sha shook
her braids. "You'll never make it."

"She's right," the Artificer agreed quickly.

"What do you suggest?" Salina asked, looking from one to the
other. "We can't let them leave before the bombs go off."

The Artificer cursed and looked up from the timepiece he pulled from his dark-green coat. "I told Buc I needed more time to fine-tune the mechanisms." He scowled behind his spectacles. "The bombs should all sync with one another provided they place them in the order I told them to. Should take about a tenth of a bell, but I warned them it could be less. Much less. Even then . . . the Plague Walkers will be long gone."

"Small win if we destroy their bastion of power after they've left," Salina said.

"And so forth," the man agreed.

"I've been waiting," Chan Sha said, striking a long match, "a long time to pay these bastards back for what they did to my crew."

She touched the flame to the match cord she'd strung through her braids, which began to hiss and spark, smoke wreathing her head as she shrugged the dozen pistoles hidden beneath her overlarge cloak into place. *Feels good.* She picked up the rotating blunderbuss Salina had long since reloaded and slung it over her back. She felt almost as she had when she'd had a deck beneath her feet and a hundred souls in her charge, all pulling the same oar as herself. All taken away by the Ghost Captain and the Dead Gods, and none, her own Goddess included, giving so much as a fig. *Fuck them all.* Grasping the rope, she swung herself out and over the edge, wincing when her bad leg smacked off the brick wall.

"Wait for my attack before you open with those long muskets, and for Gods' sakes remember to account for the height and drop of the ball." She nodded toward the man who'd once been her assistant. "He can give you the calculations."

"Chan Sha! You'll never make it." Salina stretched and grasped her arm. "Even if you reach them, you won't be able to escape in time." Concern twisted Salina's features. "Not with your leg."

"Don't you remember what I said, Salina?" Chan Sha bared her teeth. "My lives always end the same.

"In blood and flame."

22

I slid the bomb into the niche where two sections of the roof came together. The pillar below the niche was load-bearing, as were all the others I'd stuck bombs to. Up this high, the wind clutched at me, grasping me as if a friend, but if so it was a false one, because Sin or no, I wouldn't survive a fall from this height. Holding fast to a quad-horned, goat-faced gargoyle with one hand, I pushed the bomb farther back so that an errant gust wouldn't shift its position, then twisted the brass knob atop the gearwork. The gears made a grinding sound as they were pulled back. When I released the knob, they began clicking, counting down toward their explosion.

Crack! The musket shot was loud in the relative calm that existed this high up. A moment later a duller boom sounded, then two more, a pause, then a fourth and fifth in quick succession, the gunfire echoing off the masonry so that it sounded like an army was firing out front. *Not an army. Chan Sha and Salina.* I glanced down at the knob, turning slowly and clicking away, and bit back a curse as another musket crack ripped through the night air. I took off, sprinting along in the shallow gutter that ran around the perimeter of the cathedral. I'd one bomb left to plant, in a gutter that paralleled the one I was on, save it was another span or two below me, closer to the ground.

"Sin?"

"A little less than three-tenths of a bell left, and you're going to need to turn the timer on the final one on two-tenths."

Fuck, I'd better hurry.

"Aye," he grunted.

I redoubled my efforts, Sin making my legs burn and twinge as magic flooded them. My hearing went and my vision was reduced to only a dozen feet in front of me. I saw the ledge of the gutter turn the corner an instant too late. Though I put on the brakes, I overshot and had to throw an arm out to catch the pipe that ran down between gutters to the ground. My feet left the masonry as I swung out, wind whistling in my ears as my hearing returned. A thousand needles jabbed my arm as it took the entire weight of my body and changed the direction of my momentum. I flew back over the ledge, slamming off the sharply angled slate roof.

"Oof!" My breath left me as my ribs screamed from the abuse. I rebounded, tightened my grip on the pipe to keep from flailing back out into the air, and slammed, slightly more gently, against the roof again. "Double oof," I muttered.

"Second tenth bell in five . . . four . . . three," Sin said. I bit back a curse as I shrugged the pack off my shoulder, thrust my hand inside, found the timer, and turned it all the way over. "One," Sin said, the clicking sounding on his voice.

A volley of pistole fire made me glance down, and this time I let the curses fly. In the center of a ring of Shambles a lone figure spun, highlighted by the broad beam of light coming from the cathedral, sparks of fire ringing her like a halo and pistoles leaping in her hands. *Chan Sha. Godsdamn it.*

Something white-hot glanced off the pavement in front of a Shambles, taking out the creature's knee; the undead fell to the cobblestone and began pulling itself, stone by stone, toward the figure. A shot from the rooftops dropped one Shamble but a different shot missed—I saw it ricochet off the stone. Chan Sha stumbled, went to one knee, and continued firing.

Dropping the pack at my feet, I brushed my cloak back, dug into my purse, and drew out my slingshot, already fitting a ball into the sling. Drawing back the triple-strength band until I felt the protest of the steel-strengthened posts, I let Sin guide my angle and released. A long breath later the Shambles who'd been wielding a pickax overhead behind Chan Sha dropped, head spilling one way, ax and the rest of its desiccated body the other. Crowing, I fit another iron ball into my sling and drew back. The only sure way to kill a Shambles was to sever the brain stem. You could knock appendages off, even cut a Shambles in two, but they'd still keep coming, still keep trying to kill you—like the crippled one that was now within one more pull of putting a rusted knife through Chan Sha's side. I released and my eyes burned, magic bringing the view up close so that I saw my ball drive through the top of the dead woman's skull, tearing away the little ragged curl she'd left on her bleached head, and continue down through the mandible and into the chest cavity, exiting out somewhere in her sternum and ricocheting off another Shambles's shin.

After that, Salina, the Artificer, Chan Sha, and I made short work of them. *Twelve. Thirteen. Four—*

"Uh, Buc?"

"Aye?" I let the sling relax as Chan Sha blew the head off the last Shambles.

"Coming up on one-tenth of a bell remaining."

"What?" I glanced down at my feet. "Oh. Shit."

Returning my slingshot to my purse and snatching up my pack, I eased off the ledge, wrapped my legs around the pipe that ran down to the next level, and pushed away, sliding easily down to the lowest gutter. Sin was counting down the seconds and there was no time to run to where I needed to drop the damned bomb, so I eyeballed it and flung the entire pack, cursing when it caught on the gutter instead of bouncing. The bomb flew out of the pack and went tumbling awkwardly along the gutter until it hit the edge, right where I'd been aiming for, and to my amazement, spun to a stop.

"Fuck me," I muttered.

"Eld would call that luck," Sin said.

"Luck wants to claim it, they can show up and do so," I told him. "Till then, I'll take it." I spun around, took two running steps, and hurled myself into the night air. The cobblestoned courtyard rushed to meet me, and I pulled myself into a roll, something I'd first practiced years earlier, after reading a book on tumbling. *Number seventy-four.*

Old Buc would have broken a bone or three, no matter how well she landed, but with Sin, I came in at an angle. My upper back barely skimmed the cobblestone as my momentum carried me on, boots slamming into the ground just long enough to launch me forward, my legs taking only a fraction of the full impact before I rolled on. With each rotation, I slowed, shedding momentum and feeling gravity tug at me, until I came up on my feet and stopped, swaying back and forth, with Chan Sha a dozen paces away.

"What the fuck happened to us doing this on the sly, woman?" I shouted at her. Beyond her, in the distant shadows, I saw Bar'ren running, crouched, back toward the safety of the building where we'd left Salina and the Artificer. *Smart man.*

The taller woman twisted her head, match cord burning bright amongst her braids, then gestured with a pistole. I glanced back toward the cathedral, my next insult dying on my lips as a black-and-orange–striped cat the size of a gondola leapt over a dozen figures filling the cathedral doors. Muskets cracked behind us; one ball glanced off the step just before its front paws but the second caught it full in the face, sparks flying from its steel fangs. It shook its head as if annoyed by a fly and then its glowing, yellow eyes fixated on me. It roared, its gaping maw bright with metal. The sound pushed at my chest like a physical hand.

"Oh, fuck." Chan Sha had been trying to hold the Dead Gods within the cathedral until the bombs went off. *Which they're about to.* "Double fuck." If that cat-thing didn't tear us limb from limb first.

"All the fucks," Chan Sha growled as she reached my side. The cat sank into a crouch.

"That's my line," I grumbled as I dug into my cloak pocket

and palmed a grenado, which I heaved, Sin's strength burning through my arm. The semiglass ball flew through the air as if it had been fired from my slingshot, smashed onto the steps in front of the Veneficus and the rest of the Dead Gods' mages, and exploded in a sheet of fiery, white flame. A hoarse shout was drowned out by half a dozen screams. Pulling out my slingshot, I dug around in my purse until I felt a ball the size of my thumb. Just as I fit it into the sling, the cat roared again, and I pulled hard—muscles protesting as Sin's magic began to wane—to full draw and released. Half a breath later the monster leapt through the flames . . . right into the lump of silver I'd sent into the air. I saw its white, cavernous chest cave in, a dark hole appearing in the fur; the force of the impact punched through the beast, turning its leap into a backward somersault into the flames. The cat's roar turned to a screeching cry, and through the fire I saw several figures grab the cat's legs and pull it into the cathedral. One last, cloaked figure seemed to stare at us for a moment before reluctantly joining the retreat. The cathedral doors slammed shut and silence fell, save for the crackling of the dying fire.

"G-G-Godsdamn," Chan Sha muttered, half falling.

"You said it, sister," I grunted, catching her. For a moment we half stood, half knelt against each other. Then I remembered the bombs and realized the dull throbbing in the back of my head was actually Sin's voice counting down the seconds.

"Thirteen . . . twelve—"

"All the motherfucks!" I leapt to my feet. "C'mon, woman—move!"

"Can't. Leg. Useless," Chan Sha gasped.

I spent second eleven considering leaving her there before I grasped her by the arm and heaved, throwing her over my shoulders so that her boots just cleared the cobblestone in front and her hands in back. A match cord fell from her braids and lay smoking on the cobbled stone. *All right, Sin. You're of Ciris herself. A full-blooded Goddess. Time to prove it.* Shrugging to center her weight, I took off, Sin's magic suffusing my entire being; I felt as if I was simultaneously being branded and stung and burned, and yet . . . it hurt in a way that made me long for more. The world turned to a blur as I ran; I felt Chan Sha's body bouncing as I fought to hold her in place. Salina's shout carried to me and I risked a glance up through some of the locks that had pulled free from my braid. Bar'ren was just being helped off the rope by the Artificer, but there was no way I was going to make that in time. *Ten seconds.*

"*Run!*" I screamed, sparing a breath I didn't have to warn the rest, then plunged into the alleyway between the buildings, running all out and then some. A dozen blurs passed me—Sin Eaters heading toward the cathedral, one calling out a question, clearly thinking me one of their own—but I ignored them, dropping my head and running for all I was worth. Sweat sluiced off me, filling and stinging my eyes; my breath no longer came from my lungs but moldered there, a burning fire deep in my chest. *Six.* I came to an intersection, barely managed to throw myself to the right and then back to the left, and continued sprinting away between buildings, my vision flecking with stars and dark spots.

"*Buc!*" Sin screamed. *Three.* "You have to stop, you're going to kill yourself. The human body can't take this much magic."

"W-won't," I growled between my teeth. Sister flashed through my mind. The little boy in the factory. Eld. *Eld.* I'd left too many people to die in raging infernos of flame and burning masonry. *Two.* Aye, I'd been about to kill Chan Sha yesterday, but today was a new day. A different day. *No more.* To win this war, I was going to need allies who'd die with their backs to the wall, killing even as they were killed. How could I ask that of them unless I was willing to do the same myself? The question was so alien I didn't realize it was mine until several realizations fell upon one another in a cascading avalanche of madness. I dropped Chan Sha in the arch of a doorway.

One.

The world leapt, the ground rushing up to meet me, build-ings creaking and crashing all around me, all sound swallowed by an unending roar. *The bombs went off.* I fell to my knees, and something inside me gave out. *I'm in the middle of the street.* Sin's voice was broken and fragmented. *My magic.* Steam came off me in waves, turning the clay between the cobblestones to burn-ing mush that scalded my skin. *I'm on my face.* I couldn't get up, couldn't move, couldn't breathe, and it was all right. This time, I hadn't left anyone behind.

No one.

No more.

Nothing.

23

The cathedral is a smoking ruin of rubble, our dead immolated within. Whether by this Sicarii's hand or the Sin Eaters', I know not, but Ciris is onto us. She must be, to have acted so swiftly. Tell the Plague Mistress, brother. She must send word to our ship off Southeast Island that they may spread the plague from there at once. I fear you'll not get another missive from me. I am the last Dead Gods' mage in Cordoban and I intend to hunt Ciris's ilk here with the same fervor her Sicarii hunts ours. Blood calls to blood.

—Petre

Eld read the letter again, the cipher so ingrained in his mind now so that it was as if he were reading Imperial. *It worked.* His heart pounded in his chest and he sat back slowly in his chair. Outside, the smithies were loud at their trade, filling the air with ringing as they fashioned both weapons of war and more mundane items. Usually the sound began to grate after a time, but at the moment, with the hammers pounding in time to his heart, Eld found them almost soothing. *It must have worked. That has Buc's hand written all over it, to destroy the cathedral with the Plague Walkers yet inside.* It was what he'd hoped for when he convinced Yilsra to carry his missive. She thought it depressingly sad that he wanted to let the woman he loved in his former life know that he had moved on. Two classes ahead of him, Yilsra had chafed at not being given an assignment, so when Eld, in his new role as Ismiralda's lieutenant, got her name added to the list of those being sent to Cordoban, she'd agreed to secretly seek out his former love.

Eld felt a pang as he began copying Petre's missive—with a few minor changes—onto a tattered, worn piece of parchment. It was likely Yilsra had perished in the flames. *Buc may have struck the match, but I killed her.* Eld fought the warring emotions within him to a standstill, his quill a flurry across the page. He'd always been a decent hand with a pen, but after his Reawakening, everything came so much more quickly for him that it was but the work of a few moments to fill the page with cipher text. Yilsra and the rest were zealots, unquestioning of the council and the Archnemesis's means or ends, and while Eld enjoyed the company of several of the mages and liked a few—like Petre—quite a lot, they wouldn't consider giving over.

His recovered memories told Eld that before nearly dying and being saved by the blood of the Gods, he would have been torn apart by having to live this sort of double life. It wasn't easy, true, but the cunning the blood gave him blunted the worst of it. There were days when he feared he'd become an addict, like those who smoked and drank kan until they were in a stupor, only his drug of choice was the blood that, as Plague Quartermaestro, was at his disposal. Only Buc, and his memories of their time together, kept him from worrying too much about that.

Holding up the two pieces of parchment, he scanned the lines, noting the similarities and differences, before holding the true copy up to the chandelier above his desk. The edge caught, twisted, yellowed in the fire, then burned. Ashes floated down around him as Eld began translating the cipher from the copy he'd just made, making plain what was hidden. He was nearly finished when someone pounded on the thick, wooden door. Before he could speak, the door opened, flooding the dim room with sunlight. A short woman, as wide as she was tall, stomped into the room, creaking in the steel-studded leather cuirass she wore over leather pants with twin blades hanging at her sides. The day's heat made her face run with sweat. Red-faced, she bawled, "Rise for the Plague Mistress!"

"Easy, Nanten," Ismiralda said as she walked in after the woman, her bone-white dress and black skin a study in contrasts, the plunging neckline doing wonders for the willowy woman as she sauntered across the room. "I told you before, you needn't do that," she added over her shoulder as Eld stood up.

"Mistress," the woman said, the volume of her voice just below that of a bull's bellow. She stepped outside, pulling the door closed behind her, making sure Eld saw her glare.

"Take no offense at her loyalty, Eldritch," Ismiralda said.

"Of course not," Eld said, forcing a smile.

"I do try to rein her in, but—"

"Her loyalty mirrors my own," Eld added, leaving unsaid that the Plague Mistress could have commanded Nanten not to barge into every room screaming her name, threatening to draw a blade wherever Nanten saw a slight, but he wasn't that foolish. Not anymore, at least. "What can I do for you, Mistress?"

"Ismiralda," she corrected him, her mouth quirking in a smile. "In here, at least." She glanced past him, and he knew she'd catalogued everything behind him, from the multiple ledgers open on the stands to the cold fireplace to the ink stains on the birch desk and all that lay between them. Including himself. "You do like the dark, don't you?"

"I've always found the undercroft comforting," Eld said. Which was true. "There's a feeling of peace, so close to the Gods' bones." Which was a lie. The undercroft was rarely visited, though, so for a man who wanted to assure he didn't grow attached to those he meant to see dead, it was a Godsend . . . in a manner of speaking. "And too much candlelight is a danger to my work," he added, gesturing at the ashes scattered across the table.

"I can see that," she said, reaching across the table to dust ash from his soft, grey jacket. Slinking into the chair across from him, she crossed her legs, exposing a dark ankle that he tried—

and failed, given the broadening smile on her face—not to look at. "You've news?"

"From Cordoban," he confirmed, sitting back down. "None of it good, I'm afraid."

"Tell me," she demanded.

"The letter is marked three days ago, which suggests the wide-winged gulls we're using as messenger birds are working. It's from one of my class, Petre. And . . ."

Swiftly Eld outlined the doctored version he created. In this version, the Plague Walkers completed their ritual only to discover the plague was so deadly it killed them and the Dead Walkers assisting them before they were able to leave the cathedral. Sin Eaters attacked at the same time and, with weakened defenses, the cathedral was overrun.

"Blood and bone," Ismiralda spat when he finished. "Send word at once to our mages awaiting word off Southeast Island. They are to remain in place until we provide them with fresh instructions on how best to complete the ritual." She shook her white braids, knocking them against the chair's arms. "I guess the island will have to be our next test. Gods send we don't lose the lot. What a disaster."

"The bright spot," Eld said, "if we can call it that, is the plague ritual works."

"Too well, it seems," she murmured. "The Veneficus will use this against me on council, arguing it was my fault that our mages were dead and dying when attacked."

"I did leave out another potential bright spot," Eld said. "Petre was spared because he was part of the hit team that went after Sambuciña Alhurra."

"What?" Ismiralda sat up in her seat. "Let me see."

"Aye, she's been hiding there ever since the Servenzan disaster." Eld turned both the hastily forged cipher and the translation around so she could read them. "Apparently this Alhurra girl got on the wrong side of the futuwwa and their library and they sent word on the location of the al-kasr she was hiding in." Eld tapped the closed book on his desk. "Per the council's standing orders, they sent a team to eliminate her, which they did with extreme prejudice. Petre stayed behind to ensure the palace—more of a hovel, really, from the description—burned to the ground."

"Alhurra dead," Ismiralda said, looking up from the pages and showing her teeth. "That ameliorates things somewhat." She arched an eyebrow, black eyes boring into his. "How do you feel about that, Eldritch? Your former partner killed at the hands of your brothers and sisters?"

"She was never blood," Eld said, focusing on certain words as he'd been practicing since reading Petre's original letter and deciding the direction the forgery would take. "There's another consideration," he added.

"Oh?"

"It could be that Sicarii survived the Lighthouse's fall, as I did," he said slowly, "but I think it far more likely it was Buc. Which means—"

"Sicarii, too, is dead," she mused, kicking her ankles.

"Ciris won't know any of that," he reminded her. "We could . . . *create* a new Sicarii, one that would keep Sin Eaters looking over one shoulder."

"While we come over the other." She paused, studying an imaginary speck on her robes. "Are you really so sanguine after all the years you spent with her?" She looked up. "Recall, I saw your memories, felt them. You loved the girl."

"A different man," he said evenly, stating simple fact. "I've been reborn, Ismiralda. You are my blood and besides, from what I remember"—he tapped his temple—"she treated me badly."

"At the end, if nowhere else," Ismiralda agreed. "That would never happen here," she assured him. "Blood calls to blood."

"The truth of blood," he said, speaking the catechism by rote, "the purity of blood. What are your commands, Plague Mistress?"

"Send word to the plague ship and gather my Dead Walkers.

The Sicarii plot is an intriguing one that may bear fruit, but we can't afford distractions now." Eld kept the disappointment from his face; it'd been worth a shot to slow her down. "We've much work to do, you and I," she continued, "to attune this plague such that it kills only those not of our fold."

"It may be, Ismiralda," Eld said slowly, "that the Plague Walkers will not be able to survive the dosage we are using. To be a carrier, one must needs be sick, but able to move about. I believe there are ways to render us resistant, if not outright immune, although we'll need trials to confirm. That might help us develop the antidote for our worshippers as well."

"Run your trials," she said, leveraging herself up. "If the Plague Walkers must give themselves to death, to reunite with our Gods so that the rest might live . . . so be it." She marched to the door, robes swishing, and paused, glancing back. "That last, Eldritch, needs stay between us."

"Of course, Mistress," Eld said, bowing his head, a loose strand pulling free from his ponytail and falling so that it obstructed his view of her, rendering her just a shadow. He suppressed a shudder. "Our plague ship lies in wait, none the wiser. We've time yet, for our next move."

"Whatever it takes," she told him, and then she was gone, Nanten slamming the door behind them.

"Aye," Eld said grimly, staring at the lies he'd written. "Whatever it takes."

24

"The last time I woke like this," I said, sitting up in the gently sway-ing hammock, "I'd been out for days after overdoing it." I swung my legs over the side and put my feet on the polished, wooden floor. Standing up, I felt the sway that told me we were at sea. "On a ship then, too." I crossed to the small table built out of the wall and drew the towel off the tray, revealing smoked fish covered with a spicy-looking red paste and half a dozen varieties of fruit, some of which I didn't recognize.

"That's a dragon fruit," Sin said when I picked up the nearest one. "The fruit is the speckled, white part, the vibrant pink the pith. You and I need to have a talk, Buc."

"I think," I said, biting into the dragon fruit and cursing when juice ran down my chin, "you're forgetting who is in charge here." I slid onto the small bench nailed to the wall and began shoveling food in my mouth. "I give the orders and you obey. I choose what magic is used and how, and you supply it. Or else I send you back to the hole I banished you to last time," I added, spraying crumbs from the hunk of bread spread with a creamy layer of something delicious.

"That's a chutney," Sin said, rolling his eyes in my head. "You're supposed to put the fish on the bread and eat the lot together."

"Mm-hmm," I said, reaching for the carafe of water that proved to be chilled wine.

"And you can give all the orders you want," he growled, "but you nearly killed us both in Cordoban."

"Nearly doesn't equal did," I pointed out, digging into the fish.

"I can't trust you, Sin, and especially not if you're going to hold back in the moment. If I didn't do what I did, we *would* have died."

"You don't know that," he protested. "Dropping Chan Sha in that archway was smart, the whole building could come down around that and it still would have held. We could have done the same a few houses earlier and not pushed ourselves past the point of collapse. We're powerful, you and I, aye. You want to call yourself a demi-Goddess and I'll not name you a liar anymore, but, Buc . . ." His voice dropped. "We're not truly immortal. We aren't Ciris—and even if we were, clearly she's not immortal either, seeing as you intend to kill her. You're going to need to decide if you want to live to see this through or sacrifice yourself in getting there."

"I'll live to see it through," I promised him, picking my teeth with a fish bone. "Doesn't mean sacrifice won't be part of it, though."

"If it requires it, sure, but you're too damned quick to decide it does," he snapped. "You can't blame yourself for your sister's murder any more than you can for that boy or for what Eld *chose* to do. I'm not saying," he added, cutting me off, "you can't feel hurt, be hurt, carry that wound with you . . . but the blame is going to make you do something fucking stupid."

"Like scale a cathedral, plant a dozen bombs, take on a changed Veneficus, and carry a woman almost double my size across half the rii?" I asked.

"Something like that," he muttered dryly.

"I'll take it under advisement," I said, pushing myself to my feet, the tray littered with skins and pits and bones. Whether it was because I'd spent months traveling by sea or because of Sin's magic or some combination of the two, I'd lost my seasickness, despite the sway of the ship. Old Buc would have sicked up everything that I'd just taken down. Instead of throwing up, I took the carafe with me, drinking from it as I navigated to the footlocker against the other wall. "I don't trust you, Sin."

"Aye, you didn't trust Chan Sha either, but now you're giving her a chance," he said. "I've been trying to discern what I've done that's so much worse than what she's done. I didn't torture you and Eld in the hold of a ship or threaten to make you walk the plank. I didn't try to betray you to the Ghost Captain, nor attack Eld. I certainly didn't come to Servenza Godsbent on murdering the pair of you. I did none of that, and yet . . ."

"I never believed Chan Sha was other than what she was," I told him, tossing the empty carafe on the hammock. I closed my eyes, took a deep breath, and then began strapping on the blades I'd found lying atop a pair of dresses in the locker. "She didn't betray me, because there was nothing there to betray. You, on the other hand—"

"Buc—I'm sorry," Sin said after a moment's silence. "You and I are never going to see as one on Ciris, but as I told you before, I know I fucked up. I've never had a host like you, didn't know it was possible for a host to refuse Possession. That's never happened in all the millennia of Ciris's existence, and I took the failure as my own. I . . . am learning to make allowances, but I can't bridge this divide by myself, I need you to be open to meeting me part-way, at least."

I paused with my dress—an emerald-green riding dress of Servenzan cut, with divided skirts—half-done up. *Allies?* It seemed a long shot. I could feel the fragility of the steel within me. Mine and his. I had pushed us too far, but could I ever hold back where the Gods were concerned? I'd known, even when I was no more than a street-rat girl working cases with Eld, that it was going to take everything in me to achieve my goals. That girl would never have hesitated, but I was beginning to believe there was a difference between intelligence and wisdom. I'd always been whip smart, but now I needed to be wise. More than that, I needed to be cunning.

"Give me that chance to earn your trust back," he whispered.

"I'll take it under advisement," I said again, buttoning up the final loop and settling the dart gun Arti had invented against my wrist so it was out of view under the tumble of silk lace that trimmed the green hem. "Now, let's go see where the fuck we are."

"We change allegiances?" I asked Salina, gesturing toward the Southeast Islander flag, yellow with a red island in the center, that fluttered from atop the main mast. I'd been on deck for only a moment, leaning against the rail, before she and Chan Sha approached. The frigate we were on was a hive of activity, with sailors swabbing the bright, white oak decks, dressing lines, inspecting guns, and shifting crews for the midday watch. There were half a dozen mates that I could see, keeping a close eye on all; the captain was a foreboding man who strode in a circle around the command deck, his brass peg leg echoing off the deck as he observed his crew from behind the helmswoman. "Last I remember, the Company was registered under the Empire, Servenza specifically."

"The captain shares your concerns," Salina said, pulling her thin, honey-colored cloak tighter about her as the full sea breeze caught at her light-purple dress.

"Man practically turned the color of the flag when Salina told him to strike it," Chan Sha added. "Can't say as I blame him. Do that without the proper writ and there's not much say between privateer and pirate."

"You would know."

"How are you feeling, Buc?" Salina asked, leaning against the rail beside me. Her brown eyes took me in from head to toe and she smiled, but the expression didn't reach her eyes. "You gave us a scare."

"You nearly burned the magic out of you," Chan Sha said, her wrecked voice turning her words into a growl. "Ask me how that feels, you foolish woman." She shook her head disapprovingly, braids held back by a crimson bandana that matched her blouse.

"I feel as fine as a fresh-minted coin," I protested. Turning so I could rest with my back to the rail, I shrugged when Salina snorted. "I'll allow that we all know a fresh-minted coin gets clipped as soon as it passes the banker's slippery fingers, so aye, mayhap there's a clipped feel to my head at the moment."

"Mayhap," Salina repeated.

Chan Sha snorted from my other side. "Bar'ren will be glad you found your feet. Moving you through Cordoban, onto a schooner, and from the schooner to our present craft wasn't especially fun."

"Are you calling me heavy?"

"Insomuch as you've a thick skull." The woman laughed.

"How far have we come?" I asked, letting the jab go. I'd have been annoyed lugging one of them around, too. *Though I did save Chan Sha's life.*

"We're four days out of Cordoban, beyond the Cordoban Confederacy's recognized waters," Salina answered. "Yesterday morn a passing schooner bearing the broken-chained flag of the Free Cities stopped to tell us the news. War's been declared between Normain and the Servenzan Empire."

"Ah." I nodded. "Given that, sailing in unclaimed waters, heading for an area almost equidistant between the two, might be dangerous for any ship what flies the Normain or Imperial flag."

"Hence the change," she agreed. She squinted up at the flag, flapping in the wind. "It was bound to happen. After Normain's handiwork in Servenza"—Chan Sha shifted beside me, her burnished black, leather pants gleaming in the sun—"the Empress had no choice but to respond in kind until they offered an apology and reparations. Gods, even an apology from Normain might have stayed her hand. No one wants war."

"War means profits for some," Chan Sha said.

"No one wants war," Salina repeated. "After the tenth in line to Normain's crown was assassinated—and then the fifth—we thought for sure they'd declare against us. Word came as we were leaving the Cordoban harbor: the fourth in line was murdered in the capital. The dagger left in the body had the Imperial sigil embossed on the hilt."

"Well, that's as bold as brass," I muttered. "Equal to the fuckery that happened with the Doga," I agreed. "I suppose by that point they were the ones awaiting an apology."

"And with none coming . . . war," Salina finished.

"Wise, then, to pass ourselves off as Southeast Islanders," I admitted. "If my features tell true, my mother was a Southeast Islander."

"I think you're both looking at this through one of the Artificer's spectacles adjusted to the rose lens," Chan Sha said. She arched a thin eyebrow when we looked at her. "You really think Normain is going to respect the nominal independence Southeast Island claims from the Empire? Were I a land power that's been bested in every other sea war fought against said Empire, I might be inclined to try my hand at some of the softer countries first. Say, an island nation known more for trade than fighting. Might be I land an army there, put my acknowledged abilities at soldiering to the test, and win a prize that lets me claim victory and sue for peace without ever having to take on this aforementioned Empire."

"There's an affinity not just with the Empire, but with the Cordoban Confederacy as well," Salina said.

"The Confederacy's Federates will argue themselves blue in the face, and well before they decide whether it's to be red war or turning a blind eye, it'll be done and dusted."

"The pirate—former pirate," I amended at Chan Sha's glare, "makes a convincing argument, Salina."

"Normain wouldn't risk a war on multiple fronts," Salina said, matching the other woman glare for glare. "This flag will give us the freedom of movement we need . . . unless you think we should somehow transform the ship into one of Normain's jib and have us all dress up like the Artificer for the nonce?"

"And sweat my arse completely off?" I snorted. "Not bloody likely." I turned to stare across the endless blue waters at what might or might not be a blob on the horizon. "So, what happened after I, uh, overextended myself? Where are we?"

"Piling on sail toward the coordinates you deciphered from that dead Dead Walker's note," Chan Sha said. "Not a crack crew, but they'll do." I nodded. Coming from her, that meant they were probably within a rope's breadth of being up to Imperial navy standards.

"Aye, considering both their captain and first mate took ill before leaving Servenza and had to be replaced last minute," Salina said.

"Why not replace the ship?"

"I figured you'd want the best blend of speed and firepower we had, and this was the finest in port. You'll appreciate the thirty-two over-under barreled cannons," she added.

"And they have a mortar," Chan Sha said, gesturing toward the large gun mounted on an iron swivel table just in front of the final sail. One of the mates, a short woman in cutoff shirtsleeves and dark trousers, was balancing on an overturned bucket and shouting at the sailors manning it, putting them through their paces. "I trust this time you won't have any reason to keep them from firing?"

"Fire away," I agreed.

"After you passed out," Salina continued acidly, her tone clearly directed at Chan Sha, "we planned to return to the al-kasr, but Bar'ren discovered Sin Eaters surrounding the place, waiting in ambush, so we fled to my ship. Unfortunately, I wasn't planning on a world war when I left Servenza, so I sent some, uh, hasty messages prior to our slipping out of the harbor, resulting in us upgrading from a schooner to this frigate. We met her a day's sail north of the Cordoban Confederacy. The *Skua*." She patted the rail.

"When you say hasty," I said, "you mean utilizing the Company's Sin Eaters?"

"Aye," Salina said after a moment, suddenly interested in the drills the crew were running.

"Meaning Ciris knows the *Skua*, a heavily armed frigate late of Servenza, went haring off to a point somewhere between Southeast Island and Cordoban?"

"Aye. Buc, look—"

"Perfect," I said, no sarcasm in my voice as I interrupted her, my thoughts aligning as the blob on the horizon began to take shape, transforming into the coast of a massive land mass—in this case, Southeast Island. I saw the captain making our way. "Bloody perfect."

"You're not mad?"

"Your wits still addled?" Chan Sha asked on top of Salina, both women staring at me.

"Not at all," I assured her. I rolled my loosely braided locks between my fingers, letting the plan coalesce firmly in my mind. "Ciris thinks she knows something about us. She'll extrapolate from that to form her own plans. Knowing that, we can make a plan within a plan and catch her out."

"How do we do that?" Salina asked.

"I'm not quite sure. First, we need to send that plague ship to the bottom, to buy us enough time to end the undead bastards for good."

"How do we do that?" Salina asked again.

"Um . . . put enough holes in their ship that they sink?"

"Not that, kill all the undead bastards for good?"

"Signoras!" The captain doffed his red bicorne, revealing a mop of black curls, shiny with wax and only a shade darker than his skin. He swept his arm back up theatrically, adjusted his hat at a smart angle, and gave us a roguish grin that ended just below the patch over his left eye. His gesture was somewhat ruined when he overbalanced on his brass peg leg and had to grab the railing while his lower half wobbled in navy-blue pantaloons that matched his blue, gilt-trimmed jacket. "I trust you breakfasted well?"

"A very sizable repast," Salina said, "given the Company gave you such short notice."

"We followed the instructions you sent and our warehouse by the docks was well-stocked with provisions, Chair," he said, lowering his voice. *So he hasn't told his crew who they're ferrying. Why?* "It's true we weren't expecting to meet you until next week, after you were to have concluded your business in Cordoban, and my ship was in the midst of having its hull scraped, but Mankin always makes it a practice to be prepared, signora. I would have brought finer wine, but my personal casks were removed to make room for . . ." His dark gaze swept the deck, settling on the Artificer, who was aft of us, studying the helmswoman or, more likely, the gearwork in the wheel. Bar'ren leaned against the opposite railing. "Your strange little man's *requests.*"

"Arti insisted you'd want some of his, uh, stores, from Servenza brought aboard," Salina said in answer to my raised eyebrow.

"Some," Mankin growled, his thick lips twisting. "The man filled practically a quarter of the hold."

"We thank you, sirrah, for your noble sacrifice," I told the man dryly.

"You'd be the signorina Buca?" I opened my mouth to correct him, saw Salina's slightly raised eyebrow, and nodded. "Well, Buca, I and my officers are Company lot, and the crew and ship as well, but once I step aboard, I become responsible. I've some questions about what your man has belowdecks."

"Oh?"

"It's one thing to ask me to fly a flag I've no claim to." He gestured above him. "But quite another to"—Mankin stepped forward, unsteadily on his false leg despite all the practice he must have had, and leaned toward me, dark eyes flashing as the sun crossed his face—"quite another to bring on obvious mage work without the marks the mages put upon them," he hissed. "Were Ciris to find out she'd—"

"You may want to ask yourself, Captain," Salina said, her voice suddenly sharper than the leg he'd just made for us, "if perhaps Ciris isn't involved in all of this already? We employ her Sin Eaters across the known world, aye? We've undertaken missions at her request. We are . . . what's the saying amongst the black flags? Thick as thieves?"

Captain Mankin studied her for a long moment and then gave her a shorter, curter bow than the one he'd led with. "As you say, Chair. We'll be into Southeast Island within the next hour or so if the wind holds. I should see to the crew." He made to turn, then paused, looking closely at me. "Just see that you don't turn us pirates with your actions."

"He came with a good recommendation from my sailing maestro," Salina muttered, gripping her yellow cloak, "and he's a long history of serving the Company, but I was expecting more 'Aye, Chair' and less mouth."

"Aye," I said as he stomped away, leg echoing over the deck, "looks like his leg isn't the only thing made of brass."

"What?" Salina asked.

"The pair on that bitch. Telling me off like that. And the Chair of the Kanados Trading Company."

Salina burst into laughter that made Mankin's back stiffen, and Chan Sha snorted. "Captains are the master of their domain," she said, spreading her arms wide to indicate the ship. "Have to be. Chair of the Kanados Trading Company is many things, but a nautical captain she ain't."

"You were awfully quiet," I said.

"Don't need to give that old cully a reason to suspect I know more of sailing than he," Chan Sha said simply. She blinked and glanced away, settling back against the railing and taking a moment to adjust her crimson blouse. "I miss it," she whispered.

"Setting aside the captain's brass . . . whatevers," Salina said, chortling, "you didn't answer my question, Buc. Or should I say, Buca?"

"Buc," I growled. "Which question was that?"

"Once you sink this plague ship, how do you intend to sink the rest of the Dead Gods and their mages?"

"I'm not quite sure," I admitted. The books I'd read in the Forbidden Library had told me what was required to have a chance at Ciris. On the Dead Gods, I only knew that it required me to gain access to their Wellspring, the font of their power, but where or what that was, I didn't yet know. "Gods, Salina, I only woke up half a bell ago."

"What's their strength?" Chan Sha asked, tapping her pink lip with a lacquered nail.

"The blood of their Gods," Salina said. "Obviously, that's what they use to transform into beasts, and that strange book they use to control the Shambles is infused with it, if my sources have it aright."

"That's it!" I pounded the railing. "I know how we'll take them out, ladies."

"Sail ho! Sail ho! Belay that . . . Sails!" The lookout's cry interrupted my moment of smug triumph, and all three of us looked to where the lad's outstretched arm pointed, just east of the growing island before us. Toward Normain. "A brace of frigates and . . . and a man-o'-war."

"Where away?" the captain shouted through a bullhorn. The Artificer winced beside him, then produced a long, thinly fluted horn from within his sky-blue jacket and offered it to the larger man. "Where away?" the captain asked again, his voice amplified thrice over and aimed straight toward the lookout.

"Four points off starboard . . . they've caught a glimpse of us. I can see the reflection off their 'scopes!" There was a long pause. "Winds got their flags out—Normain! They've changed course, aiming to intercept us just afore the island, Captain!"

"I told you, there's no neutrality in war," Chan Sha muttered.

"Aye." I licked my lips, Sin's magic burning my eyes so that I could just dimly make out the suggestion of sails creeping up over the horizon's edge. "You may get to use that mortar after all."

25

"It makes no sense, signora," Mankin growled, gesturing across the bustling deck toward the approaching coastline. "They glassed us at least half a bell ago when we did them, perhaps sooner, given the curvature of the horizon and the sun's positioning. Even if we enter yon little bay afore them, they'll know we're there. You don't want to get trapped with a man-o'-war riding in on your rudder, she'll turn us to kindling."

Salina's eyes flicked past him to me and I moved my eyes back and forth. *No.* "Keep to the coordinates you were given," she told him haughtily, her chin raised so that she stared down her nose at him as if he were the shorter of the two. She drew in a breath that accented the cut of her lavender dress. "We've a meeting that cannot wait."

"Signora, they may well catch us by then!" the captain snapped, snatching his hat from his head. "What do you suggest we do?"

Chan Sha opened her mouth, but I reached out and touched her arm and she shook her head but held her tongue. I did not.

"Change your heading two points to the north so you make full sheets," I said loudly, my voice almost physically pulling him around to face me. I gestured toward the little notch in the coastline. "When we look to be making past it, hard over and switch your sails."

"What exactly will that gain us?"

"Time," I said, arching an eyebrow. "Do you need me to explain tonnage, draw, and knots?"

"What'd you do, read a book, woman?"

"Several, in fact," I told him. *Woman?* He'd been quick to lose the honorific when his temper was up. "Aislin, Gatina, and Frobisher," I added. I left unsaid that the last captain who'd listened to me had ended with his ship blown up and him and his crew with it. I also left unsaid that without instrumentation I'd be relying on the Sin in my mind. Some secrets you tell and some you keep and both of those seemed to be the latter. "We're more maneuverable than that floating tub yon and the frigates won't want to move outside the protection she offers."

"That floating *tub*," he sneered, "boasts eighty cannon and a pair of mortars both aft and stern. The frigates may only be twenty-eighters, but combined that flotilla has three times the cannon of the *Skua*."

"Then you'd best prepare for battle," I said.

Mankin glanced at Salina. "You heard us, Captain." She crossed her arms, drawing her cloak tighter about herself. "You've been taking Company coin, but that comes with its own price. So you'll do as we ask, when we ask. Need I ask again?"

"No," Mankin said after a moment. He jammed his hat back on. "No, you bloody don't, signora." He marched off, stomping his peg leg and bawling orders.

"A good crew," Chan Sha said as the ship turned over as I'd suggested. "Smart one, but that captain spends more time searching for reasons not to obey than to just give over and have done."

"Well," I drawled, "he is a man." I glanced at Chan Sha. "What would you have done, had I let you speak?"

"As you said." She shrugged. "I'm guessing the plague ship is hidden in that little notch of a bay yon. If she's keeping a lookout on the coastline there, they'll have spotted all of us and be wondering what to do."

"Lay up and wait or sail out."

"'Pends what wager they want to toss," she agreed.

"I'm not following." Salina forced a smile, but her pale skin had taken on a slightly greenish hue. "What will they do?"

"They could remain anchored with their sails furled and hope we pass them by," I explained.

"If we notice them," Chan Sha said, "it'd be like a shooting gallery. They've no reason to expect us to attack them, but if those Normain ships fire on us, like it looks like they're aiming to do, then they've no reason to expect we won't. Even a good crew gets trigger-happy when lead fills the air."

"You think they're really going to try to sink us?"

"Board us, at least," I answered. "Otherwise they wouldn't have turned to cut us off."

"And now we're running right at them," Salina murmured.

"Not quite at them."

"Buc's directional change favors us over them," Chan Sha said. "If that plague ship decides it doesn't want to chance it and does run, it'll have to appear damned soon."

"Aye," I said, studying the ever-growing shoreline. "Too many unknowns, but we need a plan. A flexible one, but one with teeth." I patted the mast we stood under and pushed off it. "Like this ship, really. You two think it over, won't you?"

"Where are you going?" Salina asked.

"She's right," I told her, gesturing toward Chan Sha. "What? You are," I told the pirate when her mouth slackened. "The crew's what we need. The captain, however, leaves us wanting."

"Buc!" Salina hissed. "You can't just take over. They've a name for that."

"They do," Chan Sha agreed, eyes hard. "Mutiny. And complaining fuck or no, the crew isn't likely to side with us over him. Not when his plan is guaranteed to keep them alive and ours would see them whipped and hung even if they survive this melee."

"Another quarter bell and we'll be too close for that to remain true," I pointed out. I swept my braided hair out of my face and ran a hand back along the shaved side of my head, giving them an impudent grin. "But rest assured, I've no plans to hurt a hair on Mankin's head."

"Then—?" Salina asked.

"I didn't ask you what your brilliant plan was, did I?"

"What brilliant plan?"

"The one I just said you two needed to come up with," I said, flashing her a grin. "How to sink the plague ship, whether it sails or doesn't, and how to keep us from sinking along with her. I think that's enough to keep you busy, so don't ask me about mine, savvy?"

I left the pair of them before either could say any more, ambling casually across the deck to the Artificer. "Say, Arti, what'd you take to cure your seasickness?"

"Seasickness?" he asked, blinking behind his spectacles. "Buc, I don't get—"

"Aye?" I clapped him hard on the back and leaned forward as if concerned, speaking more quietly. "You have any more of those darts with the mollusk poison on them?"

"You took them all, remember?" he asked, straightening his sky-blue jacket. "They're probably scattered across your study back in Cordoban."

"Godsdamn it." I scowled and looked away. *I may have to do this the old-fashioned way.*

"Recall that even were we to fight off the two hundred souls on deck," Sin whispered in my mind, "we'd still need to crew it afterward. Against three ships with thrice or more again our numbers."

"Point," I replied. "Hmm."

"I do," the Artificer said, producing a silver kan case from his jacket, "have a vial filled with the poison of the antiguous jellyfish. It's not as subtle as the mollusk—it'll burn—but it's as deadly."

"Exactly the antidote for my flip-flopping stomach," I said loudly, palming the vial he held out. "Why don't you go see if Chan Sha and Salina have need of any of your wares?"

"I also have several new inventions I was working on," he muttered absently, stowing the case back in his jacket as he meandered off.

I caught Bar'ren's eye and motioned with my head. "Keep close to him," I said as I passed him. "The Artificer has a great mind for gears and new imaginings, but it'll do us no good if his head gets separated from the rest of him when the shooting starts."

"I'll keep watch over him," Bar'ren promised. "Perhaps I should pick up one of those guns if there is to be shooting."

"You ever fire one before?"

Bar'ren shook his head.

"Then I'd leave well enough alone or you'll end up shooting your eye out."

"I believe you," he said solemnly, sighing. His eyes searched the shoreline that was becoming more distinct with each wave, his darkened skin wrinkling.

"What?"

"I—" He licked his lips. "I always imagined there would be more in your world, but it seems the seas are as vast here as they are around my island."

"If we sail out of this in one piece we're going to where all the land went," I told him. "Along the way we can get you some target practice if you really want a pistole of your own. Now, go make sure Arti doesn't fall overboard."

I watched the older man follow after the Artificer, his eyes still on the approaching coastline. They say you can't teach an old man new crafts, which I always thought was bullshit, but the last thing I needed was for Bar'ren to be distracted by the new world thrust upon him. *Even if my plans make full sheets, there are any number of ways they can be run aground.*

I made my way along the rail toward the dais where the helmswoman, the first mate, and Captain Mankin all stood. Mankin kept a constant stream of instruction going, some directed at the helmswoman, who made minor adjustments to the wheel, her bronzed arms whipcord strong as she held the course. Her mouth showed a grin, but I could see from the way her vest rose and fell that the seas weren't as even as they appeared. The first mate had gathered her loose blond hair back into a ponytail that made her bicorne sit at a rakish angle. Wearing gold-trimmed, blue jacket and pantaloons that were the twin to Mankin's, she kept shouting orders through the long, thin horn the Artificer had gifted them.

I glanced out and ahead, to where the three ships bore down upon us, the frigates in-line with sails trimmed to allow the man-o'-war to set the pace. From what I knew of Normain, that monstrosity of a ship was their second largest, which suggested the rest of their fleet was somewhere close by. The question was, were they simply setting up a cordon or was Chan Sha right and this was the beginning of an invasion? Either way, I'd a feeling the Empress was going to end up owing me by the day's sunset. With my body hiding my hands, I undid the button on my right sleeve and exposed my gear-wrought dart gun. The same one I'd used on Chan Sha. Carefully, I drew out a dart and slid it into the vial the Artificer had given me. If I pricked myself, Sin could save me from the poison, but we were still recovering from my Cordoban heroics and I wanted to save our strength for the fight ahead.

How much, Sin?

"Just the barest edge of the tip should make him nauseous, a little more to knock him out. More . . . there."

I carefully loaded the drugged dart into the launcher on my wrist and pulled my sleeve back down so that one would have to look closely at the inside of my hem to see the edge pointing out. Finished, I walked on, circling around to the rear of the dais, behind the three officers standing atop it, caught up in their work. The crew were moving stiffly, clearly unhappy with the thought of facing off against three ships that had them outgunned. *And they don't know about the fourth.* Despite that, they cleared the decks, ran the guns out, and tied off the lines with an efficiency that belied their expressions. Chan Sha was right: if I tried to mutiny, they'd likely turn against us, which meant putting a blade twixt Mankin's ribs was out for now.

Having him drop dead seemingly of his own accord would give the sailors, always a superstitious lot, reason to doubt our chances even more. Having him take ill and have to go to his quarters was only marginally better. Still, actions speak louder than words, and Chan Sha and I would show them what was in store for the plague ship and the Normain.

I waited until Mankin stepped away from the others to draw a drink from a nearby barrel, then marched over, calling a greeting to the helmswoman. As I passed the captain, I snapped my wrist, firing the dart launcher at him.

"How holds the wheel?" I asked, stepping up beside the helmswoman.

"True, signorina," she said with a smile, her light-blue eyes dancing over my features before returning to the wheel. "Always true."

"You know your ropes," I agreed, glancing past her to where Mankin was rubbing at the back of his neck and cursing about mosquitoes. Sin's magic burned in my eyes and I saw that the thin reed of the dart had broken off, as designed, leaving the tip lodged within his skin. A red welt was already rising and Mankin was going to feel a lot worse in a few breaths. "How long before the mast?"

"Near a dozen years," she said, shifting the wheel slightly. "Have you served, signorina?"

"No, but I've been to the Shattered Coast and back—"

"Godsdamn it," Mankin snarled, stomping past us, one hand clamped on the back of his neck.

"And to Cordoban besides," I finished. "The captain doesn't seem pleased."

"That's just Mankin," the first mate said, joining us. She stood head and shoulders taller than me or the helmswoman, made taller still by her bicorne. "Your signora's pissed him off, not taking his advice."

"I wouldn't say she's not taking his advice," I said. The other woman snorted and the helmswoman was suddenly very interested in the wheel between her arms. "She's told him what she wants and left it up to him to figure out how to do it."

"Your lot would see it that way," the first mate growled, her pale features taut beneath the shadow cast by her hat.

"My lot?"

"Landlubbers." She jammed a finger toward the approaching flotilla. "Even with our mage-marked mortar we'll be lucky to put enough holes through one of them before they're on us."

"What we need," I muttered, "is a distraction." Mankin was making a long walk around the deck, seemingly determined to glare down every crew member personally.

"Shouldn't he have keeled over by now?" I asked in my mind. "Given me that distraction?"

"Aye, he's made of sterner stuff than I realized," Sin muttered. "Iron will or no, the man's got to be a dozen breaths from passing out and in terrible pain besides. The sting of an antiguous jellyfish has been compared to being stabbed with a poker still red-hot from the forge."

"That's what I thought," I said. *Strange.*

"Sail ho!" the lookout bawled out. "Coming from the bay!"

"Not quite the distraction I had in mind," I told the first mate, clapping her on the back. Sin added some power to my arm and the other woman staggered despite her height. "But it may do." I marched off, leaving her before she could recover, heading to intercept Mankin so I could catch him before he smashed his face off the deck.

"Buc!" Salina called, then shaking her long blond braid, obviously annoyed with herself. "Buca, I mean!"

I shifted direction, making for where she and the others stood, still watching Mankin, who seemed in no hurry to topple over. *Damn him.* The crew moved at the direction of the first mate, falling into line alongside the cannons. *I'm running out of time.* A sailor dodged past me, coil of rope over one shoulder, smoldering match cord attached to a rod leaning against the other. Chan Sha gave the woman a dirty look and curled her lip.

"Sloppy," she growled, her grating voice harsher than usual. "If the cord goes out it's useless and if it throws a spark at the wrong moment it could prove deadly."

"Aye, well, you can dress her down in a moment or two," I told the pirate. Glancing past her, I arched an eyebrow at Salina. "You've a plan?"

"The plague ship just came out of the bay and Chan Sha says that thanks to the wind's direction, they have no choice but to run parallel to us. They'll hope to slip past the oncoming flotilla or at worst brave one broadside at range, and they'll be home free."

"Ah." I nodded, watching Mankin cut past us back toward the dais. He looked pissed and distracted, but not like a man who was about to collapse from poison. *How?* "So we fall in-line with them, making it appear we're together and drawing the flotilla down on them."

"That's the thrust of it," Chan Sha agreed, crossing her arms, tanned wrists poking out from where her crimson shirtsleeves were cuffed back to allow a cleaner draw of the pistoles that hung from her belt. "When the flotilla opens up, we can use our mortar to try to drop a few rounds on the plague ship's deck and slow it down, so the flotilla can pounce."

"A fresh war with a crippled ship in front of them and us too far back to help," I mused. "They won't be able to resist the chance to score the first kill."

A shout from Mankin swung us all around. "You've the deck," he told his first mate. A whistling shriek flew over the masts, and the water two score paces on erupted in a fountain as the shell hit.

"Man-o'-war firing mortars!" the lookout hollered.

"I'll be in my cabin," Mankin said in the immediate silence, and then stomped off, his brass leg nearly upending him as he stepped down from the dais and marched toward the door at the rear that led to his quarters.

"Really?" Salina snorted. "Now the man decides to leave?"

"About damned time," I muttered. *Oh.* I straightened up and adjusted the cross-slung leather satchel so it hung properly on my hip as several things suddenly slid into place in my mind.

"What next?" she asked.

"You lot have a good plan, now it's down to the execution." I gestured. "I'm going to have a word with the good captain yon." Another whistling shriek cut short as a geyser on the near side—toward the approaching ships—leapt into the air. *At least their mortar crew are terrible at grouping us in.* "Don't follow."

A squall was blowing in, casting a pall over the seas around us. The sun slipped from view and the resulting greywash made the white, oak decks look like bone as I made my way toward the captain's cabin. The man hadn't gone down like I'd hoped, nor had he been amiable to Salina's orders. The latter wasn't much in and of itself, but the former was significant. I passed the helmswoman, giving her a half salute while the first mate called up to the lookout to know when the next salvo was likely to come. The good captain had asked after our mage marks and he was fresh come to the ship. *After the last captain and mate took ill on the eve of the voyage.* I felt the ship turn sharply—as sharp as a vessel this large could, anyway—and a wave smacked the side, peppering my face with spray. *Through the door. There should be a two-step drop.* I didn't know the layout of the cabin, but I'd have to chance it. *Roll, use the jamb to push left. Stiletto?* I brushed seawater from my face with the back of my sleeve. *Ready, Sin?*

"Ready."

I knocked politely on the door, then turned the handle and threw my shoulder against the wood. Sin's magic burned through me, fire pumping in my veins and muscles as I fell through the doorway into a forward roll. My back smacked off a step and my legs scissor-kicked, connecting with the doorjamb and sending me rolling to the left. I heard something whistle over my head and through the space where I'd been a heartbeat before. As I ended my roll, I sent a chair flying, then rebounded off the far wall and came to my feet, spinning, and tossed my stiletto with a flick of my wrist.

Boom!

Mankin's pistole went off, taking a chunk out of the wall a pace to my left, sending splinters and smoke flying through the air. Either chair or blade had connected; I saw that he was rubbing one wrist ruefully against the hilt of the cutlass he held in the other hand. He stood on the two legs he'd been born with, the discarded false peg leg behind him. He nodded when he saw me taking it all in.

"How'd you know?"

"That you were a Sin Eater?" I asked. "Easy enough." I laid out the clues I'd found and added, "But only a Sin Eater could keep the toxin of the antiguous jellyfish from driving them to their knees. Bet that burned like a motherfucker."

"It did. It does." His eyes narrowed. "You think you engineered our little private audience, Sambuciña, but you're the one that's mistaken. There's someone"—as he spoke, his bass voice lightened, somehow gaining depth and strength even as it shifted octaves—"who'd like to meet you." He stopped holding his wrist, rolled his shoulders, and when his gaze met mine his eyes were pure gold with no iris to break up the light that emanated from them. "I am Ciris, Goddess of All, and you, little thief, have something I've been longing to reclaim."

"Ciris," I spat.

"Goddess of All," she repeated through Mankin's mouth.

"Aye, I heard you the first time. You would steal my world, so it's a bit rich hearing you name me thief." Her golden eyes flashed and Sin's magic changed my vision so that I wasn't blinded. "You want your Sin back?" I sank into a crouch, letting a blade fall into my palm. "You're welcome to try."

For a moment we stared at each other. Then two Goddesses went to war.

26

One moment Mankin's possessed body was on the far side of the cabin, the next Ciris was upon me, but I'd been expecting her to close after my taunt. I stepped in, Sin's speed blurring my vision as my legs burned, and slammed my stiletto up into Mankin's solar plexus.

Clang!

Ciris had pulled the cutlass across her body. My blade met the flat of hers and scored a rent up the center of Mankin's open jacket, the white shirt beneath turning red, but it was only a scratch instead of a killing blow. I leapt up, wrapping my legs around Mankin's thick torso, letting my left arm's momentum carry the stiletto up past his head, then reversed my grip on the weapon, driving it toward the back of his head. At the last moment Ciris twisted and I had to let the stiletto go or I'd have driven it into my own shoulder. I caught Mankin's neck in an armlock, trapping the cutlass between us, my limbs shaking from magic. Steam rose from me in wisps, Sin unloading all the heat the magic generated.

"You think to usurp me, child?" Ciris asked, her lilting voice strange coming from Mankin's strong jaw. His lips twisted as he jerked in my grip, the trapped cutlass keeping him from cutting me open wide, but also preventing my choking him out. "Use my own magic against me? You see but a pace before you in the dark and call yourself wise. You see nothing, you ken nothing, and when I've reclaimed my Sin from you, you'll be nothing."

"You"—I bit the words off—"talk. A. Lot." And then I head-butted the only living Goddess in the world, driving my forehead into Mankin's broad nose.

"Mmphh," Mankin squealed, spraying blood in my face. Ciris swung him around in a tight circle and the cabin spun past me in a blur as I clung to him. I felt my wrist click as something gave. Pain slashed up my arm and I flew off, spinning over the desk and slamming into the wall with a loud thump that knocked a picture off its fastening. I squirmed to the side as Mankin's cutlass flashed and bit into the floor where I'd just been, sending splinters into the air. For a few moments we played cat and mouse, me rolling first to one side then the other, Ciris laying about with Mankin's cutlass, scoring the wood a dozen times over until she swore in her tongue and leapt onto the tabletop.

Leg. Table. When's the next swell?

"Now," Sin squeaked as Ciris missed—just barely—again.

I lashed out, kicking the edge of the table hard as the ship rose with the wave. Mankin overbalanced and came windmilling toward me. I palmed the flat-edged piece of steel I kept sheathed on my left wrist and drove it hard upward, and Mankin screamed as he landed on top of me, his bulk driving the breath from my lungs.

"Pain's a bitch, isn't it?" I gasped.

"His pain," Ciris hissed, her liquid, gold eyes flashing to the finger's length of steel I'd driven through his wrist, severing the nerves to the hand. The cutlass lay useless on the floor beside him. "Not mine."

She thrust stiff fingers at my eyes and I blocked her blow with my right arm, and we went at it hammer and tongs, my face stinging from a slap, Mankin's busted nose dripping blood all down the front of my dress. Ciris slipped inside like a swirling tempest and backheeled me, sending me spilling down to the floor with Mankin's heft on top of me. I slammed my head off the deck so hard Sin cut off with a yelp, and the backs of my hands smashed my eyes so that stars burst before them.

"Pain's a bitch," she hissed, "isn't it?"

"Smash my brains out and you'll never get Sin back," I told her, barely able to hear her over the ringing in my ears.

"I *am* Sin," she growled, Mankin's throat constricting with her power. She slammed me off the deck floor again. And again. Each blow made Sin grunt and scream and I felt something in my neck crick when he cut out completely at the last blow. "I will smash you to pieces and drink him from your blood, child. I will—"

"Look out!" I shouted.

Mankin's lips curled in disgust, Ciris thinking it a parlor trick, until they disappeared in a blur of wood and blood accompanied by the sound of hardwood cracking his skull. Mankin was thrown to one side; his limp body rolled twice before it caught the edge of the table. His head thwacked woodenly against the wall, blood spurting where a chunk of skull was missing.

"T-took you long enough," I said.

"You knew we'd come?" Salina asked over Chan Sha's shoulder.

"How?" the former pirate asked, inspecting the new bend in her cane.

"Easy," I said, pushing myself up so I could lean against the wall. I could feel the back of my head swelling; my entire skull felt simultaneously too loose and too tight. "Easiest way to get me to do something is to order me not to do it. Figured you were the same." I gingerly felt the rear of my head, wincing. When I brought my hand back, blood as dark as my skin was bright on the lighter skin of my palm. I winced. "Only I would have done it faster."

"Aye, well," Chan Sha said, her dark-green eyes flashing from me to Mankin's twitching body and back, "you're welcome. How'd you let him get the drop on you?"

"He's a Sin Eater," I said.

"Damn it," Salina spat, dropping beside me. "You knew that?"

"Of course."

"And took him on by yourself?"

"Aye." I put my hand on her shoulder and levered myself up, using the wall for support. "I would've had him, too, save I didn't reckon him calling in reinforcements."

Chan Sha's braids fanned behind her where they weren't held against her scalp by the red bandana as she cast a look around the cabin. Her eyes swung back to mine and she gasped when she realized what I'd meant.

"Ciris."

Her voice was loud in the silence that followed.

"You're jesting," Salina whispered after a moment.

"Afraid not," I said, hobbling over to Mankin's body and reaching down to pull my edgeless blade from his wrist. "She wasn't pleased with me having her Sin without the grace to fall down and worship her. Can you imagine?" I asked lightly.

"Welcome back," I whispered in my mind as I felt Sin return.

"T-thanks," Sin said. "That hurt. What happened? Is She gone?"

"For now," I told him, mentally gesturing toward Mankin's body, which was beginning to twitch harder. "I'd imagine his Sin is still out like you were . . . I take it that until he regains consciousness and his Sin, Ciris can't come back either?"

"She can't," Sin confirmed, his voice high and tight. "Even if she did, that level of head trauma won't have the good captain up and about anytime soon."

"C-C-Ciris," Salina stuttered. The whites of her eyes were large and she trembled as she attempted to holster the pistole in her hand; it took three tries before she was able to slide it into place on her hip and draw her amber cloak around her. "What do we d-d-o now?"

"We've just committed mutiny," Chan Sha breathed. She leaned back against the tilted table and slapped her leather pants leg. "Sin Eater or no. And we're going to be in battle any moment."

The ship shuddered and the mortar roared outside. "Are in battle. We're fucked."

"No, we're not," I said, reaching forward and plucking the grenado I'd spotted inside her jacket's inner pocket. It was almost like the others the Artificer had made back in Cordoban, save smaller, and the timer on it had but one click to it. "Drag Mankin up on the table," I ordered. "Take care not to get his blood on you."

The two women did so, grunting and complaining about his weight until I reminded them that if he regained consciousness, he'd bring Ciris back with him. "There, now you hold this," I told his limp form, folding his hands around the grenado and turning the dial. "Done and dusted," I said, picking up the cutlass he'd dropped.

"Now what?"

"Now," I told Salina, unable to keep the grin from my face despite the throbbing of my head. "We run!"

I ran out behind the pair, slamming the door behind me and screaming, *"Incoming!"* as we threw ourselves across the deck. A moment later the captain's cabin exploded in a burst of flame and wood and I curled into a ball as the air whined with scything shrapnel. *Ow!* It rained down around us for several breaths and my ears were still ringing slightly when I got to my feet. The first mate stood gaping at us—past us, really—at the smoking wreckage of the cabin, mouth moving soundlessly, then took a step forward, and with the motion, found her legs again and began sprinting across the deck.

"Stop!" I shouted, but the woman ran on, bicorne spilling from her head, her long blond ponytail streaming out behind her. I saw her reaching for the sword at her side as she leapt down onto the main deck, only a handful of paces from me. "Stop!"

A long nine smashed the top of the railing to my left, bounced once on the deck, then took the first mate's head from her shoulders in a wave of blood. Her body rolled, along with the ball and her skull, until the railing brought them up short, catching the first while the last two disappeared over the side.

"For once," I said, "I'm glad no one listened to me today." Salina looked at me, tugging at her skirts where they were pinned to the deck by splintered wood. I grunted as I pulled a shard from the back of my hand. I flexed my fingers to make sure the nerves weren't damaged, then used the bit of wood to dig some of Mankin's flesh from beneath my fingernails. "Damnable luck, all around."

27

"Avast!" I shouted, my Sin-enhanced cry halting the disenchanted crew, who'd begun gathering around the command deck in a way that suggested they were contemplating surrender or a mutiny of their own. "Hear me, shipmates!" I leapt up and balanced on the rim of the water barrel that Mankin had drunk from a short quarter bell before. "You've been discomfited, aye?"

"Discomfited?" asked a shirtless man with bronzed skin and thick, black chest hair that ran down in a line to his faded, blue trousers.

"Upset! Pissed off!" The crew rumbled assent. "Ye should be. Yon captain was new to you, to all of us," I said, spreading an arm. "Normain's war is with the Empire, not the Company, and you're all good Company crew, aye?" Fewer rumbles told me how far that loyalty went, so I changed tacks. "Now the captain's been slain and your first mate's blood is upon my breast!" I added, pounding my chest. It was mostly Mankin's, truth be told. "We none of us asked for this, but the fight is here. Would we turn sail and run?"

"Can't!" a short woman hollered. "Wind'd be against us!"

"It would," I agreed. A practical lot, sailors, when it came down to it. "We're sat at the table of fortune, mates, and a dice cup has been thrust into our hands whether we will it or no. *If* we're to make a final toss . . . we need it to come up all sixes, aye? Mankin was a good salt, no questioning that, but who sailed the Shattered Coast?" I asked, raising my hand. Three-quarters of the crew raised theirs, all casting looks over their shoulder at the ships bearing down on us. I was wasting precious time, but if I didn't win them over, time would be the least of our worries. "Who kens a pirate queen called the Widowmaker?"

"Pirates don't have queens!"

"She's dead!"

"She never existed!"

I let the shouts go on and then roared them all down with Sin's magic loud on my tongue. "I don't think any ship she took debated her royalty! She's not dead and she's real, my cullies. Very real!"

"Bullshit!"

"Which one of you said that?" Chan Sha shouted, leaping up beside the helmswoman.

Her bandana had been replaced with a tricorne of the same leather as her pants and jacket; her braids were wreathed in flame and smoke so that she appeared a wraith in mist. She flicked her jacket back and spread her arms as a dozen pistoles appeared on either side, hanging by cords.

"Aye, I flew black sails, an' I'll leave it to you lot to decipher if that was at the Company's behest or not. I sailed through thicker than this and came out the other side. I've traversed the Ring of Fire, danced with cannibals, and sunk more ships than you've had beneath your boots. Yer in need of a captain and"—she blew the smoke from her face so they could see her grin—"I'm in need of a crew."

"She speaks true," Salina said into the stunned silence. "As Chair of the Kanados Trading Company, I vouch that this is the Widowmaker. You've all signed on to the Company and been paid wages and promised more besides for this voyage. I'd tell you I'd double it, but I'm the fucking Chair. I'll triple it and any victory treasure that comes from today will go to you and you alone!"

The crew all began buzzing, some nodding, others crossing their arms and looking unconvinced, several gesticulating fiercely to any who would listen. After a few moments they coalesced around the short woman I'd seen running the mortar crew through their paces earlier. Barely taller than me, she seemed even shorter standing in front of the three largest men on the ship—clearly they had her back; just as clearly, she didn't think she needed them. Her cutoff sleeves revealed, on her crossed arms, a number of tattoos, including a rather graphic one of a man doing something that was anatomically impossible.

"Not impossible," Sin whispered.

"W-what?" I shook my head. "Another time."

"You may be the Widowmaker," the woman said, her voice deeper than her size suggested, running a hand through her shorn, brown hair. "An' you may be the Chair"—she nodded at Salina— "but if we die or end up rotting in a Normain prison ship, all the coin in the world won't mean a Godsdamned thing."

"They've already killed your captain," I reminded her. "And your first mate. Do nothing and death seems assured. Surrender, and rotting in the hold of some barnacled hulk seems assured. Your only choice is to fight."

"No." Chan Sha's voice drew every eye. "I'll not have a black-mailed crew at my back. You want a chance?" She pointed at the coastline we were paralleling. "Swim for it. Take the rowboats if you've a mind, but we aren't slowing to drop them, so they'll likely be smashed to bits. The currents are strong here, but some of you might make it. I'll even adjust course to draw as close as we dare without taking soundings.

"Or," she drawled the word, "you vote me your captain and Buc there first mate." I growled and she showed her teeth. "I've a plan, mates. It involves you and that crack-shot crew I saw drilling earlier putting a few holes through that first Normain frigate."

"Sink the frigate, won't matter against that man-o'-war."

"True enough," Chan Sha agreed. "But we've another ship that appeared at a damned convenient time. We've got more sail than her an' if we made full sheets we'd pass her. Pass her and the man-o'-war will have a new target."

"What then?" one of the hulks behind the mortar woman asked.

"We see what the wind and waves deal us and go from there," Chan Sha said. "I won't lie to you. That"—her face hardened—"I promise. Sail with me and you may die or you may find yourselves with enough coin to get whore-drunk for a year. Or risk the water. Your choice.

"But you decide . . ." The former pirate's hands snapped to her sides, coming back up with a pistole in each. "Now."

"The wench has a way with her," Sin whispered.

"She does," I admitted. "Always has, damn her. Say, you didn't hold back, against Mankin. Against Ciris."

"I—I didn't," he said slowly, as if just realizing it. "I shouldn't have tried, but it all happened so fast. . . ."

"You're a shard of her, capable of slowing time to infinitesimal moments," I snorted.

"I mean, I shouldn't have been at all equal to Her," he said. "Even in Mankin's body, She should have run roughshod over us."

"I'm not sure she didn't," I said, touching the back of my head gingerly.

"You don't understand, Buc," Sin said, his voice worried. "I was part of Ciris. I remember who She was. What She was. What She is. You sail the seas, She and I sailed the skies themselves. She should have torn us limb from limb and shaken me out of your skull."

"But that didn't happen," I protested.

"It didn't," he agreed. "I don't know why."

"Widowmaker!!!" The crew's roar made the deck tremble, or perhaps it was my imagination, but they streamed forward, surrounding Chan Sha. The woman seemed taken aback for the briefest of moments before she schooled her face into the one I remembered from what seemed like ages before: the Widowmaker, the most feared pirate who ever sailed the Shattered Coast.

28

The crew leapt into a frenetic flurry of action, guided by Chan Sha using the Artificer's horn. She kept the mates of the watch and the mortar woman beside her and paused briefly to give them special instructions. In a surprisingly short time, barely a quarter bell, the deck was cleared save for the gun crews. Repair crews waited just below, ready to rush out to fix damage, help the wounded, or lend a hand wherever needed. Three men and one woman, stripped to their underclothes, stood by the rail, waiting. When Chan Sha bade them luck, the crew turned their back and the three leapt over the side, only the woman managing a graceful enough dive that I thought she might survive the several-hundred-pace swim in seas choppy from the approaching squall.

"I named you first mate because they'd never have accepted a landlubber as captain," Chan Sha said when she'd sent her officers off.

"I know."

She glanced at me, eyes searching my own. "Naming you first mate gives you a chance to save things if I'm killed."

"I know."

"You're not pissed?"

"I know Frobisher and all the rest, up here." I tapped the shaved side of my head. "You *know* them in your heart. I can run this ship, aye. I'd wager a fair amount of coin I could do it better than Mankin and half a dozen like him. But I can't do what needs doing here. That's why I brought along the Widowmaker," I told her, flashing a grin.

"You . . . planned for this?" she asked.

"This exact situation?" I chuckled. "You sound like Eld. I planned for all manner of things, Chan Sha. Just be glad some of those things included you."

With a wordless comment that was more like a grunt, Chan Sha raised a telescope, the gears spinning as she adjusted the aperture. I nearly made a joke about her eyesight, given the man-o'-war loomed large just beyond the plague ship that was desperately zigging and zagging, trying to shake us off their backside. Chan Sha had told the helmswoman to stick to them like a limpet and the woman had taken Chan Sha at her word. "Give this to Charli," she told the cabin girl beside her, handing the telescope over. "She'll be able to see the tops'ls and not much else beside. Cheat for'd. On my command. Got that?" The girl leapt away, flip-flops kicking up behind her, plaited curls making a flag of her own. "Can I borrow your eyes?" Chan Sha asked me.

"Only if you promise not to play keepsies with one." She rolled her good eye and I snorted. *Sin?* My eyes burned, muting the throbbing in the back of my head, and the man-o'-war leapt forward almost as if it were up against our ship. Through our rigging and the massive ship's rigging it was difficult to discern the frigate behind it, but I could see the prow with the figurehead of a grim man wearing some strange hat that looked like crisscrossed bicornes. The rest of the deck was hidden by a swell. "Target acquired."

"If you've got the windage and elevation," Chan Sha spoke with the horn to her lips, the Artificer's work amplifying her voice so that it carried across the deck, "fire!"

The mortar on deck belched flame, the roar and thump of the shot loud and muted at the same time, and our ship shuddered before cutting through the sea again as it had been. I saw all of that from my periphery, eyes focused on the slip of the frigate within my view. A geyser spouted from the sea just behind the man-o'-war.

"Two score paces off the prow!" I shouted, Sin helping me with the distance.

"I'm right here," Chan Sha said dryly, relaying my words through the bullhorn. Another round halved the distance, another sent the frigate out wider behind the man-o'-war, but Sin gave me the adjustments and the mortar crew knew its work. "Fire," Chan Sha repeated.

I saw the frigate's figurehead disappear in an explosion of wood and sea-foam. "You've got her, just," I told Chan Sha.

The Widowmaker called out her own adjustments this time and the next round dropped on the main deck. The third round impacted farther back, and the frigate heaved over, all of her sails turning as she tried to run from our mortar. I glanced over to see Chan Sha and Salina wearing the same feral grin I felt on my own lips. The Artificer merely looked ill, and Bar'ren interested but slightly bemused.

"She's running, lads 'n' lasses. Fire for effect!" Chan Sha shouted. The mortar thumped thrice more. One shot took the railing off and not much besides, the second shot went straight through her decks down to the hull, and the third sent the frigate's mast careening down across the front of the deck. The ship began to list, tilting farther over with each wave that slammed into her sides. "She's done," Chan Sha whispered.

"That's done." I jumped down from the water barrel, joining the others. "Now we just need to send that plague ship to the bottom as well, and with any luck Ciris will believe us dead. That's why I shouted warning," I added at the looks Chan Sha and Salina gave. "Before you, uh"—I glanced at the helmswoman—"took action. She'll know what he knew about our situation and assume us sunk."

"She's a bloody Goddess," Chan Sha hissed. "She won't believe any of that unless the Sin Eaters she's *sure* to have contacted on Southeast Island yon find the wreckage of our ship. If that happens it will mean we've run into trouble ourselves."

"Small favor indeed," Salina murmured.

"She'll assume us sunk," I continued as if I hadn't heard them, "because she *will* find our wreckage. I intend her to. We just need to take over another ship first."

"Another ship?" Salina gulped. "Which one? That one?"

I followed her finger to the plague ship we were rapidly overtaking on our right, putting the Dead Gods between us and the rest of the Normain flotilla. "Hardly," I drawled, feigning that haughty Servenzan noble tone. Salina rolled her eyes. "Gods, woman, it could be crawling with the plague." Chan Sha muttered and I turned to her. "Are you going to have the crew run out the guns?"

"They're run out," she said dryly. "We're approaching the tip of the island where the coast turns north . . . time this right, and we'll have enough space to peel left and give them a taste of the grape. Hopefully their crew isn't as good as ours, but we'll likely have to brave a broadside and then we'll be past them."

"Good plan. When are you going to do that?" I asked.

"Soon as you stop asking me questions," Chan Sha said. She clapped me on the shoulder and limped past me toward the crew manning the cannons on our right. Salina and I exchanged looks, both of us chuckling. The *captain* raised her arm, giving us the finger, and began giving orders to the crew. The cannons were raised slightly at the moment the helmswoman began throwing the wheel to the left. In a ship this size, more than a few moments elapsed before we started to peel away from the plague ship that was first just beyond us, then nearly level, then finally level. Across her decks the crew were moving, but in a haphazard fashion, and with my Sin-enhanced vision I could see why: the deck was teeming with Shambles. My view was obscured in fire and flame as the cannons erupted across our decks, the whole ship shivering from the concussion

"Change over!" Chan Sha shouted.

"Switch!" the crew answered back, the gears of the cannons practically singing as they rotated, putting a fresh barrel in place.

"Raise one . . . fire!" Chan Sha called. This time the sound was slightly quieter, the shiver more pronounced as they fired solid shot instead of canister. "Well done! Well done!" The crew roared their approval back at her and I couldn't keep the grin from my lips. Nothing motivates more than success. "Now," Chan Sha began, striding back toward us, calling instructions through her horn, "turn us back again and we'll swing around them all and see what the wind and waves think our next move ought to be.

"We should have a moment before the smoke clears," she added as she reached my side. Frantic shouts rang out through the smoke shrouding the plague ship and she arched an eyebrow. "Did we hull them that badly? What in the bloody mizzen tops is that about?"

"I'd say it must be the man-o'-war, but surely we'd have heard that?" Salina asked.

"Aye," I said dryly. "She's forty-odd cannon a side. Being the second largest ship in their fleet, I'd imagine she has over-under cannons like our own, so eighty cannons at once. Quite the cannonade."

"Clew up!" the lookout shouted as we began to draw perpendicular to the slowly clearing shroud of smoke. The approaching squall seemed abruptly nearer: lightning sizzled across the sky and several moments later thunder answered it. "The 'war's anchored!"

"Her name," Chan Sha gasped. "Why?"

"Why isn't the plague ship at the bottom?" Salina growled. Her features were smooth but I could see the worry in her ramrod-straight back. Aye, and why not? It was only my third sea battle and I still wasn't entirely comfortable with the fathoms of water lying beneath us either. I preferred knowledge, and the seas were one dark unknown.

"There's your answer," I said, pointing as the wind finally dispelled the smoke. "They're flying a damned Normain flag."

"Aye," Chan Sha said. "It must have been caught 'round the mast at first to have not unfurled, and either our broadside or the lookout shook it loose." The white flag with its innumerable dark-blue crowns outlined in gilt thread stood out against the darkening sky. "The man-o'-war saw right before it rammed her and then it had a choice: hull her or drop anchor and hard over."

"The captain doesn't look happy about her decision to spare them," I said, Sin's magic giving me a view of the red-faced, brown-haired woman who was screaming at her crew.

"She's ordering them to raise the anchor and sight the mortars on us," Sin told me, lip-reading from across several hundred paces of open water.

"They're prepping their mortars, Chan Sha," I relayed.

"They're disadvantaged?" Bar'ren asked.

"Going to take them a moment to get their anchor drawn up," I confirmed. "Until then we can outmaneuver them."

"Which we've essentially done," Chan Sha said. "They can try their mortars, but these are made for sea battles, designed to use the ship's momentum and direction to make sighting easier. At a standstill, it's much harder to get the aiming right quickly. Especially with us moving at pace . . . we could run now if we wanted to."

"Save we don't know how badly that plague ship was damaged by our broadside," I reminded her. "And we've a need to change our ship, remember?"

"Why not take the large one, then?" Bar'ren asked.

"Too large," Chan Sha said. "Even could it be done, we don't have the crew to run her the way she demands. First bad storm we come across would tear the sheets from our masts if it didn't send us to the bottom."

"They've almost got the anchor up," the Artificer said, an audible tremor in his voice.

"At least the frigate's separated," Salina pointed out.

The frigate had broken off to avoid running into the man-o'-war or the plague ship flying Normain colors, but it had drawn too close to shore. As it attempted to recover, the plague ship began to sail past. Suddenly, the plague ship ground to a halt and the frigate drew level with it. Figures threw themselves across the small gap, several falling, and Sin's magic showed me a score of Shambles pulling down terrified Normain sailors. Rope hooks shot out, pulling the two ships closer together, and several Dead Gods' mages swung across until a woman with ashen-grey hair ran along the side of the deck, swinging a broad cutlass, taking heads from Shambles with one swing and cutting boarding ropes with the other. *There's a brave lass.* The frigate leapt away from the foundering plague ship.

"Things just got interesting," I said, looking back and forth between the ships. "Arti, do you have those experimental charges in the hold?"

"Aye, but Chan Sha said to leave them as they haven't been tested," the man said, dry-washing his hands. "There were . . . accidents before and so forth."

"Well, what better time to test them than now? Yon man-o'-war will be the experimental arm and we'll be the control, if we're lucky," I joked.

"Buc—" Chan Sha began.

"I'm open to suggestions?"

"Let's mortar the plague ship and be done."

"You keep forgetting that a bloody Goddess knows we're aboard this ship," I spat. The helmswoman gasped and Chan Sha rolled her good eye. "Add to that I just saw Shambles jump aboard that frigate a moment back."

"Gods' blood," the helmswoman whispered. The frigate had begun sailing aimlessly as fighting erupted across its decks.

"Better their blood than ours," I said dryly. "Unless you want to face off with that man-o'-war in a fair fight, use the charges. 'Sides, the Artificer's gotten loads better at exploding things since we've been palling around."

"Those charges are from Servenza," Chan Sha said. "Back when he was working for me."

"Oh." I nodded thoughtfully. "Sometimes, you have to roll the dice. And mayhap we sail toward shore in case things backfire."

"Literally," Salina said.

"They've a better than two-in-three chance of working," the Artificer said primly.

"What happens if it's the one in three?" Bar'ren asked.

"Boom," I said, grinning to hide the twist in my stomach.

"Eloquent," Chan Sha murmured.

"But accurate," the Artificer admitted.

"Do it," the Widowmaker said after a moment. "I figure we've got worse odds than that if we face the man-o'-war in anything approaching a fair fight." She sighed. "Well?" Chan Sha clapped her hands. "Go, man! Run! Off with the pair of you!" Both men looked startled, then took off, Bar'ren sprinting effortlessly. The Artificer looked like a lump of flesh stuffed in a sack, but despite that the short man was on Bar'ren's heels as they disappeared down the hold. "Tell Charli that I've some timed charges coming for her," Chan Sha said, bending down to be of a level with the cabin girl, who had returned from her previous mission. "She's to fire a grouping now and adjust with the new."

"Won't the new have dif'frent tra-tra-trajec'tries?" the girl asked, fumbling with the word.

"Whip smart, you are," Chan Sha said, flashing her teeth. Surprisingly, despite the pink scars and patched eye, the smile softened her features. "It will and Charli will be pissed about it, but I don't want to fire one more of those charges than is needed, and this will at least get her close. Off you go now," she said, slapping the child on the back.

"Smart girl," I said, watching her dash off in her flip-flops.

"Aye, but she's just a lass," Chan Sha said, her smile hardening. "You order us to abandon ship in the middle of a sea battle in the hopes of boarding and overthrowing another ship, and the safest bet is she'll never get any older. You can't bloody exchange ships in the middle of a fight."

"All in a day's work for a pirate queen, isn't it? 'Sides, more than that little girl rides on today," I said, pulling my eyes away from her retreating form. "We've got to win if she's to see tomorrow."

"She'll never get that chance if she's dead," Chan Sha snapped.

"You think she doesn't know that?" Salina growled. The other woman stepped between us, standing on her tiptoes to be level with the former pirate in her heeled boots. "Buc's already seen that half a dozen different ways. That's how she is. She sees every fucking angle. Could be the girl lives. Could be she dies. The Gods never gave a fuck about her or the tens of thousands like her. Gods' truth, I didn't either," she added, looking away. "Buc calls the shots, savvy?"

The mortar thumped, Charli sending out a test shot, and the ship shuddered.

"Aye. Aye," Chan Sha said after a moment. "Captain."

"No, I'm the first mate," Salina said.

"An' I'm the swabby."

"I was going to allow you chamber-pot tosser," Salina said, her face stern before it dissolved into laughter. "You're second mate. Wait?" Her brow crinkled. "Is there a second mate? How many mates are there?"

"Three. Usually," Chan Sha said. "All right, you've won me over." She glanced past Salina to me. "You convert everyone you meet?"

The mortar thumped a second time.

"Just the useful ones," I said dryly, looking past them. "Arti and Bar'ren are back."

"'War's on the move!" the lookout shouted down. "Two points and sails unfurling."

"That much berth will take a moment to get moving," Chan Sha said. "Still . . ." She told the helmswoman to adjust course to steer us between the plague ship and the frigate—which was enveloped in a cacophony of gunfire and smoke as the battle between sailors and the undead raged.

The man-o'-war's deck belched flame; the dull thump of its mortar firing reached us a moment later, followed by a high-pitched whistle that ended in the sea several score paces away, between us and the larger ship. "She's way short and we're running away from her," I crowed.

"You're not wrong," Sin said. "I'd estimate a sixty count to bring them close enough to walk their rounds onto us."

"Bit tight at that," I replied.

"Aye," Chan Sha said, "but they're likely an eighty count away from getting too close for comfort." She brought the bullhorn up to her lips. "Charli!" Chan Sha called. "Got yer groupings?"

The mortar thumped a third time, and a few breaths later the round whistled through the air, splashing just aft of the man-o'-war several hundred paces away.

"That'll do!" Chan Sha said through the bullhorn. "Listen to the Artificer and load the charge. Fire when ready!"

"You really think there's a one-in-three chance that explodes in the tube?" Salina whispered to me.

"If there's one thing you should know about the Artificer," I said slowly, "it's that he—"

Boom!

The mortar spat flame, the round practically on fire as it leapt from the tube. We all watched its fiery arc, up and over until it disappeared in the sky and then reappeared several moments later, shrieking down to meet the prow of the massive Normain ship. The crew were silent, on tenterhooks. Though the deck kicked up, for a moment there was no other sign of impact. Then suddenly the figurehead blew out and away, a small fireball chasing after it through the hole it'd created. Our deck erupted in a roar of approval.

"—underestimates himself," I finished, practically shouting to be heard. "Vastly."

"So the odds aren't that bad?"

"Likely nine in ten," Chan Sha said, glancing toward the front as the second round launched. "I believe that round just unseated their front mortar and they haven't even tried the back. Brilliant! Like the Artificer," she added. "A brilliant little man, but when he fails, he does so just as brilliantly."

"Aye," I muttered. "So the fewer shots we fire, the better." I cursed when the second round tore through the sail before carrying past the railing. A small geyser leapt up a moment later when the charge went off, and the big ship rocked back and forth. Its rear mortar returned fire on the same wave.

"Incoming," I warned between gritted teeth.

Our own mortar crew had to wait a moment for the tube to cool, despite sponging it out thrice, before loading the next round, and we were all watching so intently it took a moment for my Sin-enhanced ears to recognize the sound coming down on top of us. *Gods, I forgot to listen to myself.*

"Incoming!" This time I shouted the warning.

Everyone tried to grab hold of something, and a moment later a screaming demon fell from the sky. The round fired from the man-o'-war struck atop the main mast, shearing through the flag and the crow's nest, and taking out the top quarter of the topsail, along with the lookout, in an explosion of splintered wood, burning sail, and bits of flesh. Through it all, Chan Sha stood like a statue, ignoring the downpour of ruin around her. Beyond her, our own mortar fired again.

"Might be," she said when she caught my eye, "we need to think about changing ships after all."

"Aye—"

There was an explosion on the man-o'-war's deck as our shot landed just back of midship; a breath later time seemed to grind to a halt as the ship's deck buckled, the planks snapping into a hundred disparate parts. A fist of fire leapt up from below, fingers unfurling into a hand that swallowed the deck, the masts, and the entire ship in one massive inferno. The concussion caught me full in the chest, stealing my breath away.

Booooommmm!!!

"Gods," Salina whispered in the ensuing silence, "what happened?"

"We caught their powder magazine," Chan Sha answered in a like tone. "Ship like that has enough firepower to take down a coastal fort, but she's also the world's largest powder keg waiting to touch off at the wrong spark."

"Well," I said, staring at the two burning, sinking halves of what had once been the second largest ship in the Normain fleet. "I never wanted that ship anyway."

"Which ship then?" Salina asked. "Not the plague ship, surely."

"The frigate?" the Artificer asked as he and Bar'ren joined us. He muttered an oath at the sight of the dying ship beyond us. The man loved inventing, but loved a sight less what his inventions wrought. "We could—"

"Both," I told them. "We'll have both."

"How in Her name do you intend to do that," Chan Sha asked, pointing at our shattered main mast, "with us half-arsed at the moment?"

"She has a plan," Salina said, half smiling, but her eyes showed fear.

"I have a plan," I confirmed.

"A dangerous one," Salina whispered.

"Aren't they all?"

29

"I'm not sure—" Salina cut off as our small boat caught a wave, went airborne, then smacked off the water. A small cry slipped past her lips as she held on to the seat. "I'm not sure," she continued, her sodden braid clinging to the side of her neck, "that I like this plan."

"Why not?" I cackled, the wind blurring my eyes as the sea spray slapped me in the face. Our lifeboat whumped across the waves, almost bouncing from the top of one crest to the next. "We're practically flying!"

"I know," she groaned. The rest of the crew packed into the longboat groaned along with her as each landing sent half of them sprawling into the other half. All the while trying not to impale themselves or one another on their swords and axes and trying to keep the powder dry in their pistoles and blunderbusses.

The gearwork rudder I clung to cackled along with me, the turnkey mechanism requiring a Sin Eater's strength first to wind and then to hold steady enough to chart an even course. The fins it connected to in the water blurred, churning the sea behind us. Closer to our ship, the rest of our longboats made a slower pace, relying upon oars and physical labor to follow after us. I let us bounce off half a dozen more waves, then released the tension in the mechanism. It spun out in one long, whirring grind, lowering our pace from breakneck to merely fast.

"We're coming up on the frigate, mates!" I jumped up onto the back of the boat, swayed for one perilous moment, then caught myself and pointed. "You lot with the grappling guns make ready, rest of you take a moment to find your stomachs again." Several of the crew were at the sides, hurling, and Salina joined them. It takes a lot to make a sailor seasick and she'd never stood a chance. Even with Sin's magic holding my equilibrium, my hands still felt the phantom vibrations pulsing through them from holding the tiller. "You're about to have yer shot! Aim for the rear railing yon . . . fire!"

A tall lass stood up, speargun leveled, and the thick shaft shot out at an angle as we passed the shadow cast by the rear of the frigate. We all felt the jerk when it caught. A moment later three more crew fired grappling hooks; two shot through the railing and held, the third bounced off the side, useless. A few called out jokes at the man's miss and he glared at them with his good eye.

"Probably shouldn't have given that task to a blind man," Sin pointed out.

"Most squeeze an eye shut to fire," I muttered.

"Maybe he lost the eye he kept open."

"Mayhap," I agreed.

"Two are almost as good as three," I said out loud. "Make us fast and the first up behind me will drop ladders down."

I leapt down and strode through the crew, trodding on one man who didn't make way fast enough, my elbow driving the curse from his lips. Show weakness around this lot and they'd follow me nowhere. Least of all onto a ship fighting for its life against the undead. I could hear the low rumbling and hiss of the Shambles above and a higher-pitched roar from one of the Veneficus. Judging by the sporadic gunfire, the battle had already reached its zenith and was winding down, which was to the good for my plan, but I needed there to still be enough confusion that neither side would realize they'd a new boarding party to contend with until it was too late.

"What you going to do with that?" a fat man half a head taller than me asked, pointing at the slingshot I held in my left hand. He slid a large scimitar through his belt with one hand, while reaching down to pet a dog that barely reached his knee but looked all muscle beneath its thin, coal-black coat. "Play twiddly sticks?"

"I just brought us across the open sea with a gear-wrought tiller that would have broke your wrist if you tried to hold on to it, lard arse," I told him, flashing a smile that didn't reach my eyes. "If you can haul yourself up there"—I nodded upward—"you'll fucking see what I can do. Leave the pup, though, no place for a dog in this fight unless they're a bloody Veneficus."

"Queenie knows her way in a fight," he growled, patting the top of her head. Another dog, this one an actual puppy—with auburn fur and big, floppy ears—poked a head out from the drooping collar of his tan shirt. "Georgie, too."

I opened my mouth, but the dog built like a brick shithouse showed me its not inconsiderable teeth and I decided to let it go. "Now," I told the rest of the crew, "remember the plan. We need to create a bulwark atop until the rest of our compatriots catch us up. Then we'll take the ship." Nods all around.

Salina handed me a short, snub-nosed pistole loaded with a grappling hook.

"You know," I said to her, quietly, "you really should have come in the second wave."

"I've a feeling being close to you is safer than being out there," she said, gesturing at the rest of our miniflotilla.

"I'm not sure about that," I said half under my breath, and aimed the pistole at the railing.

"What are you going to be doing while we do that?" Salina asked.

"Doing what I do best, 'Lina" I said.

The pistol leapt in my hand, the hook whirling through the air before it shot past the railing, and I heard the fat man make a sound in his throat echoed by his dog. Half a breath later I pulled the trigger again and the treble grappling hook flew back, thunking into the railing, all three tines caught. One of the dogs whined inquisitively as if surprised.

"Being a Godsdamned pain in the arse," I finished. "Wait for the rest to catch us up and direct them, aye?" Salina opened her mouth to argue and I shot a pointed look at the others. If she questioned me, they would, too. Salina got it, swallowed her tongue, and nodded instead. "The rest of you lot . . . after me."

I pressed the trigger again and my arm nearly wrenched itself free of my shoulder as I shot through the air as the line reeled in. I just got my boots up in time to catch myself against the ship, and within moments I was at the railing's edge.

"Ready, Sin?"

"We've already gone toe-to-toe with a Goddess. What's adding on a hostile crew, dozens of Shambles, and a Veneficus or two to boot?"

"That's the spirit."

"Careful, Buc," he muttered. "A few meals, no matter how large, didn't get us back to even. We've not much length left to the edge of our rope. Again."

"Noted," I whispered, both of us knowing that wouldn't stop me if push came to shove. Behind me I could hear the grunts of the crew climbing up the ropes. They'd reach the railing soon enough and I had to make sure it was cleared for them. Once we got most of the crew aboard, our numbers would tell and I'd have less work to do. *Until then . . .*

"Well, this *was* my plan," I said, throwing my left arm over the railing, slingshot still in hand, then climbing over. I stood up, gooseflesh breaking out at the scene before me.

The dead and dying lay sprawled all about me, a haphazard mishmash of detritus that had been full of life moments before. Smoke clung at just above eye level, held down by the squall that had finally caught up to us. Rain began to sweep across the deck, water running in grim colors of black and vermillion where the ichor from fallen Shambles blended with the lifeblood of the Normain crew. A woman's body lay broken back across a cannon, her skirts blooming in the wind in an obscene way that turned my stomach. Here and there knots of men and women, back-to-back, fought desperately against several dozen Shambles. The Dead Walker, a towering figure in a white cloak that was stained with blood and gore, stood midship with their back to me, bent over their glowing book, sheltering the magical object from the rain.

For a moment I was transported to Chan Sha's ship, over a year ago, the Ghost Captain's undead legions cutting through her crew. I could feel their skeletal fingers clutching at my flesh as they sought to hold me down and turn me into one of them. *Never. Again.* I started moving before I realized it. *Sin.* I tore the grappling hook free from the railing, sending splinters flying, and drew the hook back into the muzzle of the pistole. Thrusting the gun into my armpit, to hold it, I plucked out the side loader and thrust in a new powder cartridge that I'd pulled from my satchel. By the time I was within a dozen paces of the Dead Gods' mage I was ready. I sidestepped to where a swivel gun was mounted on the edge of the deck, leveled the pistole, and pulled the trigger, sending the hook buzzing through the air.

The Dead Walker roared in pain and surprise when the grappling hook punched completely through the right side of their lower back. They dropped their magical book and collapsed to the deck. Playing out line, I swiftly wrapped the pistole thrice around the thick, iron swivel mount, then I pulled the trigger. The Dead Walker screamed, his guttural shout turning desperate as the pistole dragged him backward, the treble hook caught against his spine. He clawed at the deck, trying to command legs that no longer obeyed to dig into the rainswept wood. He called for his Shambles, but without his book they paid him no heed. Finally, as if realizing someone must have been responsible for the hook through his guts, the Dead Walker glanced back, thin, pale face twisted in a rictus of pain, and his dark eyes shot wide open.

"Aye," I told him, wedging the trigger into a crevasse where the mount met the larger swivel gun so that it would keep reeling him in. "Didn't see that coming, did you?"

"W-who?" the tall man gasped, blood flecking his lips. The question barely reached my ears.

"Who am I?" I strode past him, brushing aside his feeble attempt to trip me, and dug a round ball out of my satchel. Drawing back my slingshot, I turned, aiming at him, and when he flinched, I swung back around and let fly.

The ball went straight through the strange, glowing book the Dead Walkers used to command the Shambles.

The undead surrounding the remaining crew fell where they stood, the strings attached to them suddenly cut. I turned back to the dying mage. "Couldn't let you slip into one of their bodies," I explained. The man, who was caught fast against the gun mount, had one arm behind him, grasping blindly for the gun; the other he'd buried in the gaping wound in his abdomen, trying to wrest the hook from his spine. I drew a shiny, round lump from my satchel and thumbed it into my sling.

"W-w-h—"

"Best not to name names," I said. "Lest one of yours finds enough of your blood to peer into your memories. Let's just say I'm the stuff of your kind's nightmares." I drew the sling back until I could practically feel the steel-reinforced handle creaking. A dull explosion sounded from starboard and suddenly the grey sky lit up, reflecting the towering inferno that had erupted when Chan Sha had rammed our ship—laden with barrels of the Artificer's Serpent's Flame—into the plague ship. Any plague that might have been incubating was now being burned to a crisp. I released the silver nugget and the back of the Dead Walker's head exploded. "And I'm just getting started."

The Veneficus shrieked as it swooped down from the crow's nest above, sending me diving to the deck. I glanced up through a few errant, black strands of hair and saw the creature hurtling down. Its wide wings were tipped with steel razors that kept it from achieving true flight, but it could glide above the deck as it attacked the dozen remaining crewmembers. A man bawled as one of the wings sliced across his body; he collapsed, fell trying and failing to hold his intestines in. One sailor fired a blunderbuss, and the creature squawked and swerved, its outstretched talons missing the group. A roar of humanity cried out from right beside me, and I glanced back, expecting to see my crew, but there was nothing. . . .

A moment later more of the Normain crew rushed out from belowdecks—I guessed they'd been preparing for a final stand. Lightning lashed across the sky, revealing a ragged party brandishing cutlasses and blunderbusses. I could practically feel their elation at surviving despite the odds.

A flash of white caught my eye—the bloomers of the woman bent backward over one of the cannons. A moment later I realized the cloth wasn't moving because of the wind. The woman came upright slowly, ashy hands clutching at the smooth-barreled cannon. Her skull was a ragged, decaying thing with one desiccated eye swinging wildly around its socket. *Oh, shit.* All around her, figures that had lain prostrate on the rolling deck began rising, clambering awkwardly to their feet, scraps of decaying clothing catching on their ragged bones. *It's a trap.*

"It's a trap!" I shouted, but my cry was lost in the Normain crew's ebullient reunion and the hoarse cries of the undead as they rose in scores around the living. Some sailors shouted warnings that went unheeded until the Shambles swept across the flank of the crew who'd emerged from below, taking half of them down in a flood of bone and steel. The survivors turned and their blunderbusses swept the deck, billowing gun smoke obscuring everything save for the rain lancing down into the shrouded deck.

"Buc!" Salina's call made me spin so fast my neck cricked. Behind me the deck was packed with my longboat's crew. Salina levered herself over the railing and more sailors scrambled up from a dozen rope ladders—the rest of our longboats had caught up. "What do we do?"

"Save what's left of the crew!" I thrust my sling into my satchel and drew a pair of gleaming stilettos. "To me! The lot of you, to me!" The living Normain crew rushed forward, terror written plain across their features. "Form up! Those with swords or axes to the front and crouch down. If you've a shooting iron, stand tall behind them. When we reach them, front rank drop and the rest of you lot give them a taste of lead."

"Bugger me," the fat man from the boat said, holding his black dog back with one hand and a cutoff blunderbuss like a pistole in the other. The fact that he'd made the climb with dog and weapon made me revise my opinion of him. He was fat, aye, but there was hard muscle beneath. "We're not going into that." He gestured at the dispelling cloud that was punctuated by flashes of gunfire and the unbroken hiss of the Shambles. "Surely not?"

"You'll have one Godsdamned story to tell the next time you go whoring," I assured him. "Aim for their heads, lads 'n lasses! Only way to kill the undead is to sever their brain stem. If you see anyone holding a glowing book, shoot the book, then the person."

"Glowing book?" the man asked as the sailors filled in past him and around me.

"Ready?"

"Aren't you forgetting something?" Salina asked as she joined me, twin rotating pistoles in her fists.

"Watch out for the flying were-hawk that's about," I added. "What? Oh . . . let's kill the undead motherfuckers!"

"That," Salina agreed, trying to hide the fear that made her pistoles shake.

"Charge!"

My crew roared with me, running across the deck in an uneven line that broke briefly here and there when someone tripped over a body or slipped on the wet deck. The smoke had lifted to reveal the Shambles fighting over the last of the frigate's crew who hadn't managed to reach the safety of our ranks. Whoever was controlling them didn't realize their ambush was being ambushed until my sailors reached them. The front rank dropped to the deck and the second fired a ragged volley, then another and another, turning the Shambles into shards of bone and rags that littered the deck with their black ichor. Then the front rank stood up and closed with the remaining Shambles and it was all over save for the dying. Or the undying. Redying? The dead died again. And that was that.

Or should have been.

I saw a big burly Shambles with half its face flayed away barrel through two of the crew, a screaming, kicking cabin girl grasped tight to its chest. *Stiletto. Notch in the handle will throw off the release. Compensate. Thirty paces. Cross breeze. Adjust and put some muscle behind it. Brain stem exposed. Slightly to the right of center neck.* The undead thing lumbered toward the railing and the fat man barked a cry.

"Queenie! Defend!"

The coal-black dog came out of the smoke like a nightmare, smashing into the giant Shambles. Queenie crashed right through the dead thing's leg, taking a chunk of bone and sinew away as her momentum carried her down the slick deck. As the Shambles spun around on its remaining leg, I flipped the stiletto in my right hand to grip it by the blade. *Sin.* I leapt forward, throwing the knife, which scythed through the air and slammed into the back of the brute's skull. Shards of bone exploded everywhere as it began to fall, its good leg giving way. The giant, undead creature crashed into the railing and held there for a moment until, as if in slow motion, the railing cracked like a gunshot and the pair tumbled overboard, the cabin girl's piercing wail echoing against the hull until she hit the water.

By the time Salina's "Buc, no!" reached my ears I was already moving, racing across the deck, Sin's magic burning my legs and feet. Within a breath I was at the side and without pausing I leapt overboard. For a moment it felt like I was floating; then I plunged toward the dark sea below. A hawk's scream drew my attention to my right, where the Veneficus glided toward me on steel-tipped wings, its human eyes glaring out at me from a twisted, beaked maw. *Holy shit fuck!*

"I've got you," Sin said, his voice tight as his magic burned through my mind and time crawled to a standstill, allowing me to see, in finer detail than I wished for, the blood-soaked razor blades that were the Veneficus's feathers. The beast was nearly upon us and I didn't have much in the way of options. "You've a blade," he reminded me.

"So I do," I whispered in my mind. *Ready.* Time snapped back in a rush and I flung the stiletto in my left hand across my body. Even Sin's strength was unable to put much power behind the throw, given my awkward position, but what we didn't have in power, we made up for in accuracy. The shrike screamed as the stiletto caught it between the eyes, hilt—Godsdamn it—first, and it swept by just overhead, its cry making my ears ring. It hit the side of the ship, burying its talons in the hull, before springing away on the next gust of wind.

"Mind the sea," Sin said, and I got my arms into a semblance of a dive just as we plunged into the dark waters. I kicked my boots free and surfaced, grabbing a desperate breath as I scanned the waves around me. *There!* I saw a partially submerged form floating a dozen paces and two waves away. Striking out—Sin's magic made my entire body burn—my vision and hearing were swept away and I could feel my heart pounding in my chest as steam formed from the heat we were shedding. A deep, gnawing hunger that went to my marrow told me how close I was to the edge of that rope Sin had warned me about. *I have to save her.*

"We'll save her," Sin said, as we reached the still form. "Just remember we have to keep enough strength to get us both back to the ship."

"Don't throw away our shot, aye." I grabbed the back of the girl's dress, pulling her toward me and leaning back, spreading myself over the surface with her atop me. "You still with me, little one?" The girl coughed against my chest, spat out a mouthful of water, and coughed again, her dark mop of curls hiding her face from me. "Get it out," I told her. "Breathe."

The Veneficus's shrill wail drew my eye, and I saw the monster sailing high on the wind, undulating wings keeping it almost in place as it circled above the ship, casting about for us. I saw when it spotted us, the way its head moved to focus on us, wings tucked as it began to dive. So I was watching when lightning rent the sky, tearing a silver trail in the dark clouds, a trail that seemed to begin with the steel wings of the Veneficus and ended halfway toward the horizon. For a moment the Veneficus was silhouetted against the sky, pure silver as it was lit up by the white flame of the lightning, and then a black cinder fell from above like a stone, bits of char breaking away as it tumbled into the sea with a steamy hiss.

"Looks like fried bird for supper," I muttered, blinking, stars and the outline of the lightning-struck Veneficus superimposed on my vision. "Girl, you going to make it?"

"I'll make it," the girl said as she pulled herself half out of the water, "but you won't." I realized that the glow I was seeing wasn't from my lightning-blinded vision but from the book almost concealed within the bodice of her dress. And the voice wasn't that of a little girl, but a woman. "The Archnemesis knows of your fondness for saving girls, Sambuciña." Skeletal hands reached up from below the waves on either side of me, grasping my arms and legs. "Only you never quite manage to save them, do you?"

A dozen Shambles bobbed to the surface, two floating on dresses that were flooded with air, and the woman I'd thought a cabin girl drove a fist into my stomach, driving me below the next wave. When I came back up she was seated on the pair of floating Shambles like a raft. Six or more of the undead clawed at me through my sodden dress. I fought back, driving an elbow through the skull of the one holding my right arm, and the pressure against my back went away. Swiveling, I caught a wave straight in the face that made me swallow a lungful of salty seawater and spoiled my jab. Another Shambles leapt atop me, driving me back down into the water as another wrenched my right arm back again.

"*Sin!*"

"Die, girl," the Dead Walker spat. "We know you better than you know yourself." I wriggled in the grasp of a score of bony phalanges. "The fool who thought she'd best the Gods themselves. Think on that as you drown. Send her to the bottom, my loves," she commanded. The Shambles dragged me down, water breaking over my head despite my struggles.

Stiletto. Left hand. Side toss through her wrist. Sever the nerves. Drop the book. Then—

"Buc!" Sin's shout was loud in my mind. "You tossed the stiletto already. We're going to drown! Do something."

"Anchor her in mud and silt and stay with her for eternity." The Dead Walker's voice was loud in my ears, louder even than the uneven beat of my heart. "Do it, do it n—"

The woman's voice snapped like a cut cord and I broke free of the surface by the barest inch, drawing in a painful breath that gave my brain the oxygen it needed to piece together what the fuck was happening. The hands on my legs released and I kicked hard, shooting out of the water high enough to see a whaling spear jutting out the chest of the Dead Walker, who lay atop the rapidly deflating skirts of the undead she'd used as a flotation device. Just beyond her a boat oared through the water, a tall man in a white fur standing on the gunwale, something large and shiny cradled in his arms. A moment later a plume of smoke and steel leapt out of the object, whipping through the air toward me. The bony, rigid fingers clutched painfully tight around my right arm gave way, and a Shambles floated up beside me, a massive beveled hook thrust through its torso.

"Grab hold!" Chan Sha shouted. "Grab hold, you brave, stupid woman!"

"You can do it, Buc," Sin whispered. I reached out, managing to slump over the rope and just get my wilted, chilled hands around it.

"I got you." The faintest tingle of magic warmed my hands enough to grasp the rope, and a moment later I lurched through the water as they drew me in.

"Maybe," Bar'ren said when I reached the side and he pulled me up out of the water, "you should give me a gun next time."

"A-aye." My teeth chattered as he hauled me into the longboat. I glimpsed Chan Sha, now holding the grappling gun Bar'ren had been using, as I leaned against the sideboard, sucking air in greedily. I forced myself to wink at the man. "B-biggest damned gun you've ever s-s-seen. N-next time."

"Next time?" Chan Sha asked.

"You destroyed the plague ship?" She nodded. "And our ship?" Another nod. "Then," I said, sitting up a little straighter, conscious that the crew she'd used to pull off her part of my plan were staring at me, "we're going to sail our newly acquired Normain ship into the heart of their power. The Dead Gods' power," I clarified when she arched a brow. "Into their famed catacombs. And when we leave, not one will draw breath, living or otherwise. Suffer the dead to die."

"I can get behind that," the former pirate said after a moment. "Toss that pail of fish guts over the side," she said, speaking over her shoulder. "If any are still alive the sharks will see to them." She winked her good eye at me and stood up. "Suffer the dead to die."

30

"They'll keep," Chan Sha said, stepping into the captain's cabin and pulling the door shut on the growing revelry out on deck. "We found a man what has a way with silk and thread and ensigns that can have us a close-enough-it-won't-make-a-difference merchant Normain flag by morn. Name is Mik DeGorge. Says you're a hard one," she added, looking at me. "That you set him against those Shambles and that between you and the undead he'd face the rotting bastards every time."

"Big man with a pair of dogs?"

She nodded.

"Ah, well, don't let him fool you. Mik is stronger than he looks." I plucked at the bird carcass on my plate, the third I'd eaten since we'd settled the ship down. "More cunning, too, apparently."

"Former pirate," she agreed. She waved a hand. "Anyway, I've promoted Charli and told her off on them having more than three drams of the rum and no open fires on deck."

"What's that?" Salina asked, pointing at the leaping orange glow just visible through the slipshod windowpane of glass.

"Let them have their fun," I said, in answer to Chan Sha's curse. "Captain," I added. "Today they almost died half a score times over—some of them *did* die—and tomorrow? We all could. Come tuck into this fried duck and broken rice with gravy and fixings and let's have us a palaver."

"A palaver?" Chan Sha hesitated, then shook her braids and limped over to the table, sliding down onto the bench beside Bar'ren. The Artificer slid down until his elbows hit the wall and then made the sound a put-upon man makes. I'd noticed it's a universal gift amongst the gender. "Her name," she said, ripping a leg free from the roast bird, "I don't know how your lot stay so damned thin with this rich-as-fuck food, Arti."

"We only eat one meal," he said. "Actually we eat two, but the first is only a—"

"Merely making conversation, not looking for an oratory on Normain bowel movements." She cut him off. Salina snorted and Chan Sha flashed a grin. Taking a bite out of the drumstick, she spoke around it. "Now what do you want to discuss?"

"Compare notes, take stock, figure out the best way to make our approach."

"We drenched our old ship in Serpent's Flame and set it ablaze, nearly set our remaining lifeboat on fire in the process, and sailed her right into the aft of the plague ship," Chan Sha said, licking her fingers. "You did what your demi-Goddess arse does best." She tossed the empty bone down on the plate and sat back. "We're still breathing. What more is there to say?"

"As surprised as I am to hear me say it, you know, in another life I might have actually liked you," I told her.

"Back atcha."

"Hmm." I shook my head, feeling my wavy hair fan out behind me. I'd taken it out of the braid to let it dry after my soaking in the sea, and also because Normain fashion didn't cater to braids. By the time we reached shore, I needed to look the part of a Normain woman, fancy hoop skirts, tall heels, powders, makeup, and all. *Or will the Dead Gods be expecting that? Should we try to pass as Cordoban?* "What can you tell me about the Archnemesis?"

"Eldest of the Dead Gods' Eldests, which is saying something," Chan Sha said. Her mouth twisted. "Likely a man, but no Sin Eater has ever laid eyes on him. Potentially a myth because no Sin Eater has ever laid eyes on him, but more likely he's never left the catacombs they call an undercroft. Least not since the Goddess awoke."

"That's what Sin said," I agreed. He also said the man had access to hidden knowledge of the Dead Gods that dated back to before the Gods, Dead or New, came to our world. From back when they'd floated amongst the stars in the night sky. That had sent a chill down my spine that was still lodged in my stomach. Salina had gone silent, the Artificer couldn't stop dry-washing his hands, and Chan Sha looked ready to pick a fight with anyone, including herself. Bar'ren, sitting tall and straight, and still as a carved statue, was the only one who seemed unaffected.

"That complicates things," I said instead.

"Why?" Chan Sha asked, piling a spoonful of broken rice and gravy onto her platter. "We'll kill him same as the others."

"My thinking, too, but turns out he may have had access to all of Eld's memories."

Chan Sha's hand froze with the spoon midway to her mouth.

"There was a cabin girl today. . . ."

"And that's when you lot showed up and saved the day," I finished.

"The cabin girl, our cabin girl, made it through without a hair out of place," Salina said quietly.

"I made sure of it," Bar'ren said simply.

"At my orders," Chan Sha added, shooting him a look with her good eye.

"If the world took as much care of children as you lot, you wouldn't have me," I said, drawing their attention. I smirked. "It'd be a better place, aye?" Everyone laughed at that.

"If this Archnemesis knows everything Eld knows about you, Buc," the Artificer said when we'd all wound ourselves down, "and they have centuries of wisdom to draw upon . . . does that mean they know everything you would do?"

"We know he lived for centuries, we don't know if he is wise," Chan Sha said.

"And even though Eld *is* wise and they have his memories, he's still a man," Salina said, sipping from her wineglass. Her third glass, judging by the color in her cheeks. "Men think they know a woman's mind half the time, but the truth is they know less than half of the half they think they do."

Bar'ren snorted, the Artificer cracked a grin, and Chan Sha set her glass down, chuckling. I couldn't keep my own lips from twisting, and after grinning at one another like fools for a moment we all broke into another round of laughter. I cut off before they did, suddenly realizing I couldn't remember the last time I'd laughed this hard with friends. *Friends?* The last time must have been with Eld, surely? He'd been my only friend, then. Only friend until I thought him dead.

"What am I?" Sin asked.

"A brain fart?"

" . . . "

"You're . . . growing on me," I told him. Truth was, they were all growing on me. I wasn't ready to lean on them, didn't know if that was possible for me, but I wasn't necessarily using them either. What had I told Chan Sha we were doing? *Palavering.* I was including them in my plans and, for the first time, I saw the value in that. Having partners beyond Eld—who'd felt like an extension of myself—allowed me to be everything I'd always been, but to accomplish so much more.

I'd changed. Me, the smart-mouthed street rat who was quick with a word and even quicker with a blade. I wasn't sure I'd recognize the Buc from one year ago, let alone two. *That's my edge.* Eld's memories might actually lead the Dead Gods down the wrong path altogether. I swallowed the lump in my throat. I'd changed so much. *Lost so much. But . . .* A chill ran through me and my skin broke out in gooseflesh.

Is it enough?

31

"'Allo, Eldritch."

"Hexia." Eld nodded to the short woman behind the librarian's desk.

"What brings you down here to my dusty realm?" she asked, kicking her booted heels up on the desk as she flashed him an even-toothed grin. Her cheeks looked pinched, almost hollow; the chandelier above cast shadows across her sharp, pale features. Her short, auburn hair framed her ears in a way that some would have found attractive. Eld might have, too, if he didn't have other things on his mind—and if he couldn't see the way her eyes kept focusing and unfocusing, her fingers tapping absently at the steel book in her lap. It was dim now but would glow blue when she activated her Shambles.

"Looking for a book."

"Then you came to the right place," she said, closing her eyes. "Always knew you were a quick lad."

"A specific book."

"Even better."

"The Plague Mistress wants to learn more about the properties that interfere with the Gods' blood."

"Ah." Her eyes snapped open, almost liquid gold in the candle-light. She sat up. "Beyond silver, you mean."

"Silver does a little more than interfere," Eld said dryly. "I think the idea is to find something short of poison. For the antidote."

"My illustrious predecessor would have been able to tell you catacomb, passage, and shelf where to find it," Hexia said, her mouth curving upward in a semblance of a smile that was completely incongruous with the anger in her eyes. "Before Sicarii turned the cathedral in Colgna to a pyre."

"I've been given to believe," Eld said quietly, glancing at the bound notepad in his hands so she wouldn't see the lie in his eyes, "that she's been put on a pyre herself now."

"Really?" she drawled, leaning forward. "Cordoban, wasn't it?" She smirked. "Don't say, Eldritch, you don't have to . . . it's writ large across your features." She leaned back and put a lacquered fingernail to her lips. "Hmm, I really can't help you, although I could send one of my Shambles with you to carry a lantern." She slid her finger fully into her mouth and began sucking on it. "And another," she said, speaking around her digit, "to carry any books you find. They require exercise, my lovelies, or else their tendons dry up like old cork and break. Aye, two for you and one more, to keep me company." She popped her finger out of her mouth with a loud smack.

"I appreciate the offer, but I think I'm better off on my own."

"Alone?" Hexia shook her bangs. "You Veneficus are a strange lot. I'm tired of being alone. When I'm with the dead and they're with me it's like being surrounded by family, only this family will never betray you, never question you. I don't know how you stand it, being alone."

"We are a strange lot," Eld agreed, adjusting his dark robes so she couldn't see how his shoulders had stiffened at her antics. The rest of his brothers and sisters seemed not to notice that all the Dead Walkers were bent, mentally, or that the Veneficus often fondled vials of blood, itching for the ecstasy and pain of Transfiguration. Glancing down, Eld realized his fist was clenched around a vial. *Gods, I'm becoming one of them.* "I, uh, should probably get looking for that book," he said, tucking the vial back into its sheath on his belt.

"Likely," Hexia agreed, back to sucking on her finger while staring at her dark book as if willing it to light up and connect her with the undead. "Say, Eldritch!"

"Aye?" He paused in the doorway that led to the library catacombs, the dry air sucking at the moisture in his eyes, nose, and mouth.

"Try row eleven, toward the end of the stack. Not sure why, but that's sticking in my head. Books on poisons and the like. Make sure you take a lantern with you . . . don't want to be in the middle of a stack if the candles blow out. Easy to get turned about and never find your way back." Hexia grinned. "Unless you want to join my lovelies? Oh, the things I'd have you do to me, Eld. The things I'd do to you."

He stood there for a long moment, not sure what to say. In the end, he didn't have to say anything; Hexia had closed her eyes and was swaying slightly, to music only she could hear. *Bloody weird.* Eld marched down the passage to the sharp left turn that opened up into a long hall with dozens of rows of shelves, some to the left, others to the right. Lanterns hung from poles at every row and candles ensconced in skulls jutted out from the ceiling. The room looked as if carved from wood, but it was actually carved from the bodies of the Dead Gods.

Their anatomy didn't true up with his own, so it was difficult to say exactly what this had been before, but with the marrow gone it'd been turned into essentially a cavernous library. Here and there a cadaverous skull grinned light at him from where it was carved into the catacomb's ivory-colored bone walls. He grabbed one of the lanterns, twisted the wick up, and bent to light it from one of the skulls. Marching on, he soon found the row with the strange symbol that meant eleven in whatever language the Dead Gods had used to communicate when they were still alive. Now their language was as dead as they were.

Books lined the stone shelves that had been carved into the calcified bone, four shelves from floor to ceiling on either side.

Pausing to pluck one out at random, Eld realized everything he'd just done. Walked through what was essentially a crypt. Used a corpse's skull to light his lantern. Reading. And through it all he'd felt . . . *comfortable.*

"Bloody weird," he repeated. "And I'm becoming one of them."

He slid the book—an arcane tome on the flammable properties of different tree bark—back onto the shelf and kept walking. The Plague Mistress had tasked him with finding more promising antidotes than the others had come up with so far. It'd been a tertiary task, almost an afterthought. His primary mission was putting together the plan by which they'd disseminate the plague through the world. The secondary missions were, of late, kill missions. They'd taken out half a dozen Sin Eaters, three falling to his hand—claws, really—alone. A tertiary task, but he hadn't been lying to Hexia . . . he needed some time alone. Some time away from the others.

Else they'll see my heart's not in it and wonder why. Eld picked up another book and thumbed through the pages, coughing at the dust he stirred up. Sometimes he worried his heart was too much in it, and yet . . . *And yet I've become a traitor to everyone and everything I've known since waking.* He knew he should have died and the Dead Gods had saved him from that. *Not for altruistic reasons, that's for certain.* Still, there was something seductive about the Dead Gods. He wasn't sure if it came from some chemical within the blood he and his fellow priests consumed, if it was the indoctrination they'd all undergone or the camaraderie of living a life no regular person could understand, or some fucked combination of it all, but sometimes he caught himself doubting his memories of Buc. Had he really lived a life, before?

She was still out there, still carrying the torch and pushing for her lofty, crazy-arsed aspirations. She'd kept on even after she thought him dead. *Of course she did.* Buc was indefatigable . . . he loved that about her. *Love.* That's why he was doing this. Pretending to help the Plague Mistress while undermining her at every

234 • Ryan Van Loan

turn, sending false orders, obfuscating reports, painting a portrait that didn't exist. Love was most of it, but also he knew, even when he doubted, deep down, he *knew* that the Eld of old would have fought the Dead Gods and the Sin Eaters with his dying breath. *Blood and bone, I did fight them with my dying breath.*

"I just wish I felt closer to that Eld," he muttered as he put the book back. The stimulant effects on the male erection caused by a certain blend of kan might be interesting, but it wasn't going to provide an antidote to the plague. The others working with him were more focused on increasing the potency of the plague, figuring there'd be time enough later to reverse engineer a cure. He intended to prevent a drop of the contagion from making it beyond the walls of their undercroft, but if he failed—and the odds were that they'd act before Buc reached them—the world would need that antidote. Not the primary reason he'd come down here, and it hurt to know it wasn't even a secondary one, but still, he was trying. *Despite how much I've changed. Maybe because of it?* He was—

A voice carried across the stacks. An all-too-familiar voice. The Plague Mistress. *Perhaps Ismiralda will know if I'm in the right stack.* Eld followed the sounds to where the row broke off in a jagged whirl that was permanently stained with a shade of green so bright it nearly glowed in the darkness. A wound, perhaps the mortal one that had felled this God, now used as a passageway. The Plague Mistress was walking toward him along the wound, green shadows making her black-as-night skin glow as brightly as her white braids did.

"I owned that you were right," she said to the towering, wraith-thin figure that marched beside her, slightly hunched over so that their head wouldn't brush the ceiling. Beyond them a doorway at the end of the passage melted before Eld's eyes, seemingly disappearing into the void. "You usually are. Irritating that way."

"Comes with the millennium, Daughter."

The other's laugh set Eld's flesh to crawling and he ducked

back into the stacks, heart suddenly loud in his ears. He knew who the other figure was. *What* it was. It had been present the day Eld was remade, in a ceremony at what was believed to be the heart of the Dead Gods, the Wellspring. For a moment he was back there, surrounded by the Eldests whose nails cut into his flesh as they half supported, half dragged him into the pool suffused with blood darker than midnight. Coming into contact with that much blood had nearly broken his mind and sent him reeling into the wilds of insanity, but a voice had found him and guided him back, a voice that had taken rich pleasure in his pain. That voice belonged to the man who drew steadily closer to him now. *The Archnemesis.*

"The lad will be the youngest Eldest in a generation," the Plague Mistress said.

"And that little mind witch's hold on him?" the man asked, his tone as sharp as the sound of bone snapping between teeth.

They're talking about me. Eld froze. He blew out his lantern and crouched down, trying to sink into the floor. *Gods, send them down a different row.*

"Considerable," the woman answered him, the deference in her tone enough to make Eld's head spin. The Plague Mistress bowed to no one . . . save the Archnemesis. "We unwound it by degrees, of course, as you suggested."

"Her magic is insidious . . . I was right to take an especial interest in his case."

"You were." They paused, only a few steps away. "Slowing his healing, letting him live with the pain of being reborn without being allowed to complete the ceremony, forced him to depend upon us."

"Even mind magic has its limits," the Archnemesis said, his strange, lilting voice almost purring. "Eld may have clung to an ideal, but a memory won't succor pain. Only blood will do that. He's ours, then?"

"He's been ours since the day you turned him," she said. "Blood and bone. Fortunate, too. Without the lad, we might have lost the entire mission." She took a breath. "*She* marshals her troops. Normain and the Empire are at war and if that's not her direct hand, I'm a Shambles. All too soon she'll come at us head-on, and despite the increase in recruitment, we've not the numbers to meet her. This must needs succeed and—"

"Patience," the Archnemesis whispered, his voice the sound of bone grinding against bone. "Time has always been on our side, Daughter. The Enemy thinks herself clever, but once discerned, her machinations are little more than straight lines. This *Buc*, a potential thorn, lies dead. And war has ever been a gift to us, allowing us unfettered access to both new recruits and Shambles. Normain, at least, will come to us for healing, and once our plague is unleashed, the Empire will have to lean upon us as well. Patience, dear one, will see us out. Isn't that what we were just shown in the Archive?"

"You are wise," the Plague Mistress said after a moment.

"I am old," the Archnemesis said, "almost old enough to have seen our Gods when they smote this world with their mighty fists. Old enough to remember discovering the Archive and the truth about our eternal war. For the first time since She awoke, we have the means within our grasp to end it."

"End it we shall," Ismiralda said, the heat bright in her voice.

"We shall," he agreed. "Come, let us return or the council will begin without us."

"Aye, and that lout will be calling for marching on the Empire."

"That 'lout,'" the old man said as they passed Eld by without noticing him, moving toward the entrance he had used just minutes ago, "is your brother. Veneficus always wish to pit their strength and power against their foes. He's a prisoner to his gifts, Daughter. Much the same way . . ."

Eld stood up after a moment, leaning against the shelves and hoping he wouldn't fall and bring them running back. Ismiralda had taken an obvious interest in him—without that, he wouldn't have been given the position he was in—and of course they'd searched his memories and knew of Buc. *Our relationship.* Somehow he'd never realized just how interested in him the Plague Mistress and the rest of the Elders were, and now he felt a fool. *Buc would have seen this straight off, been on her guard.*

"Perhaps I'm not so cunning, Dead Gods' blood or no, as I thought," he murmured, straightening up, glad to find that his legs would bear his weight. What now? His lantern was cold and dark. If he walked straight back the way he'd come, he should be able to find his way out. He fancied that when he squinted, he could just make out a flicker of candlelight far off, but . . . *Last thing I need is to get turned around and lost down here. Hexia would love that.* Or run into the Archnemesis and the Plague Mistress. He glanced at the green-lit passage. *There must be candles along here at some point.*

An idea popped into his mind. *The Archive.* Eld made for the wall where he'd seen the door disappear. *You'd be proud of me, Buc.* If his hunch paid off. If it didn't kill him in the process. If the other two didn't return. A lot of ifs. *Is this cunning?* It felt half like stupidity. Eld thought of what Buc would say to that, and chuckled, the cavern echoing with his laughter. Eld had been wrong, the Archnemesis had shown him that. Buc wasn't a memory, she was as real as he was, separated by hundreds of leagues, aye, but he knew her better than he knew himself these days. He didn't need cunning, he just needed to answer a simple question.

What would Buc do?

32

Eld's mind worked furiously as he approached the wall, its bone-white exterior turned nigh incandescent from the bright-green stain covering every surface save that wall itself. *What pass codes have I been taught? Puzzles? Catechisms?* Would it only open for the Archnemesis? The man had said he was the one who discovered it. *The Archive.* A hidden library. It was sure to be guarded closely and might require more time to break in than he had now, but he could make a start at least. *Baol. Gramorr. Mmemnon. Talshur. Vos.* Each of the divine had their own prayers, but would it require a piece of each or—

He reached the end of the wound, the harder calcification of the bone making it clear that whatever had carved an almost spherical hole through the God had found it impossible to cut past one of the foundational bones of its malformed body. Eld hesitated, then reached out to touch the wall, preparing himself for whatever test he would face. The surface was surprisingly smooth to the touch but he felt it for only an instant as the wall shivered and . . .

An opening appeared as the bone shimmered and disappeared, revealing a black hole in the white carapace.

"That's it?" Eld cursed. "It just opens?" He was still kicking himself for being a fool when he realized that the darkness was absolute and he had no lantern. *Damn.*

"Why isn't the green stain casting light beyond the door?" He ran a finger along the opening's edge, as smooth as glass, and his finger disappeared—the tip, anyway. Eld swore and pulled his hand back. His forefinger was intact. "What the fuck is this?"

For several moments, he stood there, staring at the black hole and willing it to reveal its secrets. When nothing happened he scuffed his boot, debating within his mind about whether he should abandon this here and now while he was still in one piece or risk the darkness before him. *What would Buc do?* "Which Buc?" he asked himself aloud. "The Buc I first met would run . . . the Buc I last left would stay." *Would the old Buc have really run, though, with these stakes? Or would she have called this a worthy toss?* Eld glanced at his finger, which didn't appear worse for wear. "What is it the knee-breakers from the Tip say? In for a copper, in for a lira?"

Eld took a deep breath, felt something break in his fist, and hissed at the sudden pain of the glass vial—crushed now in his grip—slicing through the palm of his hand. He'd been holding it without realizing. Again. Pins and needles and a burning sensation rushed through his hand and arm, and then flooded his body, giving him gooseflesh and an erection that strained his underclothes. *G-G-Gods.* With their blood suffusing his mind, he stepped forward without even realizing it.

Eld went from blinding darkness to bright light in a single pace, blinking against the harsh beams that flooded him from a dozen glowing orbs embedded around the doorway—or was that a continuation of the wound? The chamber was nearly spherical, its smooth, featureless walls covered in swirls of vermillion and grey in a thousand shades and gradients and dotted with bright-green stains. Other than the lights, the only thing in the room was a curved space in the bedrock (bone rock?) that looked something like a daybed, except for the sharp angle at the top. A person would have to lie upon their stomach to use it. Eld walked in a slow circle, his head buzzing from the Dead Gods' blood, which was intended to be ingested, not absorbed through a dozen cuts in his palm. After a few times around he realized he'd have to lie down on the damned thing.

Easier said than done with a raging erection that wouldn't go away, but Eld managed to seat himself—carefully—on the triangular, jutting bit of rock, his lower half angling downward, the rounded point of the rock resting in the pit of his stomach, touching his belly button, the rest of his torso angled down the other side. *Now what?* Eld drew in a deep breath, conscious of the way the rock pressed against his stomach, and waited.

And waited.

Nothing? Eld growled and slapped the rock with both hands. When the bloody one touched the stone something shot him in the gut so hard he lost his breath. *NO!* Something was *inside* him, going through his stomach, into his core, wriggling around. He couldn't move, but he could feel *it* moving. He fought to open his lips but they wouldn't open and his tongue wouldn't respond. The high-pitch ringing in his ears resolved into a moan building in the back of his throat. The grey rock before his eyes transformed into a thick, voluminous bar of white light that swallowed everything.

Eld floated in light.

Weightless, bodiless, pure thought and emotion twisted together in a knot. Dark spots slipped past, took form, made strange patterns. *Words.* The language of the Dead Gods. One caught his attention as it passed; he would have hissed at the sight had he lungs or lips. The word paused, then rushed toward him, filling his vision with glyphs made of dried blood that spelled one of the few words he knew of the Dead Gods: "Enemy."

The glyph swept over him and the knot that was Eld joined with it, suddenly surrounded by a dark chasm with pinpricks of light dotting the circular horizon that seemed to orbit about him. He glanced at one of the pinpricks and it expanded, revealing a miasma of shiny silver circles and fluid grey blocks that constantly changed shape. Jets of green and red shot from the rapidly expanding light, and when a dot or block was touched by a plume of color, it exploded in a fire that was instantly snuffed out. Eld shook himself somehow and the dot flew away, rejoining the others in the inky soup surrounding him. Another dot—a swirling marble of green, blue, and wispy white—grew steadily larger in his field of view. More green and red jets appeared, followed by fire. More spheres, in more colors, burning. Worlds with strange architecture that bent in angles and dimensions Eld had never seen before. All ended in flame and ash and . . . sadness?

Then, a place he recognized. The island of Servenza, blue seas, the mainland, Colgna, and farther south, the thick, green forests that gave way to cultivated lands and . . . Normain. Eld was so happy to see something he understood that he twisted about, losing sight of those familiar lands, looking up, into the sky. His sky. Where another dot floated, sliding across the blue, into the purple bruise of evening, into the full night sky of velvet black, into the golds and pinks of dawn, on and on. Eld followed the dot around the world; it touched neither land nor sea, neither rose nor sank from its place in the sky. The seasons changed; he saw the Ring of Fire blossom in a crimson rose, the petals turning to black ash, the swirling scraps of cloud thickening, forming new patterns.

The dot slowed.

It was a silver glob or maybe a globe of light, rotating even as it also spun over the land and sea below. The sphere gave birth to a dozen lines of razor-thin light, then a score, a hundred, thousands. Thousands upon thousands. Half a hundred of these razor blades coalesced into a telescope mounted in the middle of the air, seemingly floating below the clouds but above a domed mountaintop.

What?

Before the thought was fully formed Eld felt the knot that was himself thrown physically out of the world he'd been a part of just a breath before. It shrank from view, black night swallowing all. He blinked—or would have blinked if he had any physical form—and a fully realized map in vibrant colors and textures appeared before him. The Shattered Coast, fluttering on the undulating waves of the map to the west; Servenza, with her interconnected isles, in the center; and the mainland's long-running coast to the east. Just above Normain proper, in the hinterlands that ran in fingers, outstretched as if to grasp Colgna beyond the Burning Lands, a telescope was embossed on the map. Save it wasn't embossed, but a three-dimensional, moving thing, turning slowly, pointed at a slowly rotating light that moved infinitesimally overhead.

The stars shone beyond the rotating light, the Keystone bright in the tail of the Dragon, the Lances of the Divine just beyond. *Fall day*. The map shimmered, and now the sliver of light was far from the Keystone, but still near Normain, just beyond the sea that fed into the swamps that eventually drained into those same hinterlands. *Spring's birth*. The telescope's aperture suddenly shot out a beam of light that connected with the rotating dot, forming a . . . rope.

"Gods' breath." He gasped the words aloud and was abruptly back in the empty, round room, flat on his back beside the strange curved rock, chest heaving as he fought to catch his breath. It took him several moments, maybe many moments, for his lungs to fill properly. A few breaths later his head began to pound and he wiped at the tears filling his eyes, flinching when his fingers came back bloody. Rolling over onto his stomach, he felt a stab of pain and cried out. Probing gingerly he found a thimble of blood in his belly button, half-dried and cracked. None of that mattered. None of it. Because Eld had realized what the Dead Gods had shown him.

The Enemy. In the sky overhead, safe from mortal threat save for twice a year, when the telescope created a rope that allowed her to be reached. To be fought. To be killed. Eld struggled to his knees, leaning against the stone, taking care not to touch it with his hands. "I—I—I—" He drew in a shuddering breath, his mouth working at this foreign sound in his mouth. "I—I," he tried again. "I f-f-found you," he gasped. "Found your sanctuary. Buc and I will—"

Eld cut himself off, didn't dare say anything more aloud, not this close to the Dead Gods. He could practically feel their hatred emanating from the bones around him, from the rock he'd been sucked into. To say nothing of the Enemy and what she might be able to discern. A scrap of a memory caught in his mind, something Buc had told him. The Ghost Captain had said Ciris was untouchable save by Sin Eaters. *They must have a way of using that telescope to reach Her. To climb that . . . rope?* Even understanding the smallest part of *what* She was froze the marrow in his bones. First they'd need a Sin Eater. *Buc. Where are you?* Once they were reunited, once this plague was wiped away and the Dead Gods with it, there'd only be one target left to fill their sights. One that'd been looking down, watching this entire time.

The Enemy.

Ciris.

33

I walked the streets of Normain with a parasol over my shoulder to protect me from the sun. One hand held the handle of the cream-colored umbrella; the other rested on the little purse that hung from the thin belt of black leather embossed with gems—some real and others fake—at my waist. Everyone gave me a wide berth. Perhaps because they could see the handle was actually a hilt—a version of a cane sword—or perhaps because the damned hoop skirt I wore made coming within two paces of me a dangerous gamble for either of us. Even with Sin's magic, I'd nearly fallen when the cocoa brown–trimmed hem—meant to hide the dirt—caught on the uneven cobblestones despite the flat-heeled boots I wore. The capital of the country—and its namesake—was the oldest city in the world and its age showed in its architecture . . . and in its roads.

The port behind me was a muted hive of activity, much of it overseen by a bevy of commissioners in uniforms quite similar to the blues of the Constabulary back in Servenza. This lot were a grim bunch, the men twirling thick batons in one hand, often using the other to write instructions on the desks strapped to the backs of the apprentices who followed along after them. The women were worse, unholy terrors who could triple a dockage fee for the wrong look or misstep of protocol. As I put the port behind me at the next bend, the crowds disappeared and Mercantile Row lay before me in staid sobriety with only a few passersby.

With summer turning into fall I'd not have needed the parasol's protection, save Normain was a discreet culture, which meant hiding everyone in piles of thick fabric. A woman stepped out from the bankers' guild hall I'd just passed and pulled her short jacket tighter about her when she saw my outfit, which was cut too close for her liking. I took a deep breath in, the two—two!— corsets I was wearing making my chest more obvious than it otherwise would have been and her eyes widened. *Milksops.* The outer corset I wore was the latest fashion and not really a corset so much as a tighter top with close-cropped sleeves that would have been considered outlandishly prim in Servenza but was nigh scandalous here. I glanced back and saw the older woman practically running the other way, her grey-streaked locks flowing behind her as she tried to flee from the impropriety of my dress and behavior. Despite her haste, I noted how she flowed almost seamlessly from one patch of shade to another, not allowing the sun to touch her. I stepped into the shade of the building as well, but I'd more pressing matters than antagonizing the locals.

Perhaps because of the ridiculous amount of clothing they wore, I'd noticed most folks kept indoors until midafternoon, and the real masses wouldn't appear until nearly sundown, when lamps and lights would turn the night into a carnival-like atmosphere as the inland section of the city turned out to do their business of the day, or night, as it were. *A Servenzan feast day . . . if Servenzans were all prudes.* The architecture of the city down by the port echoed what I'd been told I'd find in the Old City—the section built around the actual skeletons of some of the Dead Gods. The streets were narrow and winding, buildings were made of dark brick and stone piled up several stories on either side, and there was rarely a bit of flat ground to be found as the road undulated up, then dipped down before rising again as it followed the curvature of hills buried centuries prior by the city's foundations. *Or perhaps it's the Dead Gods below?*

"This whole peninsula is likely built upon their backs," Sin said. "You're going to want to leg it."

"In these skirts?"

"If she's after what we suspect . . ." Sin trailed off, and I moved faster, imitating the shuffling step I'd seen other women use to keep their boots or skirts from catching on the cobblestone when moving at more than a slow saunter. Not that Normain women sauntered. "When they fell from the sky they broke the land in scores of places," Sin continued after a moment, "and likely created the river the Normain widened over the centuries to make this a true island."

"You could be right." A turn in the road showed a view of the cliffs flanking the port below. The Fingers were aptly named, bone-white joints jutting out from the cliffs as if their tips were shorn off by a gigantic blade for reaching too high. A trio of lighthouses decorated their bony lengths, fires beginning to bloom in their tops as the sun slipped lower in the sky. "It would explain why this place is so broken." It wasn't even the chipped cobblestone so much as how, as we'd navigated the coastline up from the south so as to make it appear we sailed from Cordoban and not Southeast Island, I saw that the land itself was scarred, broken, and furrowed with pockmarks that had never quite healed . . . like a pugilist's face after losing in the final round. Almost like the Dead Gods raged and cast about with their waning strength, futilely clinging to life as the land and sea swallowed them whole.

"She's taken the right branch," Sin said.

"So we didn't lose her."

"No. Right . . . there."

I followed his mental direction to see a woman—her face a shade blacker than my own and looking darker still against her lavender dress, her black locks tied up in gossamer netting that matched her billowing skirts—passing behind a lamppost. *Toward the Old City.* Also where the old money lived, which made sense, given the style of her dress and the ridiculous amount of thread o' gold that held her skirts together.

My own skirts were fine enough that I attracted no special attention as I headed along the road that widened and led to the

Old City. Yesterday, dressed much the same, I'd ventured deep into the new city, which was still as old as Servenza and home to dockworkers, lower artisans, and common folk. There, I'd drawn too much notice.

A platoon of dragoons in crimson-and-gold uniforms marched past me, their golden spurs jingling a background tune to their crisp marching, the ridiculous plumes they wore in their hats making them look like children dressed in adults' uniforms. As I hid my smile behind my gloved hand, the commander at the front, her bicorne's plumes of gold and blue nodding in step, glanced at me, and I felt the weight of her gaze. I didn't have to fight hard to stop smiling, then. Behind her I could see the front rank, eyes front but constantly searching, even here in the heart of their power. *Veterans, these.* They looked like a ship out of water now, but put them on a battlefield atop horses, armed with pistole, saber, lance, and sawed-off musket, and they'd not be so funny then.

As the last of them went by, I looked ahead and saw the woman in the lavender dress glance over her shoulder before disappearing beneath the archway that led into the Old City proper. I recognized her expression—she was moving in for the kill. Biting back a curse, I rushed forward, earning more than a few pointed looks from the people I brushed past, mostly men and women walking with their children. Most were likely the husbands and wives of the soldiers garrisoned within the tenements on the upper side of the city. The art of following someone without them knowing required hanging back farther than most reckoned, but not so far back one lost them entirely. As I almost had. *I need to focus.* When I reached the archway I realized why the woman had seemed to disappear as if by magic: there were steps cut into the side of the hill, steps the same color as those I'd seen in the Dead Gods' cathedrals: the color of bone. The Old City wasn't built upon a hillside, nor was it built upon the bones of the Dead Gods. The Old City was built *within* the skeleton of the Dead Gods. One, at least, and perhaps as many as three, according to the book I'd read on Normain architecture. *463*. Filipa Roun was a famed builder herself, responsible for Frilituo's newest cathedral, and I'd a feeling if the Dead Gods could get her out of retirement, they'd have her rebuild the cathedrals in Colgna and Cordoban. If I had it my way, they'd be a sight too busy to worry about that sort of frippery.

I collapsed the parasol as I moved deeper into the Old City, the woman I was trailing always just about to turn a corner or vanish into a dip in the street. She no longer seemed worried about her back trail, which allowed me to draw closer, no longer playing cat to her mouse. *Full lioness.* As I walked, the streets began to fill with a different sort of person: men in top hats and coats, buttoned to the throat, that clung to their waists and then swept out like fans thanks to thick wires hidden in the fabric; women in skirts that were double and, in one case, triple the width of my own. There was no need for shade here as the sunlight was broken up by the very bones of one of the Gods, their curves arching several stories overhead. Inns, taverns, and merchant shops were built on the street level, and winding staircases carved into the ribs led up to what were once watchtowers and forts, now palaces and schools of learning.

All of this would have felt as austere and morbid as a funeral, save for the decorative plant life that grew everywhere. Creepers, moss, flowers, and other greenery grew down over the sides of the buildings, forming tapestries of pink and purple, orange and red, yellow and white. Lengthy vines dangled from the rib bones above, almost as if they were trying to reach the street below. I took it all in, trying to get a feel for the ebb and flow around me, the pulse of this strange city, unlike any other I'd been to before. Cordoban had been different, aye, but it had felt like a sister to Servenza. The two cities weren't remotely the same, but in a sense, they rhymed. Normain had a meter all of its own, and one that made me feel completely outside of my element. I wasn't sure if I hated it or loved it, but it was a new page for me to read, and the open page is one temptation I've never been able to resist.

"C'mon, Sin," I whispered in my mind. "Past time we caught her up."

Anyone who tells you that skirts were designed by women is a liar. Wide skirts, leastwise. That they were designed by a man intent on slowing us down is the only damned explanation I'll pay coin for. I resorted to gathering my layers—no easy feat with a wired hoop skirt—and scurrying to halve the distance between us. Even with Sin's help, it was hard to get closer; the woman was moving faster now, too, her head no longer on a swivel but focused with a predator's gaze on something ahead of her. *Or someone.* We turned down a side alley that ran between the joints of the dead deity, angling almost back the way we'd come before doubling back and emerging at a crossroads that formed one of the main thoroughfares. Sin flashed a map of the city in my mind so that it was almost as if I stood upon the image. To the left the streets ran ever upward, along the spine of the fallen God, to the series of palaces known as the Aperator, which housed the royalty of Normain. Until recently their line of succession had run to over one hundred, but the Empress's assassins had whittled them down to double digits.

To the right, where my target was walking, a bifurcation in the skeleton lead to a thin but broad-boned ramp carved in fluted decorations. The ramp led up to another set of bones that fanned out over the oldest sections of the Old City, while the thicker bone it left below looked almost like a tube: carved steps led down into the bowels of the city, to the sanctum of the Dead Gods and their mages. Several dozen spans of open air separated the two massive thoroughfares, and the archway should have collapsed under the weight of the buildings and foot traffic, but somehow did not. Architects had been trying to reproduce the arch for centuries and all had failed. Roun came the closest in Frilituo's cathedral entrance, but even she had been forced to include supports.

The woman surprised me when she took the fluted walkway up toward the inns and manors. *Did she miss the turn or did I?* I followed, putting a pair of older gentlemen—whose conversation about the brothel they'd just come from indicated they were anything but gentlemen—between us. The walkway's width allowed for a fairly wide street even with buildings on either side, though these buildings were mandated by law not to rise more than two stories . . . the Normain didn't want to press the magic of the ancient bones too far. It was even wide enough to have a few alleyways, and it was the second of these that the woman turned into. *Ah, I missed it.* I left the two old perverts and slid into the dimly lit alley. She was already turning into the back street that ran parallel with the main road, along the edge of the curtain wall that kept drunks from falling to their deaths. Despite the lack of light, or perhaps because of it, I saw something glint in her hand.

Damn. I was farther back than I should have been. *Fucking Normain architecture has to be so interesting.* I wouldn't reach the corner, unless . . . time stilled. Sin's magic burned bright in me and everything came to a halt save for the long, languid sound of my heart just beginning its beat. *Drop parasol. Two clasps, one button above. Catch parasol down alongside leg. Cross draw at last moment. Throw sheath into face. Follow through. As you please, Sin.* Time snapped back with a rush of sight and sound and the beat of my heart.

I let go of the parasol handle. Before it had barely begun to roll off my shoulder, my hands were behind me, fingers manipulating the skirt fasteners hidden by my faux corset top. The button came off in my hands—*whoops*—and the hoop skirt fell away from me, revealing my dark brown trousers beneath. I caught the parasol by the hilt, a hand's breadth above the stone walk, and was off in a flash of legs, finally free of that gaol dress. I made it to the corner, ears buzzing, legs burning, in another beat of my heart, and saw the other woman, also moving preternaturally fast, heading for the top-hatted figure I'd meant to follow until I realized they already had a hanger-on.

Not going to make it. I drew the sword from the parasol sheath, still running full out, my boots smacking off the cobblestone like raindrops. *On the upswing.* Both feet left the ground and I hurled the arm's length of blade end over end.

Straight at the woman's back.

She spun at the last moment, her skirts a flash of color, the bright something in her fist resolving into a cinquedea, a short Servenzan blade five fingers wide. She parried my thin blade, grimacing in pain when the force of my throw ripped her dagger from her hand moments before I piled into her, leading with my shoulder. I felt the breath go out of her as we went airborne; a dry, soundless cry left her lips when we landed, me atop her. For a moment we were frozen, staring into each other's eyes, and I could see her surprise beginning to give way to anger.

Gravity took over and we went arse over each other, slapping off the pavement once, twice, thrice. I ended up on top again and dug my boots into the ground, throwing an awkward punch at her jaw. She caught it in one hand and I had to grasp my wrist with my other hand to keep her from breaking it. I felt more than saw her other fist hooking at my head and dropped against the woman's chest to avoid it before popping back up and cracking her in the mouth with my free hand. Her lip split and she spat blood at my eyes, intending to blind me. I blinked and that was all the respite she needed.

For the space of a dozen breaths we went at it hammer and tongs. Jab blocked by inside forearm. Overhand hammer strike taken on a turned shoulder. Jab. Jab. Cross. Hook. Neither of us managed to land more than the odd blow; otherwise it was all a lot of deflection and body manipulation. The woman's face grew ashen from having the wind knocked from her lungs and then having to fight for her life; lack of breath drove her to desperation. Her open hand, fingers outstretched and stiff, lanced toward my eyes—I jerked my head back almost too late and pain blossomed just below my cheekbone, where her fingernails had caught me. *Sin. Now.* Ignoring the cut that wept blood, I caught her hand in both of mine. My body was on fire from the fight, from the pain of being punched and cut and from Sin's magic, but at my command liquid fire poured through me and I moved in a blur even my own Sin-enhanced vision couldn't follow, trusting more to feel than anything else as I pulled the woman's arm tight against my body, then leapt up and twisted. I fell backward and perpendicular to her so my feet were on the ground on the other side of her chest, her arm caught between my legs. I slammed off the pavement, yelped, and used my momentum to put a hard arch in my back.

The woman's arm snapped and she yelped, too. Louder. A lot louder.

I let go of her arm, rolled off of her, and came to my feet, right arm outstretched, pointing at her.

"How?" she gasped, holding her ruined arm. "You're too fast to be a sister!" Her eyes rolled in the back of her head. "Her name, it's *you!*"

"Aye," I agreed, flicking my wrist so that the dart gun attached there fired in a puff of air. "I'd tell you to send my regards," I added, as she fell back against the stones, the dart's feathers just visible against her skull, "save that's not practicable. Hope you understand," I told her corpse. "Would ruin Ciris thinking me dead and all that."

The man the Sin Eater had been about to murder had come running back at the sounds of the scuffle. The fight had been so fast that he was just now reaching us, stumbling to a halt, arms windmilling in his soft, grey jacket as he caught himself. His cream-colored top hat rolled off blond locks that fanned out down past his broad shoulders. I saw his eyes widen, his lips move soundlessly, and couldn't keep the smile from my lips if I'd wanted to. Only, I'd never wanted anything less.

"Hallo, Eld."

34

"Buc?" Eld's oft-broken nose crinkled and his sapphire-blue eyes widened. "Buc!"

He took a step toward me and I leapt over the corpse into his waiting arms. Buc Alhurra, throwing herself at a man like some fool girl out of a copper romance novel! It was delicious. When he caught me, my momentum turned him, and for a moment we twirled around together as we'd done so many months before, dancing at the Doga's Midwinter ball back in Servenza. His grey Normain jacket was rough against my face; the cut below my eye protested loudly, and my body was still burning from Sin's magic, but none of it mattered. We came to a breathless halt, Eld laughing and crying and me giggling against his chest. For a long moment, time stilled and I breathed him in. *Eld.* Pure and simple, and the aching chasm in my chest suffused with something I'd thought dead. I didn't need Sin's magic to hold that moment. When you find someone who fills that void within you, for whom you would sacrifice anything, knowing they would do the same, because they already have . . . well, that's a magic all of its own.

"Gods, I've missed you," he said, his voice thick with tears, speaking against the part in my hair, his lips pressing against my scalp. "For so long, I thought I'd dreamed you, Buc. You've no idea."

"I think I do," I said, remembering the message from Eld that Sin had replayed in my mind a hundred times over. "A little, anyways." I looked up into his blue eyes, as vast and clear as the seas,

254 • Ryan Van Loan

and couldn't keep the smile from my lips. "It's you," I whispered. "Really you."

He nodded.

"At last."

"At last," he repeated.

"Uh, Buc," Sin whispered. "No wish to intrude, but the Sin Eater that was stalking Eld a moment ago? The one you just killed?"

"Oh," I said, letting go of Eld.

"Oh?" he asked, brow wrinkling.

"Can I borrow your sword?" I asked.

"M-my sword?" Eld glanced around at the empty alley. "Is that a euphemism or—"

"Euph— Fuck's sake, Eld." I snorted. "Your sword. The steel one at your side, not the one twixt your legs."

His cheeks burned red and he stepped back, pulling the slightly curved, double-edged, basket-hilted sword free. Reversing the hilt, he offered it to me.

"Honestly," I muttered, taking it from him. "Men."

"I—I didn't mean . . . It was just, after we were holding each other. Godsdamn it," he said, swiping at a few strands of his blond hair that had fallen over his face. "Why do you need a sword?"

"Because, my sword shattered when she parried it"—I gestured toward the shards sprinkled about the alley—"and the last Sin Eater I met called Ciris to them, and fighting her was an experience I've no wish to repeat." I circled around her body, glancing up at him. "I missed that," I added.

"You met Ciris?" His voice broke. "Wait . . . missed what?"

"You being all polite and blushing like an innocent maid," I said, winking. Then I brought the blade down hard, both hands on the hilt and Sin's magic suffusing my arms. The woman's body jerked, a glut of blood gushing from her torso as her head rolled free, ashy features frozen in surprise. No one ever thinks they're going to die, especially a mage. Likely there was a lesson in there for me, but I'd never fancied myself immortal. "Can't be too careful," I explained. "Sin Eaters have regenerative powers beyond the ken, and I say that as someone with said powers."

"Aye," Eld said dryly. "So I've learned."

I cleaned the sword on the dead woman's dress, then tossed it back to Eld without a thought—and my Sin-enhanced throw sent the long blade hurtling past him. Eld caught it by the hilt, whipping the blade up and around and driving it into the sheath at his side in a motion so fluid that for a moment I didn't follow it. *Damn.* "Any thoughts on what to do with the body?"

"I'll have it taken care of," Eld said. He picked up his top hat, brushing it off with his gloves before settling it back atop his head. With the grey jacket flaring out over his black leather trousers, he looked every inch the Normain gentleman. Save for the three leather pouches along his belt on the opposite side of his sword, where his pistole normally would have been. They were just the size for vials—the vials Veneficus drank from to transform into were-creatures. He saw my gaze and glanced away, cheeks burning again, showing a scar I didn't remember, white lancing back from the edge of his cheek to his ear. "I really should be getting back or else they'll wonder if something like this happened to me."

"Like what? Running into your former partner in crime-solving who saved your arse from a would-be Sin Eater assassin so the pair of us could team up to assassinate the Dead Gods themselves?"

Eld stared at me and then burst out laughing. "Gods, I've missed your tongue, Buc." He shook his head. "Something like that, I'd imagine, aye." He shrugged. "I've been walking the city every morn through afternoon as I said I would in my last letter, awaiting your arrival. You did get my last, aye?"

"Obviously," I said slowly, drawling out every syllable, and glanced pointedly at the headless woman between us.

"Of course you did," he muttered. He looked up, his blue eyes cloudier than they had been a moment before. "It's been harder and harder to justify the time when everyone is arrow-focused on the plague and—enough time for that later," he said, half to himself. "You took too long in finding me, today, we'll have to discuss our next move tomorrow."

"Pardon, here I thought I'd traversed the city following the Sin Eater who intended to slit your throat and saved your hoary old arse," I mused, touching a gloved finger to my lips.

"I'd have handled her," he said, waving the Sin Eater away as if she hadn't been one of the most dangerous creatures alive moments before. "I told the Eldests that dressing as citizens wouldn't hide us, that we should walk freely in our robes, but the Eldests don't believe that *they* can spot us, same as we do them. I felt her presence before I led her into the Old City. Find me first thing tomorrow and we'll walk and talk."

"I'd love that," I admitted. "I'm not sure it's quite wise, though?" I waved an arm around. "Enemy territory. Heart of the Dead Gods' power. Arm in arm with a woman in possession of a shard of Ciris."

"Possession," he whispered. "Buc . . . are you? Did you?"

"Still in possession of my smart-arsed tongue," I assured him. "And brain. Say, Eld, before you go . . . would you help a woman out?"

"I said I'd take care of the corpse."

"Not that!" I glanced back up the backstreet I'd sprinted down. "I, uh, need help putting my skirts back on."

"Oh, of course," Eld said slowly, his eyes running down my body as if just realizing I was wearing leather pants that hugged my curves so tight they might as well have been a second skin. "Uh, after you," he suggested in a thick voice.

"You just want an excuse to look at my arse," I told him as we walked toward where I'd left my skirts. He snorted and I smiled, keeping my eyes straight ahead. "Well, you know what they say on the streets? The first time is free. What they don't say," I added, bending down to pull up that damned hoop skirt that was half standing on its own, "is that's because after the first time, you're hooked."

"They're not wrong," he whispered as I turned around, pulling the skirt up around me. I felt his hands on my waist, then against the small of my back as he fastened the clasps, suddenly all thumbs. After struggling for several moments he managed to get the clasps back in place. "You're missing a button."

"I like it rough," I said without thinking.

He barked a laugh and I leaned back against him. I felt him tense and was suddenly aware of the slabs of muscle, carved like a marble statue, that flexed beneath his clothes. Eld had always been one of the strongest men I knew, but this Eld would have bent the old Eld like false iron. And old Eld would have tensed at getting so close to me, but I could feel this was tension of another sort. There was something between us now. *Magic.* It wasn't the first time that'd separated us. Sin's magic had nearly undone our friendship back in Servenza, but this was different—the gulf felt more solid, less permeable. *Disparate magic.* And close to a year where each thought themselves alone.

"Eld?" I bent my head back so I was looking straight up, and he bent over so his eyes were staring straight into mine. "I'm letting you go for the night, aye? But I'm never letting you go again."

"Buc—"

"Never," I cut him off, "again." I stepped away from him and he let me go. "Savvy?"

"Savvy," he said after a moment.

"Good. Tomorrow come to the Inn of the Sailor's True Four . . . you know it?"

"I don't, but I'll find it. Along the port's walk?"

"Aye, some reference to a nautical knot all sailors learn."

"That I do know," he said with a smile that didn't reach his eyes. "I'll be there. I promise, but, Buc? Take care." He let out the breath he'd been holding since we met. "There's so much you don't know. So much we didn't know. The Dead Gods are dangerous."

"I'm aware," I said dryly.

"No, you're not," Eld said, his voice low. "You think you are. I thought I was. We were both fools." He glanced up at the darkening sky and cursed.

"Tell me tomorrow," I said. "Until then, I'll act as if we're back in Gilderlock's vault."

"Before or after we emptied it of all the loot?"

"Eld, you wound me," I mocked. "Those were our customer's valuables that we were merely . . . safeguarding." He smiled for real and I gave him a quick nod so he couldn't see me drinking him in like a woman forty days lost in the desert. "Tomorrow, then."

"Tomorrow," he agreed, tugging at his top hat. Making a smooth, military about-face, he headed back toward the Sin Eater's corpse, back to the path that would eventually lead him down into the sanctum of the Dead Gods. Back home.

"Did you notice," Sin asked, as we watched Eld disappear around the corner, "how he kept one hand on the pouches that held those vials?" I nodded. "And how he made jokes with the woman's corpse at his feet."

"I started the joke."

"And how," Sin spoke over me, "he looked at your bare throat at the end, when you were in his arms with his back to you, staring into his eyes." I nodded again. "He's become a predator, Buc."

"He's Eld," I said, tears spilling down my cheeks. "He's changed, aye. He's taken wounds, deep wounds, and they're not yet healed. And if he's a predator—" I laughed mirthlessly, wiping at my cheeks. "—then what am I? He contains multitudes, Sin. As do I. And that complicates things," I admitted as I squared my shoulders. I remembered the way Eld's eyes had shifted, from my eyes to my throat, the way his mouth hardened. Sin was right.

Eld was changed, but we'd already faced greater odds and bested them. We'd do so again. I didn't know what the future held, but I knew this one thing. We'd face it together.

And that was all that mattered.

35

"What, come to tuck me in?" I asked when Chan Sha and Salina slipped into my room at the inn. The Normain were sticklers on propriety, in public at least, which meant despite Salina booking the entire inn, our bedrooms were separated by window-facing drawing rooms, and the small, common dining room was down the central stair, requiring us all to eat in the open. "Or do you have more thoughts on what this Wellspring is of the Dead Gods and how we're going to kill them all?"

"No more than before," Salina said, pulling her purple robe tighter about her. She looked younger, softer, with her hair completely out of its braid and brushed to a golden sheen in Normain fashion. "I've been preparing messages and funds to go at a moment's notice once we meet with Eld. He'll likely know far more of this Wellspring anyway."

"Eld," Chan Sha said, "is why we've come." Her white robe hung open, showing the red silk pajamas she wore beneath.

"Aye?" I leaned back against the headboard, crossing my ankles beneath my pale crimson robe—it matched the sheets—and gestured with one hand. "Say on."

"We all know Eld is a man of his word," Salina began.

"Was," Chan Sha corrected, shaking her braids—she said she was Cordoban to her toenails and no dress would hide that, so she'd kept her locks braided. "That man died or close as. This one was weaned back to life on lies and manipulation with a heady dose of their Gods' blood to make it palatable." Her dark-green eye softened when she saw my expression. "He may not even know what he does, Buc."

"This again?" I rolled my eyes. "I thought I squelched this when I came back earlier. If Eld had turned traitor, why send a letter warning me of the Dead Gods' plot? A letter that also warned me of the hit team coming to kill me," I reminded her.

"Was it a warning or an attempt to set you up?"

"He sent one to 'Lina, too."

"It was almost too late, save I had access to Cannon Ships," Salina said.

"You, too?" I growled, and the other woman suddenly became interested in the wallpaper that was patterned with roses and thorns, with colorful birds perched amongst the branches.

"The Dead Gods don't do things by the half measure," Chan Sha said. "They know the Company is closely allied with Ciris in deed, if not word. It may well be those letters were intended to bring the two of you together so that their hit team could take you both out, and if that failed . . . send you running toward their second trap with the plague in the cathedral."

"All of that would make sense," I agreed, "save Eld's warning allowed us to foil the hit team *and* destroy said cathedral. Which you both were a part of, aye?"

"It's a possible explanation," the other woman agreed. "But there's more."

"I figured there would be," I said dryly. "Given you ran through this argument with me not more than three bells ago and I dismantled it piece by piece. Neither of you are fools . . . usually."

Chan Sha's cheeks took on a rosy hue and her expression froze. "It was always a possibility that you'd defeat that hit team, but if we suppose the letter was a fail-safe, meant to reach you *after* the attack, then we could also extrapolate that the cipher on the body we found that led us to the plague ship was another trap."

"You're telling me that the Dead Gods' brilliant scheme was

to tell us all their bloody secrets so we could destroy their plans and prevent them from releasing the plague they're bent upon unleashing?" I snorted. "Much smarter and they'd slit their own throats by mistake."

"It was a pretty damned big coincidence," Chan Sha continued, her voice a harsh growl of frustration, "that said ship waited right where a Normain flotilla was sailing with enough firepower to sink us thrice over. We shouldn't have made it out of there alive."

"Chan Sha, you're ascribing much of chance to forethought and it's growing tiring." I sat up straight. "Normain would had to have agreed to lend their second-most-powerful ship to the Dead Gods," I said, holding up a finger. "They would have had to agree to declare war against the most powerful Empire in the world— one they've lost two wars against in the past century." I added another finger. "And they would have had to have been so committed to this charade that neither side adequately supported the other, which allowed us to destroy them piecemeal. If all four had acted in concert, we wouldn't be having this conversation because our bones would lie fathoms deep upon the seabed." I closed my fingers into a fist. "Now that we've dispensed with the conjecture . . . why don't you tell me what your fear really is?"

The two women exchanged looks. Salina shrugged as if to say she had told Chan Sha so, and Chan Sha took a deep breath, visibly pulling herself back from the brink of an outburst.

"My fear is you're in love with a memory of a man what no longer exists," Chan Sha said at last. She crossed her arms. "You don't realize how dangerous the Dead Gods are because so far you've only encountered their lackeys. Their Eldest have each lived for a century or more. Their leader has lived for a millennium.

"Buc, you may not realize their worth, but they've seen yours firsthand. And I know"—she tapped her temple—"what they are capable of, how deep the currents of their machinations run. Everything you ascribe to coincidence may very well be true, *but* it may also be they're showing you respect, stacking up layer upon layer to draw you into the heart of their power where they can destroy you once and final."

"Eld told me today that I didn't realize how dangerous the Dead Gods were," I whispered. I glanced up. "Why would he do that if he was against me? Why not kill me then and there? Why not ambush me in the back alleys? He said he could take care of that Sin Eater's corpse . . . surely he could have taken care of a pair of them?"

"What does Sin say?" Salina asked, breaking her silence.

"Sin said he's a predator," I admitted after a moment. I sighed. "But then, so am I, and I've been one longer than he has. Chan Sha, if you want me to believe that all of this was the Dead Gods playing the long game, that they pulled Eld from the rubble of the Lighthouse—where *you* tried to kill me," I reminded her, unable to keep the heat from my voice, "just so they could draw me in close enough where it's a coin toss whether I bury my dagger in their chest before they do the same to me?" I shook my head, running a hand through my loose locks, felt the stubble beneath my undercut. *Sharp.* I needed to be sharper than I'd ever been before, see all angles and cut off every string the powers that be thought to tie to me. That was why I'd let both women into my inner circle, not just in bits and pieces as was my wont, but fully inside. I couldn't afford to miss anything.

Silence filled the room. "I might could find my way to believing it's a factor to weigh," I said finally. "I might could believe that they've been manipulating Eld without him realizing it." I glanced up at the chandelier above, blinking against the light. "I can't and won't believe that he's a willing accomplice," I continued. "I've given you the chance to prove you've changed coats, Chan Sha, and you've changed them so many times you've a wardrobe full. You question Eld's word? Then let's see what he has to say tomorrow. I'll give him the same chance I gave you."

"You're blinded by your feelings for a ghost," Chan Sha muttered through clenched teeth. "Aye, I know you won't hear it," she added, cutting me off. She rolled one of her braids between her fingers. "Forewarned is forearmed, though, so at least I've said my piece. We'll see what the morrow brings."

"Fair enough," I said in a voice that belied the rage I could feel building inside me. This was the woman who had helped drive the wedge between Eld and me. The woman ultimately responsible for what had happened to Eld. I could have tortured and flayed her and left her begging for death and none would have gainsaid me. *Well.* I wouldn't have gainsaid me. Instead, I'd given her a chance and this was how she repaid me?

"She's trying to reward your trust," Salina said, and when I pulled myself out my reverie, I realized Chan Sha had left. Salina walked around the footboard and sat down on the edge of the bed, crossing her legs, her robe parting to reveal a smooth, pale calf. She put her palms behind her and leaned back, studying me. "In her own way, she's looking out for you."

"You agree with her? About Eld?" I asked. "You didn't say so earlier."

"No . . . mayhap? I don't know," the other woman said, shaking her loose blond hair. "Buc, do you really know that Eld is the same man as before? That you can trust him as implicitly as you once could?"

"I know, 'Lina," I assured her. I saw the question still bright in her eyes. "I do."

"I always liked Eld," Salina said after a moment, looking past me. "He seemed a good man, honest and decent, but . . ." She looked closely at me, her amber eyes almost glowing in the candlelight. "I didn't do everything I've done for the past year for Eld. I never knew him save from afar and he's been gone a long time. I did what I did, offering council, taking up the mantle of Chair, fighting all these Godsdamned bureaucratic back-alley street fights, stacking machination upon machination as we agreed, tilting scales here and there . . ." She pulled in a deep breath. "I've done all that for you, Buc."

She smiled. "I did it for the tough-as-nails street rat you were then and for the formidable woman you've become."

"We've both come up in the world," I said softly. Eld burned bright in my mind, his newfound strength, the speed with which he moved, how he'd seen things clearly in ways that the old, too-linear Eld would have missed. "Doing that will change you. Change you a lot."

"Aye." Salina reached out and squeezed my bare calf. "We have, it's true. We've changed together, Buc, drawn closer over these past months." She leaned forward. "I don't know what the Dead Gods' plans are, nor how deep they run or how Eld figures into them. I do know that you and I can finish this thing, once and final. You've made me a believer."

"What, in the religion of Sambuciña?" I laughed.

"Perhaps." Salina giggled. "I only ask this, Buc. When Eld draws near to you, set aside the man you knew in the moment, and see him as any other. If you trust him still, then Chan Sha's mind's been twisted into so many knots that all she can see are plots everywhere." She chewed on her lip. "But if you don't trust him, Buc, if you see something beyond what he's saying . . . you have to forget the man you once knew. Either way"—she moved forward so that we were a palm's length apart—"know that I trust you." There was a fierce light in her amber eyes. "You know that, right?"

"Of course, 'Lina." I leaned my head back against the headboard and glanced up at the ceiling, took a deep breath, and nodded against the wood. "It's good advice and I'd be a fool not to take good advice from the Chair of the Kanados Trading Company, wouldn't I?" I laughed and looked back to her. "But then it wouldn't be the first time I've ignored good advice, I suppose."

"You're no fool, Buc." Salina leaned away, opened her mouth to say something else, but stood up instead, smoothing out her robe. "Save where matters of the heart are concerned," she added, resuming her study of the wallpaper.

"That's why I have you," I told her. "Are you well, Salina?"

"Aye," she said, pushing away from the footboard she'd sagged against a moment before. "A good night's sleep and I'll be as fresh as a newly minted lira."

"I could—" I yawned. "—get behind that. I appreciate your concern," I added. "Both of yours. I find it Godsdamned annoying, but I appreciate it."

"Sleep well, Buc," Salina said, her mouth moving in a faint smile.

"Sleep well," I echoed, and then she was gone.

"Well?" I asked Sin aloud. "You were right that they weren't satisfied with my recounting. What do you think now? Can I trust them?"

"You know what I think about Chan Sha," he said after a moment.

"Aye, I thought the same until the past fortnight," I admitted. "But she's been there when the dice were tossed, even if she held the wrong cup. Same as Salina, really. We're all in this together."

"Chan Sha is cunning," Sin said slowly. "Eld is different, but different doesn't mean nefarious. It could and often does mean dangerous."

"The world is dangerous," I reminded him.

"Just so." He was quiet for a long moment. "You understand what brought them here tonight, aye? Why Salina stayed behind?"

"They think I'm blinded by my feelings for Eld. I get that. Salina knows how little my experience runs with relationships beyond Sister and Eld. She's a good friend."

"That's your take?" he asked quietly.

"Aye, why?"

"It's just—" He snorted. "In that case, the only word of lie Salina spoke was at the end. You are very much a fool, Buc. Especially in matters of the heart."

"You're both damned strange," I told him, frowning. "I'm just polite enough to not point that out, would that you two had the same manners." I felt him choke on his next thought and smiled, rolling the knob that lowered the gearwork caps over the candles above, extinguishing them with a muted hiss. "Sweet dreams, Sin." I rolled over onto my side, pulling the pillow tight beneath my head. I knew what I'd be dreaming of. *You're a fool, Buc.* Who, I'd be dreaming of. *A happy fool, then.*

36

Eld nodded to the pair of Dead Walkers standing guard over the cathedral's doors like grim statues. Both wore their bone-white robes with the hoods pulled up to hide their faces in shadow. They made him pause in the doorway until, after an endless moment, one nodded and the other followed. Only then did Eld reach for the large door handle, swinging the massive door, which filled half the archway from the floor to the third span above and opened almost effortlessly. He paused again, waiting for the horde of Shambles standing just inside to shuffle around until they had cleared a narrow ribbon of stone floor for him to use as a walkway.

We're wearing ourselves thin. With the war breaking out in earnest, the best of their Veneficus had been deployed to cathedrals across the world in teams of three or four, each team with a Dead Walker and a hundred Shambles to provide support. That left the home guard light, with half-trained Veneficus who'd never been in a real fight and Dead Walkers who were old enough that they preferred the company of their undead to the living. Had Eld tried to open the door before they granted permission, there was no telling if they would do nothing or if he'd be fighting the swarm of undead that currently surrounded him. He was grateful that they kept their hoods up to hide their tics and outright *off-ness,* lest they frighten off parishioners.

Not that any parishioner would come after the third afternoon bell. Services were increasingly limited and none would have been allowed to reach the cathedral, let alone enter. The Shambles were held in readiness for the mind witches that had begun slipping into the city, both in pairs and alone. *Like the woman Buc killed.* He'd felt the mind witch's presence at his back, the itch between his shoulder blades as she drew closer and closer—one of the Dead Gods' gifts. What he hadn't felt was Buc just beyond her. Eld tried to keep thoughts of her from coalescing in his mind as he cleared the last of the undead, a particularly tall woman whose putrefied eyes were leaking a green ichor that smelled fouler than it looked and made his stomach turn.

Tried and failed.

Eld could still feel her weight in his arms, smell the clean, stone-fruit scent of her skin and below that, Buc herself. Seeing Buc in the flesh, with her sharp cheekbones and that rare smile that always made her look up to something that spelled trouble, had been a revelation. *No, not that. A Transfiguration. Reshaped me into something wholly new.* He shivered, his arms breaking out in gooseflesh beneath his jacket. Before now, he'd begun to think his feelings had changed, after everything that'd been done to him or by fickle distance. Seeing her standing over the dead Sin Eater had been a shock, but the bigger one had been when she leapt at him. For a brief breath, midair, he thought she was going to murder him, but that hadn't been the shock. Even realizing he wouldn't try to stop her murdering him hadn't been.

No, the shock had been how touching Buc had given color to the grey, stilted feelings he remembered of her. Almost as if someone had thrown a bucket of paint filled to the brim with every color known in the world over the pencil sketches of his feelings. Eld knew the memories of his past life were real and true. Despite his doubts at first, he'd come to believe in them, but . . . there was always something in those memories that felt old and hollow. *Like a sail that wouldn't make full sheets no matter which direction it turned.* He remembered loving Buc, but he didn't feel love, not really. He still believed in her plans, else he wouldn't have turned traitor to the Dead Gods, but he'd begun to seriously consider that perhaps he'd finally achieved what he'd failed at before: loving Buc in friendship instead of something more.

Then Buc had been there. A thin wisp of a woman, all lithe muscle and occasional, surprising curves. A leopard on the high plain, beautiful and deadly. She'd undone whatever final blood magic the Archnemesis and Ismiralda and the rest of the council had cursed him with, giving light and color and movement to his memories. They filled his heart, and he had known, even before he set her down after that first spin: *I love her still. I never stopped. Only thought I had.*

"I hope that grin you're wearing portends good news," Ismiralda said, snapping him back to reality. She pushed herself up from the altar, stumbled, and caught herself against the carved bone that ran in strange swirls and whorls across the cathedral at knee height. Beyond the altar, the shattered face of Vos stared back at them from the shadows, the work of centuries to piece back together and still only just recognizable. From her instability and the flecks of blood on her hands from where they'd rested against the sharp bone, Eld guessed the woman had been praying for hours. The Plague Mistress's own smile—even, white teeth bright against her ebon face—never quite reached the black eyes that bored into his. "I've need of it, Eld."

"No antidote," Eld said quickly, to give him a moment to think. *Damn it, Buc.* That's why he'd been trying to avoid thinking of her, because every time he did he lost his mind, like a fool lad. "However, I feel confident we're closer after yesterday's trial on the rats. Perhaps within the next week."

"Leave the antidote aside," the woman said, licking the blood from the back of her hand. "Is it enough to weaken the virulence of the plague so that our Plague Walkers can suffer it?"

"It should be," Eld said slowly. "It's a fine line, as you well know."

"Weaken it too much and the infected will fall ill, but perhaps not mortally so," she said.

"And it may not bother the Sin Eaters at all," he pointed out.

"As it stands it's so strong it may kill us all in the process."

"That's the crux of it," he agreed. "We've no word from our ship set off the coast of Southeast Island, which I fear suggests they suffered the same fate as the Plague Walkers in Cordoban."

"Losses we can ill afford," she growled, slapping the altar and opening a fresh cut on her palm. "What of Normain? I heard they took losses near Southeast Island . . . could it be our ship was caught up in the mind witches' war?"

"I investigated those rumors," Eld said, struggling to keep from shivering at the chill that ran down his spine. *I only learned of that this morning. What else does she know?* "There does appear to have been a skirmish between the Imperial navy and Normain, but it was on the far side of the island, not where our ship was to lie in wait," he lied. "I've sent word for our brothers and sisters to search the coastal line, to see if they ran aground, but that could take days to confirm. If they died at sea . . ."

"We may never find them," she finished. "None of this brings me joy, Eldritch."

"I had another thought," Eld said, "that might do that. What if we were to inoculate all of our priests and priestesses . . . and then release the plague?"

"Inoculate?" She frowned, studying the blood that ran down the cracks in her palm. "I am unfamiliar with the word. How?"

"'How' is a good question. 'Why,' a better one," Eld said. Ismiralda's eyes shot up at his tone and he suddenly realized how Buc must have felt every moment of her life. "What I mean," he added quickly, "is that if we use this methodology, we need not wait for an antidote or on ways to weaken the plague any further."

"Say on," she whispered.

"Inoculation is something I came across in a book. It's a theory proposed by—that is"—he moved on at her growl—"it involves infecting one with a small dose of the disease, a weakened version, if you will, allowing them to fall ill and then recover. Once recovered they are immune to the more virulent form."

"You're suggesting we make ourselves immune, then unleash the plague."

"Precisely."

"That's the why." She arched a white eyebrow.

"The how is a bit trickier," Eld admitted. "We need to inoculate all of our people and, because we have no way to know if a true antidote is possible, we need to have means of both producing and renewing this inoculation indefinitely. We'll need to ensure that all new blood taken from the Dead Gods carries this strain in it."

"You're talking about using the Wellspring?" Ismiralda choked, and her other eyebrow joined the first.

"I know, it's a bold step," Eld said, looking away before she saw more in his eyes than he wanted her to. "We could trial it first, parcel out vials here and there, perhaps in a year—"

"We don't have that kind of time," Ismiralda snapped. She drew in a deep breath, straining her tight robes, then let it out smoothly, staring past him at something only she could see. "We don't have that kind of time," she repeated after a moment. "You're certain?"

"I'm certain the method we used with the rats, combined with a modified ritual that ends after the contagion is activated but before full activation is achieved, will produce enough disease to cause illness, but not death," Eld said. *Keep watching the shiny coin I've just closed in my left fist.* "I've reworked the formulae thrice and had your Plague Walkers confirm it as well. If the council approves, we can introduce this into the Wellspring and the properties of the pool will ensure its continual presence." *And you'll never notice it's actually in my right.*

"You have three days."

"Three days?" Eld felt his eyes pop. "Mistress, that's not possible. The amounts of blood and contagion, to say nothing of the rituals we'll have to perform to convert the Wellspring, are significant. The rituals alone could take three days."

"They won't," she said, stepping closer to him. "They can't. In three days, you will transform the Wellspring into not just the source of our power but of our salvation, Eldritch." Ismiralda held her bloody palm out to him. "Taste."

"M-Mistress?"

"Taste my blood and know the truth of my words."

"The truth of blood," Eld said, bending his head over her hand, licking the sharp, iron tang from her skin. A day before he would have done the same and felt nothing. Now he felt dirty, unclean. "The purity of blood," he intoned evenly.

"In three days," she whispered, her mouth pressed against his ear, "our brothers and sisters will carry this inoculation to all of us. In five days"—she bit the top of his ear, holding it in her teeth as she spoke—"the Plague Walkers will follow after, on every ship we can beg, steal, or borrow. A month from now, the world will shudder and the Witch and her kind will fall to their knees before us." She tightened her jaw, puncturing his skin.

Her breathing quickened, warm and soft against his neck. If he moved now she would lose control. After a moment her breathing slowed and she nuzzled his ear, licking the blood from his wound. "You taste sweet, Eldritch," she purred. "Do all you say you will and you'll taste *all* of me. You and I will conquer this world in the name of our fallen Gods. Together."

"It will be as you say, Plague Mistress," Eld said huskily as she marched away, keeping his head bowed.

Over my twice-dead body.

37

When Eld didn't show the next morning, no one said anything, but Chan Sha had the look of a cat amongst day-old chicks. He didn't show the next day either, and ships began leaving the harbor as if half of Normain had decided to seek safer climes. That day, people began to fall silent when I entered a room and tension settled upon us like a coastal fog. I didn't doubt Eld, but I also knew he would've kept his word if he could, which meant something had happened, and I'd no way of knowing what. I woke up on the third morning to the sound of someone slipping through my window and had my slingshot back to full draw before my Sin-enhanced vision showed me Eld, pale and haggard-looking in his bone-white robe, sagging against the wall. . . .

I knew we were in trouble.

"What's so bloody important that it couldn't wait till sunrise?" Chan Sha growled, limping down the stairs that led to the common room that connected our suites. She paused on the landing, her good eye widening and her robe fluttered open, revealing her pajamas beneath. "You."

"You!" Eld gasped, pushing himself up from the table. He began to reach for the leather pouches at his waist, then switched, resting his hand on his sword hilt. "How is it that you still draw breath?"

"A question I ask myself every day," Chan Sha muttered. "I'm here at your girl's request."

"Buc?" His eyes shifted to mine and then back to where Chan Sha stood. "You remember how she tried to kill us, aye?"

"I remember," I said quietly.

A racking cough shook him. Wincing, he cleared his throat. "She practically did kill me atop the Lighthouse."

"Not sure that's really fair." Chan Sha smirked. "I seem to recall it was Buc and the Artificer blowing up the whole damned building that did that. I nearly died myself, that night."

"After all that," Eld said hoarsely, his voice taut from anger, "why is she not dead and buried?"

"They left you your memories," Chan Sha said, before I could answer. "They didn't have to do that, you know. I may be just another human, now, Eld, but before, I was a Sin Eater of Ciris."

Eld bared his teeth.

"I knew all She knew of the Dead Gods and their blood magic. They could have made you new as a day-old babe, allowed you to make new memories . . . instead they let you keep the old ones. The ones where you and Buc teamed up to destroy them all." She strode down the stairs, leaning heavily on the banister because of her bad leg.

"Why would they do that?" she asked as she reached the table, then tapped her pink lip with her forefinger. "Why go and leave a loaded pistole like you lying around? Just waiting for someone to pull the trigger?"

"So that's how it is," Eld muttered. "The former Sin Eater, former pirate queen, former Sicarii, wants to question my loyalties and allegiances?" He snorted, wiped at his nose with the back of his hand, and smiled, the shadows beneath his eyes giving his features a maniacal twist. "In case you hadn't noticed, there's a war on. The Dead Gods could have wiped my memory clean, aye, but then I would have been as good to them as that day-old babe and they don't have a score of years to wait for me to relearn everything."

"That's not all of it," Salina said, squirming on the bench beside me when Eld shifted his glare to her. "Surely they had more reason than that. They could have pulled any number of the dying from the wreck of the Lighthouse, but they chose you."

"They chose half a dozen of us," Eld muttered. "I was the only one who survived the blood they forced down our throats." He shook his head, his hair pulling free of the loose ponytail he'd gathered it in. He leaned forward, resting his palms against the table. "But you're right. They wanted the memories I held, of Buc and me and our machinations. They let me live despite who I was, not because of it."

"So they could return to those memories if they ever needed to," Chan Sha said.

"Likely," Eld agreed with a shrug.

"Which means they let you live *because* of who you are, fool. They could seek out the memories you've made since waking," Chan Sha continued. She paused, half seated on the bench. Her unbuttoned top swung open, revealing her tanned chest. "The ones where you were plotting treason with Buc. The ones—"

Everyone moved at once, Chan Sha pulling a pistole from behind her, drawing back the hammer as Eld swung a fist that suddenly held a blade, and me, moving faster than either of them, catching Chan Sha's wrist in one hand and Eld's in the other just before his blade took her hand off and her pistole took his head.

"—where you know right where Buc and the rest of us are at this very moment," Chan Sha finished through clenched teeth.

"Don't know why Buc didn't kill you already, but I'm glad of the opportunity," Eld growled back, his bloodshot eyes burning bright with murder.

"You know," I said, forcing my voice to be light despite the fact that my arms were afire with Sin's magic as I strained to hold the two at bay, "you could just ask Buc. She's right here in front of the fucking pair of you, after all."

"B-Buc," Eld said, the murderous haze leaving his eyes. "I—"

"Am acting like every other Veneficus I've ever come across," I told him. "But you're not like every other Veneficus. You're Eld. Be better."

"I—" Chan Sha began.

"Oh, you don't get to talk," I told her, baring my teeth. "You just tried a full-on frontal assault against a Veneficus. You're not a Sin Eater anymore, Chan Sha. Eld would have taken your hand clean off and likely followed up with your head for good measure. Aye!" I shouted, cutting her off. "You might have blown his brains out first. But then," I growled, "I would have taken you down to the harbor, tossed you in, and watched the sharks tear you limb from limb.

"Now—" I took a deep breath. "—you're going to lower the hammer on your pistole and put it down on the table. And Eld, you're going to do the same with that shiv you pulled from your sleeve, because while I do appreciate the homage to my habit of carrying blades all over the place, I don't appreciate you murdering one of our allies."

"Allies!"

"Eld." I twisted his wrist and he gasped. "Drop. Your. Blade." It hit the table with a thunk. "Chan Sha?" The woman eased the hammer back and set the pistole down when I released her wrist. "Bloody perfect. Now, you're both going to sit down, stop disturbing this shit excuse the Normain call breakfast, and we're going to have us a council of war."

I sat down and Salina passed me a golden, baked scone, glistening with honey. I took a bite and while the explosion of flavor made me make a noise in the back of my throat, the thing was so small—barely the size of my palm—it was gone in a second bite. "So, Eld . . . is Chan Sha right?" I asked, spraying crumbs. Salina muttered something about manners that I ignored. "Can the Dead Gods sift your memories whenever they want?"

"They could try," Eld said, sitting so straight he looked a soldier on the parade ground. "It's not like I would have no say in the matter."

"But if they overpowered you?"

"Aye, it's possible. Even if they killed me, so long as they gathered enough of my blood, they could sift through many, if not all of them. But," he added, snapping the linen napkin on his plate open and spreading it over his lap, "crucially, they haven't done so. Because"—his mouth twitched in the semblance of a smile that didn't reach his cheeks, much less his eyes—"they trust me. Think me one of their own. Playing that charade is why I'm late and why we haven't much time at all. None really."

"Wait," I said, holding up a hand. "Before we get on with this, I want to make sure we all understand one another."

"We're here to kill some mages and burn their places of worship, and thereby their Gods, to the ground," Bar'ren said. "What's not to understand?"

"I'm with the cannibal," Chan Sha said, smiling to show she didn't mean the insult.

"You understand what we're doing, but not why," I countered. "Which is why we had this"—I glanced at the pistole and blade on the table—"disagreement a moment before. I know why you're here, every one of you. You're here because I allowed it." I let that sink into all of them, Bar'ren looking confused, the Artificer beside him accepting it, Salina and Chan Sha both turning shades of red, and Eld just . . . waiting.

"But you're also here because each and every one of you is required for the task ahead. If we're to be successful, you need to understand that down to the marrow. I'm going to do something, then, that I rarely do. Ask . . . well, any of you, really, if you don't believe me." Chan Sha snorted and Salina laughed.

"I'm going to explain myself."

"Chan Sha's still drawing breath because she's knowledge of more recent events regarding the Dead Gods than my Sin does," I said. Sin shifted abruptly in my mind. "No fault of his; being locked on a shipwreck for a century or two will do that to you." *And I need to give them more reasons than she could have been me if I hadn't found Eld.* Sin settled. "Beyond that, she's proved how dangerous she is, playing her Sicarii role. Aye, and nearly murdered us a dozen times over," I added when Eld choked on his scone. "Were the tables reversed, I'm not sure I wouldn't have done the same. In fact, when they were reversed, I almost did.

"I lost my mind when I lost you, Eld," I said quietly. "The only difference between Chan Sha and myself is that I won." Chan Sha made a noise in her throat and I spun around to glare at her. "What else would you call it? I had you strung up, could have slit your throat, and I didn't. I let you live. That's the difference between you and me." I took a breath and added, "If it helps you square that at all, I let you live because I saw where your path led and I didn't wish to fail."

"You've a way with compliments, girl," Chan Sha said through clenched teeth.

"Chan Sha wants what she lost: her family," I explained. "She won't find that with Ciris, but she might find it here . . . if you stop thinking like a Veneficus and stop trying to kill her, Eld.

"The Artificer"—I shifted focus, ignoring the way Eld's cheeks suddenly burned as if sunburnt—"is here because he likes inventing things and so long as the Gods, old or new, exist, they'll find him a threat. He's also here because we found him first."

"I'm an engineer," the short man said, cleaning his spectacles with a grey cloth. "I think about things, create things, understand things, but none of that requires bravery and so forth."

"I remember you," Eld said dryly. "That rifle I used was your creation?" The man nodded and Eld whistled. "Finest weapon I ever held. The floating balloon was pretty brilliant, too, until it wasn't."

"Storms are marvelous and dangerous things," the short man said, by way of apology.

"Bar'ren wants revenge . . . he's an instrument of his Goddess. That is," I told Eld, "he comes from the Arawaíno, the natives on the island that helped us fight the Ghost Captain."

"You're the one who . . ." Eld closed his eyes, tapping his temple.

"You're the one who gave Buc the canoe!" The older man nodded. "But what brought you here?"

"The aforementioned Goddess," I said dryly. "And this forever war we're all caught up in . . ." Swiftly I told Eld Bar'ren's tale.

"Blood and bone," Eld whispered, "this really is coming full circle, isn't it?"

"Which brings me to Salina. Congregant of the Church of Buc," I said, squeezing her arm. "Nearly the founding member, save yourself, Eld." The other woman tensed beneath my hand and I let her arm go. "When we fell apart in Servenza, she was there for me, and I don't know if it happened through osmosis or what, but Salina believes in the same dream we do: a world without Gods plucking at hidden strings, manipulating us against one another. A world where wealth doesn't reside in the clutches of older generations who will do anything to maintain their power. A world where we, every single one of us, has a chance. I don't know why you bought in, 'Lina, but I'm glad to have you."

"It was because of you," she said quietly, her eyes full of some meaning I couldn't discern. "You didn't convert me, I chose your arguments, your evidence. I chose you."

"Now, if only we could get the world to follow," I said, returning her smile. "Which brings me to you, Eld." I reached across the table, stopping just short of his hand. "When I lost you, I went after Chan Sha, and when I lost her and my chance at revenge, I really did lose my mind. Everything I touched, I destroyed. Sin Eater conclaves. Dead Gods' cathedrals. None of it made me feel better, and while there was something satisfying about watching them go up in flames, none of it brought me any closer to unseating the Gods themselves, nor was it preparing a brighter future. You were always my guiding star, Eld, and without you, I was lost at sea.

"I need your help, Eld. Now more than ever—the Dead Gods have pulled you in close, close enough for us to bury the blade, and I need you to help make the blow land true. And I need the sanity you give me. Alone, I'm not sure I would have lived to see the end. Still not sure I will," I admitted. "But for the first time, I want to. I really do."

Eld said nothing for several moments, then took my hand. "When they gave me back my memories, they tried to keep you from me. The past several years were a haze and I was slow and dim-witted until I found myself writing in strange letters that made no sense. A cipher. Not of my devising. But of yours." Eld sniffed loudly. "You gave me back my memories, Buc. Gave me back my life. Even then, it was an old, grey thing, while my new memories after waking were young and vibrant. Until a few days ago, when you shattered that illusion just as I know you'll shatter the illusion that the Gods are invincible, immortal, as constant as the sun. I'll be with you every step of the way, until the end."

"Promise?" I asked him huskily.

"Always."

38

"My plan began and ended with the Wellspring," Eld said. Chan Sha cursed and Salina spilled half the tea she poured while Bar'ren muttered something darkly in his tongue. Eld cocked his head slightly. "I say something wrong?"

"Still polite, I see," I muttered. "Something you said, but not wrong," I explained. "The Wellspring . . . it's too long a story for the moment, but I read a secret book in Cordoban that said the only way to destroy the Dead Gods was to destroy this mysterious Wellspring."

"It didn't say," Salina added, "what the Wellspring was."

"Or where it's located," Chan Sha put in.

"Ah," Eld said, nodding slowly. "I'd be interested in that book, now that I've inside knowledge of the Dead Gods and their magics."

"Sin and I could transcribe it for you," I said, stifling a yawn. "Would take a day or two. I thought you said time was short."

"It is," he said, pulling himself back to the moment. "My mind is full of fog and my limbs feel all rusted up."

"Drink one of your vials?" Chan Sha asked.

"Wouldn't help," Eld said, clearing his throat. "The Dead Gods are, in fact, it turns out, dead."

"And water is wet."

"Merely pointing out that they can't be killed," he snapped at Chan Sha. Eld coughed, then bent over, hacking his lungs out into his hands.

"Their power," he said, when he finished and had wiped his

mouth with his napkin, "died with them, for the most part, but it remains behind in two forms: blood and bone. The bones are fairly well useless on their own . . . that's why half of the capital here is built upon and amongst them. Combine their bones with their blood, though, and you can do all manner of things."

"Like what?" I asked. "Beyond commanding the undead or changing into were-beasts."

"Healing comes from the combination of blood, bone, and human tissue—without that last it would do nothing or, worse, would kill you. Transfiguration is the ritual they use to turn you into one of their own and it's only then that you can commune directly with the blood of the Gods. Anyway, they can use it to recover memories, predict the weather, and any number of useful things, likely more than they realize. They can also create poisons."

"The plague," I guessed.

"The plague," he agreed, wiping sweat from his brow. "The Wellspring is a room in the heart of our citadel in Normain. If the legends are true, the Wellspring taps directly into the heart of the last God to die; its blood is pumped into a pool from which all of the Dead Gods' magic flows. The reservoir is massive, the blood we require but a drop in comparison, and therefore practically limitless, but without the Wellspring, there would be no blood. No blood . . ."

"No magic," I muttered.

"Exactly," he agreed. "I devised a plan requiring every Dead Gods' mage to inoculate themselves using blood directly from the spring, with the idea that we'd poison it first. There's a specific ritual required, involving one of our acolytes becoming contaminated with the plague, then bleeding themselves nearly dry into the Wellspring, along with various ingredients and commands to change the nature of the pool."

"If you change the blood, would it still do what it's done before?" I asked.

"You mean unlock the static magic potential of objects?"

"Aye, like the hair of animals or what have you."

"It's a minor change, less to the property of what the blood is and more to what the blood does to us naturally, without any manipulation for specific magical aims," Eld explained. "That's why I suggested inoculation . . ."

I listened raptly as Eld told us of this Plague Mistress and her new creation of the Plague Walkers. I'd known much of this from his letters, but hearing him explain what they were about made the hairs on the back of my neck stand on end. *He's right. They are more dangerous than I gave them credit for.* Familiarity had bred contempt and after engineering the deaths of a score or more Veneficus, to say nothing of the Ghost Captain, I'd begun to think them easy meat. Take the right precautions, bring plenty of silver, and it was all done, save for the dying. Or so I'd thought.

"They're an ageless foe," Sin whispered. "We fought them in the stars above your skies, back when we were legion and they large enough to blot out the sun. Now we're but shadows of the shards of the powers that we once were. For all that, we haven't yielded, not once bent the knee. Aye, and neither have those hoary bastards, despite them moldering in their graves."

"I'm not sure what scares me more when you speak like this," I said in my mind. "That you say *we* and I can feel I'm included in your use of the word or that you think the Gods have fallen so far and yet they hold such power that it makes us look like babes beside wizened old crones."

"Call Ciris a wizened old crone, next you see her," Sin suggested.

"I'd rather call her by past tense," I said. "Because then she'll be dead."

Eld finished his explanation. "I was to have three days to work on it, three days to get in touch with all of you and figure out how we were to poison the Wellspring."

"We wondered when you didn't show up," Salina said when he paused. "But it makes sense now."

"I have a thought," the Artificer began, dry-washing his hands furiously the way he did when he meant he really had a fully realized plan, likely with schematics drawn and ready to show.

"Belay your thought for a moment," Chan Sha said, leaning in. "Eld said he had three days to work on it and that was three days ago."

"Aye," I grunted. "What are you holding back, Eld?"

Eld grinned and I saw his gums were bleeding. "As I said, that *was* the plan. When I awoke that first morn after we met, Buc, it was to discover my Plague Mistress pacing back and forth in my room."

"In your room?"

"She was too excited to wait," Eld said slowly. "You see, she'd taken my plan to the Archnemesis and he used his millennium of knowledge to improve upon it. In ways that were detrimental to my real plan."

"Here it comes," Chan Sha growled, slapping the table.

"Say on, Eld." *Do you think this Archnemesis will mind if I call him an old crone?*

"There's only one way to find out," Sin said, answering my unspoken question.

"An experiment of sorts."

"For science," he agreed.

"By requiring everyone to become inoculated before they deployed the plague, I'd hoped to slow everything down," Eld explained. "First, it would allow us the chance to poison everyone, but failing that, the Dead Gods' priests would need to wait until everyone overcame the bit of plague they were exposed to before deploying the real plague. That was my undoing," he admitted.

"Your Plague Mistress wanted the Plague Walkers gone in five days," I speculated, "and realized it'd be more like thrice that before they could leave, if they didn't want to kill their own when they unleashed it."

"Precisely." Eld paused, chewing on his lip. "In truth, this plague has never been tested on humans other than Dead Gods' mages. Everything they think they know has been filtered through me. It could be their plague is nothing worse than a bad cold, but I've a feeling it's as deadly as they believe. Deadlier even."

"Eld's finally learned to tell a fib." I whistled. "A damned big one, too."

"Aye, well, once the Archnemesis heard of my plan, he devised a better one. That morning, they'd already been to the Wellspring, the Archnemesis working with a coterie of Dead Walkers and our secret library—"

"Secret library!"

"Give over, Buc," Salina said amiably, "or we'll never find out how fucked we truly are."

"What she said," Chan Sha muttered.

"Another time," Eld assured me. "They used their combined knowledge to introduce an inoculation into the Wellspring . . . I'm not even sure if the Archnemesis waited for the council to approve it. They were all so damned excited."

"So they've already inoculated the pool?"

"They did and they made us all drink of it that morn." Eld gave me a weak smile. "It made us all sick as fuck, despite the modifications the Archnemesis made to the ritual and despite the incredibly small dose they gave us."

"Hence your convictions it's deadly," I growled.

"Aye."

"Are you catching?" Everyone slid away from Eld at my question. "Eld?"

"No," Eld said after a moment, and the tension bled out of the room. "Part of the ritual saw that we weren't, for fear of repeating the mistake they think they made in Cordoban and accidentally killing their own too soon," he added. "Even with our illness, the Eldests were too excited at the moment having finally arrived, and mages were sent out with inoculation vials intended for every crypt and church and cathedral in the world."

"That's why half the fucking harbor emptied the day before last," Chan Sha said, punching her leg.

"You said it was the war," Bar'ren reminded her.

"It was," I whispered, "just the real war, not this farcical one between the Empire and Normain."

"The r-r-rest of the harbor will empt-t-t-y t-tomorrow," Eld said, his teeth chattering.

"Is that why you look like a bag of smashed arseholes, Eld?" I asked, cracking a smile I didn't feel. "Are you going to make it?"

"He'll be fine," Salina said, proving I hadn't hid my feelings despite the smile. "You will, won't you?"

"I only feel like death," Eld assured us, his clammy skin almost as pale as his robes. "It's the alternating between fever and chill, aches and weakness, that are the worst of it."

"I'm more interested," the Artificer said, "in why they changed up your plan, Eld? If the rest of the harbor empties tomorrow I presume that's because they're sending out the Plague Walkers?"

Eld nodded shakily.

"Which suggests," the Artificer continued, "they aren't worried about the lag time between inoculation and introduction of the contagion and so forth. That seems . . . troubling."

"Troubling, the man says," Bar'ren grumbled.

"The Archnemesis and his cronies came up with an ingenious modification to my plan," Eld said. "An alternate antidote to the one I was working on. Not an actual cure, mind," he added quickly, a wry twist to the corner of his mouth, "because they've gamed this out a hundred different ways. A thousand. They know Ciris will win if they don't change the short game, so they've lost all focus save for that. No cure, but rather a return to the process of Transfiguration that renders us different from other humans. A blood pathogen that is attuned to the blood within our veins. It not only heals us of our current illness, but unlocks the plague at the same moment . . . essentially turning us all into Plague Walkers."

"Gods," I breathed.

"But why?" Salina asked. "If I'm following correctly, this will fundamentally change every Dead Gods' mage forever."

"You're following along just fine," Eld assured her. He brushed a few sweaty strands of hair from his face and shrugged. "They ran the sums. Making us all carriers spreads the plague exponentially faster, hitting the Sin Eaters faster. They'll lose their connection with their Goddess because their Sin will be consumed with keeping them alive."

"They'll castrate the Sin Eaters' power," I whispered.

"End the war in months, not years," he agreed.

"But if Sin Eaters will be that close to death," Salina gasped, "what does that mean for the rest of us? The rest of the world?"

"If you're all lucky, we'll have come up with an antidote by then," Eld said. "I should warn you that I've spent almost all my time dedicated to that and . . . I've nothing to show for it."

"You didn't have the Artificer then," Chan Sha said. "Or me or Buc or the rest of us."

"What happens if there is no antidote, Eld?" I asked. "According to your Plague Mistress's calculations?"

"We'll have a much smaller pool of worshippers to work with," he said wanly. "Enough to fit on Servenza proper."

A dumbstruck silence greeted his pronouncement. The Dead Gods were risking worldwide genocide to finish off Ciris and end their ancient grudge match.

"That makes things simple enough, then," I said, rapping the table. "They plan to activate the Wellspring tomorrow morn? We'll give the bastards what they've always wanted: to be like their Gods. We'll kill every motherfucking one of them.

"Tonight."

39

"Your plan will still work, Eld," I said. "Poison the Wellspring and they can't activate its potential tomorrow. We just need to . . . expedite things. What's deadliest to a Dead Gods' mage?"

"Silver," Eld said, suppressing a shudder. "Something in it undoes the very fabric of our magic, and since we are imbued with that magic, enough silver undoes a mage from the inside out."

"All right, so we need silver." I glanced over my shoulder at Salina as she got to her feet. "Loads of it."

"I'll lay claim to all I can within Normain," she said, drawing her damp blond hair back over her shoulder. "I know the Company stores some in our holdings, in both the harbor and our palace in the Old City. I'll have our commissioners buy up the rest within the capital, but it won't be an inordinate amount. And"—she sighed, her mouth twisting—"it'll cost a fuck ton of lire. Given the issues the Dead Gods have with it, it's a rare metal in Normain. Rarer even than gold."

"It would help," I muttered, "if we knew precisely how much you needed to procure. Given how deadly silver is to the Dead Gods, perhaps it won't be that much."

"It'll be diluted by the volume of the pool," Chan Sha pointed out at the same time Sin did within my mind. I felt more than heard his curse. He and Eld were of a like mind when it came to the former pirate queen.

"I may be able to help with the calculation," the Artificer said.

"How so?" I asked. I plucked another scone off the table and began munching as I reached for more tea. I'd a feeling Sin and

I would need all the fuel we could get for what was to come. "Do you know the toxicity levels for Dead Gods?"

"I don't. They keep that sort of information secret for obvious reasons and so forth," the little man said. He adjusted his spectacles and glanced at Eld. "Do you have a vial of blood untainted by animal or bone?"

"I do have one, for healing," Eld said, touching one of the pouches on his belt.

"May I see it? I had a different use in mind a few moments ago, but now . . ." The Artificer trailed off before shaking his head clear a moment later. "For testing purposes?"

"If you're using it for testing purposes, you'll be doing more than seeing it. And Eld may need that healing, Arti."

"I can spare the vial," Eld said with a smile that looked incongruous against his drawn features. "Without the other elements, though, the blood is good for little else unless you know how to perform our rituals, I'm afraid."

"Superstition and nonsense," the Artificer said with a wave of his hand. "Most of what your kind consider rituals are really nothing more than age-tested scientific experiments with various elements preexisting in nature."

"Meaning?" Salina asked.

"Meaning that Arti can use a small amount of the blood with increasing amounts of silver to discover the toxicity levels required to kill and then apply that exponentially to the volume of the pool." I glanced at Eld. "I don't suppose you have the dimensions?"

"The Wellspring is said to be unfathomable," Eld said. Chan Sha cursed and he winked at me. "Luckily I've taken a page from your book, Buc, and found a tome on architecture that outlines much of the Citadel, including its crypts and the accompanying cathedral." He shrugged. "It won't be exact, Artificer, but I can give you a pretty good estimate."

"That will help," the shorter man said simply. "Bar'ren, will you assist me? For a native you've a deft hand with measurements and the like."

"I think that's a compliment," I offered to the older man, who looked bemused. "So now we know what we'll need to poison the Wellspring, but how do we get to the bloody thing?"

"I've a plan for that," Eld said.

"You've a plan for everything, it seems," Chan Sha snapped.

"Aye, maybe I've one for you, yet," he growled.

"Easy, children," Salina said.

"Pardon," Eld muttered. "There are several subterranean canals running beneath the city, arteries of the Gods, if one can believe it, and while they aren't exactly secret, they aren't well known either. We use them to transport larger supplies via barges, as they run right into the crypts of the Citadel. I'll give the crew some coin as a thank-you for their hard efforts and suggest they have a drink before they pilot the final barge, and while they're having their celebratory glass we'll sneak you lot aboard and into some of the barrels they'll be delivering."

"That sounds neither practical nor comfortable," Chan Sha said, arching an eyebrow. "Even if we gain entry, surely they'll discover us at your Citadel's docks?"

"You're thinking like a mortal, Chan Sha," Eld said. "Which I guess is progress, eh?"

"Since when did you become the arsehole of the pair?"

"You bring it out in folks," Eld said.

"He's not wrong there," I admitted, and both looked at me. "She asks a fair question, Eld," I said after a moment.

"The one major flaw that runs through all of the Dead Gods' works is their arrogance," he said. "They believe their stronghold impenetrable, that the arteries and channels of their Gods are sacrosanct and therefore impossible to be used against them. They also trust all of their priests and priestesses to be committed, blood and bone, to their cause." Eld coughed into his hand and looked up, blue eyes bright. "All of which means none will question when

I bring in supplies needed to complete the upcoming ritual." He
shook his head. "Getting in will be easy. Gaining entry to the
Wellspring that is literally at the heart of the Dead Gods' power,
introducing the silver we'll be loaded down with, and getting out
alive? That's the hard bit."

"Well, that's bloody well good to know," Chan Sha snorted.

"I thought so," Eld said. "What, did you expect this to be an
easy day's sail without a cloud on the horizon?"

"I didn't expect to be trusting my life to a Godsdamned Veneficus."

"And I didn't expect to trust Sicarii with Buc's life . . . but here
we are."

"You two really aren't going to leave over, are you?" I chuckled. "I thought the hard part would be poisoning the Wellspring,
but it might be keeping you two from giving us away with your
nattering."

"So," Salina drawled. "What's left to be done? I've missives to
send and inventories to go through if I'm to find enough silver in
a single day."

"I think that may be it, at least for the nonce," I said. "I'll
be—actually I'm not sure what I'll be doing." I paused with my
mouth open. "The irony of having a crew so damned intelligent
and capable is I'm not sure I have a lot to do."

"I'll remember that," Salina said, dryly, turning to head back
upstairs.

"Salina?" Eld's voice caught her. "Do you have a ship and captain in the harbor that you can trust? With your life, if needs be?"

Salina turned back around and exchanged a look with Chan
Sha. "Might be that I do. Crew's certain, the verdict's still out on
the captain." Chan Sha rolled her eyes. "Why?"

"I'll explain later," he said, pushing himself up from the table.
"If you can give me the name and portage I will have something
delivered to them this afternoon. I-it mustn't fall into anyone's
hands, Salina."

"Very well," the woman said, searching his eyes for a moment. Her gaze flicked to me and then back to Chan Sha. "Give it to him."

Chan Sha took a nub of a pencil and scrap of parchment from the Artificer and scrawled down the name of the vessel we'd come to Normain in, the one we'd captured in pitched battle between the Dead Gods and the few remaining Normain crew.

"What are you playing at, Eld?" I asked him.

"Just trust me," he whispered.

"There you go," Chan Sha said, sliding the scrap across the table. She pushed herself up and began limping after Salina. "I'll see the ship is waiting," she added over her shoulder.

"If you truly don't have anything to do," Eld said when they'd gone, "I do have half a bell free, until the shops I must visit to cover for me being out this early will open."

"What are you suggesting?" I asked, speaking around another scone.

"Would the signorina care to take in the sunrise over the city with this honorable sirrah?"

"Honorable, eh?" I laughed, spraying crumbs. "A few years ago," I said, wiping my mouth on my napkin, "I'd have tossed what's left of this cold tea at you."

I got up, smoothing my emerald-green robe, and walked around the table to meet him. *Are you the same old Eld? Or are you just trying really hard?* Taking his arm, we went up the stairs, not stopping at the landing that led to the suites, but continuing up the spiraling hardwood staircase to the roof. As we climbed, I felt Eld leaning more heavily against me. *Sin.* Together we took his weight and I could hear his breathing ease as we reached the top. We went out the flame-streaked, oak door and into the purple-blue dawn, with the sound of the sea just reaching us. The city began waking, starting with the sounding bells out in the harbor as a ship crept out, its sails unfurling like a woman shedding her robe.

"You've been very clever this morn," I told Eld, watching the ship begin to gather speed and pull around the horn that led to the sea itself. I leaned against the brick lip that ran at shoulder height around the top of the roof and looked at him, tall and pale, almost translucent in his bone-white robes in the dawn light. "Very clever."

"Is that a compliment?" he asked, arching an eyebrow.

"Of the highest order. Clever to devise a plan that needed very little in the way of adaptation despite your Archnemesis's alterations. Clever to reach us in time. Clever to convert even the doubters in my crew—"

"I'm not sure I've assuaged Chan Sha," he cut in.

"If you hadn't, she'd have taken that pistole with her when she left," I said. "And clever," I continued, "to do it all without allowing any of them to realize that you're a plague carrier. You told them as much when you described the inoculation process and not one of them realized how deadly you'd become."

"I'm not actually contagious," he protested, taking half a step toward me. "I said as much. The inoculation doesn't make me deadly to any but myself."

"Aye, exactly," I growled. "So how do you plan on healing yourself if we poison the Wellspring?"

"I—" He sagged against the lip of the wall beside me. "I'm not exactly sure," he admitted, running a hand down the reddish-blond stubble on his cheeks. "I haven't thought that far."

"Lucky you, I've got a morning with nothing to do." I took his hand, the familiar callouses from his sword sliding against my own, from handling stilettos and daggers. "I'll figure it out, Eld."

He squeezed my hand and I looked out to the harbor again, blinking back tears. *Gods, am I going to fall apart whenever I'm around him now?* We'd nearly lost each other more than once already during my fight against the Gods, and now that we were so close—to each other and to winning—I didn't want to lose him, but I also knew we couldn't lose the battle. Not with these stakes.

"Why'd you ask Salina for that ship?" I asked, before my thoughts could linger in places where there was nothing to be done. "I know you asked me to trust you," I added when he hesitated. "And I do . . . but a woman's curious."

"Especially when that woman is you," he said, showing his even, white teeth when he grinned. "I've had an awful lot of time to think lately," he said after a moment.

"That's despite plotting the destruction of the world? And plotting to foil the plotting to destroy the world?"

"Aye," he chuckled, "despite that. I've been wondering if perhaps the true danger isn't in us losing so much as it is in our winning."

"How so?"

"Because, Buc—" He drew in a breath. "If we win, we'll destroy several of the pillars propping up much of our world. Aye, those pillars are more chains than anything else, but I fear we're going to knock the balance of power so far out of alignment that we never give the world the chance to stand on its own that we've been hoping for."

"You're not wrong," I admitted. "I've had the same fears myself. It's why 'Lina and I have been working on setting up systems of education to change things with the next generation of children growing up, but . . . that's a longer-term plan and just one small step up the staircase."

"I intend to hide several crates packed with artifacts—bone, sinew, and the like—used in the Dead Gods' rituals," Eld said, speaking quickly as if to keep me from stopping him. "I've set them aside for the after. I know, I know, it can't be allowed to fall into the wrong hands, but I'm wondering if, with the Artificer and the rest of us, perhaps we can't find ways to replicate much of what the Gods did that was of use to society without the corruption? Without the manipulation?"

"I'm not sure anything the Gods have touched can be redeemed," I snapped, suddenly conscious of the fact that both Eld and I had been very much touched by the Gods. "At the same time, the Artificer's inventions are based on Ciris's work and many physikers' potions have their origin in the Dead Gods. I suppose that ship has sailed and we may as well keep our options open." I glanced crossways at Eld. "What else are you hiding from me, Eldritch Nelson Rawlings?"

Eld's waxen features softened, the light illuminating his sapphire eyes, and he leaned forward. "Only that after being apart from you for so long . . . being beside you now is like a drowning man breaking the surface and catching a breath he never thought to find."

I leaned forward to meet him, our noses touching. "And yet?"

"And yet the thought," he whispered, "that we're likely to die killing the Dead Gods in a few hours isn't exactly leaving me trembling with joy, Buc."

"No?" I pulled him close and kissed him on the lips. His stubble brushed my chin and an electric buzz shot through me. He returned my kiss, opening his lips, and for a long moment we were one. "Something else for me to work on," I whispered breathlessly when we broke apart.

40

"The silver will work," the Artificer said, his eyes magnified to thrice their usual size by the lenses strapped like goggles around his head. He tapped the bubbling beaker until a small dot of gleaming liquid slipped down a thin, angled length of glass tubing, gravity carrying the drop across several paces of granite flooring before reaching a curved, glass vessel with a thimbleful of liquid purple—blood of the Dead Gods—pooled at the bottom. The dot fell into the blood, an infinitesimal gleam against the wine-dark liquid. The blood tremored, splitting into a dozen shades of purple that turned first auburn, then almost straw-colored as the dot splintered into a thousand pieces. Within a few moments, the mixture was a clouded amber soup.

"Too right it works," I said, bending down beside him in a dark-purple, ruffled shirt that I'd left hanging out over the soft, grey trousers I'd tucked into black, heeled boots.

"That's the problem," he said, sucking on his teeth. "Too well and so forth."

"What do you mean?"

"Eld was right, silver undoes their blood from the inside out," the short man explained. "The pain will be immediate and intense and if you want the mages to die . . . we'll need to find a way to mask it for as long as possible or else they'll stop after the first few drink of the Wellspring. I've no doubt, given enough time, they'd figure out how to cleanse the source and then we'd be back to where we started. Worse off, really."

"So we need a way to dull the pain . . . what about mollusk poison?" I asked, thinking of my time in Cordoban.

"Won't work," the Artificer said, pulling his goggles off and tossing them onto the workbench in the small sitting room he'd converted into a laboratory. "The, uh, elements? The elements in mollusk poison would eat at the silver and the silver would eat at it and render the blood almost back to its original state. Most of the poisons I've thought to try share that complication; what we need is some sort of analgesic—"

"Isn't that what most poisons are?" I asked.

"Aye, of course, but we need something different. If we could mimic the effects of kan leaf when it's smoked, only amplified greatly, that might work," Arti said, tapping his lip with an inked finger and leaving a smudge behind. "I'd need weeks to conduct the experiments, though."

"Weeks we don't have," I muttered.

"What is this analgesic?" Bar'ren asked, stumbling over the word.

"A sort of pain reliever," I said. The older man looked ill at ease in his Normain-style garments. Generally, as he did today, he wore as little as possible and left his jacket unbuttoned. He'd been quiet since we'd reached Normain—helpful, but watchful and reserved. Whether that was because he was well and truly out of his element or because of something he'd learned from his Goddess's visions, I wasn't sure. We hadn't talked much and he spent most of his time with Arti.

I explained further. "Physikers use different roots or ointments to dull a toothache or other minor pains, but those are mild at best, so many physikers use kan or diluted poisons for greater hurts. We need something like that, but far stronger." The older man nodded. He brushed his mane of white hair back as he stood up, then ducked out the door and disappeared down the corridor without a word. "Stick up his arse? What was that about?"

"You understand people far better than I do," the Artificer said with a shrug as he began writing a list of ingredients known to reduce pain.

"If that's true, then we're both fucked," I joked.

"And so forth," the short man muttered, shaking his balding head as he studied the parchment.

"What about oil of eulips?" I suggested, looking over his shoulder. "And feverfew and what's that spice you used to mask the scent of Serpent's Flame? Cardurry? Doesn't that have pain-relieving properties?"

"I should have thought of that straight off," he grunted.

"You're too close to the work, is all," I said, clapping him on the shoulder. The man had a tender disposition and the last I needed was him losing his nerve.

"Feverfew causes vomiting in some," he said, adding it to the list.

"Now that you say it, so does eulips if ingested. Number one-twelve." Arti glanced at me. "*Separating Herbs and Their Lore.* I may have let a few drops slip into a certain butler's cup in Frili-tuo when Eld and I needed a word alone with a noble's daughter concerning a murder." I felt my mouth twitch. "I guess someone should have told him it's topical in application."

"I imagine he figured it out soon enough," the Artificer said dryly.

"Aye, leastwise his chamber pot did."

The door banged open, interrupting our laughter, and Bar'ren stepped in with two large haversacks, one thrown over each shoulder. Despite their bulging sides, he carried them effortlessly. When he set them down on the floor, one spilled open, dumping a bunch of dried leaves onto the granite flagstones and filling the room with a faint whiff of mint and sugar and some smell that I'd never caught before. Not unpleasant, but off, somehow. He picked up a leaf and held it out to Arti and me. Its star shape nearly filled his palm; it was withered to almost black, save for a glimmer of green in the very center.

"We have a plant that grows in the center of our island, a tree, really, whose sap fire ants love to suckle from," he said. "The old trees' bark is too rigid for them to penetrate unless it is dying, but the young trees are soft yet and the fire ants come in swarms if but one of them catches the taste of its sap. Their groves would soon be overrun, save something curious occurs. As the ants drink the sap, they begin to lose their straight lines, wandering about aimlessly, and whatever scent they give off that the others follow becomes confused. Oftentimes one will find entire swarms marching into the sea along a dozen disparate winding paths that can almost always be traced back to these groves."

"It's a defense mechanism," I said after a moment. "Something in the sap, likely the same thing that attracts the ants, disorients them and prevents them from destroying the groves entirely."

"It is so," Bar'ren agreed. "The leaves of these trees, when dried and crushed into powder, can be ingested in small amounts to ease large sufferings."

"How small?" the Artificer asked.

"How large?" I asked at the same time.

"My Sha'amen, who taught me all I knew, broke her ankle so badly as a child that it could not be mended and became infected," he said after a moment. "Her Sha'amen had to cut it off with a hot blade, but before your kind came to our shores the knives we crafted were of obsidian and flint and dull iron."

"Ouch," I grunted.

"She said her Sha'amen stripped one point from the star-leaf and brewed it in tea, and when she drank it, her entire body went numb from sunrise to sunset," Bar'ren said.

"Impossible," the Artificer gasped. "That's more potent than mollusk poison or a sea serpent's venom."

"Not quite," I said, speaking slowly. "If it were, it would kill, and I imagine that were one to ingest enough they'd simply . . . stop breathing."

"It is the way, sometimes, for those whose pain cannot be

cured, who desire the next path, to speak with the Sha'amen," Bar'ren said, his voice rumbling deep in his chest. "It is no small thing to seek paths never before trod, where none may follow and none return. If, after a time, the Sha'amen agrees, a whole leaf is brought, crushed, and mixed into a fruit paste. Then there is a celebration and a saying of goodbye."

"Savages," the Artificer whispered so low that only with Sin could I hear him.

"I've read of this leaf," I said, shooting him a look. Given what I'd seen of kan fiends in Servenza who lost their minds and died starving in the gutters with bright, kan-stained teeth and ribs that stuck through the rags they wore, I wasn't sure we were in any position to judge. "Arasmeth said she'd been told of a five-pointed leaf in the depths of the Shattered Coast that could heal all manner of ills, dull any pain, and that the, er, natives, used it to dull their wits at being stuck on small specks of land in the vastness of that sea." *I guess Arti isn't the only one who thinks their lot savages.* "She thought it just a myth, a wild tale of sailors."

"She was a fool," Bar'ren said. "The Mother told me to take all of my people's stockpiles with me when I left our island. A fool would have disobeyed, but I am no fool, and now you see the worth of my lands."

"That's why you insisted on taking your things in the longboat along with my artifices," Arti said. "I thought they would be the feather that sunk us all."

"We're *all* fools sometimes," I said, looking at the short man. "Present company excepted," I added when Bar'ren glared at me. "Your Goddess certainly wasn't, putting her trust in me as she did." The Sha'amen looked nonplussed and I shifted tack, glancing at Arti. "That's a lot of leaves there . . . but will it be enough?"

"It depends," he said slowly. I could practically see the calculations flashing across his eyes. "Depends on how much silver Salina can bring to me . . . but I think, aye. This may be exactly what we need."

"Do you have the figures? How many stones?"

"Tonnes," Arti said, handing me a slip of paper.

I glanced down at it and felt my eyebrows shoot up. "Well, the Chair is going to make the Company earn their reputation as the most powerful trading company in the world today." I patted Bar'ren on his rock-hard shoulder. "Well done, Sha'amen."

"And you, Sambuciña," he said formally.

"Show him"—I nodded at the Artificer—"how to put this leaf best to use. I'm going to track down Salina and that silver and then it's time to prepare for tonight. I've a few loose ends to tie up between now and then."

Like how we're going to defeat Gods who have lived for millennia past their deaths—and their were-creatures and undead. How I'm going to cure Eld before we poison them all. Living would be a plus, too.

"All in a day's work for a demi-Goddess," Sin whispered.

"I'd say if I pull this off I've earned the right to full Goddesshood, but then I'd have to off myself, so . . ." My mind swam with possibilities. But first, I had to see a woman about some silver.

41

Full dark had set in, bringing the rumblings of a storm with it, and the salt air was heavy with tension that portended a violent night as our flat-bottomed boat entered a fissure in the cliff face of Normain's Old City. *Let's hope it's our deeds and not the weather that's violent.* After some discussion, we'd decided to commandeer a barge rather than try to steal aboard one belonging to the Dead Gods. The few crew we had for the task weren't as skilled with a barge and poles as they were with a sailing ship and sheets, so progress was slow, though steady enough. Bar'ren stood beside me in his white, fur stole and black, leather pants, cradling a repeating crossbow of the Artificer's make in his arms, the handle of his obsidian-studded mace jutting out behind his left shoulder. His tanned, weathered face looked like it had been carved from the same stone we sailed between. *Likely thinks his Mother sent the weather, that nature mirrors our purpose for a reason.*

Chan Sha stood on the other side of him; the unlikely pair seemed to have bonded in our battle with the plague ship. The former pirate queen was dressed in a crimson outfit the color of dried blood. Her open jacket trailed down to her calves; the vest she wore beneath it was festooned with grenadoes; and she clicked and clacked with every step as the two dozen pistoles she wore hanging from ropes across her shoulders bumped into one another and into the mechanical apparatus strapped to her back. The arms were folded in now, but I had seen in Servenza what that spider's fangs could do, with their scything blades for fingers. *I'm sorry, Marin.* I'd promised the woman—murdered by Chan

Sha, back when she went by Sicarii—justice, but I'd really meant revenge. A not-so-small part of me still thought that was what was needed, despite Chan Sha being useful to my cause.

Salina sat on a barrel in the shadow of the boat's wheel, features concealed by the green hood she'd pulled up over her blond braid. The handles of her pair of sawed-off, rotating blunderbusses poked up over her shoulders, giving her a hunched look that seemed to match her mood. Something had changed in her since we'd come to Normain, but the woman wouldn't tell me what it was. *Closest she's been to death save Cordoban? And Southeast Island.* It could be that, but I didn't think so and Sin didn't either, though if he knew something, I couldn't find the thought in him. She'd worked her magic in coming up with nearly three tonnes of silver in half a day's time and she was here now; that was what mattered.

The Artificer held another crossbow, nearly a twin to Bar'ren's, save this one had three, smaller grooves carved into the top where the bolts went instead of one. He claimed it would fire three bolts at one time, then reload itself from the cylinder attached to the bottom. Sin had shown me the secret to its firing, utilizing an ingenious canister of air compressed so tightly that it pumped gearwork that handled both the loading and cocking of the bow. That Arti had figured out how to do all of that thrice over in the same instant was . . . "impressive" wasn't a large enough word for it. He felt my gaze and looked back at me, reaching up to flick the lenses on his spectacles, sliding a lens over them that amplified ambient light like moon or starlight. There was none of that here in the dark canal—one of the fallen Gods' arteries—that cut beneath Normain. All light came from flickering lamps in wall sconces and half a dozen lanterns hung aboard the boat. More shadow than light, when it came to it.

I was dressed similarly to Chan Sha, but my grey jacket was drawn tight about me, held fast by a single button—gilded, but I'd blacked it out with ash—that I could flick open if needed.

Arti's smaller, alley-piece crossbow hung beneath my armpit and I had a pair of boarding axes thrust through my belt, along with sundry blades about me in all the usual places and one or two unusual ones as well. I shifted in my boots to feel the blades there and spun my steel-reinforced slingshot in the palms of my hands. *Almost there.* We were approaching the final bend that would bring us to a dock just outside the Dead Gods' demesne.

"All right," I said, turning back from the railing. "Everyone gather 'round."

"We're already by you," Chan Sha said.

"Formalities must be observed, woman. We're about to sneak into the heart of the Dead Gods' power. The same undead bastards that have been trying to rip us limb from limb across half the world." My gaze swept across them. "A year ago, I wouldn't be saying any of this to you, because I'd be slipping down this canal alone. A year ago," I said, dropping my voice, "I mistook intelligence for wisdom, need for weakness, and hedging for increased odds. I'm as surprised as you lot must be to discover that even I make mistakes." Chan Sha snorted and Salina giggled while both men fought not to smile.

"Truth is, the only way we'll succeed tonight is if we do this together. Might be, none of us come back out this canal, but I promise you this . . ." I drew in a hard breath, feeling the rage I'd been keeping frozen within me ever since I let Chan Sha live begin to crackle from its frozen chains. "I promise you that tonight, the Dead Gods die!

"We go in together, we come out together, or we don't come out at all." I finished quietly, and Salina and Chan Sha took up positions on either side of me.

"Well," Chan Sha said, "here's the thing. There's only one of us what can kill Ciris, and that's you."

Salina added, "We might all die tonight, but you can't."

"Remember that, when things get bloody," Chan Sha concluded. "We won't let you die. Not tonight leastwise."

"What? Is this mutiny?" I growled, and one of the passing crew members stumbled at my words.

"Call it an intervention," Chan Sha said. Her good eye stared into mine. "I knew you were trouble the day I pulled you and Eld from the drink, Buc. I just didn't know you were the kind of trouble that could free the world. Dying tonight, back-to-back, sounds fun and all . . ."

"But winning sounds better, aye?" Salina asked.

"You can't die either," I told her gruffly, reaching out to squeeze her arm.

"I've already arranged that should I disappear, you'll be the next Chair," the woman told me. "If you don't like our terms, there's a simple fix," she added.

"Aye?" I grunted. "What's that?"

"Engineer a plan so astounding in its brilliance that we never have to come to blows with any of these undead bastards."

"Simple enough," I muttered. Pointing past them at the approaching dock, I nodded. "Well, this is the first step in that plan."

"Eld's not going to like it," Salina whispered.

"No," I agreed, "he's not." I cleared my throat. "Make ready, you lot. We're here. Steady as she goes."

"You heard the woman," Chan Sha said dryly. Some sailors moved to the rails while others adjusted poles and oars; a moment later we drew to a stilted halt for a beat before continuing to edge along the channel, turning clumsily toward the dock. *Sailors, not polers.* "Wait for her command."

"You know, Frobisher made me think I could command a ship," I told Salina, "but it was Royale Aislin who made me *want* to command one. The bitch had a way about her . . . let's find out if I do as well."

"You're late!" Eld hissed when our flat-bottomed boat bumped railings with the nearly identical one he stood on. "The crew will be back any moment," he added, gesturing toward the long, thin, floating dock that ran for several score paces along the edge of the canal wall. At the far end, a series of ladders and steps led up to a gangplank that stretched out of view toward the surface. A voice cried out and several others joined them in a bawdy tune. "They're coming now," Eld said, cursing.

"We've had a slight change in plan. Too much silver to be exchanged quickly." I handed him three of the Artificer's timers. "Place those along the deck and give them a turn. Can't have anyone following after," I explained when he arched his eyebrows. He coughed hoarsely into his elbow, juggling the grenadoes and their gearwork trappings. "And be quick about it," I added, pushing our boat away from his, my legs and arms burning with magic that stole my hearing away so that I almost didn't hear his question.

"Because you wouldn't have liked it," I whispered in answer.

Our ship nosed past Eld's, Chan Sha at the wheel, and began to swing broadside to where the floating gangplank ran along the wall. The returning barge crew were all on the boards now, in a merry mood after Eld's generosity. There were nearly a score of them, singing and slapping one another on the back, no more than forty paces from us on the walkway. A few were pointing at our barge as we slowly cruised along.

"Make ready," I called across the deck, and the crew pulled off the tarps that had obscured the mounted, rotating crossbows that the Artificer had had brought from Servenza and transferred from one ship to another. It was these, not Bar'ren's leaves, that had nearly sunk one of the longboats. The heavyset sailor with the pair of dogs who said he'd follow me anywhere had proven as good as his word; now he took a position behind one of the crossbows, the coal-black dog at his side, the tan one poking its head out the back of his shirt as if wondering what all the fuss was about. *You're about to see, little guy.*

Eld came vaulting over the aftmost crossbow, hitting the deck in a ball before rolling to his feet, hacking as he rose.

"What are you doing, Buc?"

"Leaving nothing to chance," I told him. "Fire!"

My crew obeyed without hesitation. A handle on the side of each crossbow rotated the notches; a large cylinder beneath that required two sailors to load supplied both compressed air and bolts, turning the bows into automatic weapons that filled the air with hissing, scything steel. The barge crew on the docks didn't even hear what was coming, though one tall lass gestured frantically toward us before her body jerked and danced and she collapsed into the water. Within moments the wooden dock was empty save for spent bolts, while around us, scraps of cloth and a few darker forms floated in the canal.

"Well done," I called out.

"Well done?" Eld growled. "Buc, they were innocents! Men and women just doing a job!"

"I don't think you can work every day transporting the machinery of war along secret canals to the Dead Gods' Citadel and claim innocence," I told him. He stared down at me, still looking sickly from the plague; his blond hair, gathered in a loose ponytail, was dark with sweat and his eyes burned from fever or anger, I wasn't sure which. "But I do wish you had a little more faith in me."

I nodded toward the gangplank and Eld turned back just as a dozen men and women broke the surface, shedding the goggles and breathing tubes that had kept them hidden beneath the murky water. They began pulling limp bodies out of the water.

"I don't understand," Eld said as one of the hidden swimmers pounded the chest of one of the fallen crew, making sure he was breathing.

"Blunted tips," Chan Sha said, tossing a spare bolt at him. "Same that furriers use to stun animals when they don't want to lose part of the fur to a wound. *I* wanted them all dead. Cleaner that way."

"You would," Eld growled. "They're just concussed?" he asked, looking from the bolt in his fist to me.

"They are," I assured him, "and they'll be tied up by the time they're awake." I left unsaid that my crew had orders to drown the lot if they were discovered. I'd spared them for Eld, but I was only willing to bend so far. Behind us, a dull whump was followed by the sound of the other barge taking on water. "I couldn't take any chances, Eld. Not on them finding or betraying us nor on you sparing their lives."

"This is what you've been planning," he whispered.

"No, this is just the beginning," I told him. "I'm stacking every odd possible in our favor, Eld."

He stared at me for a moment and nodded slowly. "I hope you are, Buc. We're going to need them all."

"Aye." I slid my arm around his. "Every fucking one."

42

"Your lot are really hung up on death, aren't they?" I asked, shining my lantern on the skulls tucked into the ivory-bone walls at regular intervals. Some grinned back at me, their empty maws filled with guttering candlelight, while others were as dead as their owners, having burned themselves out who knew how many ages ago. "It's all dead and dying deathiness."

"They're not my lot," Eld said, burying a cough in the crook of his elbow. The muffled sound echoed through the chamber. He glanced up, wiping his mouth against his sleeve, and shrugged. "They are a little one-note, now that you mention it."

"You two want to have a chat about undead worshipping cultists, do it on your own hourglass," Chan Sha muttered.

"Nervous?" Salina asked, her face carved in the look I'd come to recognize as the Chair.

"You wish," Chan Sha said.

"Nerves keep one alive," Bar'ren said from the rear.

"Then I am the liveliest man alive," the Artificer grumbled in front of him.

"Arti? Was that a joke?"

"And so forth," he answered me.

"C'mon," Eld said, stepping past me. "We're nearly there. There are only a few tunnels between the next cavern and the Wellspring."

"Come here often?" I asked him, picking up the thick hawser rope that I'd let drop for a moment. The small wagon the Artificer had rigged up was light but sturdy. It needed to be to haul the silver ingots we'd loaded atop it as well as Bar'ren's leaves and a few more sacks filled with more of Arti's gearwork inventions. Despite the greased wheels, my Sin-enhanced strength, and Bar'ren and Salina pushing from the rear, it'd been a slog, moving up the slight incline of the passageway. The bone beneath my feet was slightly rough, so every step caught at my boots, clinging as if it didn't want to let go.

"Not by this way, no," Eld answered me after a moment. "When I was an acolyte, I was brought to the Wellspring through an archway opposite where we'll come out."

"A worshipping-your-Gods-at-the-heart-of-their-power sort of thing?"

"No, more like self-immolation. They bathe you in the pool and the blood seeps into every pore," he said, speaking lightly, though his features drew taut. "I was drowned in the pool, my skin on fire despite the wetness, my screams making small bubbles in the froth I churned up. Just as I felt my life flickering out of me, they brought me back."

"Gods," Salina breathed, more leaning than pushing against the cart.

"I was one of the lucky ones," Eld said. "There's some that never break the surface alive."

"W-what happens to them?"

"Shambles," Eld said simply.

"Well, the Dead Gods' mages are an economical lot," I muttered. "Let's give them that."

"It's considered a great honor," he said with a grin that didn't reach his eyes.

"I bloody bet it is," Chan Sha growled.

"Well, if we're done freaking ourselves out, let's remember that after we're finished with the Wellspring it literally will burn them alive and no one will ever have to fear being stolen from death only to be forced into worshipping dead beings from the skies above," I said.

We all seemed to slow down as if by hidden signal as we reached the edge of the new cavern; a mass of darkness ate the light from our lanterns so that we could see only a few paces into the space. When Bar'ren came to a stop, his boot steps chased after, their dry scuffing like a corpse's last breath, and Salina rubbed at her arms, Chan Sha suppressing a shiver beside her. *Sin.* My hearing shrank and my vision changed so that suddenly the lanterns were white splashes that washed out parts of my vision while the darkness took on an eerie glow that let me see the sprawling cavern before us. Boxes and casks were stacked along the wall to our right, each row higher than the last, the final row stretching to where I could see the vaguest suggestion of a ceiling. Three main arteries—and given we were within the body or bodies of the Dead Gods themselves, they were likely literal arteries—branched off. The one to our right ended abruptly in a pair of black, iron doors that rose from floor up to just past head height, open space above their wrought-iron spikes. The left and center passages both bent sharply after a dozen paces, obscuring what they held. The air was tinged with a musky smell like an animal's cage that wanted fresher straw.

"What now?"

"That way"—Eld pointed straight ahead—"leads to the kitchens." I knew he couldn't see that far but his finger lined up exactly with the entrance. "I'm going to slip ahead in this passage to the left and check to see if Hexia is at her desk. Hopefully she isn't."

"Hexia?" Salina asked.

"The librarian," Eld explained.

"Librarian?" My ears perked up.

"Another time," Chan Sha said.

"She's a Dead Walker anyway," Eld added. "You two wouldn't get on."

"I dunno, we'd have books in common at least," I whispered. "What's behind those doors over there?" I asked, gesturing at the wrought-iron gates.

"You can see that?" Eld's brow furrowed and he muttered something about magic under his breath. "You don't want to go in there. That's one of the storage rooms for Shambles. The ones kept down here are older, which makes them both slower than fresh corpses and far more powerful in one of those magical ways that seems to make no sense."

"Noted," I said. "Plan is you go off and check on Hexia while we wait here?" Eld nodded and I shook my head. "You're not going alone. We need her killed outright if she's there and I can't take a chance on you being noble or polite or something equally foolish."

"You can't come," Eld said. "I can sense Sin Eaters, save for you . . . they give me and other Dead Gods' mages an annoying itching feeling. I don't know if I can't sense you because we have so much history together or if you're actually invisible. So I don't know how Hexia will react to having you near."

"A fine time to let us know that we've brought a bright, blazing fucking magnet with us," Chan Sha growled.

"It doesn't work that way," Eld said, shaking his blond locks. "Buc would have to be close enough that we'd have other problems to worry about for them to sense her, but if Hexia *is* there and she *does* sense her, it will make things complicated."

"Take Bar'ren with you, then," I suggested. "He can hang back in the shadows and if Hexia is there, you'll have a crossbow at your back. If she's not, send him back to collect us."

"All right," Eld said after a moment. "Can you see at all, Bar'ren?"

"On moonless nights during the rainy seasons, I have hunted boar by feel and sound alone."

"Look at the balls on this one," I muttered, remembering how a certain hoary boar had nearly ripped Eld and me to pieces on Bar'ren's island. In broad fucking daylight. "Just show him where the wall is, Eld, and he can go by feel."

Eld nodded and Bar'ren passed his lantern to the Artificer

and unlimbered his crossbow from where he'd slung it across his front. Salina stepped up beside me, her cloak pulled tightly about her. "It's strange," she said, watching them disappear into the inky blackness, "to think the Dead Gods' mages have names. That they're people, too."

"They're like people in the same way a nurse and a white fin are both sharks." Chan Sha chuckled mirthlessly. "Power changes people, you should know that by now, Salina. Magic is all kinds of power that you can't ken until you have it."

"In the same way," I added, touching Salina's arm to keep her from snapping at Chan Sha, "that you likely imagined what being Chair would be like only to discover it was something else entirely when you got it. Aye?"

"That makes a certain kind of sense," Salina agreed. "I'm just not looking forward to finding out how different that kind of power is."

"You already have," Chan Sha said. "In Cordoban and against the plague ship. There's just more of them here."

"Oh, that's all." Salina laughed ruefully.

"Let's do something about that," I muttered. "Show me your wares, Arti." The shorter man produced a large haversack from within the wagon. I dug around in the bag and pulled out four or five Serpent's Flame grenadoes and a roll of thin wire. "Chan Sha, you remember how to set these up?"

"Aye," she said. "I remember what they did to my gangs atop the Lighthouse, too. That's going to be one Godsdamned loud bang, Buc. Might be it would draw every undead fucker here."

"If those doors open and a horde of Shambles come stumbling out, I want them on fire," I said. "They're so old they'll go up like kindling, and once the front of the pack catches, they'll all burn. 'Sides, if they do come out those doors, then I think every undead fucker will already know someone's come knocking."

"You've another escape route in mind," Chan Sha guessed. "We aren't coming back this way, are we?"

"We might." I shrugged. "If a mouse wouldn't trust itself to one hole, why would I?"

"C'mon," Salina said, taking the grenadoes from me, "let's get this done."

"I'll show you how to do the first pair," Chan Sha said, catching the wire I tossed her, "and then you can rig some up on the other side and we'll meet in the middle."

"You all right, Arti?" I asked as they headed off, lanterns held high.

"No," he whispered, drawing a hand through his thinning blond hair. "I'm scared shitless and I know that because if I could have, I'd've shit my pants already."

"Well, this whole damned expedition has done wonders for your sense of humor, at least," I told him. I clapped the man on the shoulder and gestured back the way we'd come. "Keep an eye on our backside and stay close to me and you'll come through this with enough jokes to turn jester if you wish. Savvy?" The man turned away and I added, "Mind you drive a wedge against the back wheel while you're at it. Last we need is for this damned thing to start rolling away."

"You do this well," Sin whispered in my mind.

"Aye?" He'd been quiet after he and I spent several hours planning for what was to come. I wasn't sure if it was because he worried I wouldn't trust him when the lead started flying or if it was because he thought he'd done all he could. "Do what well?"

"Lead. You sent Eld off with a minder, which is smart given his personality. You saw Salina was nervous and put her and Chan Sha to work, doubly smart, given what lurks beyond those gates. Getting the Artificer looking toward the light, where he can see what's coming instead of imaging all sorts of nonsense waiting in the darkness keeps him useful for longer, though he will panic at some point—which you know."

"He won't panic," I lied.

"Sure he will, but with luck it won't be until after a point when his panicking doesn't matter. You know, Buc, if you weren't de-termined to be such a raging arsehole, you could have led a gang or a regiment or a crew or a trading company," Sin said.

"And now, because I am a raging arsehole, I'm leading a hit team to assassinate the Gods themselves," I told him.

"I'm just saying that it's damned impressive given you're not twenty yet," Sin said. "I shudder to think what we'll be like when we're forty. Or sixty."

"What *we'll* be like?" I smirked. "That mean you've finally de-cided to help me murder your old gal Ciris?"

"There's the arsehole," he muttered. "Let's focus on killing the already dead Gods first, then we'll talk about the Goddess."

"I've got time now," I told him.

"Not the place for it, Buc."

"You've stopped trying to Possess me," I whispered, "but I re-member you threatening me with some other ritual that sounded an awful lot like suicide."

"That was before Ciris showed up and tried to rip me from your mind," Sin said after a long moment. "Do you remember the Ghost Captain saying that Ciris was insane? Driven that way by losing me?"

"Uh-huh."

"I don't think he was wrong. At least not all the way wrong. The way she came for you, even if she'd succeeded—" He swal-lowed hard. "—I'm not certain she wouldn't have destroyed me while destroying you . . . and I'm not sure she cared."

"What are you saying?" I asked him. "The Ghost Captain seemed to think reuniting you with her would make her call off the war, once she realized her enemies were dead, but he also tried to plant a hidden bomb in your altar to kill her, so it doesn't seem like he believed that you were her missing conscience."

"I'm not that." Sin barked a laugh. "I think that by splintering herself into the shard she hid in that altar, she damaged some-thing in her mind. Something that isn't fixable."

"What you're telling me is after we kill some dead Gods, we have to kill an insane God?"

"I don't think you can kill her, Buc," Sin said, cursing. "I know you don't believe that, but after this is over, maybe I can help you understand why it's impossible."

"Is this why you wanted to wait until after we kill the Dead Gods to talk?" I asked. My mind spun with a thousand different questions, each answer of which would spin up another thousand questions. "Because now I get it."

"Bloody wonderful," Sin drawled.

Before I could reply, Eld appeared from the darkness, Bar'ren at his heels. "Hexia's gone, the way is clear. We have to move. Now!"

"Trip wires, set!" Chan Sha and Salina jogged up to us, Chan Sha's trot more of a hitching limp. The former pirate's braids swung as she nodded. "Let's do this."

"C'mon, Arti," I said, tapping the man on the shoulder. "Eld, take the lead, I've got your shoulder. Chan Sha and Salina, stick with Arti." I clapped the little man on the back again, trying to drive some of my confidence into him. "It's level here, so you shouldn't need my help with the wagon. Bar'ren, watch our back trail?" The older man nodded, holding the crossbow against his white, fur stole as if it were an extension of himself. "Right, we're nearly there, folks. Full midnight and half a bell to showtime."

"The only thing is," Eld whispered as we moved out along the passageway to our left, the wagon's faint vibration hiding his voice, "Hexia's gone, but her tome is still on top of the desk."

"Is that strange?"

"Would you leave your slingshot lying around?"

"Oh. Damn. Something's up."

"Seems like," he agreed.

43

The Wellspring appeared as if by magic. One moment we were in yet another dark, winding tunnel, then a sudden turn revealed a subterranean cathedral sprawling before us in shambling magnificence. Bits of calcified sinew and tendon hanging like stalactites flickered purple and blue and green, while thicker pillars rose here and there from the floor, also reflecting the strange, blue glow of the pool itself. The Wellspring was a vast, irregular circle; flat bone, scraped clean, spread out from the glowing water in a semicircle for a score or more of paces until it met the seats. Rows of pews were carved into the bone, rising with each level like a theater, and a wide path, worn smooth from centuries of use, flowed from far up in the back, through what must be the archway Eld had mentioned, all the way down through the chamber to the Wellspring.

Eld kept walking for several paces until he realized he was alone, and paused, glancing back at where the rest of us were frozen. He swept his loose locks over his shoulder with one hand and marched back, a grin spreading across his wan features. "It does knock you back for a moment, doesn't it? At the first glance, anyway. Aye and at the tenth, too."

"I—I wasn't expecting anything the Dead Gods made to be so beautiful," Salina whispered. "It's like a starry sky."

"Aye," I grunted. In a way it was, with whatever it was inside the stalactites that caused them to twinkle against the curved ceiling above. I licked my lips. It also looked like hundreds of eyes leering down, cursing us for violating their most holy of sanctums. "Like everything with the Dead Gods, it's pretty in a creepy-as-fuck sort of way."

"You're not wrong, girl," a voice hissed from somewhere in front of us. A moment later a hooded figure rose from the far side of the pool where they'd been kneeling, uncoiling like a snake as they stood to full height. I'd mistaken them for another stalagmite. "Who are your friends, Eldritch? Come to pray with me for what we are about to do?"

"Who the fuck are you?" I shot back.

The figure stalked around the edge of the pool, following a channel cut into the bone, like a thin, dried moat. Throwing back their hood, the figure resolved into a woman with skin as black as midnight. Her white, braided hair, which hung to her waist, glowed in the Wellspring's light, and her skin gleamed. She bared her teeth when she saw me. "Sambuciña," she hissed. "The girl lives, Eldritch, which means"—she shifted her gaze to him—"you've been playing us all along. The Archnemesis was right, I should have sifted your memories again, but I thought you one of mine."

"I was one of yours, Plague Mistress," Eld said quietly. He'd shifted into a stance I recognized from a dozen earlier fights, only now I saw something that hadn't been there before. The way he held himself suggested that dark violence was a breath away. "Only, I was Buc's first."

"You've cost me much, Eldritch," she said, clicking her teeth together.

"Plague Mistress?" I asked. "You're the one that schemed all this. The one that would see the world die so that you might live."

"If I kill you all," the other woman said musingly, half to herself, "and if the Gods smile on me, *he* might not learn of it until after I've been named Highest on the council."

"The last bitch who ignored me ended up with an ax buried in his chest," I growled. "You remember your old friend the Ghost Captain?"

She practically snarled at me, then glared at Eld. "I'll leave enough breath in you to watch me rip *her* head off, Eldritch." She upended the vial she'd hidden in her hand and smiled bloodily when she finished. "It'll be the last sight you see before I turn you into a Shambles."

She leapt forward and Eld was already sprinting with his sword out, and they went at it like a pair of vipers at the bottom of a pit.

I'd fought Dead Gods' mages and I'd fought Sin Eaters and a few times I'd seen them fight one another, but I'd never seen anything like two Dead Gods' mages fighting each other. I knew she wasn't a Veneficus, but the vial had given her supernatural speed and strength. They slid around each other: she inside Eld's swinging blade, he spinning away from the vicious elbow she threw at his chin and catching her shoulder in his fist, wrenching her in a circle and using his momentum to throw her to the ground. She skidded across the floor, caromed off a pillar, and somehow found her feet, reversed direction, and came at him again so fast even my Sin-enhanced vision couldn't quite follow the blur of her motions.

Somehow Eld did, because he dropped his blade from nerveless fingers that had caught her stiff-fingered blow—she'd aimed for his throat—and cried out when she caught him with a low kick to the knee that dropped him to the floor. He scissor-kicked in midair as he fell, catching her thigh and sending her sprawling over him; then they both flipped around onto all fours and launched into a grappling match that was impossible to follow thanks to their billowing cloaks, tangled limbs, and swirling hair as they rolled across the floor toward the pool.

"Arti!" My cry snapped him out of his slack-jawed staring. "That vial you tested the silver with. You brought it, aye?"

"Oh," he said soundlessly, nodding as his hand plunged into the pocket of his vest. He dug it out and tossed it to me. "Catch! And so forth!"

"Eld!" I caught the vial, spun around, and threw it without thinking. "Over your head!"

Somehow in the maelstrom of fist and limb, Eld's pale arm shot out and caught the vial. The Plague Mistress used his distraction to squirm out from under him, sliding onto his back and sitting back hard, her forearm across his throat. "I said I'd leave you a single breath, Eldritch," she growled. "Are you ready to take it?"

Eld gurgled and threw himself backward, slamming her body between his and the floor, but she held on, tightening her hold. He gurgled again, arms windmilling, and I was just about to reach for my slingshot when he brought his fist back and smashed her full in the mouth just as her lips moved to coo victory in his ear.

As the fistful of bloody silver cascaded over her face and into her mouth, her scream echoed off the cathedral-like walls. Eld pulled free, twisting around and pinning her to the ground as her hands and heels drummed against the floor. Her cry cut off as he grabbed her.

"You first," he said hoarsely, bending over her.

Shit.

I opened my mouth to warn him, but it was too late. The Plague Mistress rose to meet him, pulling herself up the arm that was choking her, and headbutted Eld. He opened his mouth to shout and she locked lips with him and Eld's cry turned into a brutal scream that mirrored hers. He pulled away, falling onto his elbows as he writhed uncontrollably, fighting to keep his head up and his eyes on her. She pushed herself to her knees and grinned at him through broken, bloody lips, tears of blood pouring from her eyes.

"That much silver won't kill, Eldritch. You probably knew that. It *will* let the plague kill you, though. You probably didn't know that," she said, wiping her mouth clean with the back of her sleeve. "Now I'm going to—" Her words were choked off as I wrapped my arms around her neck.

"That much tongue and a girl gets jealous," I whispered in her ear. She tried to say something that came out as a muffled grunt and I felt her muscles tense. *Sin.* I felt my arms burn, the fiery, tingling pain more of a pleasure as it ran down through my shoulders into my back and hips. I put my entire body into the twist and the Plague Mistress's neck snapped like—well, like dry bone. The fracture reverberated through my arms and I let her limp form fall to the floor, dusting my hands off.

"That's how you snap a bitch's neck," I snarled.

"Buc," Eld gasped, and I was at his side before I realized I was moving. "Blood and bone, this fucking hurts," he moaned through clenched teeth. "I can feel it eating my body from the inside."

"What do you need me to do, Eld?" I squeezed his hand. "I don't know your magic. If we put you into the pool, will that blood cleanse you?"

"Not with both silver and the plague in my veins," he groaned. "With one or the other, it would work, but with both I—I don't t-t-think it—" Eld cut off, tremoring in my arms.

"*Sin!*" I screamed in my mind.

"I'm right here, Buc," he whispered. "No need to shout. I've slowed down time. We've a moment or two."

"What do we do? Is this the silver's work?"

"I know as little as you do about the inner workings of the Dead Gods' magic and I suspect the combination of silver with this plague are beyond much of their own understanding."

"You're a bloody shard of a Goddess," I snapped. "Make some guesses."

"I'd say the silver is causing the tremors and those will subside shortly when it's worn through the protections the Dead Gods' blood gives Eld. Then the plague will go to work, but it's already been in him for days, which means one of two things."

"Either he'll have fought it off and he'll just feel like death for a fortnight," I said, following his logic, "or it will . . ."

"Kill him," he finished.

"We can't afford to toss those dice, Sin. We've got to do something!"

"Aye, like what?"

"What you did with the Ghost Captain when he infected Eld with the Shamble's bite," I suggested. "Use our magic, magic we know, to heal him."

"Buc, that was orders of magnitude different. The Ghost Captain was trying to turn Eld with a bit of magic I was familiar with and I was able to craft a spell that used your body to counteract it. This . . . the Dead Gods are anathema to Ciris."

"Craft a healing spell. Sin Eaters have been doing that lately, right? You must know how."

"To heal a human of some things, sure, but this plague was developed specifically to attack Sin Eaters, remember? I can't introduce some magical cure on the fly, Buc."

"T-t-then . . ." My mind raced along a dozen disparate paths and I clenched my eyes shut as hard as I could, forcing it to move faster, commanding Sin to do the same. "We don't introduce anything," I said, opening my eyes as the solution came to me in one blinding, painful realization. "We take it in."

"What?" Sin gasped.

"Use our magic to consume the silver and the plague."

"That's not possible."

"You think it might be," I shot back, sensing his thoughts. "Cast the spell and tell me what to do."

"Now you trust me?"

"You wanted your chance, this is it." I fought back the fear that had caught me by the throat. "What do I do?"

"This is so fucking stupid," Sin said. "Even if we succeed, we'll have managed to infect ourselves with a plague that renders me useless."

"Not right away and not forever," I promised him. "We'll find a cure, but we need time to do that. Time Eld doesn't have."

"If we get ripped apart by Shambles because you're suddenly mortal again, I don't think Eld's going to thank us for saving his life."

"Eld doesn't get a say in this conversation, Sin. This is between me and you. We can do this. But I need you to take the lead."

"This is so fucking stupid," Sin muttered again. "And it's going to be gross."

"I can do gross," I assured him. "Anything to save Eld."

"That's fucking disgusting," Salina said, gagging.

"What fucking spell do you have Sin performing?" Chan Sha asked, kneeling beside me, whimpering when her bad leg nearly pitched her over.

"Sin said it's a trap," I said, looking up from the bloody gash I'd made in the side of Eld's neck. He was no longer trembling, as Sin had promised, but he'd grown so pale he was practically translucent and a rattle was building in his lungs. *Death rattle.* I spat blood and sat back, trying not to throw up as I felt some of the iron-tasting, viscous liquid slide down my throat. "Introducing small bits of himself into the wound will draw the plague there and then when I suck it out, the plague will follow."

"I didn't think that was possible," Chan Sha grunted. "I could see how the proper nanigens—has Sin explained about those?"

"The workings of the spell."

"Aye, that's the magic. Well, Sin's the magic, but he's made of nanigens, which work the magic, so you can't really separate one from the other, but . . ." Chan Sha squinted. "I never liked the theory of it all. It fucking works the same way that a pistole does and that's all I needed to know."

"Sin didn't like your analogy," I told her.

"Insulting," she agreed. "To the pistole."

I laughed despite myself and froze when Sin spoke. "If you're really going to do this, Buc, now's the time."

"It worked?"

"There's only one way to find out," he whispered.

"What if I just spit after I suck it out?"

"There are about a dozen innuendos there," he said, unable to force humor into his voice. "If that were possible, I'd have suggested it, Buc. Chan Sha's right. The nanigens in your blood, the ones I told you about when we first met, are part of me and I'm part of them. I can *sense* them in Eld and they can sense me. As soon as you suck them back out of the wound, we'll be one again, which means—"

"The plague will move out of Eld, too," I finished. *And into me.*

"Here's how it's going down, gang," I said aloud, looking up into a sea of concerned faces. "Bar'ren and Chan Sha, help hold Eld down. I don't know what's going to happen when I try to heal him. Arti and Salina, get to poisoning the well. Wait!" I brushed my hair, which I'd braided again for the occasion, back over my shoulder, using the moment to gather my thoughts. "First get a few vials from the pool to help Eld heal faster. Then poison it."

They all nodded. Chan Sha took a grip on Eld's shoulder while Bar'ren knelt across his thighs. Arti dug in one of the sacks and I heard vials clinking. Salina pulled the rest of the sacks out and set them aside. I wiped my mouth with the back of my hand and bent over Eld's bloody neck, trying not to let anyone see how much I was shaking. I was about to take on a plague engineered to render every Sin Eater in the world essentially magicless, a plague that would kill off most of the world's population. *A plague that's killing Eld as we speak.* Which made all the difference.

Eld had nearly died a dozen times over for me. Back when I thought him just a useful meat shield, he'd caught several blades meant for me. When I'd just begun to consider him a real friend— aye, and perhaps something more—he'd fought the Ghost Captain with me and nearly been turned into a Shambles for it. When

Chan Sha had donned her mask as Sicarii and led the gangs of Servenza against me, he'd shown up when I needed him most despite our being estranged, and had essentially died in the process. Even after the Dead Gods saved him for their own nefarious purposes, he hadn't stopped trying to help me.

There's friendship and love and then there's Eld . . . but I didn't want to lose him and me dying would amount to the same thing. I'd told him we needed to stack all the odds in our favor and I couldn't do that if I was weakened and dying. *If I even have that long.* But I couldn't do it without him either. Not his strength, his skill, but him. His self. *Enough. Stop hesitating. This is for Eld.* The fear left me.

I took a deep breath, felt Sin alive and all through me—perhaps for the last time—and put my mouth to the wound I'd made in Eld's neck. His skin felt clammy, the dried blood loosening from my saliva, and what I forced myself to do was what Sin had promised: gross as fuck. I sucked blood from his neck like some creature far beyond the pale. For a moment, nothing happened, then I tasted Eld's blood in my mouth and my entire face burned with Sin's magic, making my teeth lock against his neck and perversely more blood squirted, warm and metallic, down my throat.

"Processing," Sin whispered, voice strained. "The spell worked! Nanigens are back with us . . . nearly . . . no, all of them. Traces of silver, horrid ichor of the Dead Gods, and . . . something else."

"Something else?" I whispered back. "What's that mean?"

"If I knew, I'd say, wouldn't I?" Sin growled. I could feel him considering, weighing, sifting . . . all the while I felt as if my mouth was filled with cactus spines flaming hot from the Burning Lands. "It's in us. Her name, Buc, we did it. We're infected."

Eld sat up, or tried to, with three of us piled on him, gasping and retching, and his eyes widened, looking past me. "No!" he shouted hoarsely. "Stop!"

I followed his gaze to where Salina was midstride across the channel that circled the pool. She still had the empty vials in her hand, ready to fill them from the pool. Her foot came down on the other side as she turned to look at us at Eld's shouted warning.

The sprawling chamber around us shook with a vibration that ran up from the pool in an invisible, undulating wave, and the pillars' and stalactites' lights shifted from blues and greens and purples to an angry red that pulsed in time with the wave. When the wave reached the archway a klaxon reverberated with deafening ferocity, echoing through the chamber, through the entire Citadel of the Dead Gods.

"The channel is attuned to the blood of the Dead Gods," Eld said in the silence that followed. "We've just told every Dead Gods' mage here that the Wellspring is under attack. They're coming. Every Dead Walker and their legions of Shambles. Every Veneficus. All of them."

44

"That seems some important information to leave out," I said, my voice pulling Eld's eyes to mine.

"Are you bleeding?" he asked.

"No, you are," I shot back. I squinted. "How are you feeling?"

"A little weak, but fine," he said, touching his neck and frowning as it came away bloody. "Am I bleeding?"

"I suck the plague from your veins and you whine about a little blood," I growled, pushing myself to my feet. I felt no differently than I had a moment before, but at the same time I felt dirty, as if some invisible evil had coated my mind and body. As if there was an oil slick in my veins. *Later.* If there was a later.

"We don't have time for this," I snapped, fighting to keep my growing terror from my voice. *I don't want to die, not now, damn it.* "Salina, get Eld some blood. Arti, do whatever the fuck you're going to do with that tea you're brewing."

"It is like a tea," the short man said, only the quiver in his voice betraying his fear. He used a set of blacksmith's tongs to pick up a long, glass tube he'd pulled from one of the sacks. "Bar'ren, would you twist that crank on the side?" he asked, nodding at the bit of gearwork that was attached to the tube. "Mind you, let go as soon as you do . . . once the elements involved combine it's going to heat to a thousand degrees."

"A thousand?" Chan Sha hissed. "How?"

"Too long to explain," he muttered. "Magnesium sulfate and . . . too long to explain. Bar'ren?"

The older man twisted the gear and we all heard the sound

of glass breaking, and something white suddenly shot through the tube, blinding us all. The Artificer had replaced his spectacles with goggles and seemed unaffected. He used the tongs to hold the tube above the wagon, then smashed it down. The silver loaded into the wagon began spitting and crackling as it melted before our eyes. Dropping the tongs, the Artificer picked up a sack full of the crushed leaves Bar'ren's Goddess had given him and upended it over the mess in the wagon. Bar'ren grabbed the other sack and copied Arti, fine powder igniting and then extinguishing in the liquid silver that now filled the bottom of the wagon.

"All right, we run the wagon into the pool and it sinks, dispersing the silver and the numbing agent in the leaves," the Artificer said, his voice pulled an octave higher than usual from the tension running through it. "Poisoning the Wellspring. And so forth."

For a moment no one said anything. Then I held a hand out to Eld. "Seems fitting you be the one to push it in, Eld. A Sin Eater to kill Ciris and a Veneficus to kill the Dead Gods." He took my hand and Sin gave me a buzz of strength to pull him to his feet. Salina passed Eld a vial she'd just filled from the pool and he threw it back in one long pull, shivering as he did so. He handed it back wordlessly and marched over to the wagon, glancing at the Plague Mistress's body as he passed her.

Eld yelped when he touched the cart, shaking his hands, then took a deep breath and gave it a hard shove. The wagon moved a bare palm's length, then another, then the greased wheels picked up momentum and it practically flew across the floor, bumping over the channel cut in the bone and spraying small flecks of molten silver as it splashed into the pool with a spitting, sparking, high-pitched whine, like cats fighting in an alleyway. For a moment the wagon looked as if it would float, which would have been damnable luck, but then it upended, plunging deep into the glowing, blue pool and disappearing, leaving only a thin trail of silver in its wake.

A dull roar sounded in the passageway we'd come from, carrying with it a small cloud of dust and a harsh, sickly sweet scent that made my mouth twist. *Shambles.* Mentally congratulating myself on making Chan Sha and Salina set those grenadoes, I moved to the sacks and began pulling out more grenadoes and other gearwork contraptions of the Artificer's design that we'd brought along in case things went downhill. *At this rate, we're plummeting to the fucking bottom.* I could hear, Sin's magic making my ears buzz, the sounds of footsteps getting closer from above. Some running, some walking, others lurching, but all of them coming toward us.

"Sounds like the way we came in is cut off," Salina said, the lilt in her voice failing to cover the tremor.

"Smells like it, too," Chan Sha said, her nose wrinkling.

"We can't leave yet, anyway," I said.

"Why the fuck not?" the former pirate asked.

"Because the silver is leaving a sheen on the water," I said, nodding toward the Wellspring. The blue glow had brightened and grown sharper, flecks of silver melding with the blue and turning to amber. "Arti, if this doesn't change back to some semblance of blue, they'll know something is up."

"It won't be the same hue," he said, dry-washing his hands, "but as the silver dissipates, it will return to a softer shade. Knowing the plague was added could excuse it to any who notice."

"We don't come down here all that often," Eld said. "Unless you're an Eldest or part of the council."

"We need to give it time," Arti said.

"How much?" Bar'ren asked, his voice rumbling from his chest.

"I—I don't know," the man replied. He sighed and swiped at his short bangs, which were plastered to his forehead from sweat. "A quarter bell?"

"A quarter bell," Salina hissed. "By that time they'll be on us for sure."

"They already are," I said quietly.

A howl pulled our attention to the archway of the main entrance. A thin, tall figure, its robes looking bloodred in the crimson light of the stalactites, stared down at us, a dozen others flanking him and more arriving by the moment. The lead figure took a step forward, lowering its head and pulling its hood back, revealing a wraithlike human with sunken cheeks, shaved head, and eyes that seemed to glow in the angry light.

"You dare attack us here?" he asked, his voice strangely high and undulating. "In the heart of our power? What fools you must be. Did you intercept them, Eldritch? Is the body one of theirs?" he asked as he stepped forward.

He must not have seen her clearly at first, but something in the shape of the body or the robes she wore told the story, because he howled again, drawing both hands up into the air, clenching them into fists.

"Spread out. Get ready," I whispered as I walked past Chan Sha and the others.

"That's the Archnemesis," Eld said quietly, his voice pitched for our ears alone. "The most powerful Dead Gods' mage to ever live. The Eldest will be with him in a moment, each nearly as powerful as the Plague Mistress."

"Good to know," I said under my breath. "Do you want her?" I asked, louder, speaking to the Archnemesis. "Bar'ren, can I borrow your war club?" The old man reached back over his shoulder with one hand, drew the angled, obsidian-studded club out of its sheath, and held it out.

"Good man," I said lightly, taking the weapon. I hefted the club to get a feel for the weight, then spun in a circle, Sin's magic burning through me as I brought it down. The Plague Mistress's body jerked, her head rolling free across the floor, catching the edge of the circular channel and falling into it with a dull thump.

"You can have her, but she'll make a poor Shambles now," I said, shaking blood and matted hair from the weapon.

"You dare! You will beg to taste death when we consume your

flesh!" the creature howled. The mages surrounding it screamed, roared, even hissed like snakes. "Flay them all alive, but bring the girl to me!" the man cried, waving his mages forward.

"Part of your plan?" Eld asked, shouting above the din as a dozen men and women hurled themselves toward us, swarming both down the path and over the rows of seats carved into the bone.

"'Never let the enemy dictate the terms of combat,'" I quoted.

"Which book was that?" he asked.

"Number one," I told him with a smile. "Eldritch Nelson Rawlings. Haven't quite managed to finish it, yet."

"You don't say." He chuckled.

"You might want to close your eyes for this next bit," I told him, tossing the war club back to Bar'ren. "I planned for Veneficus."

"Planned? How?"

"They're predators, Eld," I explained as the others began setting stacks of thick, sharp-pointed, paper cones on the ground. "Sudden flashes and sounds disorient them, especially when they are torn between rage and fear. Light them up," I called in a louder voice.

A moment later I heard the hiss of match cord, and the dim, pulsing light of the chamber was transformed into shrieking daylight by the tonne of fireworks I'd brought in with us. The candles and rockets took off haphazardly, most spinning in any of a dozen disparate directions, shrieking and sparking. Several of the Veneficus tripped and stumbled, falling over rows of seats and clutching at their eyes. Some rockets flew true, scattering the mages as explosions rent the air around them.

When one of the Veneficus began to transform, Bar'ren leveled his crossbow and the weapon sang with a dull *tat–tat, tat–tat, tat–tat* as he fired pairs of silver-tipped bolts that slammed into the creature, making the half-transformed wolf fall slavering to the ground. The silver armament enraged the remaining Veneficus, who charged pell-mell toward us. Chan Sha dropped one with a pistole shot that blew its face into a dozen pieces. The Artificer and Bar'ren did for another pair each and I dropped four more with my slingshot.

It was all over in a few breaths: one moment there were dazzling, shrieking lights everywhere, the next, we were wrapped in a dull, crimson silence with a dozen mages lying about us, twisted in death. I opened my mouth to crow over our little victory and felt the retort die on my lips. The Archnemesis was surrounded by a dozen figures as thin and wasted as himself, several holding tomes that glowed bright blue in their hands. A horde of Shambles stumbled, leapt, or crawled toward us, depending on their level of decay, a veritable river of undead, waving rusted steel blades, spears, and all manner of cutlery. A moaning, rattling hiss turned into a roar as they ran, and their stench froze me in place as much as their battle cry did.

It was the Artificer, of all people, who broke our stupor, hurling a grenado at our enemies, the glass bauble landing in an upper row a score of paces away. A sheet of flame leapt up and the Shambles ran right into it. Chan Sha whooped and she and Salina tossed their own grenadoes, creating a wall of flame that consumed the undead.

Or should have.

Flaming corpses plunged through the sheet of fire, their tendons crackling and popping as they cooked, blades singing as they swung the blackened, burned steel lustily before them.

"Blood of the Gods," Eld whispered.

"This lot are fresh!" I shouted.

"Ciris's cunt," Chan Sha cursed, ripping at the straps across her chest. The gearwork apparatus mounted to her back shrieked and shot out a trio of metallic arms with blades in place of hands. They hung over her like some Godsdamned scorpion's tail. Slipping her hands into the straps, the woman stepped forward and the limbs snapped ahead of her, lopping off the head of the first flaming corpse in a burning dress and spearing another, his intestines flopping out over his torn belt.

Salina leveled one of her repeating blunderbusses and the gun belched flame in her arms, disintegrating a pair of Shambles. The whirring gears swung a fresh barrel into place and the weapon bucked again, dropping more of the undead, but there were at least fifty more hot on their heels, some smoldering, others infernos, all hissing and screeching for our blood.

"Eld, behind me!" I shouted, dropping my slingshot into a jacket pocket and pulling up the alley piece tied beneath my armpit. The crossbow sang, gears and compressed air working in tandem, Sin's magic burning my eyes and making time crawl so that it was almost as if the Shambles walked through an air thicker than what I breathed. *One-two-three-four pause five-six pause seven-eight-nine.* Each bolt, barely the size of the palm of my hand, found the throat of a Shambles, sending them sprawling— finally lifeless—to the ground. *Ten-click.* My right hand was already moving, detaching the empty cylinder, kicking it toward the oncoming Shambles, and pulling a fresh one from the other pocket on my jacket, slapping it into place, and drawing the nut back. *One-two-three-four-five-six-seven-eight.* This close I didn't have to adjust my aim, simply sliding from one target to the next.

"We need to get out of here! This was meant to be a hit-and-run job, not a battle."

"It's a battle now," Eld said. He stepped in front of me, slammed an empty vial to the floor, and stomped on it. Eld half fell in front of me, pulling his robes over his head; his naked torso twisted, bent, and broke with the sound of frozen marrow splitting. His scream turned into a full-throated roar as his limbs grew and sprouted hair. No, not hair . . . fur. A moment later a mammoth cave bear thrice the height of Eld rose in his place. The beast glanced over its shoulder, sapphire eyes the size of saucers glaring at me as the irises turned red and Eld—in his Veneficus form—swung around and the undead threw themselves at him.

He ignored the ones that tried to bite him, sweeping massive paws tipped with metal claws, each one a palm's length of blindingly bright steel. He carved a path through the undead, their black ichor staining the pale, skeletal floor with an inky soot. Dropping back down to the floor, Eld kicked out with all four limbs, becoming an ichor-strewn maelstrom of fur and bone.

Before I could take it all in, a Veneficus vaulted over the Shambles toward me and I had to roll to keep my head attached to my shoulders. I regained my feet just as the half-woman, half-hyena Veneficus snapped its jaws at my throat. I brought the alley piece up between us but its fangs caught the bow and ripped it out of my hands, my bolt shooting harmlessly off into the air. The creature howled, its long snout caught in the gearwork mechanism as it fell to all fours, its back legs bending and breaking as it fully transformed. To run was to die, so I did the only thing I could do: I attacked.

Long neck. Eyes too far forward. Soft spots behind the ears.

"I'm with you," Sin snarled.

Now.

Catapulting onto its back, I wrapped one arm around its long, muscular neck, grasping a fistful of loose skin. I nearly slid off when I couldn't find enough purchase on the short-furred beast, then Sin's magic burned through my fingertips and I pierced its flesh, gaining a solid grip and forcing the creature to risk ripping its own throat out if it tossed me. It bucked hard, ripping the crossbow free from its mouth, and whipped its head around, teeth snapping by my ear. *Holy shit.* Every hair on my body sprang to attention as its steel canines clacked together, spittle flecking my face. It jerked back the other way, thinking to catch me off guard, and I slammed my right hand hard against its skull. Right behind the ear.

The dart gun strapped to my wrist snapped and the beast let out a high-pitched whine, muscles tensing. Its death throes hurled me high into the air, blood fountaining behind me as I took out half the Veneficus's throat. Landing awkwardly in the middle of a bunch of Shambles, I ripped the femur free from one and laid about me, buying enough space to draw one of the axes I'd thrust through my belt. Then I didn't have time to think or breathe, every effort was bent on mere survival.

Sin's magic thrummed through my veins as I cut Shambles down, fought free of them, lost one ax in a steel-patched skull and the second in the tailbone of some jungle-cat Veneficus. Gone were all thoughts of fleeing. There were too many of them, too closely packed. Our only hope, desperate as it was, was to fight our way out. In flashes, here and there, I saw the rest of my crew. Chan Sha and Salina were back-to-back; all of Chan Sha's spider limbs were ruined save one, but her pistoles leapt in her hands while Salina wielded a bent blunderbuss like a club. Arti and Bar'ren fought side by side; the former had somehow affixed Bar'ren's crossbow to a floor mount and was firing it with his boot while the triple-shot crossbow in his arms sang fiercely. The old islander's white stole was stained black with ichor and bright with blood, much of it his own, judging by the globs in his white braids. I watched him decapitate a Veneficus with his club and then the battle swarmed around me and my vision shrunk again.

Suddenly a roar shook the air and a tall, gorilla-shaped monster with steel spikes sprouting down the length of its grey-furred spine rushed from the sullen, red darkness. Only Sin's grunted warning and sudden surge of magic through my legs let me leap clear before the thing smashed a dent the size of my head in the bone floor with its mallet-like fist. It swung around, bright, red eyes locked onto where I'd landed amidst a pile of broken Shambles. *The Archnemesis.* A glowing book was clutched in its other, all-too-human fist. Suddenly the Shambles shifted around me and I felt a skeletal hand grasp my ankle.

"That's right, girl," the monster rumbled, its twisted mouth filled with jutting, steel canines. "I'm the oldest being in this world. As old as the mind witch, almost. I am all things of the Dead Gods, their servitor. Blood and bone. Veneficus and Dead Walker. I will rend you limb from limb."

"You know," I told him lightly, hiding my labored breathing—though the steam rising from me from Sin's magic did that just as well, "the funny thing is, Archie, after the ninth or tenth time some arse-fucked beast tells me that, it starts to lose its punch." I swung the femur I'd kept in my left hand back behind me and felt it connect with the Shambles he'd called up. The hand on my ankle slipped away. "Loses its verve, as it were. You want a piece?" I called. "Get in line."

"Buc!" Sin's voice filled my mind.

I drew a silver-dipped blade the length of my forearm from the sheath strapped across my chest inside my jacket and sank into a crouch. "Let's dance, motherfucker."

"I—I'm losing my a-ability to control o-our . . . t-the plague. Have to fight it. To survive. I—I'm sorry."

"I am death!" the creature roared.

I felt Sin slip from my mind and his magic with him, and suddenly I was just a bone-tired, small woman surrounded by the undead and the Archnemesis of the Dead Gods.

"And I will consume you!"

"Fuck me," I whispered.

45

It knows what I am . . . use that against it.

The thought flashed through me as the beast rushed toward me, its long arms propelling it forward in giant leaps that closed the distance between us in the space of a breath. I made to throw myself to the right, where one of the giant pillars rose up, and at the last moment, fell flat to the ground instead.

Anticipating my Sin Eater speed, the Archnemesis bawled defiantly as he hurdled himself past the pillar, meaning to catch me out on the opposite side. I pushed myself up and threw my silver short sword at its unprotected back. It was only a dozen paces away, but without Sin's power, the blade was too heavy and awkward for me to toss like a throwing knife and the speed and force of the throw were those of a mere mortal. The gorilla-beast snapped back around, slapping the blade out of the air with a meaty fist. It howled in pain and rage when it touched the silver coating, then rushed me. *Godsdamn it.* I feinted toward the pillar again, then actually jumped behind it, and when the creature's hand snapped out to catch the pillar and arrest its charge I swung the femur I still held with both hands and felt more than heard something break. Whether it was the femur or its hand, I didn't know, but bone shattered. *Take that, f'ugly!*

The Archnemesis's steel nails caught the edge of my jacket, sending me cartwheeling end over end through the wrecked bodies of Shambles that littered the floor. My breath left me upon impact, something crunched in my side, and several stars burst in my head until I came to rest on a pile of the undead. *Ow.* I tried to sit up, mind numb, and rotting hands snapped around me, pulling me down into a bear hug that made my ribs scream. I screamed, too, for good measure. The Shambles I'd fallen upon hissed in my ear, its fetid breath blasting the haze out of my mind. I tried to wrestle free, kicking, squirming, and throwing myself around, but the damned thing had locked its hands on its opposite wrists and refused to let go.

"You're mine, girl," the Archnemesis snarled, standing up from where it'd slid to a stop, its squat, furry haunches quivering with muscle and rage.

I struggled harder, to no avail; I could feel my strength leaching out of me, likely the lack of Sin or the effects of the plague or of getting tossed halfway across a cavern like a Godsdamned rag doll. *Or all three?* I laughed at the thought before I could think. It didn't seem funny and yet . . . I laughed harder.

"Fucking mind witches," the beast snarled, scooping something up from the floor with one of its long-armed limbs and whipping it at me. The blade sliced through the top of my face, glancing off my cheekbone and just missing my eye. "Always think you're so Godsdamned clever," it continued, something metallic flashing from its hand again.

My laughter turned into a scream when the second knife slammed through the meaty part of my lower thigh and pinned my squirming leg to the body beneath me. Waves of shock, pain, and nausea rolled through me.

"Not so clever now," it cackled in a deep voice that rumbled in its chest as it walked toward me, its primate body undulating in those strange rising and falling motions that gorillas had.

"Are you, witch?"

"S-still, cleverer t-t-than you," I gasped, moving my hands down to the knife and pulling it free with a burning squelch. "Thanks for the blade."

I almost passed out from the pain, but willed myself to stay alert. The beast was going to kill me, but I was going to ram its own knife up its arsehole when it did. Eld and the others would see to the rest. *Eld.* A dozen thoughts rushed through me, banished when the Archnemesis charged me, great maw open in a frothy roar, steel canines aiming for my throat.

Something large hurtled across my vision and the roar turned into a surprised yelp, followed by a sharp cry a moment later when it hit the floor. The massive cave bear that was Eld rose to his full height. Some sort of giant, leather-winged bat creature clung to his back; Eld roared as he caught it with a paw the size of a dinner plate and ripped it from his fur, slamming the flying thing onto the ground at his feet. Before the creature could move, Eld opened his paw, and steel claws, each a stiletto in its own right, shot out, removing the bat-beast's furry, wolflike head. Then the Archnemesis was there and the two went at it hammer and tongs.

I'd like to say that with Sin still bright in my veins I would have put Archie down myself, but even I have my limits when it comes to stretching the truth. Eld fought like both man and bear, using his claws as swords, his jaws as knives, but even with the advantage of a cave bear's strength and ferocity and a fighting man's senses . . . it wasn't enough. When he caught the Archnemesis on the shoulder, the other dropped its head and rammed one of the shorter spikes on the back of its neck into Eld's sternum, hurling Eld twenty paces across the cavern. The monster scooped up a discarded glowing book, and half a dozen Shambles leapt upon Eld the moment he landed. Thanks to his size, he shrugged them off as if they were nothing more than flies, just as the rage-filled Veneficus-turned-mountain-gorilla closed the distance between the two of them.

C'mon, Eld. Get out of there! My heart was pounding so fast I could feel it practically tossing my lifeblood out of the thin slash across my face and the far deeper wound in my leg. The Shambles beneath me tried to squeeze me tighter and I remembered the blade in my hands.

Eld slammed the desiccated corpse of a large Shambles into

the gorilla's face. They both howled; Eld fell and the Archnemesis was on him in a flash of steel and grey fur. Eld's roar turned into a panicked cry and I drove the dirk over my shoulder frantically. Once. Twice. The third blow caused the arms holding me to fall slack and I got to my feet just in time to see the Archnemesis savaging Eld.

"Stop!" I screamed, throwing the blade as hard as I could. At that distance, I didn't have a hope of killing or even injuring the Archnemesis . . . but I didn't have to hurt him, just distract him.

The dirk struck him in the head, hilt first, and Eld did something to send the Archnemesis hurtling through the air, twisting in an awkward somersault as it flew past me and slammed into the floor. It rolled half a dozen times until it managed to grab the edge of the channel running around the Wellspring, and yanked itself to a stop with a roar. Eld's bear form rolled over onto all fours and stood swaying back and forth.

A piercing wail drew my gaze back to the Wellspring, to where the Artificer ran full tilt in the direction of the pool, pursued by an antlered Veneficus the size of a horse. Screaming, Arti shoved a one-legged Shambles out of his path and kept running, panic clear on his face. *Sin was right. He broke.* Bar'ren's body lay in the Artificer's path, the old man's white stole now a rainbow of gore. As I opened my mouth to shout a warning, several thoughts lanced through my mind.

At the fore was a book I'd read right after Eld taught me what letters could do when strung together. Two books actually, both by Nasau. One on mass and acceleration and the other on fulcrums and levers. *Twelve and fourteen.* I drew in a deep breath and prepared to embrace pain.

I took off in a sprint that lasted two steps; when I came down on my wounded leg, the pain practically swept me from my feet. I kept my balance, arms windmilling, and ran on in a lurching hitch that was little better than a walk. The Artificer ran straight into Bar'ren's body, tripped, tried to catch himself, and went sprawling, tumbling to the very edge of the pool. His boots slipped on the smooth edge as he tried to scoot back and scramble to all fours with his hands. The Archnemesis shook the cobwebs out of his thick skull and wobbled to his feet.

I didn't have much mass. I barely came to Eld's chest when he wasn't a cave bear. I didn't have much acceleration, with my leg screaming every time I took a step and my boot filling up with blood. But I didn't need much, not when I had the perfect fulcrum right there on his hands and knees.

I hit the Archnemesis low, below the waist, making him stumble and take a step back. Right into Arti's backside. The Archnemesis's red eyes widened in surprise as he fell backward, long limbs clutching at air. He went head over heels into the Wellspring.

That we'd poisoned with silver.

I saw his thick lips part around his canines, screaming soundlessly as the viscous pool, filled with his Gods' now-tainted blood, pulled him under. His fur and skin burned an angry red, the silver scoring his body inside and out as he sank into the depths . . . and then he was gone.

Reality came back to me in a frightening cacophony of sound. The sound of hooves on marbled, bone floor and a bull's bellow that sounded like a buffalo I'd seen at a menagerie in Cordoban. I spun around and my bad leg gave out, sending me down hard onto my arse as the antlered Veneficus galloped toward me and Arti, who had been knocked half into the pool by the Archnemesis. It seemed he had managed to pull himself out just in time to die beside me, as the beast dropped its massive, branched horns, ready to gore us to death. Two massive paws filled my vision and suddenly Eld was there, catching the beast by its antlers and swinging it around so hard that its hooves slipped out from beneath it. Its body went one way, its head the other, and the sound of its neck breaking was like a gunshot that reverberated across the pool.

And then there was. . . . silence.

An actual gunshot made me and Arti jump.

"Gods fuck!" I screamed.

"Sorry," Salina said, blowing smoke from the end of a pistole. Her pale face was ashen with gunpowder, and darker flecks of ichor and blood stained her cloak, but she seemed fine elsewhere. "Last one," she added, pointing at the broken, now dull, black book she'd just shot. "That . . . creature," she said after a moment, shuddering, "dropped it when Eld sent it flying halfway across the cavern."

"I've seen all manner of shit," Chan Sha said, limping up beside Salina, her spiders ripped free from her back along with her jacket, "in my time. Sin Eaters. Veneficus. Dead Walkers. Shambles. Pirates. Vanishing isles. Lost civilizations." She slapped the rope that hung around her neck and the dozen pistoles tied to them swung back and forth. "And none of it holds a flaming candle to this pile we just stepped in."

"So fucking true," Eld said, walking toward us. He'd picked up some torn, white robes to cover himself; his bleeding chest was still exposed. "You all right, Buc?"

"F-f-fine," I said, my teeth suddenly chattering. "Is it cold in here or did I swallow a bucket of ice water?"

"She's going into shock," Chan Sha cursed.

"Buc, you're bleeding!" the Artificer said.

Everyone rushed toward me, but Eld beat them there, trying to pull me to my feet—he stopped when I screamed. Then Salina and Chan Sha were holding me upright while Eld wrapped my wounded leg with sections of cloth he tore from his robes. He pulled hard, apologizing every time, but I didn't feel it. The Artificer produced something out of a pouch that spun hazily before me, and as he packed whatever it was into the gaping wound, my pain receded. From inside his jacket, Arti plucked out a flask. Its contents burned my mouth and throat when I drank, but its warmth shattered the ice in me and after a few long moments I felt the haze beginning to clear from my vision.

"I think," I said slowly, "I might make it after all."

"That's what we've been saying," Chan Sha snapped, her good eye betraying her fear.

"Of course you will," Eld insisted. "You saved my life. Again. You can't die on me now."

"I predict a healthy prognosis," the Artificer said, his grinning face looking strange without his spectacles.

"You still remain a significant pain in the arse." Salina laughed.

"A boil of epic proportions," I agreed, and everyone huddled around me laughed.

So I was the only one who saw the Wellspring's waters ripple and the Archnemesis—his tall, wraithlike form covered in burns, blisters, and raw flesh—rise from the water. Blood—his own and that of his Gods—sluiced from his limbs and he bared his teeth in a rictus of pain and rage, pointing a spectral hand at me.

"You cannot kill what is already dead!" he hissed.

Someone, Arti or Salina, screamed, and I shook free of my friends, pulling on the final well—my well—of my resources. My hands moved of their own accord, almost as if Sin were directing them, but he was gone from my mind, consumed by the plague, so I moved for him. For Bar'ren, dead following my orders. For Eld, made one of these abominations. For the whole damned world caught in the grips of Gods that wouldn't just stay dead.

"Let's find out, aye?" I drew my slingshot back, pulling with everything I had, barely reaching to half draw. "Tell your Gods Sambuciña Alhurra sends her regards!"

The silver ball took the creature in the eye and blew out half the back of his head. Blood, brain, and gore hissed as they fell into the bloody waters of the silver-infused Wellspring. The Archnemesis of the Dead Gods tumbled into the viscous pool for a second time, its thick waters pulling his limp body down into the dark depths, and this time, he didn't rise. The ripples subsided after a moment, leaving the surface as still as death itself.

46

"Let's blow this crypt," I muttered, leaning against Eld.

"More will be coming," he said. "Less senior mages, those guarding the outer cathedral, the acolytes . . . and when they come, I need to be here."

"What?" I blinked up into his eyes. "I didn't kill the bloody Archnemesis so you could play the last-man-standing trick."

"I've no intention of dying, Buc." He leaned down and kissed my forehead and I felt something in my chest loosen. "If we leave them to find this—"

"Massacre," I suggested.

"'Massacre' seems too tame a term," he commented, gazing at the destruction we'd wrought. Piles of bones, some burned, others bright white, littered the floor; mingled amongst them were the robes and twisted forms of the Veneficus we'd killed. "Leave them to find this and they'll test the Wellspring. They might very well find a way to mitigate the poison."

"Anything is possible," the Artificer said, adding, "given enough time and resources."

"Exactly," Eld agreed. "But if I greet them as the sole survivor of this fight, spin them a tale, I can get them to drink of it before they are thinking clearly."

"Uh, Eld," I said, "no offense, but spinning tales isn't really your thing."

Eld nodded, his cheek swelling from a blow he'd taken in his beast form. "You're not wrong, but you said you read from my book?" He grinned, his split lip bleeding. "I've been reading a book as well, all these years. Yours, Buc. I'll tell them how the Plague Mistress and the council had just put the finishing touches on the plague when we were attacked by dozens of Sin Eaters. Many of us fell, but then the Archnemesis appeared. They fled at his wrath and he pursued them. His last words were to drink of the pool and take the next ship that sails. All of us. For any port. The plague must be spread everywhere at once."

"That's not half-bad," Chan Sha said, wincing. I noticed that the vest she wore was dark on one side.

"You'll have to sell it," I said slowly. "Show them how desperate you are, how near a thing this was. Show them your anger and thirst for revenge. Show them that . . . and they'll lap it up."

"What will we be doing while you're spinning, Eld?" Salina asked. Her dress and cloak were torn in several places and she was favoring one leg.

"Blowing this crypt." He pointed back the way we'd come into the massive cavern. "Whatever *that* was must have destroyed any mages and their Shambles or we'd have been attacked on both sides."

"It took us a while, navigating all those passages," I reminded him.

"There's another way. Through the library you're so damned curious about. An actual crypt," he added. "It emerges through a secret tunnel into the middle of the Old City and usually it's heavily guarded, but I think we'll find it otherwise today."

"I don't fancy getting lost in this graveyard," Chan Sha muttered.

"You won't," Eld assured her. He squeezed my arm. "With Sin, Buc can remember everything she's told."

"With Sin?" I feigned a smile. "Of course." *Only, Sin's gone missing, fighting the plague in my veins.*

"See?" Eld began telling me which door to enter, how many rows to walk past, which to turn into, how many shelves to pass, which tunnel to look for, on and on and on. I listened intently, tried to, anyway, but without Sin my mind raced ahead, exploring a dozen other thoughts that made Eld's path only one of the potential solutions my brain wished to consider.

"That'll put you out just a street past where you killed that Sin Eater, Buc. Gods, that feels ages ago, but it was just a few days, wasn't it?" He paused for breath and looked at me closely, his eyebrows pulling toward each other. "Are you all right? I'd have thought Sin would have you patched and back in fighting shape by now."

"Sin says to remind you that I took a blade through half my leg and a dozen other serious contusions besides. And that I didn't eat enough for all of this shit."

Eld snorted. "You didn't eat enough? You eat like a horse."

"First you tell me I'm ashy, now you're comparing me to barn animals?" I twisted my head, my braids falling back over my undercut. "I thought you were a wise man, Eld."

He looked at me for a moment and shook his head. "Are you well?"

"Truly."

"Okay." He stiffened. "I can feel them coming. You need to go."

"Off with you," I said, straightening carefully so all my weight was on my good leg. I could feel sweat break out on my brow from holding myself steady. "You'll catch us up?"

"Aye. I'll meet you at the ship . . . likely beat you there."

"It's a race," I told him.

Eld half bent to kiss me, realized the others were watching, and cursed under his breath before kissing me anyway, full on the lips. In the next instant he was running up the stairs, tying his torn robes around his waist so they wouldn't fall off entirely. In the time it took for me to catch my breath, he was gone.

"Why aren't you healed?" Chan Sha asked, catching me as I wobbled.

"Is Sin hurt?" Salina asked, slipping her arm around my waist from the other side.

"Not hurt," I whispered. "Sick." I glanced back and forth between the women. "Halfway through the fight he said the plague was killing us and then he just . . . left."

"Sin doesn't just leave," Chan Sha growled. "Not unless he's burned from you or torn out," she added more gently, her hand reaching toward the patch over her missing eye before she stopped it.

"I think he's there or I'd be dead, but . . ." I took a breath. "I think the plague's consumed him. The Dead Gods didn't think they could kill the Sin Eaters outright, remember?"

"They thought they could make them sick enough to render them mortal," Salina answered.

"Or good as," I agreed. "We've got to get out of here, but I'm going to need some help."

"Obviously." Chan Sha snorted. "That's why we're here. Let's go."

"How'd you know?" I asked as we took a halting step. "That I wasn't healing?"

"We're women." Salina laughed. "Luckily for you, unlike men, we actually pay attention."

"I think Eld was paying attention." Chan Sha's rasping laugh joined Salina's. "Just not to the right things."

"How bad is it?" Salina asked, her pale features serious, eyes intent on mine.

"Well, I've got a hole in my leg, a cracked rib or two, and I've lost enough blood that I'm lucky to still be conscious." I reached up and gingerly touched my cheek. "It's this fucking scratch that hurts the most. Like a firebrand."

"He's alive!" The Artificer's voice made us all turn. The short man was bent over Bar'ren's body, a small mirror in his hand. Bar'ren lay half–propped up on a fallen Shambles, his stole and taut stomach covered in blood and ichor. Judging by the amount of dried blood caked in his braids, whatever wound had taken him down had been to the head. The Artificer held up the mirror so we could see the faintest bit of fog disappearing from the glass. "Badly wounded, but alive."

"I guess Mother Waska didn't want her Sha'amen dead after all," I said, hobbling over with the help of Chan Sha and Salina.

"He doesn't look like he's got much left in him," Chan Sha said.

"If Eld were here we could use one of his vials of pure blood with some of Bar'ren's blood and heal him," I mused. "I'd try myself, but without Sin I'm useless."

"You're just mortal," Salina corrected.

"After practically being a Goddess for the last year it's one and the same," I told her. She rolled her eyes. "Damn."

"Uh." The Artificer stood up, his hands searching through his pockets. "When Salina was gathering that blood to heal Eld, I may have, uh"—he pulled out three small, thin tubes filled with a dark, purplish-red substance—"collected a few. For science. And so forth."

"A genius and a comic and now a thief? You're a fucking onion, Arti," I told him. I nearly told him about the barrels of the stuff Eld had hidden away aboard the ship, but saying that aloud in the heart of the Dead Gods' sanctuary seemed ill-advised. *See, Sin, I'm exercising judgment . . . and you're missing it.* "Anyone know the ratio of Bar'ren's blood to the Dead Gods' required so it heals and doesn't kill?"

"I don't do magic," Salina said. "I just buy and sell things."

"And blow shit up."

"That, too," she agreed.

"Don't look at me," Chan Sha said, waving her free hand. "I just know how to kill the bastards."

"Wench after my own heart," I muttered, searching my mind. "Oh, wait. I think I know."

"Think?"

"It's in one of the books Sin speed-read for me in that secret Cordoban library," I told Salina. *The Felling Chant and Other*

Incantations. Four-seventy-five. "The author's name was spelled in
the Dead Gods' tongue, so no fucking clue who they are, but I'm
not sure it matters."

"The healing, Buc?" Arti asked, his voice cracking. "Bar'ren is
nearly gone."

"Right, right. Uh, you're going to have to do this part."

"Me?" The short man's face paled.

"You're already covered in blood," I pointed out. "It's not that
hard . . . the blood does all the work. You need some of Bar'ren's
blood. A few drops. One of his hairs plucked from his scalp.
Flesh from his body."

"Flesh from his body?"

"I don't make the rules," I said, shrugging.

"Just flay a little off his arm," Chan Sha suggested. The Artificer practically fainted and she rolled her eyes. "Hold her," she told
Salina, and the other woman stepped closer to me. "Like this,"
she said, dropping beside the old man. A dagger appeared in her
fist and she made three quick, small cuts before pulling back a
piece of skin the size of a fingernail. "And the hair," she added,
pulling one out of his braids. "The blood should be easy."

"Mind it's actually his blood," I reminded her.

"Good call, Buc." She pressed a wound in his scalp between
the braids and the blood that had already begun to dry cracked
as more poured out. "Vial. Arti! Vial!" The shorter man passed it
to her and Chan Sha carefully let a few drops slide into the tube,
taking care not to spill the Dead Gods' blood, then added the
other materials.

"All right, old man, let's see if your Goddess foresaw this,"
she muttered, turning Bar'ren fully onto his back; the Artificer
dropped to his knees to cradle the man's neck. She forced the tube
past his lips and upended it. "Any idea how long this takes?" she
asked when the man didn't move.

"Eld said he felt better immediately," the Artificer said.

"He fought like he felt better," Salina added.

"That's because he's a Dead Gods' mage," Chan Sha said. "It's attuned to him."

"The book didn't say, that I recall," I said, closing my eyes and trying to find the pages in my mind. They were there, but faded, unlike other books I'd read. I checked other texts from that visit to the hidden library and they were all the same. *Thanks, Sin.* "I think the implication was it all happened pretty damned quick. There was reference to an agent to slow down the healing, but I think that's for the bullshit they sell at the altar. Make the poor dying bastards feel they've earned it."

Bar'ren coughed, spitting blood in Chan Sha's face, and she sat back with a cry, cursing as she rubbed at her eyes. The old man coughed harder, his chest suddenly rising and falling with vigor, and his eyes blinked open. Bar'ren worked his jaw slowly and he rolled his lips as if helping them to remember how they moved. After a moment he rasped, "I think I fucking earned it."

"We've been past this row twice before."

"Are you going to follow me 'round stating things I already know?" I growled at Chan Sha. "Eld was specific that we had to start down the right one or the rest of his lefts and rights and all the rest of that bullshit sequence would be thrown off. I need to be doubly sure I'm recalling the right row."

"Ought to be triply sure at this point," Chan Sha rasped. I glared up at her and she grinned through the braids that hung in front of her face. "You want me to let you drop right here?"

"I should have had Salina prop me up," I muttered.

"Only she's not strong enough and Arti needs help with Bar'ren."

"Only that," I said, lifting my lantern so I could see the strange sigil carved on the ivory bone that rose from the floor almost like a stack in a library. *I wish you'd told me the row and not the word carved at its end.* The problem was, I could translate a few letters or words in this language thanks to the books Sin and I had read, but not many, and counting was far easier. This sigil meant "eleven," but no matter how you many times I counted rows, starting from the first, this wasn't the eleventh row. I thought it was the thirteenth. *We need to move. Worst case, we retrace our steps . . . if we can find them after we've moved through this labyrinth.* "Let's get the others."

"This it?"

"Close enough."

"Eh, worst case we retrace our steps," Chan Sha said with a shrug as she helped me turn back the way we'd come. "'Course we lose ourselves in this fucking maze, that last might be tricky but . . . can't stay here." She pulled up when she felt me stop moving. "What?"

"Nothing," I said, shaking my head after a moment. "You're just . . . not like me, but close enough to rhyme?" I squinted at her. Sweat from the pain of her own wounds made her olive skin glow, one of sundry ways she was more striking than I would ever be. *I'm more cunning than her.* "I wonder what would have happened if we'd met a few years back."

"I'd have slit your throat for threatening my Goddess," Chan Sha said simply. Her mouth twitched. "And you'd probably have put a blade in my side while I was doing it," she added. "Together, though . . . we just destroyed the Dead Gods."

"Theirs will be a slow, grinding death," I whispered. "They'll feel it coming on as their numbers dwindle. If any don't take the poison or never received the smaller dose of plague, they'll run out of vials eventually."

"It's always nice to have a little shot of liquor waiting for you after the party," Chan Sha chuckled. "Evens things out."

"But first, Ciris."

"Aye." Her grin faded. She adjusted her hip so that her bad leg was up against mine; between the two of us we could almost walk halfway normal. "About that, Buc. I've been meaning to talk to you—"

"If you're going to try to talk me out of it," I growled.

"Not in the leastwise. Ciris betrayed me," Chan Sha said, the glowing hate in her grating voice sending a chill down my spine. "I sold out every family I've had for her and when my life was on the line she abandoned me, left me for dead." I could feel her biceps flexing around my shoulder, her body quivering like a sparking eel. "I owe her a dose of revenge, but . . . there's things that you don't ken. About her, about Sin, about yourself."

"Like what?"

The other woman pursed her pink lips. "I'm not sure the undercroft of the Dead Gods is the place to be talking about Ciris," Chan Sha said after a moment.

"Don't put me off."

"I'm not. C'mon," she added, and we began limping back toward the entrance to the library, where we'd left the others. "Thing is, I don't know everything either, but I know how my Sin was with me and I know how every other Sin Eater's Sin was with them. I could feel them when we cast Transference and spoke to one another across great distances. We were all the same, all one. Save Ciris," she added. "Hers was a presence that stood out like a lighthouse on a moonless night."

"I'm not sure I'm following," I said, grunting through gritted teeth so I didn't scream when my bad leg's boot caught on the floor.

"What you have with Sin is impossible," Chan Sha said after a moment. "He should have flooded your mind so that you felt the way we do when Her magic suffuses us . . . only in that first, initial rush, you wouldn't have known what was happening and with that much magic flowing through you—"

"It'd be like a river of pleasure so deep it turned to pain," I said, feeling gooseflesh break out across my skin at the thought.

"Exactly. You'd have accepted Possession before you understood he was inside your mind and then Ciris would have joined him and you would have begun the Rite of Initiation. It takes hours and when it's over it's like . . . ecstasy," she breathed. "And torture, aye, that, too."

"Hours? Eld would have died on the shores waiting for me to come back at that rate."

"Sin didn't care about Eld, only about turning you. Leave that aside for now, what it all comes down to is this," Chan Sha said, dropping her voice and leaning in despite us being hip to hip, "none of that happened. Which either means you're the one girl in all the world capable of dominating Sin or . . ."

"Or my Sin is different from every other Sin Eater's Sin," I whispered.

"You were chosen for the investigation that led to everything that brought Sin to you," Chan Sha said, her good eye studying me.

"To free up some sugar shipments, not to find Sin. I didn't even know what that meant, back then." I snorted. "I'm not special, Chan Sha. I'm a street rat from the Painted Rock Quarto and there's ten thousand others just like me. More." I took a breath and added, "I'm just smart as fuck, quicker than I've a right to be, and at two or three points in my life, luck twisted the die to land on my number. Had the tosses gone differently, I'd be dead and forgotten." I scratched my chin to hide my discomfort as several things fell into place. "Sin, though, he was separated from Ciris in ways no other Sin was, placed in a special altar, hidden away for centuries."

"And Ciris has been batshit crazy to find him, when she learned the Dead Gods sought him," Chan Sha mused.

"Aye, that, and . . ." I shook my braid. "I wondered why I've been able to best every Sin Eater I've faced down, Sin to Sin. It stands to reason I'd be better than some, but every single one of them? Sometimes several at once, and all of them more experienced with their Sin than me. . . ."

"It stretches the bounds of credulity," Chan Sha agreed. "After we get out of this crypt, we need to have a talk, you and I. May-hap Sin will join us and the three of us can figure out what he is."

"Not what he is," I said, biting my lip until I felt it break. "What he was. What we've become. Together."

What are we, Sin?

47

"Tear him apart!" the man bellowed, dropping onto all fours as he began to transform, limbs cracking and twisting. Behind him, a score of others filled the bone-white hallway.

"Wait!" Sheira shrieked, her pale face twisted with pink scars. She put herself between Eld and the plumed bird with impossibly long, bent legs with scimitars for talons that had been a man a moment before. The woman's red hair hung to her shoulders, but patches of flesh showed where her skull had been crushed in. "It's Eldritch—one of us."

"The Plague Mistress's Quartermaestro," Xulet added in her croaking voice. Her robes hugged her curves, the smooth lines interrupted by the massive ax thrust through her belt. "What happened, Eldritch?" Her dark eyebrows drew together. "Who betrayed us?"

"I don't know," Eld gasped, not finding it hard to feign fatigue. Xulet was Cordoban and suspicious to her core. *You'll have to sell it.* Buc's words echoed in his mind. He'd been selling it for months now, but . . . *It's Eldritch—one of us.* He remembered sharing cups with his fellow acolytes after they were all raised to full priests. Moments when one of them had been on the brink of madness and the rest had sat with them, speaking softly, until they came back. Not everyone made it back. *But we did.* Laughing about the time Sheira had locked Petre in with the Shambles and gotten Hexia to give her a lesson in using her glowing book. *Petre died in Cordoban.* And all the others had been sent off to fight the mind witches and were likely dead, or soon would be. Only Sheira and

Xulet remained of his coterie. *Use them.* Eld wished the last was from Buc, but he knew whose thought it was.

Mine.

"I don't know," he repeated, gritting his teeth. "But when we find them, Xulet"—he met her eyes—"we'll tear them limb from limb and let the Shambles stitch the scraps back together." The Cordoban woman gave him a nod and the Veneficus behind her screeched a hoarse eagle's cry. "Brothers! Sisters! Follow me!"

Eld led them back into the chamber of the Wellspring he'd just left a quarter bell before, running at the fore and then, suddenly, running on alone. He turned back and saw them, raw Veneficus, newly trained Dead Walkers, and many more who were either acolytes not trusted with Transfiguration or else Plague Walkers waiting for their task, frozen in place at the sight before them. Some wept and several began screaming incoherently. He followed their gaze and felt his stomach twist. The dead priests lay twisted and torn and burned amongst piles of bones and melted sinew that had formerly been a legion of Shambles. The Wellspring itself seemed to weep, a soft grey instead of its usual vibrant blue.

"Eld," Sheira choked out, "what happened here?"

"B-betrayal," Eld muttered. *Show them how desperate you are, how near a thing this was. Show them your anger and thirst for revenge.* "The mind witch sent her Sin Eaters here, to attack us at the heart of our power. To desecrate the Wellspring!" Several gasps and one throaty growl greeted his statement. Eld pounded his chest with a bloody fist. "The Plague Mistress died sounding the alarm, died so that we might live. Then the Archnemesis called me forth and . . ."

Eld spoke until he was hoarse, describing the desperate battle where half a hundred Sin Eaters had faced down the Archnemesis and the council and nearly won, until the Archnemesis broke them and sent them fleeing back to their Goddess. "He left but one command, family. Drink! Drink of the Wellspring and then make for the harbor and take every ship that has a scrap of sail. We end this war today. Now. Are you with me?" A cacophony of screams and yells rose from those who stood before him. Eld thumped his chest, then pointed at the glimmering pool. "Drink deeply, brothers and sisters! Our Gods' blood will end this forever war, once and final. The truth of blood!"

"The purity of blood!" they shouted back at him, their voices echoing off the cavernous walls. "The sanctity of blood!"

The horde rushed past him, Sheira giving him a wide grin that made her look younger than her years and nearly broke Eld's heart. Until he remembered how she'd pleaded to be made a Plague Walker instead of a Dead One. Begged to be allowed to lay the Empress herself low as punishment for serving Ciris. Eld walked slowly after them, urging a Veneficus who was still shivering and wet through with sweat from Transfiguring to get to the harbor, patting a woman on the back who muttered about her insides tingling. All the while he watched closely to see if any noticed that the blood they drank—whether they scooped it up with their hands or knelt to plunge their mouths into the liquid— didn't provide the blissful release they were accustomed to.

"Make sure you fill up vials to take to our brethren!" Eld called out. "They'll need our help in spreading the seeds of our victory far and wide." He wandered through the carnage of the battle, kicked a familiar-looking blade, and stooped to pick it up.

"Eldritch?"

"Xulet?" Eld peered through his blond locks and stood up slowly.

"You're sure this was the Archnemesis's command? To leave our sanctum unprotected?" The woman held a cup in one hand and gestured around her with it at the rapidly emptying cathedral.

"I trust the Archnemesis," Eld said.

"Who doesn't?" Sheira asked, walking up to them.

"Xulet," Eld said.

"I didn't say that," the woman protested.

"Xulet doesn't trust anything. It's why she carries her own drinking cup wherever she goes." Sheira chuckled, dried blood cracking on her cheeks when she smiled. "I can taste the plague," she whispered as if to herself, but loud enough Eld could hear her plainly. "Can't we? We can. Like liquid death. But not mine. And not yours. Theirs? Theirs."

"If it would make you feel better," Eld said, cutting off her mutterings, "I could stay? Wait for his return?"

"I'd like that," Sheira said, clapping him on the back. "Where will you go, Eldritch? Colgna? Servenza?"

"They know me—knew me in Servenza," he said. "Colgna or Frilituo seems a safer bet."

"I hope they remember me when I march through the Grand Bazaar," Xulet growled.

"Then I'm off for Servenza." Sheira giggled. "See you back here?"

"Eventually," Eld agreed.

"All we've got is time," the red-haired woman shouted, skipping up the steps and nearly tripping on her robes before joining the last of the acolytes filing out of the cavern and back toward the cathedral proper.

"Time," Xulet said.

"Time for you to bottoms-up, sister," Eld said, pointing at the cup full of viscous, faintly glowing liquid in her cup. "Drink in the plague and become one with us all."

"It sounds of Ciris, when you put it like that."

"Then we'll slay her with a taste of her own," Eld answered.

Xulet laughed thickly and raised her drink. "Say?" she asked, pausing with the rim pressed to her lips. "If two and a half score witches killed so many of us . . . where are all their corpses?" She gestured with the ceramic cup. "I see our dead lying thick, like cordwood stacked for the flame, but none of the enemy."

"Would you believe the Archnemesis tossed their broken bodies into the Wellspring? To drown them in our Gods' blood?" Eld asked.

"Sounds too poetic for a thousand-year-old prelate," Xulet said, shaking her head.

"I thought you'd see through that." Eld sighed.

It happened in a flash.

Xulet tossed the contents of her cup at Eld's face, as he expected. He was already moving, pressing right up against her so that the poisoned blood hit only air. Xulet's other hand appeared, clutching a dark blade covered in some glowing substance—also as he had expected. Eld trapped Xulet's arm against her body, then brought the blade he'd picked up off the floor hard into Xulet's sternum, driving it deeper and deeper, angling it upward until he felt it strike home in her heart.

It was Buc's stiletto . . . the one dipped in silver.

"Y-you?" Xulet choked, blood flecking her lips as black tendrils crept up over her features. Her dark eyes were wide—clearly she hadn't expected that.

"Me." Eld held her tight against him, fighting her death throes lest they free the arm that held the poisoned blade. "I betrayed you, Xulet . . . but you betrayed me first. All of you."

Realizing he was holding a corpse, he let her fall to the floor. For a few moments Eld stood there, taking it all in, then he turned and began climbing up the steps after the others, the echoes of his footsteps chasing after him.

He found Sheira a dozen paces down the passageway, her face twisted in a rictus of pain, her lips mangled and her mouth a pool of frothy blood from where she'd chewed her tongue half-through. Eld knelt beside her and closed the woman's wild, frightened eyes. Sheira had not been put back together quite right; she'd probably tried to drink the whole damned pool when others had limited themselves to the few sips he'd advised, and the poison had caught her full on. *It works.* Relief warred with guilt, but guilt lost out. *Send it doesn't work so fast on the others.*

"Betrayal," he said soundlessly. Eld took the poisoned vials from her pouch, stood up, and walked away. This time there was no echo from his footfalls, no sound at all. He was the last one drawing breath in a charnel house that now truly belonged to the dead.

48

The eerie light cast by vibrant, green stains along the walls and across the floors and ceilings meant we'd no need of lantern light, which was good, as the sole lantern we'd found had burned out shortly after we stumbled upon the passageway Eld had referred to simply as "the wound."

"What do you imagine this hall was? When they were alive?" Salina asked, easing the sling off her shoulder and down to the ground.

"An impossibly long forearm?" Arti asked between gasps as he lowered his side. The canvas papoose we'd rigged to drag Bar'ren settled against the floor. The islander hadn't spoken more than three words since we began our escape, but I could see his head moving slightly as he looked back the way we'd come. "A femur?"

"Who cares?" Chan Sha asked, beside me. "I just want out of this rotting grave of a place."

"We can't be far now, surely," Salina said.

"We aren't, if I remember Eld's directions right." Everyone groaned. "Listen, I didn't see any of you taking notes when he told us how to climb out of the bowels of these Gods."

Beneath my open jacket, my shirt was sodden with sweat and drying blood. I couldn't grab a full breath without my ribs screaming in protest. *Crack a rib and it could pierce a lung.* That would be a damned sight worse than the mass of bruises springing into existence all over my torso. As much as that hurt, the wound in my leg was the real concern. There'd been nothing to fasten a crutch out of and though Chan Sha did her best to support me, every fourth or fifth step I had to put weight on it to keep from sprawling across the floor, and each time sent a burning dagger through my body. *I'm not going to die getting out of this Godsdamned crypt. We* won, *damn it.*

"S-should be up around the next bend," I panted. "A ramp leads up to the street and opens onto an alleyway between two warehouses."

"Let's get on with it," Salina said, bending down to pick up the strap looped through the canvas. "After today, I'm going to order others to do the grunt work."

"Your prerogative as Chair," I told her. "Doubt you'll be able to stick to it."

"Fucking watch me."

I smiled at that, and when Arti had gathered up his side of Bar'ren's canvas sling and I'd taken hold of Chan Sha's elbow, we moved on. A score of paces later, we turned the corner and a ramp greeted us, this one made of sandstone that had obviously been built by humans. The top of the ramp held a sliver of grey dawn where the door had been left ajar, and both ramp and doorway were blissfully empty. We picked up the pace at the sight, moving from a slow walk to a shambling one. I saw something dark in the middle of the ramp and risked letting go of the wall to point.

"What's that?"

"It looks," Arti said, squinting through his spectacles, "like one of those books the Dead Walkers use to call up Shambles."

"Bloody wonderful," Chan Sha muttered, her lilting gait causing me to stumble.

"Smash it," I growled, glaring at her. As it was her patched eye I was glaring at, she didn't see. "Last we need are more dead-and-uglies."

"Someone already did," Salina said as we began climbing up the ramp. We reached the book a moment later, and someone had indeed smashed it; the normally smooth, glass-like book was cracked, and shards popped out from the dead, black surface. Salina edged it with her boot. "Looks like we were done a favor."

"Aye, but by who?"

"We're not going to find out standing here," Chan Sha said, the former pirate's pink lips pressed together in a firm line that almost hid the pain writ across her features.

"It doesn't matter," I agreed. *We're all at the end of our ropes.* We needed to get up to the street, hail the first hansom cab we could fit into, and get back to the ship before we all dropped dead of exhaustion. "C'mon, a dozen paces to fresh air."

"I'll drink to that," Chan Sha said.

Salina's chuckle set us all to laughing like fools as we lumbered up the last bit of the ramp and reached the door, which was cunningly cut into the stone of what looked to be a wall. Chan Sha dropped her shoulder and smashed it open, pulling me along with her, and Salina and Arti came hard on our heels, even Bar'ren twisting half around so he could see the open sky. We burst into the alleyway, bone-tired and out of breath, mad with laughter, and Chan Sha stopped short. I limped past her, glancing over my shoulder to exchange grins with Salina. I made it several more shambling paces before something in Salina's eyes made me turn back around, and I saw a dozen men and women standing at the end of the alley, blocking our path to the street.

"I knew I felt something." A short woman in a yellow, brocade dress, the fabric slashed with crimson panels, took a step toward us, her sable skin even darker in the poor light. Her eyes, all gold with no iris, practically shone from her face as she stared back at me. "There was an extra pattern aboard Mankin's vessel, but I thought it merely feedback from my Possession," she said as if speaking aloud to herself in a high, lilting voice that I recognized at once.

Ciris.

"In the flesh," she said, answering the question I didn't realize I'd spoken aloud.

"We don't need the other after all," she said over her shoulder. "Kill the beast, Kerqard."

A small man in a bronze jacket the color of his skin whipped around, steel bright in his fist, and next to him, a pale woman, her short, blond hair curling around her ears, grunted. She would have screamed, save the woman behind her had a hand clamped over her mouth. Kerqard drove the dagger into the woman's chest again, slightly lower this time, and by the way her body jerked I knew he'd found her heart. As she collapsed to the cobblestones I realized she wore white robes like Eld's. The woman who had been muffling her cries bent and rubbed her hand clean on the back of the dead woman's head.

Broken book. Dead Walker. Librarian. What had Eld called her? "Hexia help you find what you were looking for, Ciris?"

"Was that its name?" The gold-eyed woman shrugged. "She was useful enough, in the end. You, child, were far more instrumental. I thought I'd lose some of my dearest Sin Eaters today while discovering just what these mindless cravens were plotting, but whatever it was you did down there certainly grabbed their attention."

"Sounds like you owe me one," I told her.

"Owe?" The woman's mouth made as if to grin, but her eyes blazed with the fury of a thousand suns. The Sin Eaters behind her spread out across the alley; the buff wall of a warehouse on one side and the bone of a Dead God on the other ensured there would be no escape. "I promised you what I would do to you, little thief. Back on Mankin's ship. She's fast, Kerqard; mind the blade up her left sleeve," she added conversationally. "A Goddess always pays her dues . . . and *always* collects her debts."

Ciris spoke so smoothly I almost didn't realize what was happening until the short man in the bronze jacket moved in a blur of limb and steel.

Straight at me.

Ciris was right . . . I was quick. Only, I didn't have Sin. Sin was off battling the plague that was flooding through my body like a diseased cancer—that is, if he wasn't dead already. Even without Sin, I'm faster than most would expect, but I had a hole in my leg and was on the brink of passing out. *Gods, I've nothing. Save my mind.* But thoughts were going to be little protection against the Sin Eater's blade. *Thoughts.* Almost the first lesson I'd learned with Sin was that nothing was faster than thought. Not muscle, not action, not even the ball fired from a pistole. The Sin Eater had halved the distance between us already and would be on me before my heart took another beat . . . yet nothing is faster than pure thought. *Nothing.* I knew that. The Sin Eater rushing to plunge his dagger through my chest knew that. All of them did. *And one other.*

"Chan Sha!" I screamed, sharp as a blade's edge even as I did the other thing that's nearly as fast as thought . . . nothing at all.

I collapsed to the ground as Kerqard swept across the cobblestones, blade punching through the air where I'd stood an eyeblink before. His head snapped back and everything from the bridge of his nose up disappeared in a plume of flame and smoke, then his feet tripped over my body and he tumbled forward, his momentum carrying him past me, trailing blood and brains. The echo of the gunshot reverberated off the walls like rolling thunder.

Chan Sha was beside me in the next moment, still-smoking pistole in her fist. "Bloody smart," she growled, rotating the over-under barrel so a new round was in place. "But there's not enough brains in between your ears or mine to get us out of this."

"Chan Sha—"

"Listen," she snapped, her dark-green eye boring into mine. "Looks like we've run out of time for that chat, Buc. Recollect how I said either you or Sin were different? Ciris just confirmed it . . . you don't have Sin in you. You're not a Sin Eater."

"Bullshit," I protested.

"You've an actual shard of Ciris Herself, not a Sin like the rest of us, but something that is pure Her."

"I don't—"

"Understand," Chan Sha said, smiling. "You're shit at listening, Buc. You and Sin could become something more than just a mindless Sin Eater . . . perhaps already have. You could become a Goddess yourself. That's what She fears. That's why you have to make it out of here before She pulls you apart to find that sliver of Herself trapped inside."

"That seems unlikely," I said, trying to sit up, my leg screaming in pain, Ciris screaming a few feet away, everyone screaming. . . .

"I've a debt to you," Chan Sha said, reaching into my jacket and tugging free one of my last grenadoes. "You gave me back what I'd lost more than once and thought gone forever . . . a chance to belong. A chance at family."

I frowned at the glass orb in her hand. "I told you we're in this together," I began.

"We are," the other woman assured me, winking her angled eye at me. She pressed her still-smoking pistole into my hand. "I owe yon bitch a debt, too, and today"—she lunged to her feet—"I'm going to pay them both off."

Chan Sha moved in a lurching run, braids streaming behind her. Somehow, despite her twisted leg, she was running all out and I knew—none better given the hole in my own leg—that the pain must have been on the edge of knocking her out. I wanted to call her back. To tell her there was another way. My mind, free of Sin, raced along dozens of paths that branched out across dozens more. *Think.*

"Goddess! Goddess, let me return to you!" Chan Sha shouted, waving a bare arm in the air, keeping the other pressed against the dark patch in the side of her sleeveless vest. We'd bound the wound so it was no longer bleeding, but the Sin Eaters didn't know that. "I repent!"

"Repent?" The Sin Eater possessed by Ciris took another step forward, lips curling. "You betrayed us a dozen times over."

"You don't understand," Chan Sha said, reaching her former Goddess. "It was all for family."

Ciris caught Chan Sha by the throat with one hand, cutting her off with a choked cry and lifting the woman off the ground despite being a full head shorter. "You're no daughter of ours, *pirate*," Ciris snarled into her face. "Watch what is done to this one, little thief," she said to me. "It's but a taste of what's to come."

She shook Chan Sha like a rag doll, whipping her around in the air, her body growing limp. Chan Sha's eye snapped to mine, bright with intention. Time froze and I saw Chan Sha's pink lips move, her mouth curve up into the hint of a smile. Ciris hurled her back around and Chan Sha let her hand open, tossing the grenado, which glinted in the rising morning light.

I drew my good leg up and dropped my right arm to form a solid platform, pistole falling in line with my eye. The glass orb filled the sight as it reached the apex of Chan Sha's throw. *I'm sorry.* I squeezed the trigger without realizing it, something in me breaking free with the kick of the pistole in my hand, the cacophony of the explosion making my ears ring. A heartbeat later the street erupted in a solid wall of flame, the silent fist of the shock wave knocking me flat on my back.

I flipped onto my stomach, roiling waves of heat licking at my face, as the white-hot flame shimmered and changed to a duller, angrier orange. Dark figures writhed and danced in the fire, screaming to the mindless beat of incineration, until one by one they slithered to the ground, writhing still as they were consumed. I watched. Watched as the flames ran their course, the crackling, popping intensity giving way to a dull, dying groan. Watched as the firestorm died and a former Sin Eater, one-time pirate queen, and the most badarsed woman I'd ever known, died with it. Watched through a haze of tears, the now-useless pistole heavy in my hand. *She knew.* When Chan Sha gave me the pistole she knew there was only one shot in it. No second one to grant her mercy.

I've a debt to you.

"It's been paid in full," I whispered, pushing myself up. I felt Salina's hand on my arm and I let her help me stand. For a moment we stood together in silence and then I cleared my throat and drew in a ragged breath. "She saved our lives."

"She did," Salina agreed. "At the end of it all, she was one of us." Her amber eyes were bright with tears. "Buc, we can't stay. We've got to get back to the ship and figure out what the fuck to do now."

"What? You mean facing down every deity in the world wasn't enough for you?" I asked, feigning a smile. She snorted and I nodded. "We're done here." With her help, I hobbled back a few paces to where Arti stood guard over Bar'ren. Both men looked as if struck by lightning, and I imagined I looked much the same. For a long moment no one said anything, and then I nodded and they nodded and we all got on with it, giving the dead a wide berth and leaving the alley behind us. I glanced back as we turned the corner, the flames withered down to an oily, fetid smoke, and smiled through tears.

Goodbye, sister.

49

―――――――――∞∞∞―――――――――

"Where the fuck have you been?"

"Nice to see you, too, Salina," Eld said. He felt his mouth twitch in a semblance of a smile—the same smile he'd worn earlier. *When I killed Sheira and Xulet and the rest of the Dead Gods' mages.* He was dead on his feet, hollowed out, and ready for one final breeze to carry him past the ships anchored or making way in the harbor and out to sea. *I could probably reach the Shattered Coast, given a good trade wind.* He swept his leather cloak back, exposing the leather buckles crisscrossing the crimson, feast-day robes embossed with thread o' gold he'd pulled on to forestall anyone questioning him after he left the Dead Gods' final crypt. When he set foot on the gangplank, the two sailors standing on the other side lifted their blunderbusses. He quirked an eyebrow and fought to keep from reaching for a vial. "Permission to come aboard?"

"Let him pass," Salina said, waving her hand.

Eld trod up the gangplank, nodded to the pair guarding it— who affected not to see him—and caught up to Salina in three more paces. The blond-haired woman glanced up at him, her honey-brown eyes full of some import he couldn't grasp, and pulled her blue shawl tighter despite the sun hanging above the horizon.

"Where's Buc?"

"Passed out," Salina said. "It's a wonder she held herself together as long as she did."

"She's all right, aye?" he asked quickly.

"Worried more about you than about losing half the blood in her body, I think," Salina said, half under her breath. She swept her braid over her shoulder and made for the opposite railing overlooking the harbor. "Before she fell asleep she said that if you weren't back by the time she woke, she'd come find you." Salina snorted. "Woman can't walk, but she thinks to play the hero one more time."

"Can't walk?" Eld arched an eyebrow. "What are you talking about? Sin should have healed her before you left the cavern."

"What part of her sucking the plague from your veins don't you remember?" Salina asked.

"She what?" Eld clamped his hand to the bandage on his neck. When he'd opened his eyes after the Plague Mistress nearly killed him, he'd known Buc had cured him, but the details were fuzzy. They'd been fighting for their lives and his small sense that something was wrong had gotten buried in battle and desperation. *She infected herself . . . to save me.*

"Godsdamn it," he whispered.

"Sin's gone," Salina said.

"Gone?" Eld frowned. "That's not possible."

"Gone. Disappeared." She waved a hand. "Buc said either the plague took him or he's fully occupied in fighting it off, but either way she's no longer a Sin Eater." Salina leaned against the railing, and this time when she looked at him, Eld recognized what was bright in her eyes, aflame from the setting sun. Anger. "Meantime, Eld, what have you been doing that you're hours late and dressed like a grandee of the Dead Gods?"

"Betraying those who trusted me," Eld snapped. He waved at the harbor, where a dozen ships were setting out, with more behind them. "There they go, carrying their deaths with them. I sold them all out, Salina. I know it had to be done," he said, cutting her off. "I know what they are."

He ran a hand through his hair, sweeping it back over his shoulder, and his crimson robes peeked out from beneath the black, oiled, leather cloak he wore. "I sold them on it too well. In the absence of any of the Eldests, they practically anointed me. By morning our ship will be the only in the harbor."

"Is that so bad?" Salina asked. "Isn't that what you intended?"

"It is," Eld admitted. He chewed on his lip, trying to find the words. *How do I explain that I hated and loved them in equal measure? Sheira was a Plague Walker who would have helped murder half the world, but she was also a child. She drank from the pool with a grin, never questioning what a friend told her to do. So now, she's dead.* "It's what had to happen, but . . . I spent more than half a year living as one of them. The first few months I thought I *was* one of them!" Eld's voice broke and he closed his eyes.

"I get it," Salina said. "I've never murdered an entire cult before, but I've done things as Chair that caused pain and hardship, aye, and in at least one case, the deaths of others because it suited the plans that Buc and I crafted." She sighed. "So that's why you tarried?"

"I was on the verge of leaving when what must be the last remaining Eldest in Normain found me," Eld said. "She'd been asleep with her Shambles and missed the whole damned thing."

"She slept through a Godsdamned war?"

"The things some of the Dead Walkers have their Shambles do . . ." Eld trailed off, face heating. "Makes hearing anything else difficult."

"Should have told her to go dive in that bloody pool to clean up," Salina muttered. Eld snorted and Salina held a hand up in acknowledgment. "What happened?"

"I killed her." He sighed. "It wasn't that hard, either." For a moment he was back in the library, moving between the rows with the Eldest leading the way.

"Do you feel strange, Eldritch?" Jaran asked. She reached out and pinched the back of her hand with the other. "It's almost as if my senses have been dulled."

"Dulled?" Eld asked. He slipped his hand into his cloak, past the leather pouch on his belt that held a few, precious, untainted vials, and

clasped the butt of the pistole tucked behind it. "Are you sure it's not just you acclimating to being a Plague Walker?" He cleared his throat to hide the sound of the hammer cocking. "I felt a little off at first, too."

"No," she said, shaking her curly, brown locks. "It's not that." She kept walking, trusting him to follow. "It's more like, something is leeching the strength from me by degrees so small I almost wouldn't notice it save—"

Eld leveled the pistole behind her right ear and squeezed the trigger.

"She was dead before she hit the floor," Eld said. "Never saw it coming. None expect a Veneficus to carry a weapon. We *are* the weapon." He cleared his throat and looked away. "I ran after that, went up that sandstone ramp and found half the street burned away."

"We ran into Ciris and ten of her Sin Eaters," Salina said.

"You what?" he gasped.

"Ciris."

Eld listened in shocked silence as Salina told him about Ciris having Hexia murdered—likely after torturing her for information—and then sending another Sin Eater after Buc. How Chan Sha did for that Sin Eater and then sacrificed herself with a grenado to save the rest of them.

"I—I judged her wrong," Eld whispered when Salina finished.

"We both did," Salina said. She shook her head and looked down at the railing. "The woman had a strength the likes of which I've only seen once before."

"Buc."

"Buc," she agreed.

"How'd Buc take it? Killing her?"

"Like Buc," Salina said dryly.

"With a quip and a joke, while looking away so you couldn't see her tears," Eld guessed.

"Just about." She snorted. "You know, when I first met the pair of you, all I saw was the noxious arrogance."

"That's all she wanted you to see," Eld said. "I'll allow, that's a large part of who she was then, too."

"Buc was the last woman in Servenza I'd have spared more than a glance on, but I got to know her when you two fell out. To understand her, to see the woman beneath the harsh, abrasive layer the streets had given her. And the layer below that and on and on, and I confess, I found myself drowning in her depths," she whispered. "Eld, I doubt we'll ever be as close as Buc and I are or as you and Buc are, but . . . I would like us to be friends."

"I'd like that, too," Eld said slowly, trying to discern what he was missing.

"Good," Salina said, sounding as if she meant it. She pushed herself away from the railing and paused. "But remember this, Eld. There's only one Sambuciña Alhurra in this world, so if you fuck it up . . ."

"There you are!" the Artificer called, pulling them both around. "Oh, Eld, too. This is fortunate, and so forth." The short man tugged at his purple jacket, buttoned to his neck despite the sweat on his brow. "Buc's awake and asking for you. For all of us. She said it's time we, er, 'put this motherfucker over the horizon' were her exact words, but I believe she means we need to discuss what comes next."

"Eld and I were just discussing that," Salina said, winking at Eld. "Let's go see what our little Goddess has ordained."

"I'll be along in a moment," Eld promised. He watched the pair walk back toward the captain's quarters, Salina's words still echoing in his ears. *Wait.* Several things fell into place and Eld swore. *How do I compete with the Chair of the Kanados Trading Company?*

"It's not a competition, Eld," he whispered, and the sharpness the Dead Gods had imbued him with via their blood, the edge that saw everything as a fight, relaxed. *I'm here for you, Buc. However you need me.* If he clung to that, he couldn't go wrong. He straightened up and surveyed the harbor once more; nearly all the ships were gone, scores of them racing to spread the poison that would spell the final death throes of the Dead Gods. *Of me.*

There was at least one barrel of blood belowdecks, packed alongside bits of bone and ritual artifacts, likely enough to maintain his power for decades—a century perhaps. *But will the world really need a Veneficus? Will it need me?* He pushed himself away from the railing and followed Salina and Arti, still feeling off ballast, full of guilt for betraying those who had trusted him. For all of that, Eld settled one matter. He wasn't certain if the world would have need of Eldritch Nelson Rawlings in the days to come, but he damn sure knew one woman who would.

Buc.

50

"You can't be serious!" Salina slapped the mahogany dining table. "Buc, we need a break to recover. Gods, woman, you need a week's bed rest, perhaps more. Surely, after dealing a mortal blow to the Dead Gods, we've earned that."

"We defeated Ciris today," Arti said quietly, polishing his spectacles furiously on the hem of his coat, as he did when nervous.

"We didn't," I reminded him, speaking around a spoonful of some thick soup made of offal and other nasty bits that the Artificer swore would help replenish the blood I'd lost. It didn't taste bad, quite the opposite—so long as I didn't look too closely at what I was eating. "Chan Sha did that."

"Aye, and died in the doing," Salina said. "Buc, you're not thinking clearly. Bar'ren's still barely clinging to life despite the blood we gave him."

"I can help with that," Eld said. Salina had said he was depressed after betraying his fellow priests, which was definitely Eld's style, but he seemed upbeat to me. "As soon as we're done," he added, patting the cloak that hung on the wall behind him.

"What'd I fuck up?" I asked, brushing my loose hair over to the opposite side of my undercut.

"Nothing," Eld said, "but while the proportions are more like guidelines, they do matter." He shrugged in his crimson robes, which looked the color of blood in the lamplight. "And there's an incantation or two that may help."

"I already told you," the Artificer said, "those incantations are . . ."

"Bullshit?" I suggested.

"And so forth," he agreed.

"If Bar'ren isn't up and walking two days after I have a go, I'll eat shit," Eld said, cracking a grin. "I'm not suggesting there aren't underlying principles of nature involved that I just don't ken, but I know what I'm about, Artificer."

"Wonderful. In a few days, a weakened Bar'ren will be available to us," Salina said, lifting a finger. "Arti's weapons were all used up fighting the Archnemesis." She lifted a second finger. "Chan Sha's dead"—a third finger—"you're seriously wounded, and without Sin you won't be able to climb out of bed, let alone go haring off after Ciris"—the fourth finger—"and Eld's just one man with a dwindling, finite stockpile of vials." Glancing at the palm facing me, Salina shook her head. "Buc, with those resources, how are we going to fight the only God left in this world? We've got nothing."

"It's worse than that," I reminded her. I dropped my spoon into the now-empty bowl and pushed it to the side. "The Dead Gods were one of the pillars of the world, Salina. They provided hope, security, solace, whatever it was to the true believers, few as I hope those were. Beyond that, their services gave casual believers something to do, to look forward to, much the same as they look forward to feast days. They used their healing to make coin and indebt people to them, sure, but they still saved lives. With them gone, Normain's economy is going to crater."

"Bully for Servenza," she said.

"Aye, until I cut Ciris's throat and you lose all your Sin Eaters," I said. Her smile slipped and she shivered. I did, too, despite the thick, wool robe I had around me. Arti had given me something for the pain, but I felt fragile in a way that I hadn't since before Eld found me. Or I found him. "The Company's wealth is based upon the benefits the Sin Eaters provide, using both Transference and technology. The entire Empire is."

"More reason to wait," Salina said. "Let the world recover from the aftershock of losing the Dead Gods before killing the New Goddess."

"Salina has a point," Arti said.

"She does," I agreed. "Save Ciris won't be sitting idle, letting the world recover. I read a book once that said the kingdoms of the sea abhor vacuums." *Number 244. Kingdoms and Fiefdoms of the Deep.* "Hunt white fins out of an area and grey razors will come in their place. Instead of a dozen big sharks, you'll have scores of smaller ones. Ciris is the last white fin, Salina. She's not going to lick her wounds, she's going to try to sweep up the whole world before her."

"She's right," Eld agreed. "You both are," he added at Salina's glare. "We're talking about killing the Gods, for fuck's sake. That's bound to have huge impacts on the world."

"Which was my intent from the start." I reached into my pocket and pulled out a thin cigarillo I'd bummed off one of the sailors who'd filled the cask I used to wash up in earlier. The last time I'd smoked kan had been when I banished Sin from my mind. Now he was gone against my will and my mind was racing so fast I knew I wouldn't be able to dole my thoughts out slowly enough for the rest to follow without the help of the drug.

"I was bent on destroying the Gods ever since I read Volker," I said, leaning over the candle and puffing the kan to light, "but it's only in the last several months that I've begun to really understand what roles they play in the world." I exhaled a stream of smoke. "Corrupt roles that they played for their own, selfish ends, not for us, but the world's learned to function with them and we'll be dealing a huge blow to everyone with this." I coughed as I exhaled, feeling my mind slow just enough that I thought they'd be able to keep up. "Absorbing multiple body blows in one go is enough to put anyone down."

"But you're not talking about just anyone," Salina growled. "You're talking about the whole bloody world, Buc."

"What we need to do," I said, ignoring her, "is to ensure we have alternatives ready to put in place. We need to heal the world by our hand."

"How do you suggest we do that?" Salina asked, gripping the sides of her head.

"I'm glad you asked," I said dryly, scrubbing the nub of the cigarillo out on the table.

"We can't do this overnight," the Artificer said, putting his spectacles back on and blinking owlishly at me. "Buc, replacing every service they offer will take months. Years and so forth."

"The world isn't going to end tomorrow. The Dead Gods will be months in the dying, both literally and figuratively," I assured him. "We'll likely have to give them the final push into the grave when we're ready. Until we bury them, they'll carry on more or less as they have done until it becomes clear they've no magic left. I don't know what will happen to the Sin Eaters when Ciris dies . . . will they die with her, or will they be like Chan Sha was when her Sin was ripped from her?"

"Uh," Eld grunted, "she went homicidally insane, remember?"

"Let's hope they don't all do that," I murmured. *What happens if I lose my Sin? For real, if I haven't lost him already?* I stepped hard on the thought and continued on.

"What we have in our favor that no one else has is that we know this is going to happen. So we can take steps." I picked up the thick binder off the bench beside me and dropped it on the table, making the bowls and plates bounce with a satisfying clatter. The hundreds of pages represented many sleepless, frenetic nights spent up reading and writing and plotting with Sin, and I'd ensured it was on one of the longboats when we jumped ship off Southeast Island.

"I have a few ideas of ways to leverage this in our favor. Some of it's simple enough, making trades with this knowledge in mind, establishing protocols that can be used as a 'temporary' stopgap when we lose the Sin Eaters' capabilities.

"If you know Normain is going to collapse . . . bet accordingly.

Some of this"—I tapped the stack of parchment—"relies upon your genius, Arti. We'll need to figure out new ways of doing things, from communication to healing and everything in between."

I leaned forward. "This is humanity's moment. This is our opportunity to finally control our own destiny."

"None of that can be done from here," Salina said slowly. "You're sending us away, aren't you?"

"I am," I admitted. "You and the Artificer can do the most good in Servenza, preparing for the storm that's about to come. Bar'ren's finished his Goddess's bidding, so he can go home, and I've a few thoughts about ways he can aid our cause in the Shattered Coast."

"You're not sending me away," Eld said in a tone that brooked no argument.

"Wouldn't dream of it," I told him. "Last time I did, you came back a Veneficus. I shudder to think what you'd come back as next." His mouth twitched. "You and I, Eld, are going to kill the Goddess that fell from the stars and frightened the Dead Gods so much they tried to kill her from the grave. We're going to finish the war none of us started. We're going to kill Ciris."

Salina clapped slowly and loudly and I glared at her. She shook her head, smiling. "Bloody inspiring speech, save one problem."

"I'm beat to fuck?"

"Aye."

"You're sounding like Chan Sha, 'Lina, you know that?"

"She and I . . . may have had a conversation or two these past weeks about you, Buc. Someone needs to keep you in check or you'll end up killing yourself, from ambition if nothing else."

"You're not wrong," I admitted. "All of you"—I included them in my smile—"need to do that."

"Big job," Arti deadpanned.

"I'm not sure I like this new side of you," I joked. "Look, Ciris said she can sense me," I said, dropping my voice and leaning in. *I'm praying that means you're still alive and kicking, Sin.* "I've a feeling that now she's got the scent she'll be able to follow me even when I'm not right up her arse. Once she pulls herself back together after losing her second Possessed Sin Eater, she's going to come looking.

"I want her to know I'm coming straight for her," I said, unable to keep the anger from my voice. To my ears, I sounded like Chan Sha had. *Sister.* "I want her to know what it is to feel fear."

I drew in a breath and put my cards on the table. All of them. "This won't be a physical fight, 'Lina. I realize that now. Not like the Dead Gods at all. This will be about subterfuge and wit and it's going to end the way it all started . . . with Eld and me alone against the world. Or in this case, Ciris." *Sin, if you want to join us, I'd love the company.* I waited a moment, but the void where he'd once been in my mind remained empty. "But first, I need to figure out where exactly the fuck she is."

"I may be able to help with that," Eld said slowly. "I found a hidden library within the hidden library in the Dead Gods' Citadel. . . ."

"I could bloody well kiss you," I told him. "That's all for tomorrow, but tonight, while we're safe aboard . . . can we eat and drink and laugh and think about what we've just done?"

"Killed the Archnemesis!" Arti shouted, raising his glass.

"I was going to start with a smaller toast and work up to that," I said, digging out another cigarillo.

"Not dying!" Salina cried, clinking hers glass against Arti's.

"Now that's more like." I laughed, and we all began talking and laughing and drinking and I tried hard not to look at the empty seat and think about the differences between allies and cannon fodder. One hurt a lot more than the other did. Even for a girl of ten and eight who has a funny way about feelings of any sort.

Later, much later, after everyone else had left, Eld picked me up carefully, cradling me in both arms, and carried me through the door into the next room, where my bed was. My head buzzed with the wine I normally didn't drink, and the lantern lights had a warm, pleasant glow, and all was tempered by the knife's edge of pain that ran from my leg, through my bruised ribs, all the way up to the cut on my cheek. Eld touched the thick line that ran just below my eye and I made a noise against his chest.

"You know, earlier you mentioned kissing me," he whispered.

"Eldritch Nelson Rawlings," I said, biting off each word as I stared into his sapphire-blue eyes. "Are you saying I owe you a kiss?"

"I'm simply acknowledging there was an offer." He laughed.

"There are two things you should know," I told him, as he set me down gently on the bed. "The first is that you need to take care with my leg. . . ."

"And the second?" he asked.

"The second is that I always pay my debts."

51

"If you'd told me a week ago that Normain was this fucking big, I'd not have believed you," I told Eld as our coach ground to a halt on a small rise overlooking the endless sea of grass that ran on to the horizon. On one side of us, it stretched toward a brown smudge in the distance where the Burning Lands began encroaching on Normain; on the other, the grass seemed to spill over the ragged cliffs and down to the actual sea, its brininess sharp in the air.

"Big and empty," Eld said. "The grasslands here are shallow, not much good for farming and barely better for grazing."

"And the sand demons lie a few day's ride to the east."

"Aye," Eld said with a nod as the coach we'd hired jerked free of the mud—the fall rains had arrived in earnest the day after we left the city—and turned toward the sprinkling of buildings that formed one of the small coastal hamlets dotting the coast. "The Burnt aren't far off, but typically, the route up the coast and through the outskirts of their land is left well enough alone."

"Is that where you landed?" I asked him. "When you were with the army?"

"Around there. On the Colgna side of the Burning Lands there's a break in the cliffs."

"Iverny?"

Eld looked up at that, his powder-blue Normain jacket buttoned up to his throat, a silly, silk scarf of bright red billowing out and down his chest. I teased him about it, but he did look dashing in a stuffy, Normain sort of way. He touched the bridge of his broken nose and laughed. "What'd you read, a book on coastal geography of Colgna?"

"Ages ago," I confirmed, "but it was Zadaya's *Desert Folly* that gave me the name of the port."

"Zadaya? What number was this?" he asked.

"Three-ninety-five."

"Three-ninety-five," he repeated, his forehead creasing slightly. "After you thought I died?"

"I didn't think you kept that close a tally on my reading," I murmured.

"Close enough," he said with a smile. "So you read Zadaya. I knew her to see her. She was Seetel's sister commander, one of the four regiments in our battalion."

"She said Seetel was a fool of the highest order," I said, trying not to show my discomfort at the rocking of the coach as we navigated the rutted-out slop from increased traffic that portended our arrival into the village proper. "That he'd no balls and if not for his tailor he'd have never been allowed to advance past leftenant as he'd no brains to impress his superiors with either."

"He was a polished suit of empty armor," Eld agreed.

"She said he was smart enough to avoid singular conversation with his superiors as assiduously as he avoided being anywhere near the fighting."

"True enough," Eld growled. He glanced out the cab window, his eyes distant. "Why'd you pick that book, Buc?"

"Because," I said slowly, "when I thought you gone forever, I realized how little I knew of what made you the man I missed so terribly and . . ." I took a breath, trying to find the words that usually came so naturally to me. I'd never understood what regular folk meant by being tongue-tied until I discovered the meaning of the word "love." *Fools, the lot. Present company included.* "I decided if there was to be no future with you, I'd at least understand the past."

Eld nodded, still looking through the window as the coachmen hollered for servants—which was some damned wishful thinking, given the flyspeck village we'd come to. *We're fortunate there's a proper tavern here in the first place.* "I woke up on a ship with the wounded," Eld said. "I tried to return to shore when I'd convalesced, but I was sent back to the mainland. Discharged." He cleared his throat. "Only, there's no discharge in the war, Buc."

"I'm sure there's not," I told him gently, thinking of how the streets had never really left me. The coachmen knocked on the door and Eld made to stand up. "One thing I wondered about," I said, making him pause, bent over before the door. "I read Seetel died not long after the war ended . . . but he was a young enough man and had not been wounded in battle."

"Oh?" Eld asked lightly.

"One thing I've learned, Eld, is that you can't save the dead." I stood up, taking his hand and trying to keep my bad leg from catching in those damned hoop skirts that I meant to change out of as soon as we were settled inside. I looked him in the eyes and squeezed his hand. "You can only avenge them."

"We know the telescope isn't a telescope," Eld said, leaning back in the wooden chair beside the small table in the center of the cramped room that served as both bedroom and dining room. He gestured at the map unfurled on the table beneath a triad of candles, his forearms corded with pale muscle where his shirtsleeves were rolled up. "It can't be."

"Can't it?" I asked, looking out the tiny square window that overlooked the village green. *Well, brown, after the rains.* Earlier a messenger had ridden through, crying the news that the world was being turned on its head. Had been for the last fortnight, but this far from the capital news traveled at little better than a snail's pace. The village had been a frantic swarm until the local lady or mayor or whoever was nominally in charge shouted them all down and sent them back to work with the promise of a full tribunal in the morning. Full night had come and I could barely see anything more than a pace beyond the sole lamppost in the center of the town. Leastwise I couldn't see more without Sin.

I hobbled about on my crutch, taking slow, measured steps so I could control how much weight I put on my bad leg. It'd been a week since I'd taken the wound, and while pink skin—stark against the deep brown of the rest of my thigh—had grown over the hole in my leg, it didn't feel much better than the day the Archnemesis had put that blade through me. *Likely because you're fighting off a plague. You and Sin both, if he hasn't died already.* I assumed if he did die I'd know it when I developed the symptoms Eld had been displaying when he was infected. I was determined to walk of my own accord by the time we faced Ciris, but it was more of a battle than I'd bargained for.

"Think about it, Eld," I said as I stomped over to the map. The Artificer's skillful hand was obvious, from the thin squares of latitude and longitude to the detailed notes scattered along our route. "The Dead Gods showed you the Enemy. That has to have meant Ciris. They also showed you the stars and constellations at two midpoints of the year . . . doesn't that suggest something?"

"Timing, certainly," Eld said, scrubbing at the stubble on his chin. We'd spent every night like this . . . me working the stiffness out of my leg until the pain was too much to bear and Eld playing the sounding board while we tried to decipher the Dead Gods' map.

"Perhaps something more," I murmured. "It could be a configuration of constellations at a certain time of year that would provide direction?"

"Almost like an arrow?"

"Almost," I agreed.

"But an arrow in the sky pointing to what?"

"If we knew that, we would already know where Ciris was," I said dryly.

"Then there's this glowing silver dot," Eld said, pulling the star map out from beneath the map the Artificer had drawn. "I don't have your recall with paintings or drawings or pages, but I do remember it moving about . . . I just can't quite place where it was when the image in my mind stopped." He swept his hand across the map. "I don't see it here, though."

"All right . . . the telescope shows us the sky," I muttered, hobbling over to the bed and wincing when its sagging springs took my arse half to the floor. *If we try to make love on this thing we'll end in a pile of moldy feathers on the floor.* I glanced at the door that led to my room, which had a far nicer bed that we weren't using, and sighed. "Then there's that damned rope. I know Arti got my message because of the cipher text that lass slipped in my hand at the last village, but he didn't have any suggestions."

"Aye, well, a bloody rope to the sky," Eld snorted. "Who would?"

"Enough for one night," I growled, massaging the muscles above my wound. "I'm not likely to sleep as it is, salve or no salve. We've a few days yet, before the equinox."

"Plenty of time to spend riding in damned carriages all day searching for the location," he agreed, pushing himself up from the table.

"We'll see about that," I muttered.

"Here, let me." He dropped to a knee beside me, taking the pot of salve, and slid my trousers carefully down my legs and off my feet so I was in my underclothes. "You going to take your jacket and shirts off?"

"In a moment," I said, closing my eyes. I didn't want to let him know I'd been shivering all day . . . didn't want to think what it meant that my head felt hot against the back of my hand while the rest of me trembled with chills. *Sin* . . . "That feels good," I added, as he started working out the knots around my knee. It wouldn't feel so good when he got to the wound itself, of course. I took a deep breath and steeled myself, searching for distractions.

"Tomorrow," I started to tell him. The window in the adjoining room—"my" room—smashed in and someone plowed into the furniture we'd piled in front of it, cursing as they fell.

It was the only warning we had.

Eld leapt to his feet, spinning back toward his chair, plucking a pistole from the holster slung over the chair's back, and—spinning still—flung the chair toward our own window just as it exploded. A woman slid in along with the glass shards, feet first, arms crossed over her chest. She screamed when the chair hit her and probably would have screamed again when she hit the floor, but the pistole in Eld's fist roared, and even with the smoke filling the room I knew the woman wasn't going to make another sound again.

Our door kicked free of its hinges and I saw more people plunge into the room, blurs of motion obscured by the rising smoke, charging toward Eld. The last figure aimed for me and I rolled off the bed, legs flashing in my thin underclothes, hearing their blade catch in the lumpy mattress. I pulled the rotating alley piece out from under the bed frame and managed to fire a single bolt before the figure caromed off the wall and landed atop me. One knee went straight into my wound and I screamed even as the attacker knocked the crossbow out of my arms. I barely saw their next move in time and flung my hands up to catch their hand, which held a curved dagger. I wasn't trying to contain the Sin Eater's blurring strength, simply redirect it. So instead of cutting my throat, she cut a lapel free from my jacket.

I thrust my left hand at her face and she caught my wrist, letting go of her blade in the process. The woman, pale with pointy features and eyes the color of dishwater, glared at me, baring small, even teeth as she forced my hand away from my body, obviously intending to break it. Gunshots boomed out, someone shouted, and I ignored it all, fighting against her grip, and her smile grew.

"T-they t-told you to watch out for the blade up my left wrist," I grunted. "Didn't they?" She nodded. "She told you." Another nod. "S-should have told you"—I stopped fighting and her strength sent her spilling over the side and half onto the floor—"about this!" I snapped my right wrist back and the contraption strapped there fired a dart into the middle of her forehead, the iron shaft the same color as her startled eyes. She fell against me and did not move again.

The room had fallen silent and I looked up to see Eld wrapping a long scrap of fabric around his forearm. Two bodies lay twisted atop each other, their heads disfigured by pistole shot, and a third sat clutching their ruined throat, whatever color their jacket had been stained crimson by their lifeblood.

"Eight."

"What?" Eld asked, looking up.

"Took Ciris eight days to pull herself together," I said, forcing my voice to be light despite the fact I could barely breathe. "Eight days to find me and have her mages reach us."

"Good to know," Eld said, tightening the knot by holding one end of the bit of fabric in his teeth. There was something practiced in the gesture, as there was in so many of his gestures relating to the giving or caring of wounds.

"Eld?"

He arched an eyebrow.

"How come you never really told me about the army or Seetel?"

He looked at me for a long moment and sighed. "Show me your scar and I'll show you mine," he whispered.

"Oh." I shoved the body off me and sat up. I'd told him a little. In bits and pieces, fits and starts, but never the truth. Not all of it. For a long moment I wasn't sure I was going to speak. And then I did.

"I was seven when I met Sister. . . ."

52

"Why'd we leave the coach, again?" Eld asked behind me as we stumped through grass tussocks that grew in uneven lumps with clay and mud between them. Were I healthy and full of Sin, I'd have been able to leap from one to the next, quick as you like, but I wasn't, so I was squelching through mud and stumbling over bumps of reedy grass, and either way my leg felt as if it was just another word for pain.

"I thought you hated the coach?" I asked, working my way up the rise, Eld prepared to catch me when I inevitably fell.

"I hate wading through muck even more," he muttered.

Atop the rise, the cliff was covered with short grass and rocky soil. The sea stretched out before me, the sun's rays cutting a bright line through the deep blue. A ship lay at anchor, sails furled, just off the edge of a rocky inlet that was more of a sliver carved into the coastline than an actual harbor. The schooner rode high in the water, two banks of oars sprouting like insect's legs on either side, and long tubes running the length of the hull, one on each side. Cannon Ships weren't pretty, but given their ability to use seawater to propel banks of oars in addition to catching the wind, they were damned fast. My stomach flopped at the thought. With Sin, ships posed no problem; without him, I was in for a long go of it. Fortunately, I'd no intention of sailing.

"There's a ship!" Eld said when he caught me up. He adjusted his midnight-blue, nearly black tricorne so it cast a shadow over his face, squinting. "Kanados Trading Company, by her flag." Eld shifted his gaze to me. "You planned this, didn't you?"

"Next you'll tell me the sky is blue," I said, digging into my bloodred jacket, "the sun bright"—I pulled a small mirror out—"and water wet." I grinned as I flashed the signal mirror in the cipher that the Artificer and I had agreed to. "Of course I planned this . . . I hated that coach as much as you."

A few flashes came from the ship as they lowered a pair of longboats on either side. They both sunk nearly to the gunwales when they hit the water, then buoyed back up. With only half the oars crewed and the rest of the space filled with crates, I could see that they were going to have a go of it to reach the shore, even with the help of the tide. I glanced up at the sun, nearly to the full nooning bell. *We've enough time, Buc.* I just wished I believed it. Not that I ever believed Sin when he said it, but I expected him to lie. Start lying to yourself, and it's a quick drop with a noose around your throat.

"What's in the boats?" Eld asked.

"It's our ride," I told him.

"Our ride?" Eld glanced at me. "I thought the Cannon Ship was."

"The only thing worse than that rickety-arsed coach on that rut-filled excuse for a road would be a Godsdamned Cannon Ship." I snorted and clapped him on the shoulder of his midnight-blue jacket. "C'mon."

I stepped down awkwardly—though more easily in my grey trousers than if I'd been wearing a fool hoop skirt—onto a rocky, sandy path that had been cut into the cliffside ages ago. I heard Eld mutter a curse behind me and grinned. *He should know me better by now. A plan within a plan and another if that doesn't work out.* The Cannon Ship was a last resort, but I'd no need to let Eld know that. I was still congratulating myself as I navigated a sharp bend in the scuffed-up sand when my bad leg slipped and the ground gave way near the edge. My boots slid and I felt my balance vanish.

Rocks crumbled under my feet and fell over the side and then

I hit the ground so hard all the breath left me and I was merely a passenger in my own body, sliding toward the gaping chunk torn out of the cliff's edge. My bad leg was already dangling over the air; the rest of me was sliding along to join it, and the beach far below suddenly loomed large in my eyes. My stomach flipped and I opened my mouth to scream but everything had been knocked clean out of me and I couldn't even manage a croak.

Fuck me.

A rock half-buried in the path caught my thigh and buttocks and held me fast, a full pace away from the edge, only the toe of my boot hanging out over the edge. For what felt like an eternity I hung there, suspended. My breath returned in a fitful gasp full of briny saltiness, and I giggled. *Gods, that fall gave me more of an adrenaline rush than that Sin Eater from the other night.* I chuckled. *Or Ciris.* I began to full-out laugh.

"Crazy"—a loud, hissing, crunching noise filled my ears—"woman." The noise sounded like lightning and the surf breaking as it popped in my head. "Ciris terrified me. Should have terrified you," Sin said, his presence flooding into my mind.

Sin?!?

"The one and only," he said weakly, settling into the hole that had been left in the wake of his passing. "Tired as all fuck, but I'm back, Buc."

"Holy shit," I whispered in my mind. "I didn't think you'd died because I hadn't died, but I was feverish the other night with a chill and I'd begun to worry. . . ."

"That was the burst of energy in the form of heat I needed to knock the plague back," Sin said. "It's still in us, I—I'm still fighting it, but the tide has turned."

"Turned how? I thought this was engineered to part Sin Eaters from their Sin," I said.

"The Dead Gods like to believe they know everything when they know less than a part of it, and that part not well at all," Sin muttered. He sniffed. "This plague is virulent, sure. Deadly, of course. At the end of it all, though, it's an illness like any other, and most illnesses that don't kill you right away often won't kill you at all."

"You fought it off?"

"In a manner of speaking," Sin agreed. "Your body and my nanigens fought it off. *Are* fighting it off, as any Sin Eater would."

"Mayhap," I said slowly, "or the fact that you're different from every other Sin allowed you to break free of the plague's grip."

"What?" Sin asked after a moment. I felt him reaching for memories and then he froze. "Buc, what the fuck are you talking about?"

"You . . . truly you don't know?" I closed my eyes, remembering how it had felt.

"You've an actual shard of Ciris Herself, not a Sin like the rest of us, but something that is pure Her."

"I don't—"

"Understand," Chan Sha said, smiling. "You're shit at listening, Buc. You and Sin could become something more than just a mindless Sin Eater . . . perhaps already have. You could become a Goddess yourself. That's what She fears. That's why you have to make it out of here before She pulls you apart to find that sliver of Herself trapped inside."

Sin felt pensive in my mind as he sifted through my memories—soon to be our memories—mulling everything over.

"Buc! Are you all right?" Eld shouted, reaching my side. I realized I was still laughing, less madly and more happily, but it was still clearly unsettling to Eld. "Gods, I thought you were going over the edge there for a moment."

"Aye, me too." I wiped at my eyes and took his hand, pulling myself up. I felt a familiar tingling—more phantom than real—flow through my leg, and I surprised Eld by taking a few steps on my own that were almost like walking. A moment later I resorted to limping, but it was still much improved over what I'd been able to manage before.

"Sorry, Buc," Sin whispered in my mind. There was an edge

to his voice as if he, too, were in pain. "It's all I can give you. For now."

"I'll take it," I whispered back. I almost told him having his voice back was enough on its own, but I didn't want him getting airs and thinking I actually *needed* him.

"I missed you, too, Buc."

"I hate the way thoughts work," I growled.

"Buc . . . did that fall do something to your leg?" Eld asked, catching me up in two strides and placing himself between me and the edge despite the narrowness of the path. He'd unbuttoned his jacket, allowing the crimson vest that matched his trousers to show through. We'd both reverted to our Servenzan finery now that we knew death could take us at any moment. Not that I wanted to die and I definitely couldn't lose Eld again, but . . . my mind was too sharp not to ken the odds we faced.

"Our odds just improved. Sin is back," I said, unable to keep from smiling.

Eld's eyes widened and he pulled me into an embrace in the middle of the path. "Buc, that's wonderful. Not that I'd thought to ever be glad that mind weasel was back, but . . ."

"Sin says he loves you, too, Eld," I said, my voice muffled against him. Eld let me go and I stepped back, laughing. "I think we might actually pull this off."

"I never doubted," he said, sounding like the Eld of old.

By the time we reached the shore, the longboats had landed their cargo and were returning to the Cannon Ship, bobbing up and down on blindingly bright, blue swells broken by whitecaps, the dull rhythmic, roar of the ocean echoing off the cliffs surrounding us. The half-dozen crates, all but one the size of a large millstone, seemed to have been carefully arranged on the strand, I assumed at the Artificer's orders. Sure enough, when we opened the smallest chest, a veritable encyclopedia of parchments—some bound, others loose—greeted our eyes. The top paper bore just three words, written in the Artificer's sprawling hand.

"'Read three times,'" Eld muttered. "Read what three times?"

"The instructions," I said, shifting through the papers. "On how to put the Artificer's ornithopter together."

"Ornithopter?" Eld choked, mangling the word. "That flying deathtrap the man used to lift me to that building last winter? Before he put me in that floating balloon that nearly killed me when it decided to stop floating?"

"Arti can't control the weather, Eld," I said, clicking my tongue. "And that lightning strike only gave you a slow leak—it could have set the whole thing ablaze."

"Small favors," the man said, picking up a stack of papers and gazing at them. "So, what's our first step?"

"Don't know."

"Don't know?" He frowned, glancing up at me, and froze when he saw the smirk on my lips. "What don't I know?"

"It's not what you don't know, it's what you're going to figure out," I said. "I got the damned thing here, all the way from Servenza . . . the rest is up to you."

"I suppose that's fair," Eld said after a moment, his tone suggesting something else entirely. He crossed his legs and sank down onto the sand, reading Arti's spidery instructions. I moved to where the cliff face offered some shade and sat down on the edge of some bleached driftwood. "Say, Buc, do you know how to fly this contraption?" Eld asked, flipping one of the pages over and back again.

I shrugged, brushing my braid back over my undercut. The wind from the sea promptly caught it and tossed it back over and I gave up. "Sin will."

Eld started to nod, then paused. "Wait a moment . . . you didn't know Sin would come back."

"True enough."

"Then what was your plan?"

"Wing it." I laughed.

Eld stared at me, then shook his head and bent over the papers again, shaking his head every now and again.

"I see running roughshod over Eld is still a favorite pastime," Sin murmured.

"He wouldn't trust me if I didn't." I laughed again. I slid down onto the gritty, pale sand and leaned back against the driftwood, letting the salty air fill my nostrils. The sea was different here than in Servenza. Darker, deeper, harsher—but the sounds and smells still reminded me of home. *Minus the sickly sweet scent of refuse broiling in the gutter.* "Do you remember everything that happened while you were out of my head?" I asked Sin.

"None of it." I felt him tremble. "I barely remembered myself . . . it was like I was a disembodied echo of a thought swirling through your veins. I remembered my power but could do almost nothing, like a child trying to lift a boulder."

"Well, we've a while yet for Eld to figure that thing out," I said.

"It'll take him days without us," Sin said.

"Aye, but let him get all the crates opened and then we'll see what can be done." I crossed my arms behind my head. "Time you and I caught up."

". . . Eld says that at the time of the equinox, fall or spring, the telescope turns into some sort of braided ladder reaching up. . . ."

"Up to where?" Sin asked.

As we'd talked, his voice had grown marginally stronger, which I took as him recovering at a faster pace now that he was once again properly ensconced in my head. The beach was littered with wood from the crates Eld had torn apart and he was stripped to the waist, the sheen of sweat over his pale chest making me forget what we were talking about for a moment. Muscles rippled beneath his skin as he bent to tug one of the bolt arms level, and when he straightened, sweeping his hair back out of his face, I felt something tighten, down low and deep in.

"Buc . . . Buc!"

"Aye?"

"If you can stop eye-fucking Eld for a moment . . . What was this ladder figment of Eld's imagination reaching up toward?"

"Oh." I closed my eyes, opened them for a quick peek, then closed them again, forcing myself to concentrate. "Toward a silver dot high up in the sky that moved from one end of the horizon to the other."

"Well, I'm sorry, but it sounds like Dead Gods' bullshit to me," he said with a mental shrug. "If I had been there, perhaps I could discern more, but telescopes and ropes to nowhere?" Sin snorted. "I'm not sure—"

"I'm not sure you want to start off our reunion by lying, Sin," I snapped. "Thoughts go both ways, recollect?"

"I'm not saying there's nothing there," Sin said quickly. "I'm just saying the imagery makes no sense. We'd do well to gather more information, conduct more research, before we go haring off because of something Eld saw once when the Dead Gods were suffusing him with their fuckery."

"The imagery is confusing, but it makes some sense. The telescope only turns into this ladder when the silver dot is at a point where it can be . . ." I waved a hand. "I don't know, seen? Reached? The ladder makes me think it's that, but—"

"Buc," Sin interrupted me. "I think we need to let this go. Just for now."

"Stop trying to protect your Goddess, Sin." I let him feel the knots of anger twisting within me. "If you only came back to make sure I don't kill her, then you can fuck right back off."

"You don't understand me," he muttered.

"Uh-huh. So you've said from the first moment we met."

"No, you really don't," Sin said. "I told you I lost myself when the plague took me, but I think I found myself, too."

"You're right," I grunted, "I don't understand."

"When I was fighting the Dead Gods' plague in your body, everything snapped into focus. It was a metaphor for everything else."

"My almost dying was a metaphor?"

"Exactly! The plague represented the Dead Gods, I was Ciris, and your body was the world. The plague weakened you, would have killed you without me, but I was drawing on your strength to fuel my own," he explained. "Buc, we've been weakening and sickening your world for centuries with our forever war. I—I didn't get it before," he whispered. "Not really. But I do now."

"I almost believe you," I admitted. "Because that's exactly what this is, but then I ask myself, why the fuck won't you help me?"

"If we fight Ciris now, today, as we are . . . we might as well slit our wrists and walk into the sea and be done with it," he snapped. "What if Chan Sha was right?" he asked, more quietly. "Say I *am* a literal shard of Her. What if together, you and I are becoming what She is?"

"A Goddess?" I asked, and I suddenly realized what I was sensing in Sin . . . he'd searched the evidence he knew, which included everything that he was, and he'd come to the same conclusion as Chan Sha. *He thinks we're a Goddess already.* A flash of terror lanced through me. *Us. Ciris.*

"You're thinking about this all wrong," he said quickly. "I'm not Ciris, you're not Ciris . . . together, we're not Ciris. Buc, you could never be Ciris. Ciris is unfathomable today, aye, but She couldn't have always been this way. Think! Whatever She was before shaped what She became, the same way that you growing up on the streets shaped who you've become and what you've tried to do to fix this broken world."

"That almost sounds like a compliment?" I shook my head, watching the tide break against the shoreline. "Sin, I want to kill the Gods, not become them."

"Then we should buy time for us," he hissed. "Time enough for us to become Ciris's equal. *Then* we challenge her."

I'd begun to question what exactly Sin and I were before Chan Sha had shared her theory, and certainly Ciris's actions supported the idea that there was something important about Sin, something that made him different from all the other Sins, that made us different from all the other Sin Eaters.

We've bested her twice. Only, that wasn't quite true. Both times I'd had help and both times, Chan Sha had been there. *I don't think you're coming back from the grave to rescue me a third time, Widowmaker.* Ciris had not been in her true form—whatever that looked like—either time. *And yet.*

"How has my body felt these past ten days or so, Sin? You've been fighting the plague; how goes the war?"

"It—" He choked. "It was all I could do to keep regenerating you from the inside out so you would be spared the worst of it. It took everything in me to fight for the space to give us a chance to find a way to fight it off for good."

"That's how the world feels," I whispered. "Every day I don't act is another day of suffering."

"You know better than that," he countered. "Suffering doesn't end with Ciris, just as it didn't begin with her. The Company and the scores of others who would supplant them: the Empire, the strong, the cruel, they existed before this war began and they'll exist after."

"You're not wrong," I agreed. "In the same way the plague is virulent and violent, the system the Gods have created has made them worse. They're parasites. Like worms in a dog. You know how you treat a dog with worms?"

"There are powders and tinctures—" he began.

"Poison. Good as. Feed them medicine so strong you have to hide it in meat and crushed nuts. It makes them as ill as the worms, nearly kills them, but the worms die first. Ciris is that worm, Sin."

"I don't believe you can kill Her, Buc. She's a Godsdamned Goddess."

"I say otherwise." I sat up, my back tingling from lying in one place for so long, then got to my feet. I knocked the sand from my back and knees and straightened, smiling. "I read otherwise." *474.*

Whispers and Weaknesses of the Enemy. I couldn't remember every detail of the tome Sin had speed-read in that hidden Cordoban library, but what I could remember had given me several ideas. "I believe I can cut her so deep she bleeds herself dry."

"Without dying yourself? I've run the odds and I don't see this ending with me, you, or Eld still breathing. Even if She dies and we with Her . . . what do we leave behind?"

"There's worse fates than death," I whispered. "Many have sacrificed themselves for me. Sister. Chan Sha. Eld a dozen times over. Past time for me to shoulder that burden. Sacrifice is a word without meaning if there's no cost."

"If you give me that quote . . ." Sin muttered.

"It's the truest thing I've ever read," I said, limping over to help Eld, who was clearly in well over his head, with parts strewn everywhere and gearwork glinting in the sun. "Take what you want and pay for it." He glanced at me, the sun catching his blond hair and lighting up his blue eyes, but it was his smile that made me ache.

"But," I whispered to Sin, "if we could figure out a way to bleed her dry and not die, that'd be great, too."

53

"This is unbelievable!" Eld whooped, giggling like a child who found a toy in the gutter instead of flotsam. He glanced down at the grasslands far below us, green parted by a thin brown snake of a road, the coastline a white scar on our left and a brown smudge that hinted at desert on our right. "Unbelievable," he repeated.

"Eld. Crank!" I reminded him over the whistle of the wind, which we were protected from by a thin, transparent shell—what it was made of, I'd no idea. I leaned forward in my seat to speak in his ear. "Unless you want to find out how unbelievable it will feel when we crash," I added.

He looked over his shoulder at me, his eyes made larger by the thick, glass goggles he wore strapped over them, and nodded. A moment later I heard a whirring sound as Eld wound the crank that in turn wound the gears that drove the ornithopter's long, thin, mechanical wings. As they began to beat with more vigor, we rose several score paces, just reaching the bottom hem of a fluffy cloud. Satisfied, I eased my good leg off the pedal that determined their flapping rate. The twin shafts in my hands controlled lift and drag as well as pitch and direction. I was fairly certain I could have figured it out on my own, but Sin's guidance had made it effortless.

"I'm not sure if us nearly smashing into the cliff face upon takeoff exactly counts as effortless," he grumbled.

"Killjoy," I said. We cast a vast shadow over the grassland as we flew, eating up leagues in no time at all. The sun hung low over the horizon and dusk was only a bell or two away, but we should be near whatever this telescope thing was well before that. *If Sin tells me.* I thought over our conversation on the beach and pulled up a little higher until the wind caught us and I could ease off the pedal even more.

"Eld?" I leaned forward again so he could hear me. "Eld?"

"Aye?" he shouted, cranking slowly but steadily. *Gods, he let the damned thing almost unwind itself. Men.* "Or should it be ahoy? What's the proper terminology for flying this orn-thingie?"

"I think we get to invent it," I told him dryly, my mouth beside his ear. He jumped and I laughed and he shot a glare over his shoulder before turning back around. Early on he'd discovered that looking back for too long made him ill, but whether it was Sin's magic or something else, I felt fine. "I need to talk to you about something."

"The telescope and how we find Ciris?"

"They're interrelated, I suppose," I said after a moment. "Listen, there's something you should know about Sin and me. What we are."

"Buc," he said quickly, twisting half-around so his mouth was closer to mine, "I get it. You're a Sin Eater. I'm a Veneficus. We both hate magic and we're both cursed with it . . . but if I'm being honest, we'd have died this year without it. A dozen times over. You don't need to explain that to me."

"It's not that," I told him, blinking back an unexpected tear. *Godsdamn it, I'm not going to cry.* I'd spent most of my life believing emotions were a disease that infected others and finding myself afflicted was something I was still coming to terms with. Feelings weren't awful, but they were discomfiting and distracting and that was the last thing I needed now. "It's about Sin being a shard of Ciris."

"You mean what Chan Sha believed?" He shifted in his seat. "Is it true?"

"He thinks so."

"He's rarely wrong."

"I think so, too," I added after a moment.

"Well, you're never wrong . . . but what does that mean?" he asked.

"It means that I could eventually become Ciris."

Eld stopped turning the crank.

"Not her exactly, but have the same powers . . . become her equal."

"Magic," he said beneath his breath, Sin's negligible power just barely allowing me to hear. "You may need that kind of power, Buc."

"Bullshit," I told him. "We killed the Dead Gods, or good as. We're going to kill Ciris. The last thing the world needs is another Goddess to worship."

"You've never been one for that," he protested. "Just because you have the power of a Goddess doesn't mean you have to act like one, demanding worship in return for power or safety. You could use it for good."

"I could," I agreed. "I intend to." I bit my lip. "But I read Volker and Martens."

"Made me read them, too," he reminded me.

"So you know what's at stake, Eld." I punched the side of the carriage. "We can't save the world from the Gods only to turn 'round and inflict a new Goddess on them. I used to think the Dead Gods were benign until Ciris came about, but I think they were just lazy and she kicked them in the arse."

We flew in silence then, the wind whistling past our ears, flocks of birds giving us a wide berth, with one that had the wingspan of a phoenix swinging past for a closer look before veering away at our size. I cleared my throat.

"Eld, I don't want to become a Goddess, and if I do, I don't want to abuse my power . . . but it might be that I can't help what I'll become. I-if that happens, I need you to promise me." *Gods, forgive me.* I took a breath. "That you'll help me—"

"Of course I'll help you," Eld snorted.

"—by killing me," I finished.

Eld turned back around slowly, the whistling wind the only sound. "You're serious?" he asked finally.

"Deadly," I assured him, wishing I could see all of his face.

"Buc," he groaned, shaking his head.

"I'm not asking you to murder me now, Eld." I looked at the gulls hovering over the shoreline below. *I could wish for that simple life. Well, a day of it at any rate. An hour?* "I'm asking you," I continued, "as my best friend, as my partner in all of this . . . if I ever change so much that I start to construct societies that lock children into poverty, if I ever stop trying to give everyone a chance, to reduce suffering, if I use my power for selfish ends to harm others . . . If I do that, that you'll be there waiting, blade in hand."

"You do know who you are, aye?" Eld asked, risking sickness by turning around and locking eyes with me. "Sambuciña Alhurra? The woman with a tongue sharper than any blade, and mind sharper still. A woman who has sent entire crews to their deaths to meet her goals."

"Those were means to higher ends," I protested.

Eld reached back awkwardly and grasped my shoulder for a moment, then turned back to his cranking. "Buc, you're not perfect. You're going to fuck up. When you do, people are going to get hurt. As genius as you are, your fuckups are that much larger . . . the more power we gain, the larger they'll become. Aye, and sometimes your ends will demand that others pay a price. So far, that price has been worth paying."

"Well . . . damn," I said after a moment. "Since when did you get smarter than me?"

"The word you're looking for," he said solemnly, "is wisdom."

"Get fucked," I told him, grinning, and we both laughed.

"I know what you mean," he said, serious again. "If I believe you've changed, truly, that your ends are not what they are now, that this magic and Godhood? Goddessness?" He shook his head. "If you become Ciris in all but name . . . I'll stop you."

"You will?"

"I'll have to," Eld said slowly, "because it will mean I'll have failed you as well . . . by letting it get to that point. Buc, you'll never become Ciris, one way or another. I promise you that."

"Thank you," I said.

"It's a bloody thing, the woman you love thanking you for agreeing to kill her," he said after a moment.

"We're complicated," I said with a shrug, sagging back against my seat, thankful he turned back around so he couldn't see my face. "Always have been. Always will be."

"He never would have agreed to that before the Dead Gods took him," Sin whispered after a moment.

"I know," I whispered back in my mind. I'd felt him listening. "There's a darkness in him now that wasn't there before."

"When you two met, Eld was a man in search of a cause, and he made that cause you," Sin said. "For a brief time when he lost all memory of you, his cause became something different. Not worship, I don't think, but something more primal."

"You're saying he's a predator?"

"You're all predators," Sin said. "What I mean is that the blood they gave him, the rites and rituals they taught him, made him a more dangerous version of himself."

"Eld was always dangerous," I protested.

"He was, but he was acutely aware of that and therefore careful to control himself. The same way you're careful in managing the pedal on this ornithopter, but imagine if you cut the cord to the pedal."

"The wings would go as fast as they wanted to, we'd lose control, and crash."

"Precisely," Sin agreed. "The Dead Gods cut Eld's cord when they remade him . . . it's the nature of their Veneficus to err on the side of violence rather than reason. When he regained his memories and you with them, he regained his cause."

"So the cord's there," I murmured, "but there's some slack in it."

"Some slack and fraying. He could snap. I doubt he will and over time he'll likely be able to draw in that slack, repair that cord, but that kind of work takes years."

"So Eld's lost his restraint and I'm turning into a full-fledged Goddess," I said. "Bloody perfect."

"Bloody complicated," Sin corrected. "Just as you said."

For a time we flew in silence. I felt Sin shift in my mind and I tensed. "What is it?"

"Pull us down out of this windstream," he said.

"We're getting close?" I asked, shifting the handle and sending us down, out of the clouds.

"I think so," Sin said, sifting through our memories of the pages we'd read in the library. *Along the coast broken by Her fall, the Enemy lies in wait, hidden within Her mountain where none exists. Here the pathways hidden in aire lie strongest, here She can still be sought as She once sought us. Within the mountain that is no mountain. She awaits and Her name is Death.* The map the Artificer had drawn from Eld's memory flashed in my mind. We were on top of the telescope. "I think we're here."

"I don't see anything," I said, staring over Eld's shoulder at leagues upon leagues of more grasslands. The entire plain looked empty to the horizon. "Do you see anything in front of us?"

"I don't," he shouted back, "but I was going to ask if you sense something? Almost feels like there's spiders crawling up my skin," he said, scratching at his forearm.

"He must be feeling Ciris's power growing," Sin said. "That's how She's been tracking you," he added. "She can sense the presence of my nanigens."

"So she knows we're coming?" I asked him.

"She knows."

"Why didn't you say?"

"We had more important things to discuss and the knowledge wouldn't have changed your mind."

"Fuck me."

"Eld, Sin said Ciris knows we're coming."

"Wonderful," Eld said, shaking his head. "I know *that* feeling and it's more like when you feel someone staring at the back of your head. This just feels wrong on a gut level." He frowned. "You know, I don't see any birds in the air around us like there have been since we've been flying." He looked around, shook his head. "None at all."

"Hmm, you're right," I muttered. "I wonder if—"

Clang!

We ricocheted off thin air, the blow reverberating through the entire craft, rattling my teeth. The ornithopter spun in a circle, its nose tipped up, then began to slowly fall forward, almost in slow motion, until suddenly everything snapped together as reality asserted itself and we fell like a stone from the sky.

54

I fought for control with the sticks in my hands, but they felt like lead weights and when I pressed the pedal, it went straight to the floor. The wind howled, pressing my goggles so tightly around my eyes that I felt like my head was caught in a vice; the green grassland became more distinct as we plunged straight down toward it. The gears screamed and the wings flapped uselessly, slowly wrenching themselves loose.

We're going to die.

My eye was caught by the sight of the thin hawser cord slipping between the seats, being pulled along past Eld.

"Grab the cord at your feet!" I yelled to Eld.

"What?" he called back.

"Look down. At your feet! Grab that fucking cord."

Eld disappeared below the seat and shouted something that sounded like "Now what?"

"Put those muscles to use and pull! Pull like your life depends on it," I shouted, the wind stealing my words. "Because it does."

For several moments nothing happened and then the bone-jarring thumping stopped, but if anything, we fell faster, the ground screaming up to meet us. Eld stood up, an arm's length of cord tossed over one shoulder. The sticks loosened and I pulled back on them for all I was worth, Sin's feeble magic making my arms tingle like someone had brushed a feather across my skin. *Not enough.* I braced myself, using my good leg, and pulled harder, fighting with the stick to change the angle of the wings and tail, to pull us out of this death spiral. It still wasn't enough.

"Sin!"

"I'm doing all I can!" he shouted back in my mind.

"No," I growled, "you're not."

I slammed my bad leg down hard and blinding pain erupted through me, making my stomach turn, but I forced myself to press my leg harder against the floor, riding the sudden flood of endorphins, and for a heartbeat Sin's magic burned through my arms like it had in the past and the stick came all the way back to meet my chest. The ornithopter's nose turned up, fractionally at first, then more, the gears and bolts and metal frame screeching like an old woman who awakened to find a thief in her room. The bare edge of the horizon appeared as we leveled out, no more than a pace or two above the ground, winging out across the plain.

"Ow!" Sin screamed, his voice crackling in my mind. "That fucking hurt."

"You did it!" Eld crowed, his voice strained from the effort of holding the wings steady with naught but a thin cord. "You did—"

He spun half-around, eyes wide behind his blood-flecked goggles. The echo of the musket chased after him and I saw blood flowing from a round hole in his jacket.

"Eld!"

The rope slackened again and our craft's wings beat furiously, driving us a span into the air before Eld fell against the seat, using his weight to hold the rope taut. He swallowed hard and looked back at me. "B-bastards shot me," he growled.

A cacophony of gunfire erupted, rounds pinging off the metal frame, shooting sparks out over the grasslands. A dozen figures rose up all around us, with more streaming out of a door that'd opened up from some underground lair. *Sin Eaters,* each a blur of inhumanly fast motion, which meant their rounds would be inhumanly accurate if we slowed down.

I pulled up on the stick in my right hand and our momentum sent us rocketing back up into the sky. I shoved the stick in my left hand hard over and we banked away from the sea and whatever monstrosity had tried to take a bite out of us from thin fucking air.

"Eld, you all right?"

"I think it went through and through," Eld said, twisting around to settle back in his seat. He grimaced and cursed. "Fucking hurts."

"We'll get you patched up as soon as I figure out what to do."

"Put us down and I'll kill them all."

"Too many of them," I said, shaking my head as we made a looping arc back in the direction we'd come from. "Sin Eaters, the lot of them. We've a better chance in here, moving."

"Except this orn-a-whatsit is broken," Eld said through gritted teeth.

"Except that," I agreed. Another round scythed through the air, just missing us as I leveled us off, aiming for the door amongst the tussocks of grass. "You up to using that mount the Artificer put on the front or is your shoulder fucked?"

"My shoulder's fucked," Eld said, sitting up. He wrapped the cord several times around the crank he'd been turning earlier with his uninjured arm, the slack causing us to bounce several spans up before settling back down, the wind hissing along the wings. "But I don't need my shoulder, just my hand."

"Good man," I said. "Hang on."

We came whistling through the air, a full span above the ground this time. A score of Sin Eaters were waiting, spread out across the grass, crouched with muskets and pistoles and still more climbing out of the doorway. *How many of those bastards are there?* I scooped a glass orb from the pocket of my jacket and tossed it over the side. A concussive whump sent the ornithopter up with a shove from a warm fist, and I felt more than saw the fire from the Serpent's Flame. The bump likely saved us as the remaining Sin Eaters opened fire, the gunfire drowning out all other sound, so I didn't realize Eld was firing until our foes began to twist and fall.

Eld slung himself around in his seat, swiveling the massive repeating crossbow in its mount, pouring out bolts the size of my forearm at an alarming rate. The Sin Eaters weren't prepared for the Artificer's genius or Eld's determination. I tossed another grenado for good measure and then we were past them, with a solitary shot chasing after us.

"Let some slack out of that rope!" I shouted. A moment later the wings went wild and we rose from skimming the edges of the grassland back up to a span. "Tighten her down, we're going back for another pass," I said, whipping the stick back and over.

"Buc!"

"Aye?"

"I, uh, shot all the bolts," Eld said.

"All of them? The directions said the canister holds five score."

"My finger slipped?"

"Motherfuck." We were already halfway through our arc and I could still straighten us out. . . . My mind slid through our options, Sin's magic barely there but just enough to take the mania off as I considered. *Run them down. Left, then right.* I discarded it immediately. Any real fine steering was lost with the cord and it was just as likely we'd crash as hit them. *More grenadoes.* That was an option. I glanced out over the grasslands and saw sheets of flame leaping up from the ones I tossed on our last pass. We'd have to come in at another angle entirely or risk catching on fire ourselves and that would expose us to every mind witch below with a gun. *Flames. Fan.*

"How many were left?"

"I got a dozen or so," Eld said, breathing hard with his chin jammed into the hole in his shoulder, his other hand on the cord.

"Likely another dozen left, your grenado toss was a little late," Sin added mentally.

"Good," I answered mentally.

"Good?" Sin shrieked.

"Aye," I said out loud. I manipulated the sticks, intending to head right through the flames caused by my last throw. "We're going back in, and Eld? When I tell you to, let that cord go completely and get ready."

"Get ready?" He tried to shift in his seat to see me and gave it up. "For what?"

"To jump!" I bore down on the spreading fire, the grasslands giving off an oily, black smoke as they burned. Hiding our approach. "Now . . . let the cord go!"

I felt the change as soon as he did. The wings—freed from all control—began humming, vibrating back and forth, but I had my full weight over the stick, so instead of rising, we just flew faster.

Straight into the wall of flame.

Eld shouted and at the last moment I pulled up hard. Almost too hard. The winged machine swept up, its beating wings sending the smoke and flame billowing before us, and I heard shrieks below. For a moment we hung in the air and then I threw myself forward and we swung over, the flame following the curve of the wind we'd stirred up. I repeated the process, making a jerky, half-arsed arc. Something broke with a sharp crack and I lost all control of the damned thing. We swerved away from the growing circle of fire, bounced several spans up into the air, fell, then snapped back up, the ornithopter shaking like a rat caught in a terrier's jaws. Death loomed. Up. Down. Up. Down. My leg screamed. The world spun. *We're going to crash.* I screamed.

"Jump!"

Eld moved. My bad leg slipped on the floor and I couldn't climb out of my seat. *Guess the captain goes down with the bird.* I was trying to tuck myself into a ball when something grabbed me by the back of my jacket and yanked me out of my seat and over the side. The ground rushed up to greet me as I twisted, falling, and for an instant I was looking skyward and then I hit, bouncing violently around like a rag doll. I tumbled end over end before slamming face-first into soft clay that slapped me hard.

Stars burst in my eyes, my lungs screamed for want of air, and cutting through it all was a sharp pain that told me I'd lost my leg.

I pulled my face free of the muck, sucking greedily for air, blinded by clay. My fingers found my thigh, warm with blood, and I groped along it, waiting to touch bone. I felt the knee, the shin . . . the foot? *It's still there.* I fell onto my back, chest heaving, and swiped muck from my eyes. Amber sky, bright with waning sun, stared back down at me.

"Gods," I groaned, sitting up, gingerly feeling my aching breasts. I'd taken a beating in the cockpit at the end and everything hurt, except for my leg, which I couldn't feel at all, though I was happy that it was still attached. A huge furrow had been plowed through the tussocks by the ornithopter, which was buried in the ground not far off, nose down, tail up like a big, jagged finger against the skyline. Swiveling my head, I saw Eld's still form, hunched over in the grass.

"Eld!" I pushed myself to my feet—my leg decided it actually could still feel things and I fell over with a scream. Crawling along on my hands and knees, pulling myself from tussock to tussock, I reached his side. "Eld?"

"I—I said it hurt befor-r-e, b-but I was wrong. T-that f-f-fucking hurt," he whispered, rolling over onto his back. A cut above his eyebrow had left his eye bloody and, from the way he squinted, half-blind. His shoulder was sodden with blood. "Still does."

"I've come to realize," I said, collapsing against him, "that pain is a good thing." I winced as my leg made a liar out of me. "Means you're still alive."

"There is that," he said after a moment. "I can't move my arm, but if you can reach the vials in my belt—assuming they're not smashed—I would like to take the edge off."

"One of us should," I said, wearily reaching into his dark-blue jacket and finding the leather pouches attached to his belt. "You're in luck," I added, pulling a thin glass vial out that was none the worse for wear.

Eld upended it, the Dead Gods' blood mixing with his own on his lips from where he'd bitten his tongue, and shuddered, moaning as he swallowed. I could feel him stiffen against me before he sighed the way he did after making love, and melted back into the ground. "Mmm," he buzzed.

"Better than sex?"

"Impossible," he said.

"Wise man," I muttered, sitting up again, staring back the way we'd come. The sky was lost in a column of oily smoke that rose from guttering flames that still leapt about as they licked at the grasslands around them. "I think it worked."

"How?"

"The grenadoes sort of accidentally boxed them in," I explained. "When we came over for that final pass I used the wings to call up drafts that fanned the flames and trapped the Sin Eaters."

"Gods, they burned alive?"

"That much fire likely sucked all the air out before then," I said. "Mostly they suffocated to death, though those that weren't dead yet burned."

"Being Sin Eaters," Sin whispered, "they likely all lived until the flames caught them."

"They made their choice," Eld said as if reading my mind. "Reaped what they sowed."

"Aye, dark and crispy," I said, shifting onto my knees and pulling myself up using Eld as support. "That should have been all of them."

No sooner had the words left my mouth then a woman came bursting out of the flames. She threw herself into a roll, bouncing across the grass, shedding clothes and skin as she went and coming to a stop a dozen paces from us. She ended up on her knees, facing back the way she'd come. Her dark skin was bubbled with pink and white scars and was peeled away from her body, and her hair had burned completely off her scorched scalp.

"Ciris! S-s-save me!" she screamed, then drew in a breath and screamed again, one long plea full of pain.

I reached inside Eld's jacket and pulled out one of his pistoles. Wavering on my feet, I took a breath and steadied myself until her form filled the front-sight post. I wondered if she could sense she wasn't alone; if her Sin was still with her, she probably could. As if in answer to my thought, she twisted to look over her shoulder, and though her eyes were milky white from the flames and she was probably blind, they began to glow gold.

Boom!

Her head snapped back, tossing blood and bone and brains into the air as she fell to the ground, limbs flailing.

"There. That's all of them," I said, handing Eld back his pistole. He took it and stood up smoothly, sliding an arm around me to lend me his support. The cut over his eye was still bloody, but I'd a feeling if I brushed at the crust, I'd find smooth skin beneath. *Not fair.* "Well, she knows we're here, but this close I doubt she knows more than that."

"Now what?"

"Find whatever it was we hit," I muttered, looking around. "I can't see a damned thing out of the ordinary."

"Save for that hidden door to some hideaway belowground that was filled with Sin Eaters?" Eld asked.

"Save that." I nodded. *Sin?*

"On it," he said quietly. "You were smart to think of flooding us with endorphins . . . that burst of energy brought me to nearly normal for a moment. Still there's always—"

"A cost," I finished.

"Aye . . . the plague is retaking ground as we speak. I'm not in danger of slipping away," he added, "but your recovery is not going to happen tomorrow like we'd hoped."

"You hoped," I corrected him. "I'm not playing for tomorrow. I'm only playing for here. Now. Can you help?"

My vision shifted, the green of the grass suddenly a vibrant, lime color, the sky a strange orange hue, all the colors out of alignment. A shining, steel-colored spire appeared as if by magic fifty paces off, rising like a monstrously tall, thin tower toward the sky.

"That's what we fucking ran into."

"What?" Eld asked, looking around.

"You don't see it?"

"Not a damned thing."

"Hmm . . . well, help me make it about fifty steps that way"—I pointed—"and we'll see if that makes a difference."

"Still nothing," Eld said when I pulled him to a stop, leaning heavily against his side. I reached out and touched the smooth, slick, shiny surface—it felt like oil on glass—and Eld gasped, seeing my hand pressed flat to nothing. "Fucking fuck," he whispered.

"That's my line." The steel suddenly felt warm beneath my palm and a flash of light shot up its length. I blinked against a sudden burst of dark specks that flecked my vision. Eld cursed again, stumbled back, and I had to lean against the side of the pillar in order to not fall over. A whirring hiss beside me made me straighten up and heralded the appearance of an opening in the metallic spire, as if a door had been drawn straight up within the polished steel. A faint light shone from within, but all I could see was a bit of floor that looked the same as the outside surface save for strands of glowing light on either side of the doorway, like a path.

"Well, that was easy. C'mon, Eld," I said as I hobbled across the threshold into a shadowed, dimly lit space. "She's waiting."

The whirring sound returned and I spun around just in time to see the spire seal itself behind me. Fists reverberated off the other side and I could hear Eld shouting my name . . . until another door slid down, cutting off the sound as it blended seamlessly with the interior wall. A stream of silver light fell from above, illuminating an all-too-familiar obsidian altar ten paces farther into the room.

Exactly like the one that had given me Sin.

"Yes." Ciris's lilting voice hissed from all around me, bouncing off the eggshell-white walls. "She is waiting."

55

"Come to us, girl."

"I'd rather not," I said, steeling myself as I turned away from the door.

"Come to us or I will rain fire down on the Veneficus you brought with you," Ciris snarled. "You want your chance to kill me the way you killed his Gods, you're going to have to come to me."

"I don't know how," I lied.

"We both know you do," she hissed. "Touch the altar. Accept me into your soul. Embrace destiny."

"You're coming on a little hot and heavy for my taste," I muttered. *Sin?*

"She's not in the altar, if that's what you're worried about," Sin said slowly. "I've been in this place before, I think. It's familiar. Altars are places of holding, it's true . . . but they're also places of communication and Transference."

"Like what Sin Eaters do in their mind?"

"Of a sort?" Sin shook himself in my mind. "It's hazy, Buc. I don't know if her memory within me has faded or if I've been damaged. Transference uses nanigens to tap into invisible waves Ciris emits, and traveling along those waves allows for communication back and forth."

"You can send sound and emotion," I said, remembering my conversation with the harbormaster, more than a year ago.

"Exactly."

"Can you send anything else?"

"Like what?"

"Like ourselves?"

"It'd kill us— Oh. *Oh*."

"Uh-huh." I began limping toward the altar, my left leg dragging behind me. My jacket was torn and sooty, my pants smeared with clay, and I could feel that same clay hardening and drying in my hair and on my face. *Hardly the dashing hero who saves the world*.

"Buc, you don't have to do this," Sin whispered. "There's another way."

"There's not," I said, calling him out on his lie. "So now what?" I asked out loud. "Just slap my hand on the altar and we play fuck-fuck games until one of us dies?"

"We talk," Ciris said. "We want the Sin within you, but you're a valuable vessel . . . you needn't die if you don't want to."

"I don't want to die," I admitted. "But I don't think my living is precluded on your living either."

"We know what you intended with the Dead Gods, girl. That empty husk we tortured the morning the Betrayer murdered my Sins told us of the plague that would see my servitors reduced to simple mortals. Fortunately for us, the plague ritual was never fully completed. They will die, we will live. Yours was a plan worthy of us. Ambitious. Haughty. Intelligent." She spoke them as one names lovers. "All traits of a Sin Eater, Sambuciña Alhurra. Touch the altar. Embrace Sin. Commune with us. With me. You could be the greatest of them all."

"Buc—" Sin began.

I threw up walls of iron in my mind and then bent them over onto themselves, forming an impenetrable box, and Sin's voice cut out. A prison. *Sorry, Sin*. I needed control over him for what I was about to do. . . . I'd only have one shot at this. I'd realized months ago that the Dead Gods had the right of it. Introduce a contagion into Ciris, or preferably into one of her Sin Eaters and through *them* into Ciris, and she'd die. I needed Sin for that, but I also needed the plague running through my veins. It would have killed me without Sin, but if I used Sin's powers to supercharge the plague . . . it would kill Ciris *because* of Sin.

It would kill me, too.

I'd been ready to die almost from the day I was born. That faint memory of a warm fire and a soothing voice singing me to sleep aside, all I remembered was struggling to survive, walking the gutter's edge in the Painted Rock Quarto and the Tip. I expected to die when those boys stopped Sister and me from stealing their food, but she died and I didn't. I nearly died half a dozen times, from hunger or in fights, until I met Eld. Since I'd decided to kill the Gods, death had been a constant companion, and I'd been fine with that so long as I took the other bastards with me. Now, for the first time in my eighteen—soon to be nineteen—years, I'd a reason to live.

Aye, I wanted to give the world the chance I'd never had, but I wanted more than that. First, there were books. Can you blame me? There's a pleasure in opening a new page in a book and finding a world you never knew existed before. Slipping into someone else's mind and behind their eyes. Living dozens, nay hundreds of lives you never could have hoped to have lived. Books are a magic all of their own, and doubly addicting.

I'd found a friend in Salina. I enjoyed our talks and seeing her grow into the formidable woman I'd always known her to be. I wanted to watch her, as Chair of the Kanados Trading Company, taking the Company to isles they'd never thought to chart a course to before.

Eld. Aye, shit was complicated between us. We loved each other and both knew it, but there were new edges between us and we'd still not had time to talk about what had happened in Servenza. What had Eld said? *Show me your scars and I'll show you mine.* I was looking forward to finding out what a new life might be like. Together.

I wanted to live, but in the same way one can only be truly brave if they're terrified, one can only sacrifice if there's a cost.

One street rat's life in exchange for the world's? It seemed fair odds. More than fair.

I drew in a breath and placed my hand on the altar before I could think, ready to send my death through Ciris's veins. The altar, black as night, exploded in flaming-hot light that burned my hand. Knives and heat shot through me. Up. Up. Up.

Into the inky darkness.

Into Ciris.

Up.

56

I opened my eyes on nothingness. Then something filled that nothingness, vast and bright but hidden from my eyes. Not that I had eyes. I floated in a void, nothing but pure thought blurring around a nightscape like a firefly caught in a jar. Caught within Ciris.

"You don't understand." Her voice came from all around me. "Perhaps if you are shown?"

Suddenly there was light, loads of it. I hovered above a massive, swirling vortex of white and blue, its edges curving away out of sight. The vortex drew closer and closer still, filling my vision until I realized I was descending through clouds, thin, then thicker, dark, then white, before breaking free just above a silver spire. I slid down the spire to its base, where a man was aiming a pistole at the structure. He fired, a plume of smoke and flame leaping from the weapon's mouth, then jumped to the side as the ball ricocheted off the spire and rocketed across the scarred, smoking grasslands. Screaming, the man flung himself at the spire, slamming his pistole off the wall.

Eld.

"He is in pain. Because of you. Many are in pain because of you, Sambuciña. Few know your name, but if they did they would curse the moment you first drew breath, in much the same way they curse mine or the Dead Gods now."

The vision spun, shifted, blurred, and suddenly we were in the Old City of Normain, and dead mages in the bone-white cloaks of the Dead Gods littered the streets. Men and women clung to their corpses, wailing as others jeered and laughed. Some fool man drew a sword, leaping up from a dead Veneficus, and a woman who'd been mocking a moment before shot him and they fell upon each other. The square quickly descended into a pitched battle, and beyond the combatants I could see ranks of soldiers rushing forward with pikes and muskets.

The vision shifted again. More cities. More riots. Worshippers of the Dead Gods fighting worshippers of Ciris, fighting the local Constabulary, fighting one another. Sometimes they were led by Veneficus who hadn't been caught up in the plague, sometimes companies of Sin Eaters fought back, sometimes it was women and children and men in rags, but over and over again they fought and died and screamed, and the world began to burn.

"The world depends upon us," Ciris growled. We rose, the motion making me nauseous despite my lack of a body, and soon we were once again in the clouds, sliding toward the horizon's edge and full night. "Can you feel that weight? Like a tonne of brick piled upon your mind, your chest. You destroyed the hoary bastards that kept your people as thralls to their beliefs, but you did not consider the ramifications."

"How do you know I didn't?" I asked, unable to hide the tremble in my voice from the shock of what I'd just seen. "There was bound to be chaos in their death throes."

"Chaos can be put to order. By us."

"Bullshit."

"Oh, little one. You think you can take care of this? The fate of an entire world? Every man, woman, and child? Animals and fish, plants and trees, entire ecosystems within ecosystems, and all far beyond your ken? Today you flew amongst the clouds." An image of the ornithopter rushing toward us appeared and disappeared in a crackle of lightning that left spots across my vision. "You flew for the first time, when we flew amongst the stars for millennia."

I felt small, a fly beside an elephant. The enormity of it all threatened to crush me—but there's always been something in me that won't bend. Would rather break. Only, I was done breaking, and I wasn't going to bend. So I did the only thing I could do. I pushed back. Hard.

"You care? *You?* Sin showed me where you came from. Out there in that inky void. Fighting your forever war with the Dead Gods, each so twisted around your need for revenge that you never saw us as anything more than resources to be used."

"Care?" Ciris spat, her musical voice turning harsh. "I can't help but care, girl. I know the price of failure . . . none better." For a moment the vision shifted to a strange place with purple skies where steel spires rotated in the air. A blinding, green light filled those skies; the spires fell like rotted fruit and ash swept over everything. "You think we came from the skies to conquer, but we did not. We are refugees. The Dead Gods, too . . . fleeing epic death."

"I don't understand."

"Exactly what I've been saying," Ciris whispered. "You don't. You can't. It's beyond you."

"Fuck off. I killed the Dead Gods."

"You did," she said after a moment. "Very well, we shall try to explain. Imagine you find yourself in the middle of a sea that's been chummed with dead fish. A shark appears, a white fin half the size of a galleon. You see another person beside you. The white fin attacks and you realize . . . you don't have to defeat the shark. You merely have to outswim the other."

"You and the Dead Gods," I guessed. "But what was the white fin?"

Something red flashed through the vision, past it, reaching to where I floated in nothingness. It flashed again, like a flickering candle, growing infinitesimally brighter each time. Ciris spoke after an eternity, her voice echoing with the red light. "We both came up short in the end. Even now, the Enemy are coming. We couldn't outswim Them and neither can you, Sambuciña Alhurra. The Enemy are coming."

"Who's coming?" I scanned the vision but saw nothing beyond what I now realized was my world beneath me at my feet. My head swum with the thought. "Who?"

"To name Them is to pull their gaze to you. They are ever-seeking, ever-clutching, ever-destroying, and that is all you need to know. Madness," Ciris spat. "There remains a chance, little one. It was mine, stolen from me, but if returned, there remains a chance."

"Stolen? Didn't you send Sin in that ship?"

"My first servitor thought they were preserving us," she whispered. "It's always those closest to us who betray us in the end. You already know that, though, don't you? The pirate queen betrayed you, your friends have abandoned you, and you stand before us alone. We—I—will give you a choice, girl, to prove I do care. Accept Possession . . . return Sin to me . . . and I will make you a true Sin Eater or, if you desire it, let you leave as you were before. Diminished but alive."

"Why would I ever serve you?"

"The reasons, like myself, are legion," the Goddess replied. "Think, child. I am the protector of your world and with the Dead Gods gone, there will be none better. I will keep your kind from extinction."

"There's more to life than drawing breath," I told her. "You've shown me something; now it's my turn."

I reached within me and suddenly we were on the streets of Servenza, watching a little, black girl in a ragged, torn dress that hung from her painfully thin frame like a shroud. She stumbled along the edge of the gutter, gaze searching the refuse for scraps. Her bare feet made rasping echoes on the rough cobblestone until suddenly they were drowned out by the laugher of a dozen men and women in gilded silks who appeared around the corner. One woman was telling a bawdy joke about a groom who suffered from stage fright and the others laughed even louder, though one man, dressed in white, turned a shade of red. Another man, dressed in a crimson that nearly matched the white-clad one's face, almost ran the girl over; he cursed her roundly when he stepped in a fetid puddle to avoid treading on her. His careless backhand sent her spilling into the gutter and one of the women remarked he kept cleaner stepping in piss than on that shit stain.

"That was me, the day Sister found me," I whispered.

I showed Ciris my childhood, I showed her Quenta and Marin, Denga and Govanti and dozens of others. I transported us to the heart of the Kanados Trading Company, to the palazzos and al-kasrs, peeked at the balls, Masquerades, and services at the massive cathedrals. I fed her images of those, like Eld, sent off to die in wars that made no sense save one: profit for those in power.

"Power begets power," Ciris said, interrupting me. "You know this. It is a means to an end. You've used your power to hurt and destroy. You've slain innocents and never thought twice, so long as it served your goal. What separates you from me?

"I've used the powerful in your world to enact my will because doing so gives the greatest chance of your survival."

"You say you'd save us from extinction," I growled, "but I've seen wild animals caged up for entertainment. They aren't dead, but they aren't fully alive either," I said, returning us back to the image of the little girl I'd been, bones sticking out and a haunted look to my gaze before letting that, too, fade away. "The world doesn't need a supposedly all-knowing Goddess who knows nothing of hunger, fear, or pain, who cares little for inequity so long as her will is done.

"I've done awful things in the name of something better, aye. I could say it was because I didn't know any better, couldn't see a better way, and that wouldn't be a lie. I could say it was because I decided it was necessary or even that I didn't consider it all, and that would be a truth as well."

I drew a breath. "The difference is I was a sixteen-, seventeen-, eighteen-year-old woman with hardly any power at all. If I do the same next year and the year after and the year after that and on and on for centuries, then I hope someone comes to gut me because I'll have earned it a thousand times over. That's where you and I part ways, Goddess. I won't see us die, but I won't see us caged, half-dead, either."

"I have done as I have done because it served a higher purpose—" Ciris began, and I surprised us both when I made the darkness begin to glow with my fury. She paused, then began again. "I am not given to caring as you do. It is . . . 'beneath me' is not the right term and I know that would offend you. It is—" The Goddess hesitated. "—not within my nature to search out the cures for the ills you've shown me."

"No fuck. That's why I'm here," I told her.

"It may surprise you to find we agree," the Goddess said slowly, as if surprised at being surprised. "You see where I do not and I see where you do not. Divided, we have blind spots, but together, we would encompass all. Join with me, Sambuciña."

"You want me to become your conscience?"

"I wouldn't phrase it that way," Ciris said dryly. "But think . . . if you accept Possession, you would keep your Sin and the power that comes with it and you would aid me in protecting your world. I know the value of that shard, none better. I can't imagine that the cost of losing it has been lost on you.

"You desire altruism as well, and perhaps that is where I have misstepped, but it would not be so difficult to adjust the tiller such that the images you've shown me become things of the distant past. Isn't that what you've wanted all along?"

Isn't it? I'd never thought to find myself tempted by Ciris or any of the Gods, but I'd come here knowing I was going to die. Sin had said as much—he'd run the odds and they didn't end with the dice coming up all sixes. Killing Ciris wouldn't guarantee that my hopes and dreams would come to pass. Salina could be supplanted. Arti was too malleable in the wrong hands. The Dead Gods were done for, but there were still priests and priestesses with untainted vials who could do harm. If I died with

Ciris, the world might well remain shackled by the chains the Gods had shaped for us.

"You and I seated at the same table," Ciris whispered. "Think of what you could do with that power, Buc."

Power.

Power corrupts. I'd learned that the hard way last year, sitting on the Board of the Kanados Trading Company. I wasn't a rich noble and in trying to be one, I'd nearly become as awful as they were, ignoring the plight of the needy in my pursuit of the one thing the rich crave more than fine food and even finer wine: power. Oh, I'd had good reasons, none better: saving the world. But as I'd just said, there's more than just survival to be considered. If I sat down with Ciris, I'd be trying to become a Goddess—the very thing I set out to destroy. The version of me I'd just asked Eld to destroy. *Never.*

"I believe you," I said, suddenly realizing why Ciris had put on this performance. "You want me to join with you because you need me. You need the shard within me. I've fucked up a hundred different ways, but I never make the same mistake twice. I'm not going to ruin my perfect record today."

"Turn away," Ciris growled, "and I will rend you, blood and bone, and suck Sin from your marrow."

"Fuck you—"

A thousand hot blades pierced my mind and searing pain exploded through me. Pain so intense I felt the flesh sucked from my bones, my blood boiling away. I vomited, winked out of existence . . . but since I didn't have a body, the pain only grew. And grew. Until I longed to pry my lips apart enough to beg. Me, *beg.* For death. For an end.

"Let the rending begin," Ciris spat, and the pain found new pathways to make me writhe.

"Fuck you!" I tried to scream, but it came out as a mangled whisper. The little rod of iron within my core refused to bend.

"Buc!" Sin hissed, suddenly in my mind. "You must accept her Possession or she'll kill you!"

"I told you I wouldn't do that, Sin!"

"Oh, my Sin knows," Ciris crowed. "Knows that . . ."

"Fuck her," Sin growled. I felt him step in front of me and the pain lessened by a degree. "Listen to me. To me, Buc."

"I thought you changed," I said, unable to keep the hurt from my voice. Ciris's attack had left me raw and bleeding. She was going to tear me apart and he was abandoning me? *No.* "Sin, I felt you earlier. You were different."

"I am different." He sighed. "You were right about Ciris, all along." He suddenly expanded within me, returning to the Sin I'd known before and the pain vanished, leaving me gasping, the phantom tendrils of it nearly breaking my mind. "I know the damage She's wrought," he continued, pain bright in his voice, "but I thought . . . maybe it was accidental, that she didn't realize what she had done.

"Now I know that losing everything broke us, drove us into madness. She's convinced the only cure is to control everything. Everything, Buc!" He sucked in a breath, his voice taut. "She won't be content until the whole damned world is under her sway."

"Then why are you telling me to give her what she wants?"

"I've come to realize," he said, ignoring me, "watching you over the past year, living within you, becoming you, that you're right. You deserve the chance that we fucked up. So does this world."

"That's what I'm trying to do," I snapped.

"No, you're trying to kill yourself."

"Because that's the only way!"

"I never thought I'd say this, Buc, but your emotions have blinded you."

"What?"

"Don't you get it?" Sin asked. I felt him quivering in my mind and I suddenly realized that if he broke, I'd break with him.

"You're going to commit suicide to kill Ciris, but there's a shard of Ciris missing. A copy . . . that can be returned without you."

"You're not just a copy anymore, Sin. We've grown together, become intertwined."

"Exactly! I'm agreeing with you. C'mon, Buc, you can see this, surely?"

"The last Goddess in the world just tried to rip you out of my mind, Sin." I shuddered as he stumbled in my head and for a moment the pain threatened to return. I'd known we were going to die, that's what he refused to accept. I just hadn't expected it to hurt so much. *If only.* "Fuck me. You want me to allow Possession so that you can—"

"So that I can repay everything I've betrayed before. Everything Ciris betrayed. Buc, she's flaying me alive, I can't hold on much longer." Sin's voice broke. "Its name is Possession, but its definition is trust. Trust me to repay the debt owed to you. To your world."

I owe you a debt.

Chan Sha's voice, and Sister's, and Marin's, and beside them, all the debts I'd thought to repay, the guilt at not repaying them and in that guilt, a recognition of an echo, a reverberation . . . coming from Sin. A twin to my own.

"Sin," I whispered aloud, "I trust you to do what is right."

Ciris's voice cut off and I was suddenly encased in a tomb of silence. Mentally Sin and I collapsed against each other, shaking from the pain. I hesitated, gathered myself, and felt him nod encouragement.

"I accept your Possession."

With the words spoken I was suddenly back in my body, one hand pressed to an altar of smooth blackness that pulsated with light. Sin slid through me and into the altar. If Ciris's attack had been like knives, this felt like my brain was being dragged across broken glass. I felt him gathering everything with him as he left, the pain bright, excruciating, and then just . . . gone. Ciris shouted with joyous rapture, shaking the very spire, and suddenly I was aware of my body in ways I'd never been before, throbbing with life and magic.

It felt like when Sin's magic burned within me, only amplified a thousandfold. Ten thousand–fold. Every pain and ache was gone and suddenly I was aware of how heavy the weight of the plague had been on my core. Sin had taken it with him . . . up. I could *feel* a rope of braided light shooting through the altar, through the spire's tip, and up into the skies above, where I knew Ciris flew alone, watching. With the awareness came ten thousand thoughts, but they were ordered, organized, obeyed me. *I can control them?* It was almost what Sin had done for me, but now I was doing it myself?

Almost, a small voice whispered, and then suddenly I was well and truly alone and the realization of what had just happened rocked me to my core, the vast chasm left in Sin's wake echoing in my mind. I had all of Sin's powers without Sin, without his mind inside me. The shard that had begun as a splinter of Ciris had grown to be so much more, had grown to become . . . me. *A Goddess.* What had returned to the altar was the shard that Sin had been when we first met.

A shard consumed by the Dead Gods' plague.

A scream the size of the ocean rang out from on high, showering me with cascading waves of light. Ciris's cry swelled, her tortured pain filling the altar with white flame that knocked me back a dozen paces. I tripped, fell, and slid away on my back on the floor as the altar melted into lumpy slag. "I was your *protection!*"

"You've been protecting this world to use it to eradicate the Dead Gods!" I shouted.

"*Lies,*" she screamed, the waves of light slacking to beams and then raindrops. "I was using this world to escape beyond the sky once again. The Dead Gods followers never . . . understood . . . the true Enemy. Fools. All of you. Undone by fools."

"Sin was no fool!" I fought to sit up and drew in a breath. "And neither am I!"

Ciris screamed again, her voice dwindling at the end, and the spire shook. The door opened and a figure rushed in: Eld, his fists bloodied, scooped me up off the floor and whipped back around, getting us out the door moments before it whirred shut.

A wave of invisible energy sent us sprawling across the ashy grasslands. We both flipped over, side by side, staring up at the braided rope of light streaming out of the spire that was now visible with normal vision. The rope burst like a massive firework starburst and a jet of pure, blue fire shot out of its corona, into the dusky night, and disappeared.

"What?" Eld gasped. "What happened?"

"I saw the truth," I whispered. "Or a version of it." I told him about Ciris and Sin. All of it.

"But surely," he said in the quiet after I finished, "if nothing has happened for thousands upon thousands of years, then any enemy out there is dead?"

"The funny thing about time," I said, laying my head on his chest, "is that it's relative." I felt him sigh against me and snuggled closer. "But that's a problem for another day. If ever. We've more pressing matters."

"Like what?"

"The world," I breathed, the images Ciris had shown me sharp in my mind.

I threaded my fingers through his, felt some of the scars the Dead Gods' magic hadn't healed from when he'd almost died, and thought about the fresh scar in my mind. The one left by a friend who'd been living there for a year and more. We had started off as adversaries, but almost all of my friendships started that way, come to think of it. We'd ended as something more than friends. He'd known, for far longer than I had, what was required to kill the New Goddess, and he'd stepped in when Ciris was a heartbeat away from doing what no other had managed: breaking me.

Sin had sacrificed himself, and in so doing had saved me. Given me a chance at a better tomorrow that I'd never really thought to have. The loss of him was so massive I couldn't quite grasp it. It was almost like losing Eld. I don't know when I started crying, but Eld didn't say anything, just held me. The question running through my empty mind was one I knew I'd never find an answer to. At the end of it all . . . did I convert a God?

That's the kind of shit thinking that's going to get you into trouble, Buc.

"It doesn't matter," I whispered.

"What doesn't?" Eld asked.

"The price," I said, blinking back tears. "When this all started, I thought the world was run by gold. The hard kind. I thought that, and the power it gives, would be the instrument of change, but I was wrong."

"It's the people," Eld said.

"You've a good heart, Eldritch Nelson Rawlins," I said, pushing myself up to look him in the eyes.

"You've a better one," he said, leaning forward and kissing me.

"You're a shit liar, Eld," I told him, breaking the kiss. We stared at each other. Emerald into sapphire. Sin Eater into Veneficus. Buc into Eld.

I kissed him again, felt his mouth against mine, and then rolled over onto my back, still holding his hand, staring up at the starry sky above. "What matters is that the world will have the chance it's never had before. The chance to fly with its own wings."

And I intend to see it fly true.

Epilogue

⸙

"Buc!" Salina ran into the room and threw her arms around me, crushing me against her purple dress. She pulled back and looked me over in my wrinkled, grey jacket. "You look like you need a week's sleep and week-long bath at the end of it."

"I missed you, too," I growled, then laughed. "We did it, 'Lina."

"We did," she agreed. "All of us," she added, looking past me to where Eld and the Artificer sat at the table. "Why'd you choose this place?" she asked, skirting past me to take a seat opposite Eld.

"The world's been aflame the past three fortnights and there's some looking for the ones what struck the match." I shrugged. "Who's going to look for anarchists in this flyspeck of a tavern?" I asked. "Besides, don't you remember coming here?"

"Wait?" She turned in a slow circle. "This isn't where I gave you back that pistole, is it?"

"The very same." Eld chuckled. He glanced around, stretching in his crimson jacket before resting his forearms on the table. "They cleaned up the blood pretty well, looks like."

"Blood?" Salina frowned.

"A story for another time," I assured her, dropping into the chair opposite hers. "So what have you lot been up to while Eld and I took care of Ciris?"

I listened as Salina told me about the schools she'd started, how the Company was actually capitalizing on the break in world communication caused by the Sin Eaters all falling dead, bleeding from every orifice. The Artificer, looking ill at ease in a thin

Servenzan jacket with only a shirt beneath it, despite both being a staid black, kept switching the lenses on his glasses as he told us how he'd tapped into the invisible airwaves left by Ciris. He dug out a sketch from one of his pockets, smoothing out the wrinkles to show us a drawing of a machine that looked suspiciously like a printing press, one that could reach out to other presses and send and receive printed letters.

"Salina's set up a dozen other workshops and begun paying other creators to come fill them. We've a score of other inventions just like this about to roll out. We'll change the world and so forth!"

I listened with one ear, taking it all in, but I couldn't stop grinning at the people they'd become and who they were on their way to becoming.

"The one thing I took from the Gods," I said when they finished, "is that they never tried to conquer outright. Leastwise not until the end. They conquered through need, through giving the world services we craved: healing, communication, and systems that were exploitative but gave us all a warped sense of safety. All for their own ends, of course," I added, waving my hand. "We need to fulfill those same needs, but our motivation will be for the people themselves."

"That sounds too altruistic to be true," the Artificer said, polishing his spectacles. "There will be those who want to conquer . . . who know no other way."

"Some might say," Eld said, tapping his chin, "that the Empire became an Empire through war, not need."

"They'd be wrong," I told him. "The first empire began with need, a small island nation needing friends . . . only later did it turn to war."

"And yet Normain and the Empire are killing each other despite the unrest in their streets," Salina said, drumming the table with lacquered nails.

"We should trial some of what we've done in Servenza in my home country. That may help," the Artificer mused.

"Do it," I told him. "But don't do it half-arsed. Give them everything we have. We're in this together," I added. "Perhaps the Empress needs reminding of that. We freed our world, but its fate still hangs in the balance.

"I know that's a crushing weight, the sheer enormity of it all, but we've felled Gods together. There's no one else I'd trust with this more than you lot."

I smiled and turned to leave, and Eld's voice caught me.

"Where are you going, Buc?"

"I'd hoped to read a book," I said, glancing at the obsidian glass screen that I'd found outside the spire the morning after Sin killed Ciris. *476.* A parting gift from a friend. I ran my thumb over the inscription and smiled. "And mayhap other things," I said, winking at him.

Arti chuckled and Salina snorted and Eld's face matched his scarlet coat. I swept my black cloak back over my grey jacket and shrugged to feel my blades, a number in the usual places and a few in ones that weren't.

"But there will be time for books—and other things—later. Right now, I think it's time for the last Sin Eater to speak with the Empress."

The Annotated Library of Sambuciña Alhurra

Numbered and listed in order read, with notes by the reader. At the time of the events detailed in this volume, by her own count, Buc had read 476 books and an uncounted number of pamphlets.

12

Nasau
Calculations of Force

A Cordoban scholar, Nasau wrote in a plain, crisp text accompanied by diagrams that may make a new scholar at first dismissive about the depth of her series on mass and acceleration and force, but her works remain a mainstay amongst the newest branch of learning in Colgna and Normain: engineering.

Buc's notes: *I'm not sure it takes much learning to realize that something small moving fast hits harder than something moving slow? Gutter rats figure that out as soon as their fists are large enough to hold a stone.*

14

Fulcrums, Levers, and
Other Applications of Force

Nasau's continuation of the exploration of force expands into fulcrums, levers, and several ingenious pulley systems utilized by

architects the likes of Roun when crafting the cathedral in Frilituo.

Buc's notes: *Now this is interesting. Utilizing fulcrums and levers to unseat larger objects. Hmm . . . Nasau says force, but I hear power.*

23

Jens Marten
On Religion and Power

If his contemporaries are to be believed, Marten was better at speaking than writing. Still, this is a detailed—too detailed, some might say—accounting of the rise of Ciris and the creation of the new world wrought by rival Gods, told in a straightfor-ward, if somewhat boring, manner.

Buc's notes: *Why does no one speak of this? This accounts for ev-erything I've seen on the streets. I always thought it was the hoary old Empress's fault, aye, and she deserves a measure of the blame, but in part only. These fucking Gods set everything in motion that led to the streets. They're why Sister died and I'll—*(rest of page torn away).

67

Fivvonasi
The Cornerstone of Nature: Chemical, Engi-neerical, and Physical Maths

Today's mathematicians stride upon the shoulders of Fivvo-nasi. Begun by the Frilituo as a complete primer for her young daughters; even now, students will find the text grows with them, from simple addition and subtraction through some of the most complex proofs of Fivvonasi's day. Several guilds offered her vast sums to work exclusively for them, but Fivvonasi's commitment to learning was such that she died in relative poverty before her texts were truly appreciated for the master class they are.

Buc's notes: *I keep intending to start with the basic texts instead*

of leaping into the pool of knowledge headfirst, but I can't help myself.
Maths are a raging sea for one who doesn't know how to swim and I'd
have drowned without Fivvonasi's lessons.

112

Arasmeth

Separating Herbs and Their Lore

A Servenzan with little sense of adventure, Arasmeth never left the isle of her birth despite cataloguing every herb known within the world. Utilizing the vibrant trade scene to obtain both stories and samples of herbs, her encyclopedic work is vast but limited—Arasmeth never believed an herb truly existed until she saw the plant (often dried) in her hand. The years subsequent to her death have confirmed much of her lore is, in fact, based in truth.

Buc's notes: *I really thought there would have been more about poisons in here and less about tea. Even the poison teas sound a bit boring....*

143

Eint Volker

Where the Gods Fear to Step

Eint Volker, one of the few northmen who cared more for spilling ink than spilling blood, married an elder daughter of a Cordoban lady and soon thereafter stumbled upon the origin of the family's fortunes: as agents of Sin Eaters. Even in his simple hand, the tale pulls the reader in ... agents of Ciris risking all on rickety vessels to brave the hurricanes of the Shattered Coast and ignite chains of volcanoes in worship to their Goddess. Is it fact as Volker claimed, or mere fiction, as Ciris's followers would have one believe? The reader must judge.

Buc's notes: *Half the world starved, if everything else I've read about that time is true. The sun blotted out behind an unending cloud of ash. Funny how when it cleared, the Empire grew and the Kanados Trading Company with it. And the Sin Eaters with them both. Hmm . . . what did the Sin Eaters want in the Shattered Coast that the hurricanes hid?*

189

Royale Aislin
Black Flag's Shadow

Privateer turned savior of Southeast Island, Aislin died a century ago, but not before she wrote out the unbelievable story of her life—which ended in an Imperial jail, both legs replaced with pegs. She was fond of joking that she didn't need her legs to swing, and swing she did, but not before completing the autobiography that every would-be leftenant reads before joining the Academy.

Buc's notes: *A hard woman, and now I understand the stories about her insanity. But it's only insanity if you don't win, and she won every fight, save the last.*

201

Errol Gatina
A Captain's Mast

Gatina became Maestro of the Servenzan Naval Academy, reckoned just below the Imperial Naval Academy, after two decades before the mast. An average sailor, he proved a better teacher, proving that those who can't do, teach.

Buc's notes: *If I wanted a field manual on how to run a ship, I'd have bought one. Aislin led me to believe all salts were salty, but now I wonder. Frobisher's coming up in the pile, but is she another slog?*

221

Joann Frobisher
The Silence of Black on Blue

Frobisher rose from lowly cabin girl to High Admiral of the Imperial Navy. A lifetime insomniac, she worked the deck by day and wrote her memoirs by candlelight, thrice seeking healing from the Dead Gods for her ruined sight. Amongst her numerous victories were the Battle of the Channel, where she single-handedly rewrote the rules of engagement for ships of the line, and the Fortnight War, where she shattered the Free Cities' navy for decades after.

Buc's notes: *I don't trust writers—everyone lies and writers doubly so—but I think I may trust Frobisher. I wonder how it feels to throw the ship over and deliver a broadside such that it propels the entire floating monstrosity back around for a broadside from the other cannons? Talk about a one-two punch. . . .*

244

Cisorca
Kingdoms and Fiefdoms of the Deep

The Southeast Islander was a fine diver and an even better scholar. He devised a diving bell that let him sit on the ocean floor for hours, observing all manner of life about him. It is from Cisorca that the world learned of the terrifying kraken-killer, the crimson fyre dragon shark, and how reefs were vast worlds unto themselves. Had Cisorca stuck more to reefs than sharks they might have found more of him than an arm when he died.

Buc's notes: *It's fascinating how the various worlds Cisorca discovered exist all around us, from the canals of Servenza to the cliffs of Normain and everywhere in between. The commonalities of power dynamics, balance, and predator versus prey make me wonder.*

395

Zadaya

Desert Folly

A true accounting of the fated Imperial campaign against the Burnt as told by a regimental commander under one of the Servenzan battalions. Zadaya's scything criticism of the expedition—from ill-trained troops to haphazard battlefield deployments—could almost be seen as a political hatchet job, as she targets some of the highest commanders in the field, save she saw no profit from her work. Few sales came from a nation that wanted to forget its bitterest defeat in half a century. Zadaya was last seen fighting in a mercenary company on the continent in the endless skirmish battles between Colgna and the Burnt.

Buc's notes: *Eld never had a chance with that fuckwit of a commander, I can see that now. I see a lot of him in Zadaya. He left those burning sands but they never left him. It seems like they never left her either, if the rumors of her selling her sword are to be believed.*

451

Amirzchu

A Life of Sand and Blood

One of Cordoban's most famous princesses, Amirzchu inherited a blood feud on the assassination of her father. She added two more families to the mix, drawing them in so that she could play all three whilst preparing the final thrust of her own army, which would result in their city-states being folded into her own. Philosopher, military strategist, mother, and daughter, Amizrchu's memoir is as much an enigma as the woman herself. She sought to forge a dynasty from the sands from which she came and did so, though her poisoning by her second daughter, on the morrow of the murder of her first, prevented her from seeing it to fruition.

Buc's notes: *A wench after my own heart, this one. Speed, sur-*

prise, and aggression are all things I've found work best for driving steel through flesh. Political or otherwise. Perhaps a bit too mercurial, though . . . glad I don't have any daughters.

458
Jerden
Skydances and Circles:
On the Nature of Time

A northern mystic, Jerden likely never fancied himself philosopher or scholar, but proved to be both in this treatise on the interrelationship of time, space, and activity. A believer in something known as the Wheel, Jerden spoke of time and experience as a never-ending feedback loop. He attracted a large following, including many who also used his writings to locate and utilize a particular mollusk toxin that alters the mind.

Buc's notes: *I'd have likely skipped this book once I realized it was a northerner with a new name for kan fiend, save the prose is inviting. More than inviting. I don't believe a damned word Jerden wrote while under the influence of the toxin, but I could almost wish his thoughts on time were true. It'd be comforting to know someone like me traversed this path once or thrice before.*

461
Lauxnu Lamin
An Education of a Wandering Mind

Lauxnu Lamin lived quite the unscholarly life, first working as a day laborer before stealing aboard a ship. The stowaway talked themself into being taken on as a cabin runner, rising to mate on a merchant ship before becoming an apprentice with half a dozen different guilds in Servenza. Later, they briefly returned to the seas as a privateer in a venture that saw them shipwrecked on one of the many uncharted islands in the Shattered Coast. Marooned for a season with a locker full of books, Lamin returned to Cordoban and went from m'utadi to futuwwa faster than any pupil in recorded history. Their famous work, part memoir, part framework for self-education, is an unofficial part of the syllabus of every major learning center.

Buc's notes: *It's rare a life makes me feel lazy, but Lamin lived a dozen before they saw two score years . . . seems a waste they retired to the Academy life before they saw half a dozen more.*

463

Filipa Roun
Bones of the Old City

Filipa Roun has made the study of the Dead Gods' bones her life's work, finding inspiration in their twisting grotesqueries the same way an artist looks upon a pond of lilies before addressing their blank canvas. Not content with just studying their form, Roun delves into the earliest writings on the bones' formation in an effort to uncover what unnerving physiology could have prompted the Dead Gods' anatomy.

Buc's notes: *It's almost as if the actual Dead Gods had multiple limbs, heads, and hearts . . . unless they were close kin to an octopus and the head and mandible were lost in the devastation of their fall? I'm not sure this is going to help me kill their twisted, human servitors, but to end them, I must needs first understand them. Unless I can gain access to this Forbidden Library I've heard less than a whisper of. Fuck it, maybe I don't need to, after all.*

471

Chinshu Feng
Gunpyders and Their Arts

A frustratingly incomplete text, Feng's deep dive into the mechanics of gunpower and their explosive properties has been emulated by a number of pupils, most of whom have ended up immolated, the same as Feng was upon her last experiment, which took her workshop and half the quarter with her.

Buc's notes: *If Feng's to be believed, gunpowder must needs be calculated down to the grain, but if she was actually that careful, wouldn't she still be in one piece instead of plural?*

474

unknown author, Dead Gods' tongue
Whispers and Weaknesses of the Enemy

A heretical tome thought destroyed in the conflagration of Sin two decades after the reemergence of the New Goddess, *Whispers* is little more than a series of thought experiments on the methodologies that might result in the death of said Goddess. The author's name is a mystery lost to time, but a rough translation of the tongue suggests something about a subenemy or nemesis? The translation is broken and multivariate.

Buc's notes: *My brain aches, reverberates with this knowledge. I could wish the words didn't swim before my mind, but what I can see without slipping beneath the waves suggests Ciris can be killed by what is hers. Sin. Only, my Sin would never touch her with a thought, let alone a blade. Yet I control him. . . .*

475

Akzbphifknut, Dead Gods' tongue
The Felling Chant and Other Incantations

A tome of morbid morbidity with too many consonants and few enough vowels despite the translation, on healing properties of the blood of the Dead Gods.

Buc's notes: *The author? Authors? Whoever wrote this seems to believe that intention of healing or harming matters more than the ratios of blood, bone, and sacrifice described . . . but then why*

*is half the book nothing but detailed ratio tables that make my head
spin?*

476

Sin

Read and Find Out

Buc's notes: *Damn it, Sin.*

Acknowledgments

I've written over a dozen books since I first put fingers to keys, but *The Memory in the Blood* was my first grand finale, wrapping up an entire trilogy. Dear Reader, I was not prepared for the feels. You know that feeling you get when you're deep into a series and something comes up that hearkens back to a scene in book one? Or when the character has been chasing something across a thousand pages and finally manages to catch it? When the payoff hits you in the gut and you pause mid-sentence? As readers, those are the moments we live for on the page. Turns out, it's not that different for writers. I wrote this novel during the lockdown of that first summer of the pandemic, when the world seemed to teeter upon the precipice. Closer to home, this was the summer when you all were introduced to Buc and Eld in *The Sin in the Steel*. It was not an easy time, but perversely, writing a story about characters who dream big and sacrifice everything to overturn their corrupt society and the unimaginably powerful Gods who rule it? That helped me navigate those tempest seas. Later that fall, we were able to get away to an isolated beach house whose coastal waters once played host to real buccaneers, and I was able to sit with Buc and Eld and the story I tried to tell. I think I told it true, and if it gave me a respite from the omnipresent hurricane of modern events, I hope it will do the same for you.

A quick note, before we get into who made all of this possible . . . I know some of you will wonder if the pandemic inspired the plague in the book. It did not. I wrote the first sketch of this series in 2016 and refined it in 2018. I put together the final, scene-by-scene outline for *The Memory in the Blood* in the fall of 2019 and worked out the minutiae of the plague with my agent. I've always been fascinated and terrified by plagues, and it fit perfectly within the magic system of the Dead Gods. It's a tragic twist of fate that a real pandemic hit at the same time. Netflix had something similar happen, when they released their documentary *Pandemic* the month before the first case of what would eventually become COVID-19. Truth really is stranger than fiction.

A big thank-you to DongWon, my agent, who read this from cover to cover and plucked out some key themes that let me refine some of the best moments of the book. Publishing often feels like for every pull of the oar the headwinds send you two pulls back; having someone in your corner to fill your sails is invaluable, and I'm forever grateful for DW's support and guidance. Without DongWon, no one would have ever heard of Buc or Eld (or Chan Sha!).

Melissa, my editor, is another to thank for having this story appear on shelves everywhere. Her editorial skills are amongst the best in the industry and every book has been the stronger for her wisdom and eye.

My beta readers, Arnaud Akoebel and Kristine Nelson, who have been reading my work for years and came through on a tight turnaround in pandemic times to assure me when I needed to hold steady and point out where I veered off course. Forever indebted to you!

Eternal thanks to TeamDongWon and Drowwzoo, my aunties and uncles who are incredibly talented, busy, and successful authors in their own right . . . I appreciate your wisdom more with each turn of the page.

I dedicated this book to you, Dear Reader. Thank you for coming back one more time. I said last time that this is what careers are built upon, and I mean it more than ever. I hope you forgave me for Eld. A secret about me . . . I'm a bit of a closet sap and I just couldn't let him go. I believe that none of us is an island. We all need someone. Buc was fortunate to find an entire crew to rely upon, but she couldn't have done what was needed without her partner in crime-solving, and I hope you enjoyed their reunion as much as I did. I think Buc and Eld have earned their rest on the page, but I've more stories (many, many more!) in mind, and I hope you'll pick up the next when it hits the shelves. You can find out more about my next series on my website (sign up for my newsletter if you're interested in behind the scenes stories and sneak peeks). I hope to get out to conventions and bookstores if the pandemic cooperates and meet more of you, but until then we'll always have the page.

I dedicated *The Sin in the Steel* to Rachel. In many ways, every book is dedicated to her. She's my true partner in all of this, the bedrock who gives me the strength to weather the storms of publishing and trying to make a career in this fickle industry.

The shipwrights at Tor continue to astound, and there are so many to thank, I'll inevitably miss a few, but know that everyone there is the reason why this book is in your hands. Thank you to: Rachel Bass, associate editor, who keeps everything on track and ensures I know what I need to do at every step along the production process. Jim Kapp, production manager, who interacts with the printers, among other things. Dakota Griffin, production editor, who handles the different stages of production. MaryAnn Johanson, copy editor, who returned for this book (yay!) and kept me honest . . . anything you find in the lines that doesn't make sense I probably STETTED. Greg Collins, designer. Peter Lutjen, art director and jacket designer, has done an exemplary job in capturing Buc from book to book.

Thanks to Rachel Taylor, marketing manager, who wields the keys to Tor's social media castles as well as handling marketing duties, and to Caro Perny, publicity manager, who handles all of my appearances and gives me the same attention bestsellers receive despite me being a newb . . . and who is as big a WoT fan as I am while acknowledging there's room for criticism (rare in hardcore fandom circles). It's always a pleasure to work with pros who are also fans.

About the Author

Justene Bartkowski

RYAN VAN LOAN served six years in the US Army Infantry on the front lines of Afghanistan. He now works in healthcare innovation. *The Sin in the Steel*, the first book in the Fall of the Gods series, was his debut novel and was followed by *The Justice in Revenge*. *The Memory in the Blood* completes the trilogy. Van Loan and his wife live in Pennsylvania.

CPSIA information can be obtained
at www.ICGtesting.com
Printed in the USA
LVHW101112060723
751549LV00002B/188